TO HAVE AND HATE

DONNA ALAM

COPYRIGHT AND DISCLAIMER

The moral right of this author has been asserted.
All rights reserved. No parts of this publication may be reproduced, stored in a retrieval system, or transmitted in any form or by any means, without the express permission of the author.
This book is a work of fiction. Any reference to historical events, real people or real places are used fictitiously. All characters and events in this publication, other than those clearly in the public domain, are fictitious and any resemblance to real persons, living or dead, is purely coincidental.

© Donna Alam 2019

Cover Design: Book Cover By Design
Image: Specular
Model: Chris Williamson
Editing: Editing 4 Indies

ALSO BY DONNA ALAM

The following are standalone titles, often written in a relating worlds.

No Ordinary Gentleman

Before Him

One Night Forever

Liar Liar

Never Say Forever

London Men

(Not) The One

The Stand Out

Aussie Men

In Like Flynn

Down Under

Rafferty's Rules

Brit Boys

Soldier Boy

Playing His Games

Gentleman Player

Great Scots

Easy

Hard

Hot Scots

One Hot Scot

One Wicked Scot

One Dirty Scot

Single Daddy Scot

Surprise Package

ANTI-HERO

/ˈantɪhiːrəʊ/
a central character in a story, film, or drama who lacks conventional heroic attributes.

A Quick Word

To the person holding this in their hand.
Thanks for waiting for this one.
I appreciate your patience and support and hope you'll love this perfectly imperfect pair.

*Between men and women there is no friendship possible.
There is passion, enmity, worship, love, but no friendship.*

— Oscar Wilde

PROLOGUE
OLIVIA

I'D ALWAYS EXPECTED to get married in my grandmother's garden. During spring probably, if I'd given it any real thought at all. The garden would be fragrant with bluebells and tulips, the scene like something out of a Monet painting with colour and fragrance bursting all around our guests. We'd exchange our vows at the edge of the lake as the sun set before spending the evening dancing under fairy lights that would mirror the stars.

It's funny that I would consider these details now when, a few days ago, I was no closer to finding a husband than I was to sprouting wings. Yet here I am, alone in a hotel, about to marry a man whose first name I don't even know.

There have been no invites to send, no cakes to taste, and no videographers to vet. I'm not even wearing a wedding dress.

They say your wedding day is supposed to be the happiest day of your life, but I'd have to disagree. That's not to say I'm unhappy, though. I'm more resigned to my fate. Today won't be the pinnacle of my existence, and not for the lack of champagne or the absence of friends flitting around me like butterflies in the room, but more for the fact of who I'm marrying.

Why I'm marrying can wait for another time.

"Are you ready?"

As my husband-to-be enters the room, his eyes fall over me in a cool sort of appraisal. If only I could share his detachment because how I feel about him is anything but cool.

Oh, Beckett. Let me count the ways I loathe you.

You're the bane of my existence.

A thorn in my side.

And I'm pretty sure you're the devil in disguise.

Remind me again why I'm about to become your wife?

1

OLIVIA

I'M LATE. I'd like to say this doesn't happen to me often, but I'm *always* late. Despite my absolute best intentions, and despite setting alarms on watches, laptops, and phones, and not to mention, trying really, *really* hard, I always seem to be in a hurry. Oftentimes arriving by the skin of my teeth with my hair in disarray and my shirt sticking to my sweaty back. *Exactly like today.*

But being late for the biggest day in my life so far? That's kind of special even for me. In my defence, it isn't my fault. There was a signal problem on the Jubilee line; that's the Jubilee line of the London Underground. I'd given myself an hour to get to my appointment, an hour for a thirty-seven-minute journey. I know it should've taken exactly thirty-seven minutes because I'd timed it in a dummy run last week.

So now I'm running.

In heels.

Because I don't have the seven minutes walking time I'd allocated to from the Tube to my meeting.

Damn.

I slide my laptop bag higher on my shoulder as, in my haste, it begins to bang painfully against my hip. I press my elbow tightly to the leather, though not to stop potential bruising but as a means of protecting my handouts—the hard copies of my pitch—from somehow escaping. I really don't need to invite another disaster today. I must look a horrendous mess, but as the entrance to the building is in sight, maybe I won't be late after all.

But I'll still be a mess.

"*Oof!*"

The toe of my shoe catches on a loose paving stone, catapulting me forward as my bag skitters across the ground. But that's not the worst of it because I collide with someone climbing from their car, the forward motion sending me flying over a large foot. And not a *large foot* as in a generous measurement, but as in the thing at the end of a long leg.

Long, sensible legs, I decide as I lie across the ground, staring up at the car's expensive wheel rims. Sensible is what I should've opted for. I should've ordered an Uber or a cab. Maybe even something a little fancier like an UberLUX. Then I might've arrived on time and in style to the meeting that has the potential to change my life. I might've even gotten a fancy Mercedes like the one I'm staring up at right now. And as if I haven't suffered enough, I just felt my hair tie snap.

"Are you all right?" asks a very English accent, albeit quite sharply. Hands hook under my arms, and I begin to protest as though I'd meant to throw myself on the ground all along.

"I'm fine, just peachy," I answer ungraciously.

"Sprawled across my path is neither fine nor peachy." The tone and grip leave no room for argument, but I don't let that stop me.

"I *am* fine." Twisting my upper body, I pull away from his strong grip and unceremoniously roll onto my butt.

As I push the tangle of hair from my face, my view is filled by a pair of highly polished black brogues, the kind that are probably handmade, before my gaze travels the length of a pair of well-cut grey suit pants with knife-sharp pleats. The fabric coats a strong pair of thighs, and a leather belt denotes a trim waist. Ridiculously, my eyes follow the row of tiny buttons on a matching vest, up the flat planes of his stomach, and farther still to a broad chest. His shirt is white and open at the collar, exposing a triangle of tan skin.

"I wasn't aware the footpath belonged to anyone but one of the London Boroughs," I grumble, keeping my gaze resolutely on his chin. Call me a chicken, but something tells me I should stop my perusal here. Especially if his face is as delicious as the deep tenor of his voice . . . I certainly don't mean to tilt my head at the sound of his deep chuckle.

Strong brows frown down at me over coffee-coloured eyes, narrowed for effect. The man has cheekbones you could probably sharpen a knife against, though they're a perfect frame for a mouth that, without those hard angles, would be far too generous for a man. The effect is striking. And he's all too aware of it, I decide as I focus instead on the gravel and debris pitting the flesh of my palms.

Handsome. Older. Sophisticated.

Therefore, not my type.

With a smile that's more amused than kind, he holds out his hand. "Only street urchins languish in the gutters."

I slide my hand reluctantly into his. I'm pleased to find there's no bolt of electricity as our palms meet, just the continuing simmer of annoyance at his tone. Once upon a time, I was a sucker for a man in a good suit, but these days, I recognise it isn't the clothes that maketh the man but rather the substance stuffing it.

And this is a stuffed shirt if I ever met one.

"I'm a little too old to be any kind of kid." Even if my tone suggests otherwise.

"You are young but not too young."

"Whatever that means," I reply under my breath as I allow him to help pull me upright. I feel foolish and a little angry. After examining my now grazed and smarting knees, I turn and scan the ground for my laptop when a large—like *really large*—man passes it to the guy who just helped me up.

"Thank you." I hold out my hand expectantly, protesting as the thing is passed over me, the buckle on the strap unceremoniously thumping my head. "Hey, that's mine!"

"Of course it is." The suit's smile is almost cryptic as he passes the leather satchel into my hand.

Something about this whole exchange screams *old movie*—girl falling at the feet of the leading man. But this is no meet cute, even if he is good-looking enough for the part, because something tells me he's just one moustache twirl away from being the bad guy. As my eyes flick to the larger man behind me, I'm even more convinced. *A villain and his henchman*. But this is ridiculous, and I haven't got time for ridiculousness, not if I have a hope in hell of making this meeting.

"Thanks for nothing," I mutter, shoving the strap of my satchel over my shoulder. I turn on my heel and make for the stairs, my skirt hiking around my thighs as I take them two at a time. As the glass doors swish quietly behind me, I allow myself to turn, but the stuck-up stranger is nowhere to be seen.

"Ols!" Twisting back at the sound of my name, I find Luke passing through the security point with a look of genuine happiness. Why, when after he went to the considerable trouble of wrangling this meeting, I pay him back by turning up late?

They probably won't even see me now.

"God, I'm so sorry, Luke. There was some kind of signal trouble on the Jubilee line, then I tripped and fell over, and—"

"Don't worry. It's all under control. Your meeting isn't until ten thirty."

'What? You mean you—"

"Purposely told you the wrong time." Luke grins smugly. "To make sure my favourite American would be here *on* time."

"I don't know whether to kiss you or kick you," I say as he leads me over to the reception desk that's the size of the bow of a ship. I try not to hobble across the expanse of shiny tile as my skinned knees begin to smart and stiffen. Certainly goose-stepping my way there would bring me the wrong kind of attention.

"Do I get to choose?" Luke angles his gaze my way, a smile lurking in his words.

"Maybe. If you're lucky." I duck my head and push away an unruly hank of hair that falls across my face.

"Here's a thought." Without coming closer, he positions his body in such a way it's clear he doesn't want to be overheard. "I could claim that kiss tonight, and in the morning, be your alarm clock."

"That's kind of presumptuous of you." I fail to hide my smile.

"I'd wake you in the best way."

"Stop," I protest in the vein of *tell me more* as my heart rate goes from a trot to a gallop. This is such a big day. First, my meeting, then dinner with Luke. Is it any wonder I can't help myself? "So you'd wake me up and then what?"

"Make you late again." His low tone makes me feel all shivery.

"I'm not sure you'd be all that helpful."

"No," he agrees. "But I'd be fun."

"I don't need help with being late, obviously," I say, changing the subject because there's a time and a place and neither of those are here and now. "Sometimes, I just seem to be a magnet for trouble," I add with a small sigh.

"My kind of trouble." *I hope so.* "And today is going to be your day," he adds as we reach the reception desk. I begin to sign in. "And at least you can say you're a proper Londoner now."

"Because I can complain about the Tube?"

He laughs as I'm handed a lanyard and card with the word *visitor* printed across the front. "You can't help being an Anglophile." He throws this over his shoulder as he leads me to a bank of elevators.

"You make it sound so dirty," I say as he presses his own access card against the panel.

"Maybe because you're so dirty."

I turn to him quickly when he shoots me an innocent look. "Watch it," I retort, hip checking him as the doors slide open, and I step into the empty box. *The glass box of possible doom.* I shake off a shudder, wishing it was as easy to shake off my fear of elevators.

"I just meant with your relatives being from Yorkshire," Luke says innocently. "They talk funny up there. Like they've got a mouthful of dirt."

"Like Londoners don't sound weird." I sort of scoff. Though, in truth, I love the diversity of British accents. And he's right. I am a big ol' Anglophile.

"Has your gran still got her accent?"

"After being out of the country for seventy-two years?" My grandmother emigrated to the States from Yorkshire following World War II to follow her G.I. sweetheart at age seventeen. "She absolutely has," I add with a laugh.

I guess she's the reason I love all things British and that, up until the age of fifteen, I was convinced I was destined to marry one of the Windsor princes. Secretly, I still thought I had a chance when I moved to London for college, or university, as they call it here. Which is where I met Luke and decided I'd rather take a chance with him. He's the kind of boy-next-door handsome and a good man. Take right now, for example. All this idle chit-chat is his way of trying to distract me from my nerves. Sadly for me, he always seemed to have a girlfriend and never really noticed how I watched him from the sidelines. But life is all about timing, right?

"How long have I got?" I turn my head, noting the riot that is my hair reflected in the glass as I try to ignore the fact we're hurtling skywards at a rapid pace. "Please say it's long enough to wash these?" I hold out my scuffed palms. "And fix this." I point at my hair.

"You're just angling for a compliment." In profile, his smile looks quite sly. At least, until I jab him in the ribs with my finger. "What was that for?" He turns to me, his words delivered through a stuttering laugh.

"I can't go into the meeting looking like something the cat dragged in *after* chewing on it!"

"You always look gorgeous." His low voice is all rumbly and he takes a step closer, but no matter how my heart pitter-pats, I know we're not about to get hot and heavy. Luke is too honourable. We've waited this long, so I'm sure we can both wait a few more hours.

"Business before pleasure," I whisper, placing my hand in the middle of his solid chest. His eyes darken, but he doesn't answer as the elevator begins to slow.

"I can't wait until tonight."

"Tonight," I repeat with a sigh of longing.

"But for now," he murmurs as the doors swish open, "it's time to get your game face on."

Luke points out a nearby washroom where I tend to my hands and tame my hair as much as is possible without the use of a flat iron. The thick mass that is neither red nor brown but always unruly looks nothing like the low bun I'd painstakingly crafted this morning. It turns out that I don't have another hair tie, so using the remaining pins and my fingers as a comb, I do my best to repair it before rubbing my fingers under my eyes to straighten my mascara.

Mine is hardly the kind of face that would launch a thousand ships, I reason as I study my reflection, but I'm passably pretty. The inclement English weather mostly keeps my freckles in check, and a dab of Origins Pink your Cheeks in Coralberry is usually enough to stop me from looking too pale. But right now, I don't need any of that because my cheeks are colourful enough on their own. I open my purse to pull out my lip-gloss, wishing a Xanax would magically appear instead, but it seems I'm all out of wishes today.

"A lot of people are depending on you right now," I whisper, staring at my flushed expression. Which, as far as pep talks go, it isn't much of one. So I pull open the bathroom door and step into the hall.

2

OLIVIA

"Knock 'em dead," Luke whispers, leading me to one end of a large boardroom. Just because it doesn't have the prerequisite sterile-looking table doesn't mean it isn't a boardroom. A large bank of windows flank either side of the room, one with a vista over London and the other overlooking an open-plan office space filled with furniture that seems to be a modern take on mid-century Danish interior design. At the other end of the room, a bunch of suits don't so much wait expectantly as they do ignore my presence, chatting among themselves. I know I'm not the first person to pitch an idea to them today, but I'm grateful for Luke's help in getting me through the door.

Ignoring the butterflies the size of pterodactyls swooping through my insides, I force my attention back to the man himself. With blue eyes, sandy blond hair, and a boyish smile, he's a good distraction.

"Here's to hoping," I reply brightly, though my smile feels more brittle than bright. It's make or break time. Do or die. Finance my company, you lovely bunch of people, or . . . or I don't know what. At this stage, I don't have a plan B, just a desperate need for a large cash injection.

"You'll kill it," Luke repeats. My eyes find his calm, reassuring ones and with a nod, and a deep, fortifying breath, I let my gaze slide left to the bank of windows. Beyond the glass, the sun shines down on London, glinting from buildings of glass and steel. There is so much wealth crammed into this small space.

And wealth is what I need to get my hands on today.

Even the iconic dome of St Paul's Cathedral looks brilliant this morning when it's usually a grimy grey in the daylight. With a final glance at the Gherkin, the Cheesegrater, and the Walkie-talkie, I turn back to the room, trying not to smile too much at the ridiculous nicknames these building have been gifted by locals. I feel a kind of affinity or privilege to be in on their jokes.

This is the universe's payday, I decide.

The weather is great, I have an amazing business plan, and I have an appointment with one of the best venture capitalist companies in the country. My pitch is faultless. I've practised and repeated it so often, I can probably recite it in my sleep. I've become a devotee of my business plan, and this pitch is my mantra. A mantra I'm about to sell to these dozen good people . . . most of them men.

Gentlemen, I am woman. Hear me pitch.

From the back of the room, Luke gives me a wide smile and a double thumbs up. I nod in response, so grateful to him for his help. Whatever happens after this, I'm pretty certain our friendship will be changing. Deepening, turning a little more physical, at the very least. It's kind of become inevitable, and we've been dancing around this for a while. But for the need to keep things professional, our relationship might've developed already.

Luke is, was, my college crush. My *unrequited* college crush. We'd reconnected recently, and at first, I was afraid his offer of help was a means to get into my panties. Which is ironic because, as he takes his seat at the very back of the room, his eyes following the movement of my hands as I smooth the fabric of my skirt over my thighs, I realise I'm more than ready to get to that part.

"Ms. Welland?"

My gaze glides to the man seated in a Le Corbusier chair at the front of the throng of suits—a wad of suits? A wallet of suits? I'm not sure what the collective noun should be. Around five foot eight and portly, the man is somewhere in his early fifties with a shock of silver-grey hair. His navy-blue suit is well fitted and doesn't so much scream *wealth* as sneer it imperiously. My mind runs through the company hierarchy, and I pick him out as Mark Jones, the managing partner here. The head honcho and the man to impress.

I take a deep breath and smile in his direction as I prepare to sell the suits on some romance.

Piece. Of. Cake.

I depress the button on the remote in my hand, and the smartboard behind me fills instantly with an image of a couple in love. The girl's golden hair is a mass of curls blowing in the breeze, the dark-haired man smiling lovingly down at her as he pulls a lock free from her cheek. This isn't a stock photo but an image of my best friend, Reggie, and her one true love, who I helped her find. Ladies and gentlemen, my app works, and you're looking at the very beginning of my business. But I digress.

"We're E-Volve," I announce to the quietened room, "the socially conscious Tinder."

My eyes touch on each of the main players before moving to those farther back, making everyone feel involved by spreading the connection. But I hesitate as my gaze lingers on the silhouette of a figure at the far end of the room. He's tall, his shoulders almost filling the space of the open doorway, and though his face is in shadow, I sense he's staring at me.

No matter, I intone, ignoring the involuntary shiver of awareness that ripples through me. Whoever he is, he's not part of the meeting and is therefore of no interest to me. I click the remote again, the smartboard changing to an image of the company logo as I begin my pitch with a mildly amusing anecdote from my own online dating experience.

"It's two thousand and seventeen. Covent Garden. A girl sits at her desk, staring at her phone and the profile of a man she'd swiped right on the previous weekend. His bio painted a man of diverse interests. A man well-travelled. A man whose profile and social media post were intriguing. Alluring. With tattoos and a hipster beard, the man had a retro vibe. The girl was young," I add with a small smile. "Please try not to judge."

A tiny ripple of laughter travels through the room.

"Cut to a couple of weeks later. The girl sits in a coffee shop waiting to meet the man of her dreams when a senior citizen takes the seat opposite and smiles. Those *aren't* his own teeth. The girl wonders if the man is a little lost. Maybe he has memory problems, and he only *thinks* he knows her. But then she notices his tattoos. They're old, sure, and faded, but with a sinking feeling, she realises she's seen them before. The guy she'd been speaking with hadn't used a cool filter on his social media images; he'd used originals. Photos *decades* old. Her date was old enough to be her grandpa."

The chuckles deepen, and I know I have their interest.

"This is what we at E-Volve call the realities of online dating. With our app, we connect people not by the lies of retouched profile pictures and inflated bios but by social mapping."

This is done using blockchain technology, which I'm not sure I one hundred percent understand myself, hence the need for a developer on staff. I only understand enough to have sunk my inheritance into getting my idea off the ground.

From here, I hit them with the numbers. Lots and lots of lovely numbers that will, no doubt, tickle the pickle of these here finance suits.

"Tinder has over ten million daily active users; sixty-five percent of them are male and thirty-five percent female. Fifty-two percent are single. Of course, it's unknown how many of those are shielding the truth in order to attract a temporary mate . . ."

My own personal statistics tell me *honest* and *single* don't necessarily go together.

"American singles alone fuel a two-point-five-billion-dollar online dating industry..."

I run through the rest of my business model in three minutes flat—succinct, sexy, and relevant—detailing our customer acquisition strategy, our scaling plans, and ultimately, our exit plan, the part where we make lots of money. Next, I move through the scary part. The many zeros of the investment number I'm seeking.

Me. Just me. While I may be using *we* as a pronoun, in actuality, my business is all me.

"E-Volve is about quality matches," I say as I conclude. "We're intentional about the direction of our lives. Our careers, our aspirations, our accomplishments. Why leave our love lives to chance?" I flick the screen to our logo, the one chosen by expensive marketing and focus groups. "Find your person," I say in closing. "Evolve."

My heart is beating out of my chest as the suits begin to talk amongst themselves, when I hear the phrase "business-lifestyle model" repeated.

No, no, no! This is *a make lots of money* model.

"Make no mistake, ladies and gentlemen. This is a cash-producing business," I insist. It's also as a labour of love. "We foresee our growth leading all the way to a successful exit where we intend the market leader to pick up E-Volve."

For this little company to be swallowed by another much bigger one, making me rich in the process. Though, in all honesty, I'd be happy to survive without being declared bankrupt. *And it's close, believe me.* But this isn't just about me. It's also about the people who have invested their time and their energy to get our app off the ground. The people on my small team deserve a reward for their faith. It would also be nice to stop considering ramen a food group. Maybe even buy a half decent bottle of wine from time to time.

"Matches," murmurs a man to the left of Jones, and I jump on his comment.

"Yes. Matches is definitely in our sights, given they are the biggest player in the online dating marketplace. They're our ultimate aim." Our best scenario exit strategy. They buy my company and, *cha-ching!*

Jones nods. There seems to be so much consideration in that small action that it's hard not to become excited, those pterodactyls now feeling more like butterflies.

"While I'll admit to being intrigued," he begins, "I'm not entirely sure your model fits with our portfolio."

I resolutely ignore the dip in my stomach because this is *so* up their alleyway. Even if I need to knock them out, drag and dump them in that alley myself.

"I've done my homework, Mr Jones," I respond evenly. I've considered their reputation, studied their press and website, and prepared for this response. "Given your recent investment in the Grant app, I believe this is very much in line with your portfolio. Romance may be seen as low-tech, but we both know apps available to Android and iOS are where the money is at."

I have his interest—I can feel it—my hand curling into a fist behind my back as though I can almost touch that thick wad of cash. Just as I sense he's about to answer, my attention moves to the figure in the doorway once more. Only this time, the shadowy man has been replaced by that of a woman young enough to be an assistant or intern. She bustles her way deeper into the room, handing Mr Jones a note. He unfolds it, scans the contents, then slides it into his top pocket. I suddenly feel sick. Something tells me the tide is about to turn.

"Ms Welland, I'm afraid we must adjourn for the day." A protest rises in my throat, but I manage to swallow it. "Your pitch was impressive, and you've given us a great deal to consider."

"Just don't consider too long," I reply, aiming for a kind of haughty confidence. This deal is too good not to be in, my friends. But maybe I've overshot as he doesn't answer. Instead, he inclines his head before he and his team file from the room.

"Do I want to know what he said to you as he left?" I ask Luke once we're the only two left in the room.

"Only that he wanted to see me this afternoon." As Luke answers, he tugs on his left ear. I watch on as he shoves his hands into his pockets and tips back on his heels.

"What do you think? Was he not into my pitch?" I feel my expression twist.

"Ols, no. That can't be it. Your pitch was great—spot-on! It's my job to bring interesting options to the table. I only wish I was a couple of positions higher than I am on the decision-making end because I'd snap this deal up, just like I want to snap you up."

'I'm not sure what you mean," I demur half-heartedly. It's not Luke's fault things didn't go according to plan.

"No, but you will. Tonight." He's careful not to come closer or display any connection between us as though we're being watched, which is entirely possible in an office built from glass. "It went well, really well. I promise. Don't give up hope."

"You'd make a good boss," I tell him, wishing I could say I've retained my earlier confidence. "You give good pep talk."

"I also give good pillow talk."

I conceal my ridiculous smile by beginning to pack up my things.

"My dirty talk is on point, too," his low-pitched voice teases.

It's official. This is happening tonight. The level of innuendo between us has never been this blatant.

"I'll take that under advisement. God!" I add, the word hitting the air as a groan. "I could do with a drink."

"But to celebrate, not to drown your sorrows, right?"

"I can't celebrate something I haven't achieved yet."

"Great things are still waiting for you." He pulls his cell phone from his pocket and frowns down at it. "Are you going back to the office?"

I shake my head. I can't face them right now, even if I didn't tell the team about this morning's pitch. I didn't want to build their hopes up, though they've been hinting that Luke might use his connections to get me in the door. And he has. But I'll be devastated if I haven't held up my end of things.

"And we're still on for tonight?"

"Well, if you're offering . . ." I draw out my reply. It's heavy with meaning.

"Oh, you know I'm offering. But I reckon the first round is on you," he replies with a naughty wink.

"To show my appreciation? I was kind of hoping to show it in some other way." As though drawn by invisible strings, we find ourselves in the centre of the room

"Were you, now?" he almost purrs.

"Urgh, that sounded bad, didn't it? How about I buy you a drink for business advice rendered. Let me appreciate the hell out of you." I let my gaze roam over his chest so there really is no doubt about my intentions.

"Let me take you to dinner first."

First. So much meaning in that one little word. A meaning I'm more than ready for, so I nod because I don't trust myself to answer right now.

"Eight?" he suggests, and I nod again.

"Text me the address of the restaurant."

He pauses, his expression taking on a wicked light. "Should I bring a toothbrush?" This time, my answer is a peal of laughter. "What about pyjamas?"

Blood rushes through my veins as I raise my hand, almost sliding it around the back of his neck. But as I remember where we are right now, I settle for brushing invisible lint from his bicep.

"I have a spare brush," I almost whisper, clasping my hands demurely in front of me now. I stare up at him from under my lashes. "As for pyjamas, it's up to you, but I prefer to sleep naked myself."

3

OLIVIA

RETRACING MY STEPS, I head home to my tiny flat in Shepherd's Bush, which is an area of London not as quaint as it sounds. *Especially the end where I live.* Bonus, I manage to retrace my steps without falling over this time.

It's still sunny when I exit the Tube station, though it could be raining monsoonal levels for all I care because when I pull out my phone to check my messages, I see a very welcome email.

"Yes!"

I find myself fist-pumping the air, drawing censorious looks from the pensioner pair next to me. The elderly gent wraps his arm tightly around his equally doddery wife as though I'd aimed that punch at her.

But it doesn't matter because nothing can make me feel bad right now, because the PA of my favourite person in the whole wide world (currently) has emailed to request a second meeting!

Mr Jones, I knew you were a man of discerning tastes.

Opening the door to the imposing Victorian townhouse, or terrace as they call them here, I grab the pile of mail from the console table in the hall before climbing the stairs to my little flat on the top floor. Technically, my home is in the attic of this once very grand household. I live in the rooms where the maid would've resided; only these days, my exposed brick-and-white-walled home is a perfectly bijou dwelling rather than somewhere you hide the help. It's the first place I've ever lived alone, and I love it. Sure, the rent puts a hefty dent in my rapidly diminishing bank balance each month, but I try not to dwell on the figures so much because, quite frankly, I'm not a fan of finance induced heart palpitations.

Dropping the pile of circulars, reminders, and final notices to the kitchen worktop, I pull a bottle of Pinot from the fridge before making my way to the sun terrace. I say *sun terrace* when what I really mean is the little bit of flat roof I have access to when I climb out of my bedroom window. I can't even begin to say how difficult it was to get the little table setting out there at the beginning of the summer. But it now takes pride of place in the shade of one of those grand chimney stacks that dot the London suburban skyline like a scene from *Mary Poppins*.

Pulling out one of a pair of spindly chairs, I deposit my wine bottle and glass on the intricate wrought-iron tabletop. I twist off the cap and reward myself with a generous pour. It's then that I pick up my phone.

"Ask me how clever I am?"

"Is this a trick question?" Reggie yawns, and I curse myself for not checking the time zones again.

"Did I wake you?"

"I needed to be out of bed anyway," she says sleepily. A voice murmurs from Reggie's bedroom somewhere on the other side of the Atlantic. "We're supposed to be on the road before nine."

"That's right. You're off to meet the parents this weekend."

In the background, Josh dramatically adds a little background suspense.

"*Dun-dun-dunnn!*"

"Josh says to say hi, by the way," my friend adds. Sheets rustle, a door opens, and a switch flicks. "You're on loudspeaker now, so why don't you just tell me how clever you are."

"Who have I been chasing forever?"

"Luke Bedford," she answers immediately. "The guy you've been crushing on since college?"

"I have not!"

"You haven't been chasing him or you haven't been crushing on him since college? Because I remember otherwise." This she drawls lazily, accompanied by the sound of the fridge door opening. I don't need to see her to know what she's doing. Reggie and I have been friends since grade school. Right now, I know without a doubt she's drinking orange juice straight from the carton, a terrible habit neither Josh nor I have been able to break her of.

"If I've been chasing him, it's been in a purely professional sense."

"My bad," she replies airily as the sound of glass condiment bottles clinking together precedes the slam of the fridge door. "And also, liar, liar, pants on fire."

"It's true!" I protest. "I *may* have, from time to time, and with a purely aesthetic viewpoint, mentioned how easy on the eyes the man is."

"And how much you want in his pants," she adds a little gleefully.

"But I haven't been chasing him."

"Does following him around with your tongue hanging out count as chasing?"

"You're mean before breakfast."

"And you're not fooling anyone. You'll have that man out of his suit pants before he can say *venture capitalist*. Well, just as soon as you've secured your—" Her words halt, and I almost hear the penny drop. "That's it, isn't it? You got a pitch meeting!"

"Did and done. Delivered it this morning, just a couple of hours ago."

"I can't believe you didn't tell me!" she almost screeches. "How did it go? It went well, didn't it? It went amazing, right?"

"Well enough to get me another appointment on Monday."

"Yes!" I know that burst of excitement came with an air

punch. "Your ribs must be aching from all the congratulatory team hugs."

"You're the first person I've told. I didn't want to get their hopes up." I find myself shrugging even though she can't see.

"Ollie, we've had this conversation. There is no "i" in team."

"No, but there's a *me* in team, and as it's me who's responsible for paying their salaries, the rent on our offices, and a million other things. I haven't had the heart to tell them how things have been looking." Reggie is the only person who knows the company has been kept afloat by my inheritance. No, that's not true. Luke knows, too. But it's an inheritance *not* followed by six zeros. I only came into it last year, and it's now almost entirely spent. "I've had so much riding on this meeting."

"And now you've had it. You've got this, babe."

I let out a long sigh, my eyes welling with tears that are a strange mixture of release and apprehension. "Oh, God, I hope so, Reggie. I really do."

After a glass and a half of liquid relief later, I climb back through my bedroom window just as the sun decides it's done for the day. The air is still heavy, and even though foreboding grey clouds fill the sky, nothing will spoil my night. I shave, buff, and slather myself in cream, and almost dance around my bedroom in my underwear, filled with a nervous kind of anticipation. I can't remember the last time I had sex, and when I say I can't remember, I mean on purpose. The experience really was that bad. *A one-night stand following the party of a friend, a little too much vodka, and a lot of grinding against nothing very much.*

But the ordeal confirmed my suspicions that I'm a monogamous relationship type of girl. And as I've been interested in only one man since then, but unable to do anything about it, I'm more than ready for tonight.

Still in my underwear, I add a little smoky eye to my makeup routine before slipping on a flirty little vintage Stella McCartney dress. *Vintage sounds so much better than second-hand.* With a spritz of perfume, I'm ready for a night with Luke. A night of firsts. A night that might just be the beginning of forever. What I'm not quite so ready for is a trip on the bus. I might be on the brink of multimillion-pound success, but it would be irresponsible to be anything but frugal until the ink dries on the contract.

For the whole journey along Uxbridge Road, I feel twitchy and restless, and I'm not sure the feeling is one hundred percent excitement. My wave of wine bravery has long since worn off, and my confidence waned. It's possibly my psyche's attempt at managing my expectations. I'm sure most people could relate. We've all had that one childhood birthday that couldn't quite come soon enough. The day we were on our very best behaviour for, which in turn became the party that didn't quite live up to the excitement and hype. Not that I'm equalling dinner with Luke to a gift I somehow deserve, but I have been on my best behaviour around him. Also, Reggie was right. I have had a crush on him for quite some time. And as I walk into the Brasserie where we'd planned to meet, I wonder if my subconscious had picked up on something my sentient self didn't see because as I'm led to our table, Luke's expression isn't exactly a balm to my nerves.

"Hey," he greets me, his hands clasping the tops of my arms as he pulls me in for a double air kiss. It's not the warm, enveloping hug I was expecting. Not that I was expecting a passionate embrace in the restaurant or his hands all over me, but I'm also not a colleague or a distant cousin. And earlier he said . . .

I snap back to the moment as the waiter pulls out my chair. But before he has time to turn away, Luke shoves an empty glass at him.

"Same again," he demands without tending the invitation to me. He looks dreadful. His shirt appears to have had a fight with a steam iron and lost, his blue eyes are ringed with tiredness, and his endearingly floppy hair now appears to bear a two-day unwashed sheen. *As if he'd run his hands through it repeatedly.*

"Is everything okay?" My mind slips to my pitch this morning, and my concerns that Luke had somehow snuck me in through the back door. But didn't he say that was his job—to find and introduce interesting investments? Besides, they wouldn't waste their time by calling me in on Monday if they had no interest in my company.

Maybe that's it. Maybe he wants to cool things off until after meeting number two? But that can't be it. He said any conflict of interest would be over once he'd introduced E-Volve as a possible investment partner.

"This isn't how I envisaged tonight going," he mumbles, staring at an empty wineglass on the table. *The size of a goldfish bowl on a spindly stem.*

I take a moment to gather my thoughts, my gaze now fixed on it, too. I take in the lily-white linens and the gleaming silverware. Above us, light fittings that look more like art installations don't so much provide a little ambient light as a glare. The walls are stark, the pale-coloured artwork like a smudge of cream left on a porcelain plate. I shift a little in the chair, the brushed steel cutting into the back of my thighs. Would it have killed them to use a little upholstery? While obviously an expensive restaurant, it isn't exactly the kind of place that screams seduction or romance. It's a monument to minimalism. Cold and impersonal.

"What is it, Luke? What's wrong?" I reach out across the snowy table linens, covering his hands with mine just as a black-clad waiter arrives with his drink. His presence causes Luke to snatch back his hand as though we'd been discovered half naked and not just holding hands.

"I don't know where to start." But that's a lie because it seems he's going to start from the bottom of his glass as he throws back what I assume is neat vodka and not water, draining the contents with a pained scowl.

"What can be so awful that you need to have a drink to be able to spit it out?" I'm not sure I'd meant to voice that thought.

"Timing," Luke answers cryptically. "The timing is fucking awful."

"Okay, but I still don't know what it is you're trying to tell me." Trying *not* to tell me? The restaurant might not lend itself to romance, so does the stark setting have more to do with business? "Is it about Monday?" I ask sharply, suddenly panicked. "About my meeting?" I know it's humid this evening, but the weather has nothing to do with the trickle of sweat that's broken out on my spine.

"No," he answers immediately. "If there's one thing that brings me comfort, it's that you've gotten another meeting with Jones."

"And I have you to thank for that."

"No, I got you in. The rest is on you. And you're going to do amazing."

"Why do you sound like an elderly relative on his deathbed?" I'd aimed this as a joke, but my answer sounds a little more like distress.

"*Ols.*" He gives a protracted sigh, ridiculously drawing out the shortening of my name. "I wish to fuck we'd gotten to this point before now."

I wish he'd get to the point now!

"What are you trying to tell me?" I ask, leaning back in my chair as we both ignore the waiter hovering nearby, trying not to interrupt whatever this is.

"I was so looking forward to tonight. To dinner. To taking you home and peeling you out of your clothes. I've wanted this, wanted you, for so long."

Past tense. What the hell?

"I've been single most of the time you've known me." My laughter sounds bitter as I prepare for whatever letdown is coming my way. "Meanwhile, you've been busy." And no, that doesn't sound jealous at all . . . "And then there was E-Volve, this pitch, and the help you've offered me. And we both agreed it would be a bad idea to mix business with pleasure."

Not that I'm feeling very pleasured right now.

I needed to know I did this on my own—I thought he understood. It's one thing for him to have helped get me through the door, but quite another if, somewhere down the line, his help gets misconstrued. If I end up looking like I succeeded because I got on my knees for him. Not that Luke would say such a thing. He's far too honourable.

"I worry we'll never get beyond a platonic kind of pleasure now." He lifts his head, his eyes baleful.

"Oh. Okay." The tightness returns to my stomach, my confusion no doubt written in my expression because it's not okay. Not until I get an explanation.

"I really wish we hadn't stuck to that rule." He chuckles again, and my frustration levels rise and peak.

"Just spit it out. Whatever it is. Whatever you have to say won't change how I feel about you."

"I'm going to be a father."

Oh . . . Well, except that. Because *that* does change things.

My mouth falls opens, but I clamp it closed again before I can speak, digging my teeth into my lip against the torrent of words I can sense burbling.

My first reaction? How? I mean, not biologically, but what the fuck? We agreed we'd keep things purely platonic, but I didn't for one second think that meant we should be screwing others.

He wasn't supposed to be like that.

"I'm so, so sorry." This time, Luke reaches out for my hand. I let him take it as I stare down at his large one curled over mine. His thumb rubs over my knuckles again and again as though my hand is cold to the touch. "Say something, Ollie."

"Congratulations." This is delivered more in the vein of *go fuck yourself* as I pull my hand back, signalling for the waiter to order a large brandy. People drink brandy for shock, right? "Why did you wait until now to tell me?" *What's with the bait and switch?* I want to ask him. "Are we here," I add with a glance around the minimalist décor that leans toward sterile, "because you thought I'd flip out?" Somewhere light and bright where any meltdown, breakdown, or hurling object could be seen? Possibly later reported to the police.

"Of course not," he replies, looking genuinely hurt. For a moment, I feel like a colossal bitch, a blindsided colossal bitch. "Although you do have a bit of a temper."

"What?" I force my expression to relax, my next words a little quieter. "I mean, how could you say such a thing?"

"Because I've seen it in action. Granted, not for a few years. But I remember that time at uni when you poured a pint of beer over the head of that kid in the Student's Union bar."

"He was harassing one of my friends. Besides, that was a long time ago," I answer uncomfortably. "I've grown up lots since then."

When I was younger, I literally used to see red. A mist of something would come over me, and I'd absolutely flip. These days, I have a better hold on things. I choose not to allow people to yank my chain. And quite honestly, I think it must've had something to do with hormones. In short, I'm much calmer now. I even do yoga. Occasionally.

"Anyway," he adds with a sigh. "I literally found out an hour ago and came straight here and ordered a double vodka. What was I supposed to do? I couldn't call and tell you over the phone."

"No, I suppose not," I respond with a frown. Jesus, what a shit show. It's not like I've pinned all my romantic hopes on him, but it's just that childhood birthday scenario all over again. And I was having such a good day. Not to mention looking forward to what this evening would bring. And my vibe ran out of charge last night. *Something else with the worst timing.* I somehow don't think I'll be looking for the charger before crawling into bed tonight.

The waiter uses a lull in the conversation to place my drink in front of me, though I whip it unceremoniously out of his hand before it reaches the tabletop. I take an indecorous gulp and come up coughing. Maybe that's why brandy is good for shock.

It's guaranteed to bring all snits to a spluttering end and drag all simpering misses from swoons.

I'm not swooning, and I'm not giving up on my snit.

With a start, I become aware of Luke's fingers entwining with my own again.

"Waiting for tonight has been the best and worst of tortures. Spending time with you, watching you, knowing each day we were getting closer to really doing this. I'm just so fucking bummed that it's all been for nothing." His words are almost desperate, but he's not the only one feeling let down. *Frustrated. Flat.* It doesn't matter because what was will now never be. "We haven't slept together in months, her and I, and I don't know what we're going to do going forward. I just know I'll need to be there for her. That it'll be expected of me from so many directions."

"And so you should." Please don't say you're going to try to welch on this because that would make you less than the man I hoped you were. Also, please let me finish my drink in peace because I don't have the emotional bandwidth to deal with this shit.

"But I promise you—"

"Whatever that promise is, hold onto it for the mother of your child." Because I'm looking for a man in my life, not a man-child. Or a man with a child. And associated baggage.

And though part of me wants him to define what he means by *months*—before our unspoken agreement or after?—much bigger things than this are at play now. I'm not interested in splitting hairs, particularly as I have no intention of becoming involved in any of this. My life is already complicated enough. From here on, I can't be anything but his friend.

"Whatever tonight was supposed to be, it's now in the past," I continue softly. "Maybe we were never destined to be anything other than friends."

First college and now this. I swear to myself right here and now that I'm not going to wait to act on anything ever again.

"Or maybe," he says, his eyes lingering on our hands, "we

should take this opportunity to get it out of our systems. My ex, Anna. I haven't made her any promises."

His words are halting, but his meaning is no less clear.

Urgh. Men.

"She's going to need you."

And I don't have the mental capacity to look after anyone else, I realise, because this is what I do. I take on other people's worries, problems, and issues. That's why I'm funding a company out of my own inheritance, living on a shoestring budget, wearing cheap clothes, and using public transport while the people who work for me all seem to have cars. I mean, do they think I'm conscious of my carbon footprint? That I bring my lunch because I'm environmentally conscious? I am, of course I am. But I'm also broke!

"And you have to focus on E-Volve," he says, slowly retracting his hand. "I'm sorry. I don't know why I would even suggest such a thing."

"It's okay," I answer simply, even if it feels much less than okay. But I have this meeting to think of, and I can't afford to blow it. I sigh in quiet acceptance. I won't get laid tonight. I won't get to experience the delights of Luke, but "Some things are just bigger than sex." Even as I speak, I'm pushing back my chair, and he doesn't stop me. So with my head held high, I leave the restaurant.

Outside, the air is still heavy, grey clouds trapping the day's heat while also threatening a deluge of rain. I turn left for no other reason than I want to be anywhere else but here. After the highs of earlier today, I'm feeling more than a little emotional. *Blame the brandy*, I tell myself, refusing to give in to the sting of tears as I give myself a little reality check. If it's been a day of highs and lows, given the choice, would I reverse things? Get to be with Luke while failing my pitch? If that had been the play of things, I wouldn't be crying right now. I'd be looking for a bridge to jump off.

Though it's past eight thirty, it's still full daylight. Summer days in London are long, and the sun often doesn't set until after ten in the evening. I walk without thought or direction, passing bars, restaurants, and old-fashioned English pubs where people spill out onto the sidewalks with their drinks in hand to avoid the stifling heat indoors.

Oh, for a little air conditioning.

"The Lord giveth, and the Lord taketh away!"

From the other side of the road, a drunken vagrant calls out. I want to yell back that he, maybe He, should pick on someone else today because I've had enough. I keep my eyes focussed ahead and continue walking instead.

At a pedestrian crossing, I pull out my phone as my shoes begin to pinch and I briefly consider splurging on an Uber ride home. As the green man begins to flash, the delicious scent of rosemary and garlic suddenly tantalises my nose. I realise I'm starving; I haven't eaten since lunchtime when I'd had a couple of crackers with a chunk of aged cheddar cheese. I was kind of looking forward to a fancy meal tonight almost as much as I was looking forward to being in Luke's arms. I sigh heavily as I begin to cross, accepting one of those things is off my Friday night agenda now.

But I'm celebrating as well as commiserating this evening. So I will splurge. An Uber to save my feet *and* a meal to nourish my belly. Or maybe my soul.

After all, what are credit cards for?

So I follow my nose, which leads me to a restaurant close by.

Pushing on the door, I step from the light into a much darker interior.

"Madam?" Almost immediately, I'm accosted by an imperious-sounding voice from beyond a small archway.

"A table for one, please."

"Do you have a booking?" The man steps under the dim light. He's seventy if he's a day, dressed in a dinner jacket with tails, and holding a leather-bound menu in his hand. A maître d' of the old school, by the looks of things.

"No, I—"

"I'm afraid we're fully booked this evening." His gaze roams over me disdainfully, so much so that I find myself looking down at my dress. *No stains. And, hey, this is Stella McCartney!*

"Really? You're fully booked?" I repeat, though more doubtfully.

"Quite." As he replies, his shoulders relax a bare half an inch. But oh no, honey, this isn't over.

"You're telling me you can't fit one more person inside this restaurant?" I strain to see around him to find him blocking my view. It should be ridiculous, and on any other day but this, I'd accept his explanation, no matter how annoying. But not today. And this is the straw that broke the (un-humped) camel's back.

"Madam?"

"Now, listen, you . . ."—*Downton Abbey reject*—"this is a restaurant that, by definition, sells food. I am a person who possesses money"—*fine, a credit card*— "who requires food. So how about we work out some kind of exchange?" I gesture between us quite violently, if a finger can ever be considered violent.

I guess it might poke out an eye.

"I am very sorry, Madam, however—"

"It's miss, actually." I've just had a long day. A day that's aged me.

"Nevertheless, *Madam*, we are fully booked this evening. And even if we were not, I'm afraid this establishment does not accept walk-in diners." The latter he says with such a lofty air, anyone would think he said *we rarely accept streetwalking diners*. But even streetwalkers need to eat, don't they?

I am seconds away from doing something that could well result in my removal from the premises wearing handcuffs when the door behind me opens again. *Just you dare give them a table, and I'll sue you for discrimination. After I tie those coat-tails up over your ears.* But as a hand curls around my shoulder, I turn.

"What the . . ." I begin, my words trailing off as I look up into

To Have and Hate

the face of the man I'd fallen on this morning. "You with the feet!"

"Yes. Last time I checked, I had two of them."

"What are you doing here?" The words are in the air without my permission and his answer steals any breath I have left.

"That's simple. I followed you."

4

OLIVIA

"I'M SORRY, WHAT?" And also, what the hell? And why am I now looking at his shoes? His big shoes. Because big shoes mean big feet, and big feet mean—

"Of course, I haven't followed you." At his dismissive tone, my head comes up so fast I almost give myself whiplash.

"Why would you say so if it isn't true?"

He sighs, actually sighs, as though I'm boring him. "I see your mood hasn't improved. It's quite all right, Peter," he adds, his attention moving from me to the maître d'. "The lady is my guest."

Guest what? Guest I wasn't paying enough attention.

Maybe I should be looking for hidden cameras.

"Very well, sir," Peter returns in a tone no less haughty. As for his expression, I can't tell because I'm still looking at the man behind me. Eyes the colour of fine whisky and hair like dark wheat. *Maybe I'm thirsty. Maybe that's why I'm still standing here.* Or maybe it's because our paths have crossed twice in one day. That's got to be the universe pulling strings, right?

"Shall we?" The man's lush mouth tilts in one corner in something that resembles a genuine smile, a far cry from his sardonic offering this morning. I find myself nodding in response, probably from shock.

He's still wearing the grey suit, his shirt open at the neck. For a moment, I consider what I'd look like if I'd worn the same clothes all day. The words *homeless person* spring to mind. Meanwhile, he still looks like the star of a Gucci ad campaign. Or like David Gandy's hotter, haughtier twin.

His hand cups my elbow as if I'm his elderly maiden aunt as he leads me through the archway and into a dark and sumptuous interior. The walls of the dining room are painted the colour of fine claret, the wooden floors gleaming like dark tinted mirrors. We come to a stop, the maître d' bidding me to sit. But I don't. I just stare at the oxblood-coloured leather upholstery as though the chair is alien. Raising my head, I stare at the snooty elderly penguin and then at the stranger opposite. He seems to be watching with barely contained amusement.

Am I only just coming to my senses? I feel like I've been hijacked, press ganged by polite pirates. Are they going to kill me with kindness? A very cold and sterile kind of kindness?

"I think this is a mistake," I begin, still standing, still ignoring both men. I'm no one's charity case. Besides, what happens if he's expecting company for dinner? Or a date? I know it all sounds so ridiculous, but after the day I've had, if a troupe of clowns came dancing through the restaurant, I'm not sure I'd be surprised. "Really, I can't—"

"Sit down," the stranger replies, his tone fairly dripping in boredom.

"I'm not a dog," I retort curtly.

"Just take a seat, there's a good girl."

The last person who called me a good girl was my grandfather, and it was usually accompanied by a pat on the head and a barley sugar candy he'd produce from a tin. He made it sound like a compliment, not a scolding for being annoying. So why exactly have I dropped into the seat opposite?

"That's better," he murmurs, seating himself as a waiter

appears at the table. The man opens my starched napkin with a flourish, laying it across my lap. He then presses a heavy leather-bound menu into my companion's hand.

"I owe the lady a glass of champagne," he murmurs, passing the unopened menu back. "A bottle of the Ruinart '98, I think."

He may be bossy, but he also has a very pretty mouth, and I can't seem to stop watching the shapes it makes, even comprehending the words.

"Of course," the sommelier, I guess, returns in modulated tones. "The rosé, sir?"

Both gazes turn my way, one narrowing in an echo of this morning. Before I decide they're waiting for me to answer, my trippy stranger murmurs, "Yes, I think so."

Apparently, I look like a girl who drinks vintage blush champagne?

"You don't owe me anything," I demur, my hands moving the silverware on the table in front a few millimetres to the left. My eyes also remain glued to the task.

"Not even an apology?" My head rises at his even tone. "I'd like to say this morning's behaviour was out of character, but that would be a lie."

"You mean you often trip up unsuspecting passers-by?"

"No. I usually do much worse." With a half-smile that can only be described as provocative, he adds, "I was very curt."

My responding laughter has a nervous edge because what's the difference between now and this morning? Also, being asked if you're owed an apology and hearing an actual apology are two different things, aren't they?

This has been the weirdest evening. But at least the interior of this restaurant is more comfortable than the first, even if it does reek of money. Low, soothing music plays in background, the unobtrusive waitstaff seemingly invisible until a diner lifts a finger and they reappear out of nowhere. The furniture is so comfortable it seems to suck the life right out of you, which is perhaps why our fellow diners' conversations are being carried out at levels scarcely above a hum.

The champagne arrives, and once poured, I settle for making a *v* of my fingers over the base of the glass.

"I draw the line at poisoning my guests."

Not for the first time, I realise why this kind of accent is described as cut glass. *His diction is so sharp it might pierce skin.* His sharp jaw flexes with something like annoyance as his own fingers wrap around the stem of the glass in front of him. He brings it to his mouth in an exaggerated motion.

"I'm not afraid of being roofied, if that's what you're implying. I'm also not entirely sure I'm your guest."

"I don't remember dragging you into the dining room. I invited you to join me. You accepted. By that very definition, you are my guest."

"Well, thank you." *I suppose.* Eventually, I lift my own glass and take a sip, allowing the cool bubbles to roll over my tongue. "I'm Olivia, by the way." I set the glass down but don't offer him my hand. The moment feels a little too odd to be covering the pleasantries now. *Odd.* That must be the word of the day. "Olivia Welland."

"Beckett," he offers in response with a slight tilt of his glass.

"Just Beckett?"

"Yes." I feel myself frown at his answer. "Is there a problem?" he adds. *Like the issuing of a dare.*

"I'm just making conversation." One-sided conversation. "Just Beckett? It's a little cloak and dagger, don't you think?"

"It's almost as though I live to intrigue you."

"So *just Beckett*," I enunciate in some approximation of him. "Just Beckett, like *just* Madonna or *just* Beyoncé or *just*—"

"Are you quite finished?"

Apparently, I am.

My shoulders rise and fall before I take another sip or three of my champagne. As he opens the menu, I take the opportunity to really look at the man opposite me. I know I looked this morning, but this time, I take a thorough inventory from a different perspective. For one thing, I'm not sprawled across the pavement, I guess.

He's tall and powerfully built. He looks like the kind of man who'd participate in triathlons for fun and barely break a sweat. His fingers are long and elegant, square fingernails buffed to a shine. Even ignoring his sharp suit and chauffeur-driven car, it's obvious he uses his head and not his hands for work. *If he works at all.*

He's older, but not old. Mid-thirties, I'd guess. He has the kind of face that would stop a girl in her tracks. Not because he's handsome (which he is) but because his looks are kind of intimidating. He seems to exude power, and even just perusing the menu, he looks kind of threatening. His expression focussed, like a hound on the scent of a hare.

I jump at the sound of the heavy-bound menu hitting the table.

"You look like you're about to bolt," he says.

"Is that an observation or a recommendation?"

"It would be a shame. I hadn't expected such lovely company this evening."

"Lovely?" Try combative.

"Lovely," he repeats, his gaze roaming over my face.

"I was just thinking about your looks, too." Because he *so* can't be talking about my personality. We're not exactly chatting like old friends.

"Should I prepare for an insult?" he drawls, resting his elbows on the arms of the chair, his fingers steepled. *As though his tone wasn't enough of a challenge.* "What was your verdict?"

"I've decided that while all outward signs point to you being a gentleman, I think . . . the illusion ends there." And I still didn't hear an apology.

"I sensed you weren't just a pretty face." Completely unfazed, he picks up the menu once again. "Shall we order?"

Despite the swanky surroundings, I opt for my usual go-to of

To Have and Hate

risotto, this one containing a type of mushroom I won't even try to pronounce. It's served with truffle shavings over the usual serving of parmesan. I send a silent prayer to the heavens that my selection isn't wildly expensive because it seems this isn't the kind of establishment that would sully its menu by including prices. Beckett orders chalk stream trout, which sounds fancy enough to come without a price tag, even if I do find myself biting back a smile.

"What's so amusing?" he asks after dictating his order to the waiter.

"I'm not allowed to smile?" Something inside me unfurls. No way am I telling him I'm relieved he's ordered fish. This really is just an unexpected meeting and a platonic dinner. A case of being in the wrong place at the right time. Or wrong time, depending on your perspective.

Maybe wrong *should be the word of the day, not* odd.

"I get the feeling you smile a lot, perhaps just not around me."

"Come on, we've met twice and spent. . ." I make a point of looking at the watch I'm not wearing. "Thirty minutes tops together?"

"Thirty minutes," he agrees somewhat inscrutably. "But I hope there will be many hours more."

That's just confusing. Who orders fish if they're *hoping to get to know you better*? Which, let's face it, is just boy-speak for hoping to get into your panties.

So not happening.

I don't even like him.

Right?

From here, things fall into a comfortable pattern. Or less strange, anyway. Conversation moves along with few gaps, and Beckett fills the potential awkwardness with a wry observation or an anecdote, all with a thoroughly practised ease.

"What brought you to town this morning?" he asks as the waiter fills my glass again. It's like my glass is one of those toy baby bottles I had as a kid, the kind that came in the box with a new doll. *Tip the bottle and it drains. Stand it up and it fills again.* Just like my champagne glass; I tip it to my lips, and by the time it's upright, it's full again. Like magic. But I do match each glass of champagne with another of fancy Norwegian water. *Probably harvested from a diamond glacier.*

"I had a meeting in the building you tripped me outside of. On the thirty-fifth floor." That's as far as I'll go, even if pushed for details. "I suppose you were there for kicks? Did you trip many more unsuspecting passers-by while you were there?"

"Remember, I said I do much worse. And usually in the same building." Over the rim of his glass, his eyes gleam. Maybe it's the light. Or the champagne. Maybe I should drink more water.

"What is it you do, then? You know, when you're not behaving atrociously?"

He taps a finger against his chin. "If I'm not behaving badly, then I must be asleep."

"No, seriously," I say with a giggle. Giggling. Also not a great sign. "What do you do for a living?" Because everyone works. Even rich people who have chauffeur driven cars have some kind of vocation, something to fill their day. Like my grandfather. He was a pharmacist and owned a chain of drug stores.

"I'm in finance."

"Ah, so you're in league with the devil, then?"

Our joint mirth is interrupted by the delivery of an entrée of tiny Thai style crab cakes. *More fish.*

"Here, try one." Beckett pushes the plate into the middle of the table, but I shake my head.

"No, thank you. I'm not a fan of seafood."

"Crab cakes aren't seafood," he says with an air of having heard something ridiculous.

"Crabs live in the sea. Ergo, seafood."

"They're delicious."

"I'll take your word for it."

"Try one, for goodness' sake." Both his lips and voice tighten. "Don't be a drama queen."

"Don't be a drama queen?" I repeat a incredulously. "I have this book you might benefit from. It's called *How to win Friends and Influence People*."

"I expect the spine is unbroken."

"Wha—" I think I might be making a guppy face.

"Olivia, eat a crab cake."

"How about . . ."—*you eat a dick*—"no," I add at the last minute and much more politely. I think I'm enjoying goading him.

"You're being ridiculous." His gaze narrows, his expression suddenly thoughtful, just not the good kind of thoughtful. The kind where he looks as though he's considering force-feeding me just because he can. Just because he's bigger than me.

"What if I'm allergic to seafood? What if I went into anaphylaxis?" What the hell am I doing arguing?

"Then I expect you would've have said that seafood was verboten. And I, myself, wouldn't have ordered fish."

"If I'd been allergic, it wouldn't mean *you* couldn't have fish."

"But what if I'd wanted to kiss you? And not to give you the kiss of death?"

His gaze is so intent I feel I need to wrap my hands around the arms of the chair to stop them from dithering. Touching my hair, clutching my pearls. That kind of thing. *Does* he want to kiss me? Do I want him to kiss me? Before I can fully analyse those thoughts, Beckett tears one of the tiny morsels open, dropping a piece into his mouth. His eyes roll closed as he savours it, and I must admit—to myself, at least—that it does smell really good.

And he looks really good eating it.

"Well." His attention returns, his thumb brushing the corner of his bottom lip. "So far we've established you're stubborn, you're in need of finance, and you're a colonial."

"I never said I needed finance."

He waves off my protest. "The companies on the thirty-fifth floor all deal in business finance of some sort."

"That doesn't mean anything."

"I thought I was supposed to be on first-name terms with Satan?"

"And Satan's given you the skinny?" I say with a snort.

"You are rather lovely when you're being oblivious, Olivia. Perhaps I should spell it out for you. I'd very much like to kiss you tonight."

5

OLIVIA

So much for my theory of fish and kissing.

"Play with me, more like."

My answer is immediate, the words in the air in all their brash incredulousness, because if this is the way he treats people he thinks are lovely, God knows how he treats the people he doesn't like. Yet I can't help but be flattered. *He wants to kiss me with that gorgeous mouth of his.* What would that be like, I wonder. Soft, I decide, at least to start with. Teasing and slow, the kind of kiss that makes your insides all shivery and your knees a little weak.

"How old are you, Olivia?"

"You're not supposed to ask a lady her age," I reply, wondering where the conversation will hop to next.

"Young women aren't generally so reticent. Or perhaps you want me to guess? Twenty-four? Twenty-three?"

"Fine. I'm twenty-seven." Practically. "What about you?"

"I'm older than that."

"Well, duh." Not my finest response as these things go.

"But not too old," he adds, the hint of a sparkle back in his gaze. "What about tonight?"

"Tonight, I'm half a day older than I was this morning. What about it?" I add when I realise he's not going to bite.

Bite. I bet he'd use his teeth, too.

My eyes are almost riveted to his mouth as he feeds himself what suddenly seems like small bites of heaven. Seafood seems to appeal to a stomach full of nothing but champagne.

"You're sure you wouldn't like some?" I shake my head even as he uses his fork to slice a crab cake in half before offering it to me. "They're delicious." A ghost of a smile hovers on his face as the fork dances in front of me. I finally concede, lifting my hand to take it from him, but he moves it away. I roll my eyes, then open my mouth anyway. *Don't judge.* The smell is divine, plus I really do need something to soak up the alcohol.

"I do hope you're not allergic."

I stifle a smile and use my napkin to gently pat the sides of my mouth. Not that I need to, but I need to do something because he's looking at me. Studying me, almost. *Like a butterfly pinned to a piece of felt.*

"What?" Do I have a little on my face?

"I'm still wondering about tonight." My heart jolts unexpectedly somewhere in the vicinity of my panties. *Tonight-tonight? After this?*

"What about it?" I enquire evenly.

"Aren't you intrigued as to why our paths have crossed again? Wondering what has brought us together?"

"As long as you haven't been following me, not really," I admit.

"If I'd followed you, I wouldn't be asking what brought you here tonight. Not many people are aware this place exists."

"And if they do, they know they're not welcome, right?"

"Have I not made you welcome?"

I shrug. Honestly, I'm not sure. "I'm only here because I got a little lost and a lot hungry, and well, that's pretty much the whole story. "I've had a strange kind of day," I find myself admitting, my gaze anywhere but on his. "I just wasn't ready to go home."

Our conversation pauses as the waiter clears away the dishes, which is now little more than a few crumbs and a smear of horseradish cream.

"Strange how?" he questions once we're alone again.

"Have you ever had a day when you're given something in one hand but robbed of something else?"

"I don't think we're ever given anything. We work for it. Swindle sometimes. Beg, borrow, and steal, but in my experience, we're rarely gifted good things."

I shrug under the intensity of his gaze, not knowing the answer or even the question. What the hell were we talking about again?

This time, he reaches for the champagne bottle, pouring the last few drops into my glass. "It sounds like you found a penny but lost a pound today, as the saying goes. Or was it the other way around?"

"The more I think about it, the more I'm convinced it's the penny that rolled out of my grasp." Maybe even less as far as values go.

"So, on the whole, you're having a good day."

"I suppose so," I conceded. "Even if I have drunk almost a whole bottle of champagne on my own. And on a mostly empty stomach."

"You're not drunk, are you?" His brows furrow, his gaze sliding to the space behind me. "Dinner won't be long." I realise he's looking for the waiter, probably willing our food to appear, which makes me chuckle.

"Don't worry, I'm not going to end up face down in my soup." Because I didn't order any. I reach for my neglected water glass.

"What did the pound represent? Was it business-related or personal?"

"Business. And don't ask me what. It's not a done deal yet, and I don't want to tempt fate."

"So you're superstitious, too?" He says this in the vein of *so you're ridiculous, too*?

"Let's just say I'm willing to cover all bases to get what I want."

I immediately play back the words in my head at the sudden flash of his grin.

"What about the penny? Business or personal."

"The experience was worth about that amount," I say. "Let's just leave it at that."

"Pity."

"Tell me about it," I reply.

"How about you tell me about it instead?"

I consider it for a moment. I don't know him, and I'll probably never see him again. And it's not like Reggie will be around for a debrief as she's off to spend time with her boyfriend's family this weekend. But no, I can't. It would be too weird.

"Trust me," I find myself saying, it's not a very interesting tale."

"I wouldn't have asked if I wasn't interested. I sense this penny was somehow personal. A friendship? Perhaps a romance?" I nod because it was both of those things. "A problem shared is a problem halved, so they say."

I laugh softly because oh, the irony. "This isn't the kind of problem that can be halved. It's the kind of problem that multiplies."

"Multiplies?" Beckett looks at me, then the glass, and for the first time this evening, I can actually see what he's thinking.

"No, sir. Not me. I'm not, what do you call it? Up the duff? There's no multiplication going on here. But the penny problem's ex-girlfriend is."

"Sounds positively soap-opera worthy."

"Try Korean soap-opera worthy." His expression is languid and a little seductive, and makes my little heart go pitter-pat. "And that's a secret, by the way. You didn't hear it from me."

"My lips are sealed. Whoever he is."

"I mean it," I add with a giggle as he mimes turning a lock at his mouth. Maybe I should feel bad for telling him. Maybe I'll feel bad tomorrow. Or maybe I won't care then, either. "Are you sure you want to hear this?" I find myself asking next.

"More than I want my next breath," he answers with a humorous glint.

"Okay, so, this guy I know, we met at UCL, and the attraction between us was pretty much one-way."

"Which way?"

"What? Oh. I was friend-zoned by him and barely a blip on his potential girlfriend radar because this boy is, was, total boyfriend material. I think if I chopped off his head, the words *serial monogamist* would be ingrained through his body like words in a stick of rock."

"And after today, you can see yourself doing just that?"

"Chopping his head off? You're asking if the idea is appealing. No." Surprisingly. "Not even a little bit."

"Why don't I believe you?"

"You're saying I look like a murderer?"

"I'm saying that I think you're a good actress. And for the record, so far in our short acquaintance, I've been on the receiving end of a number of your murderous looks."

"Glaring at you isn't the same. I'm not evil." I find myself glowering across the table, which just seems to make him smile more.

"Perhaps, but you're not as nice as you would have people believe."

"Wow." The word comes out as disbelieving chuckle.

"It's okay. I'm not very nice, either."

"Oh, *that* I've already realised."

"But you were telling me about your penny."

"I was. But now I'm wondering what word would run right through you."

"If you chopped off my head, you mean?"

"I'm also wondering why the prospect is suddenly so tempting."

"Ah, because I'm getting a glimpse of the real you, and most people don't."

"You know nothing about me." My tone is even, uninterested,

and completely the opposite to how I really feel. Which is shaken, though not the worried or shocked kind. More like, turned on.

"I also know nothing about your university penny, but you were about to tell me," he murmurs, all silky mouthed.

"So we're back to him?"

In answer, he inclines his head. *Please, go on.*

"Fine." On your head be it. "So, a few years later, our paths cross again. But time, he sees me."

"How can he not?" Beckett adds with an appreciative glance that makes me feel all ruffled and feathery. It doesn't mean I like him. It's just a physical reaction.

"And for once, he's not in a relationship," I add, my words almost running together. "But then he mentions who he works for, and I realise he could help me professionally."

"So you friend-zoned *him* this time?"

"There was an . . . understanding between us. You see, we've been working together quite closely."

"A euphemism?" His brow curls like a question mark.

"No. That's not what happened. We kept things strictly professional while he helped me pull my pitch deck together—"

"That's a sort of business plan, correct?"

"Bigger than that. Sexier than that. And pretty alien to me."

"So he helped. And you were grateful."

"Not in the way you're suggesting, but yes, I was grateful. Relieved." *So relieved.* "He got me a meeting to help secure financing." Which, if I'm explaining this to him, I guess Beckett isn't any kind of high-flying financier. Or maybe just not that kind of financier. What do I know? Not a lot, apparently. "And it was kind of implied that once it was over, we were free to date or whatever. There was no pressure or coercion. It's not like I promised him my body or anything. The attraction between us was kind of put to one side for a while."

I wave my hands as though the details aren't important, and

as though I didn't spend two hours of my day preparing for the night of my life that never came.

"I'm sensing a *but*."

Like a shark senses blood, I'm sure.

"The time just never came."

You know who else didn't come?

Doesn't matter.

"I should've known when I arrived at the restaurant," I murmur, toying with the stem of my glass. "The place didn't exactly scream romance. It was nice and obviously expensive but sterile." *Unlike Luke*, I think to myself, moving from my glass to rearranging the silverware again.

"Perhaps he was trying to impress you. Or perhaps he doesn't really know you as well as you think."

"Or maybe he just has poor taste," I mutter.

"Not in women."

His words are delivered so softly, I can't help but look up. Softly spoken words from such tender-looking lips. And then I'm wondering how those lips would move in a kiss. The shapes they'd make. How they'd taste. And now I definitely know I've had too much champagne.

Before I have a chance to agree or protest, and I'm still not entirely sure which would be appropriate, dinner is served. Our conversation returns to the inane. Not that Beckett is frivolous in any way, but his conversational skills are a mixture of astute observations and super sharp wit.

"I'm sure you have no end of suitable admirers," he teases as the conversation returns to my love life somehow.

Yeah, somehow.

"I struggle." At the raising of a sardonic brow, I find myself protesting with a giggle. "It's true! I can't remember the last time I had a decent date."

"Why do you suppose that is?"

"We're told, as a society, that men like the chase. They like women who are hard to get. At least, that's what we're told. But that's not true. Not in my experience."

"I suppose you have a theory."

"No. I just know men don't chase me."

"I find that very hard to believe." His eyes narrow, a ghost of a smile peeking through.

"It's true! Maybe I just don't play the game well enough."

"I'm not sure I follow."

"Maybe I'm not calculating enough, that I'm too nice or something."

"I'm sure that's not entirely true."

"That's not very complimentary," I contest, amused. At least, until I realise he's not joking. "I am nice!"

"You mistake me. It is a compliment. You, Olivia, are no insipid miss, despite your sugar-coating."

"Sugar-coat? I'm not sugar-coated. I'm just nice! A nice person."

"No, you only think you are. Or you want other people to think you are. Which is something that strikes me as odd. Nice is such a bland word. Nice people have no substance, I find. No spark. They make themselves available to others to be used as doormats. Clearly, you are no doormat. You're a dynamic and vivid woman attempting to hide behind a persona as deep as a puddle of rainwater. Perhaps that's where your problem lies."

"Wow. You're kind of an asshole."

"We're not talking about my shortcomings, though I will say nice girls don't hold any interest for me." His eyes roam over me in a lazy sort of appraisal. "They're so predictable. And such a letdown in bed. You, on the other hand. You'd be the opposite." My cheeks heat, a dark pulse beginning to beat between my legs. Where the hell did that all come from? "Does that shock you? Knowing that I want you?"

I swallow thickly. What happened to kissing?

"What you want doesn't interest me."

"See? You're not nice. Not even one little bit."

"You deserve it. You're, like, an incitement to violence."

"So I've been told." He picks up his glass. "Many times. Tell the truth, Olivia. How goes your *real* dating life?"

"I think I frighten men off." The level of relief I feel at the admission is ridiculous. "Other than Luke. He's the first man who's shown any interest in me." I blow out a breath. "In a very long while."

"The man who still sees you as the girl he met in university?"

"I suppose." My gaze dips to my napkin as I shrug.

"And why do you suppose he's allowed to think of you that way? If you're not that person anymore."

"I am that person. With him, at least."

"And with others?"

"I'm nice to my friends." It sounds like an excuse or a protest. "And to people, in general." I always try to be nice. And I'm fiercely protective of the people I love.

"But not to men."

"Men *so* don't like the chase." I find my expression twisting. "I can be in a coffee shop, on a train or a plane, or even in a vibrant city bar, my prickly outer shell seems to put every man within fifty meters off." And there's the heart of the problem. I don't really know if men like the chase because I rarely get to that point. "It's not like I mean to be mean. When a handsome man asks me if I'd like a drink, I'm really not the bitch that seems to crawl out of my mouth." I pause. "You're doing that weird staring thing again."

"Am I?"

"Like you're trying to see into my head."

"Perhaps it's because I find it hard to believe you don't mean to be rude."

I sigh heavily. "Sometimes, I don't even have to speak to frighten them off. I seem to be able to do it from across a room. A friend only has to point out that a man is staring my way or trying to catch my attention, and the bitch appears. It might be a disdainful look or a narrowed stare that keeps them from approaching me. It's no wonder I've barely dated since college."

"It's because they're not worthy of you."

"Oh, really?" And yes, I sound amused.

The waiter chooses that moment to appear like a wraith, ready to clear the plates.

"If you'll excuse me," I murmur, pushing back my chair with a sudden haste.

6

OLIVIA

Why would I tell him all that stuff?

I made myself sound like a complete basket case—a basket case wrapped in bitch.

And the bathrooms in this place? Urgh, so hard to find! But thankfully, my risotto seems to have soaked up the alcohol, so at least I'm not lurching around the place like a sailor on leave as I make my escape. My reflection, however, paints another story. I look like a woman well on the way to getting shitfaced. Mascara has gathered in the outer corner of my eyes, giving me a kind of sultry or slutty look. *I can't decide which.* My lip-gloss has entirely worn off, and my hair is back to its regular programming of frizz. Though that is less the fault of the champagne and more thanks to with my walk through the humid evening.

But this physical inspection is just a way to stop introspection because I'm not really going to let him kiss me. Am I? Could I really see myself going home with him? Sure, he's handsome, and smart in that razor-sharp way, but razors have edges that often cause pain. I've found myself saying things to him that I haven't thought through or examined properly, or maybe they're more like things I try not to think. What must I have sounded like complaining I couldn't attract a man?

Desperate, I decide. I sounded desperate.

"Oh, God," I say to my flushed reflection. "I've pretty much told him I need to get laid."

The door bangs open, and an elderly woman dressed more for a rave than retirement bustles in.

"Don't mind me, darling," she purrs, pushing open one of the stall doors as she rubs her finger under her nose tellingly. "The white stuff always makes me talk to myself, too!"

I don't bother discounting her assumption, and it's clear that unless I want to get into a conversation with an elderly cokehead, I can't stay in here any longer. But that doesn't mean I'm going home with him.

I could leave now, I think as I stand at the threshold of the dining room. I already have my purse, and I don't owe him anything. *Except my share of dinner.* But slinking away really isn't my style. Maybe he'll want to order dessert or coffee, and during that time, I could call a cab.

Yes. Change the tone, wind this evening down.

Pulling open the door, I make my way back to the table wondering how much a bottle of champagne costs in this place. And whether I have enough on my credit card to cover it. When I get there, Beckett is already pulling one of those fancy black credit cards from his wallet.

"Please let me know what my half of the bill is." I don't sit but, rather, hover by the side of the table, a little like the waiter. He's obviously waiting for his tip. Meanwhile, I'm waiting to make my escape.

Beckett scowls at me before signing the tiny slip with a flourish, exchanging what looks like a fifty-pound note for his card with the waiter.

Note to self: if my business goes bust, I could get a job in here. If I could ever find the place again.

"Well!" I exclaim, suddenly sounding all jolly-hockey sticks. "Thank you. Dinner was great."

"Yes," he replies, standing himself now.

"It was good to meet you. Again. Actually, it was weird but kind of pleasant." I can feel myself frowning. "Much better than when we met the first time, anyway. Well, I guess I'll be going."

As I babble my extraction plan, backing away from him, Beckett reaches out to touch my arm briefly. I wonder if it's some silent signal for *don't go, you're gorgeous creature* when I realise he's trying to stop me from falling over the chair behind me.

He smiles tightly in response to my apologetic mumbling, like he finds me an ordeal rather than charming. As I turn to walk forwards this time, I find his fingers curled around my elbow again as he leads me from the dining room. For some inexplicable reason, I have the overwhelming desire for that hand to hold me elsewhere else. *Curved around my hip, bringing us closer.* Why I honestly can't fathom. It could be the size of him next to me, a kind of evolutionary stirring. *The biggest and the baddest make the best mates*? Maybe I could blame the subtle spice of his cologne, or better still, the champagne.

Even though I know it's none of those things.

It's more likely because I'm horny and that I sense a night with Beckett would be like nothing I've ever experienced. No one can be that self-assured, contained and controlled without becoming a deviant when the lights go out. And I so want to find out. I guess that kind of make me a deviant, too.

At the door, his forearm brushes my hip as he reaches for the handle, the barely-there touch like a wash of awareness across my skin. I find myself leaning into him, knowing as I do my response doesn't go unnoticed.

It's not like I've been in love with all the men I've slept with, I reason as I try to make sense of my actions. That's also not to say I've slept with a lot of men, or that I've been in love a bunch of times, but I usually like the men I screw, at least. Which is possibly the reason I haven't had sex in a while. But I find I don't need a reason or an excuse right now.

The sun is setting when we step out into the humid evening, its scarlet rays escaping through the swirls of dark clouds. Beckett's car is at the kerbside, the engine idling before the driver climbs out. I inhale as I turn, ready to speak when he cuts me off.

"If you say *well* again, I'll leave you here on the pavement."

"That's one way to end an evening, I guess." I find myself smiling. There's something about annoying him that calls to me. Something that amuses the little devil sitting on my shoulder.

"Get in the car," he mutters with an air of long suffering.

We both know where this evening will end. And those tingling nerve endings from before? In the close confines of the back seat, they increase tenfold. I don't know where we're going, and it feels kind of wrong to ask. I can imagine, though. A dark warehouse somewhere far enough away from civilisation where the soon-to-be murder victim can't be heard. I catch myself smiling in the darkened window at such craziness.

But will it be his place or a hotel? The thought causes me to shiver.

"Cold?" Beckett's head turns my way, his question solicitous. I don't even get to answer, not that I'm about to tell him I'm turned on, before the driver is adjusting the climate controls. The hum of it adapts immediately.

We might be sitting side by side, but we're barely touching, so maybe I *am* on the way to be murdered somewhere? Unless he's thinking about dropping me at the nearest bus stop. I turn my ridiculous smile to the window and watch darkened snapshots of London blur by.

It's barely ten minutes before the car pulls to a stop in front of a pair of automatic gates, and in this time, Beckett has spoken a total of one word. It could be that I'm just really bad at reading the signals. If he wanted to fuck me, really have me like he said at the dinner table, then wouldn't he have at least made the tiniest of moves? A compliment? A caress?

Nothing. Nada. Nope.

The man is keeping his cards close to his chest.

To Have and Hate

My gaze slides to him, though I don't turn my head. Because if he likes to play games, I can play, too. I'll play the I'm-far-too-sophisticated-to-be-concerned game.

The gates are slow to open, and the driveway is a decent length as far as London property standards go, before the car pulls to a stop outside of what can only be described as a Georgian mansion.

Well, here we are, I almost say.

The interior light illuminates the small space as the huge driver climbs out of the car. Strangely, Beckett doesn't seem to be in any hurry to open any of the other doors. I begin to wonder where the driver has gone, not that I technically need the help. I've gotten to the grand old age of almost twenty-seven without someone travelling a couple of feet in front of me to open doors like my hands are nothing but stuffed gloves. But what I could do with is a clue as I narrow my eyes and peer out into the darkness. At least until I feel the caress of his finger against the back of my hand.

"You have freckles."

His voice is soft, the tenor of it drawing my attention as much as his touch. We both watch as his finger moves across the pale skin of my knuckles. With his head angled, I can see his hair is shorn short in an effort to keep it from its natural curl. His lips softly pout, his lashes casting dark shadows under his eyes as this thing between us, this strange attraction, swirls weighty and thick.

Then the interior light goes out.

And everyone knows the darkness brings its own delights.

His hand travels up the length of my arm, the pads of his fingers stroking over my bicep. I inhale sharply, biting down on my bottom lip, refusing to give in to the urge to sigh. Who knew the skin there was so sensitive? The sensation of his soft, touch radiates outwards, hardening my nipples under the gauziness of my dress, making them ache for attention.

Is he testing me? Torturing me? Waiting for me to make the first move?

There's only one way to find out, and find out is the least of what I intend to do as I turn and press my lips to his. His lips meet mine, more than returning the action. His hands slide into my hair, cupping my head as I find out exactly how soft his lips are. He tastes me. Teases. Savours me like I'm a delicious dish. My head lolls back against the headrest as he draws away to press kisses along my jawline, one hand slipping to my breast.

It's then I have a bit of an epiphany. Maybe his kisses are where he aims to set his behaviour to rights. The confusing hot and cold thing, the things he said meant to shock and other bad behaviours. Maybe his kisses aren't quite an apology but a means of showing me who he really is.

The insight evaporates as Beckett finds a spot on my neck that seems to be inexplicably linked to a point pulsing between my legs. I arch, pressing my breast full in his hand and his clever fingers begin to tease my nipple, soft swipes and tighter pinches, alternating gentle touches with a little pain. A nip of teeth against my ear, a slide of stubble against my neck, each movement oh, so controlled as he reads my reactions until I'm panting and wordless and minutes away from turning to liquid against the leather seat.

But with something that sounds like a growl of masculine approval, he slips his hand down my body and grips my thigh.

God, I'm so ready for this, though I hadn't envisaged doing the dirty deed in his car. It's a very nice car, but there's also a very nice house nearby, no doubt with a very nice bed ... or ten.

But those thoughts don't last either as his hand slips under me to bring my body over his. My knees on either side of his thighs, I find my summery dress is nowhere near where it should be, and due to the height restriction, my chest is heaving in his face. By his wicked expression and the way he moulds his hands around my ribs, this is no happy accident.

"God, yes, touch me, please," I whimper as his fingers graze the edge of my underwear.

"Such lovely manners." Beckett watches me lazily from under his thick, dark lashes. "You colonials are so unfailingly polite."

It takes a while for his words to register, but when they do, I drop down and rock over him, causing him to exhale a harsh curse.

"How's this for polite." My voice is husky as I undulate over his hard length, slipping my hands to the back of his neck.

"Fuck polite." Our mouths meeting in a rush as my body continues to move over his, slowly at first, but then less so.

"I think you want to," I taunt as hands grasp and teeth bite, this thing between us building in the tight space.

"By that definition, I suppose that makes you *polite*."

"I can be when the occasion calls," I rasp.

"What about when the occasion calls for you to be a fuck toy?"

"I don't know. Maybe you can tell me how that feels."

Under me, Beckett is all hard angles and slopes, and I can't touch enough of him. The dip of his collarbone as I feed my hands under his jacket, the hard caps of his shoulders, and his pectorals as I slide my hands down. The proud outline of his cock pressing against my hot centre, making my panties wet as I rock against him.

"Yes. Yes, like that." His voice rasps like sandpaper, the sound and his direction causing a fiery need to wind through my veins. I jerk at the unexpected sensation of a tug to my nipple, everything inside drawing tight like a knot.

One minute, we're writhing in the back seat, our movements hot and heavy, and the next, I'm on my back, and his hands are lifting from my waist.

Oh. This is it.

We're moving this from the car to inside his place.

Good.

Not that it hasn't been good so far.

Like a little trip down teenage memory lane if I ignore the smell of leather and expensive cologne . . . and the hands that seem to know exactly what they're doing. Endorphins still raging, I reach out and wrap my fingers around his wrist, not wanting the connection to ease. As his thumb and forefinger peel away my thumb, my mind seems to be struggling to compute what this is. I mean, *what the fuck?*

"Thank you," he murmurs, his tone as smooth as silk. Not so smooth is the way he jerkily straightens the cuffs of his shirt under his jacket.

"Thank you?" I repeat but not in the same tone as I push up on one elbow, falling back again as it slips against the shiny leather seat. My legs are in an undignified tangle as I try to right myself—my dress and my position at odds with his very proper form as he straightens his jacket, pulling sharply on the lapels.

"Yes, thank you for a very unexpected and enjoyable evening."

For an enjoyable . . . no, really, what the fuck?

I pull myself up, my movements stiff and jerky, partly because of the space issues and partly because I. Just. Don't. Get. It.

Or maybe I do, I think, my heart sinking along with my gaze. Maybe he's the kind of man who's all froth and no substance. The kind who arrives at the destination far too prematurely, if you know what I mean. But as my gaze sinks south, I note the bulge in his pants and know that is *not* the case. It's like he still has something stolen from the produce aisle shoved down there. And there's no telltale wet patch, excuse my indelicacy.

So, again. What the hell is going on here?

I just don't get it.

It looks like I'm not *getting it*, either.

"Dobson will take you home."

I think maybe I'm doing a solid impersonation of a guppy as I manage, "Take me home?"

"Yes. No doubt you have a very busy day tomorrow."

"But tomorrow is Saturday," I find myself answering. But it doesn't make one bit of difference. In fact, I'm not even sure he even he heard me because the car door is already closing behind him.

I tug at my dress as the driver's door immediately opens. My mind is still trying to process what the hell just happened as a quiet voice says,

"Where to, miss?"

7

OLIVIA

"He said thank you."

"He said what?"

"Thank you," I repeat. "Thank you for services not quite rendered, I guess." And hell, yeah, I felt cheap. "Then he climbed out of the car."

"And where was the driver while this was going on?" Reggie asks, her tone no less incredulous and almost squeaking down the phone line. I'm not sure if she's enthralled or disgusted. It's a little hard to tell because of the volume. But she's definitely invested. And yes, I know. I know I said I wasn't going to be able to speak to her this weekend, but it's not like I could spend two whole days without getting this stuff out of my head.

She knows. She gets it. I'm available for her emergencies, too.

"The driver was standing outside. It was dark, and the windows were tinted so I don't think he saw anything." Though I'm sure he heard my muttering as I cursed complaints all the way home.

"Did it not strike you as a little weird? That the guy's chauffeur was standing outside while you and the nutjob were getting freaky on the back seat? He could've had a camera or something."

"I doubt that," I reply, pulling at a thread hanging from the seam of my denim shorts.

"Not to mention that the car was parked outside his perfectly habitable house.

"I know, I guess I thought I was getting a little taster before we went inside. Urgh. It was all weird. So weird! And I was really into him, which is just weirdness on top of more weirdness because he isn't even my type."

"Rich is everyone's type," she retorts. "And rich people get a pass for being weird. They even have a different label for it. Unconventional," she adds expressively. "I'm pretty sure that covers ugly rich asses, too."

Her words make me think of the (definitely) elderly (possible) coke fiend in the restaurant bathroom. But I don't mention her appearance.

"So, is he?"

"Is he what?" I ask, my mind still in the bathroom.

"Ugly."

"Nope. The man is hot." In looks, at least. In behaviour he was so cold.

"What kind of hot? Henry Cavill kind of hot or Tom Hiddleston kind of smoking?"

"He's definitely more Loki than Superman, for sure." He's the debonair villain in a film noir. The irascible rake in a regency story. "It might've been easier if he was ugly." But this is a lie because I would have found him no less intriguing, I'm sure. *It wasn't just his looks that made me hot.* "I might not have ended up in that position at all."

Which is probably another lie.

"Ooh, positions. Kinky."

"Clumsy, more like. We were in the back seat of a car, remember those days?" While I'm still seven colours of angry and twelve more colours of confused, I'm also painting a picture that isn't quite true. I might have ended up sprawled across the leather in a less than ladylike manner, but nothing about

Beckett's moves were unpractised. "As for kinky, unless this is some kind of serious delayed gratification thing, I think not."

"He left you high and dry and didn't even share his name." Reggie's words echo my thoughts. "What a douche. What will you do if you see him again?"

"I'll be sure to run the other way." I hope.

We both fall quiet before Reggie begins to speak quite animatedly. "I think I've got it! Maybe that's his kink—getting you all hot under the collar, then withholding the D."

Beckett was contained and certainly controlled, but I'm pretty sure that's not why he left me in the car feeling cheap.

"Like a ten-dollar whore," I mutter some time later as I scrub nonexistent stains from the kitchen countertops, anger having manifested itself as an urge to clean. "Asshole. Big footed, big dicked, small-minded asshole."

Because that's the conclusion I've come to. The only kind of coming I've come near to, so to speak.

"The man couldn't cope with a woman content in her own skin. A woman who owned her sexuality was a threat to him. There!" With a decisive nod, I tell myself I'm right, and that the worktops are clean enough. On to the bathroom!

At least the energy from my sexual frustration is being put to good use.

8

OLIVIA

Another Monday, another very important morning meeting, and another last-minute dash. This time, I blame the Uber driver for not knowing there'd be traffic on this route.

"Are you sure you can't take a shortcut?"

"Madam, I have been in this country less than three months. I think it entirely better if we stick to the suggested route."

"But I'm going to be late."

I'm trying not to be a bitch despite feeling thoroughly bitchy. If Friday night was enough to make me turn into a mega bitch, this morning's experiences have sent that bitch stratospheric. First, Jorge, the developer on staff, rang to say he's discovered a glitch in the E-Volve back end. It's going to be offline for an hour, which is a pain in the ass as I'd planned on demonstrating its use this morning at my meeting.

"But late is always better than never," the driver advises with a sage waggle of his head. "Do you know that the traffic collision rate in Delhi is forty times higher than it is in London? Forty times!" To emphasise his point, he bangs his palm against the steering wheel.

"Oh, really?" I sit back in my seat deciding that straining

forward isn't going to get me there any faster. But it is giving me neck-ache.

"One death every hour!" he pontificates, his index finger held aloft. "I bless the good Lord for bringing me out of such a deathly place, and I will do my very, very best to keep my passengers safe."

"I'm sure," I murmur, my eyes sliding to the side window. No sunshine today, but I'm not taking that as a bad omen, even as the rain begins to dash against the windows. *And even if I can't throw off the funk that's lingered all weekend.* As the driver continues his sermon, I consider leaving him a less than a stellar five stars before deciding I could do without a karmic hit.

It seems to take forever to get where I need to be, and despite figuring in extra time, I'm arriving once again by the skin of my teeth. With a quick thanks, I hop out of the car and make a dash for the steps, holding my three-year-old Burberry trench coat over my head as the rain shower becomes a deluge. On Friday, I arrived at the building sweaty because of the heat and my rushing, but this time, anxiety is to blame as a cold sweat breaks out against my skin. Also, my shoes are wet.

Once inside the building, I shake out my coat, folding it inside out, before draping it over my arm. As I make my way to the behemoth front desk, I run my hand down my thigh, nervously straightening the wrinkles where the material of my skirt has pulled tight.

"Olivia Welland. I have an appointment with Mark Jones of Jones, Beckett, and Wright."

Beckett.

How the hell . . .

Oh, no. Fuck no!

My stomach sinks to my shoes. But no, the universe isn't so cruel. This is just a coincidence.

It must be.

The receptionist makes the call, murmuring into the handset.

"Oh," I hear her remark. "Okay. Yes, I'll tell her. Perhaps there was a mistake." Cue a second stomach swoop as her gaze flicks my way with a pinched expression. I straighten my spine and paste a *don't mess with me* look on my face. I'm here to do business, and business I intend on doing!

"Ms Welland? Mr Jones' PA doesn't have you down for today. Your appointment was Friday."

"Yes, that's right. But I had a call from her asking me to return today."

"Yes, of course. But what I mean to say is that your appointment this morning is with Mr Beckett."

I think . . . I think I must look like I've swallowed half a lemon, half a lemon that feels like half a melon in my throat as I swallow down the words *mother fuck* while also trying to convince myself that this isn't some massive cosmic shakedown. It's just a coincidence. Beckett is a common enough surname. Hell, Beckett might have even been his first name for all I know. Wouldn't that make more sense anyway? That he'd give me his Christian name to keep up the whole secrecy thing? Also, on Friday, he was only near the building, not in it. And he wasn't at the meeting.

"Ms Welland?"

"Yes, of course. My mistake." Because there are more men named Beckett in London than him. I mean, I don't have a phone book on hand or the time to search the internet for confirmation as I juggle my laptop bag, purse, and coat to sign in. But I'm sure finding two Becketts in the vicinity of this building is pure coincidence.

There.

No need to panic. Or stress.

I make my way to the elevators and don't even mentally genuflect as I step into the little glass box of potential death. I pull out my phone to check my email, suddenly doubting what I'd read, but I can't get a signal. So all the way to the thirty-fifth floor, I'm giving myself a pep talk.

It's a coincidence.

Get your head in the game.

Today, you're going to show him—not him-him, the other him—how E-Volve works.

How it can help people find love while also making those involved an awful lot of money.

I rub my sweaty palms against my thighs as the doors ping open on the thirty-fifth floor, and I'm met by the young intern I'd noticed last week who greets me with a warm smile.

"Ms Welland, Mr Beckett is waiting for you. Right this way."

On the tip of my tongue, I have a dozen questions balanced. Did this particular Beckett attend the meeting on Friday? What's his position in the company, and how the hell did I end up with a meeting with him?

We walk through the same sleek and stylish open-plan offices, past glass-walled meeting pods and the larger boardroom to the far end where a bank of private offices are housed. Private but for the glass walls facing the more public spaces. I count four doors that blend seamlessly with the walls they're set into. *Glass doors set in glass walls.* But at least it makes it easy to see what's in the rooms. Offices as big as my apartment with desks and chairs, and fabulous views. But it must be like working in a goldfish bowl. The woman turns left, leading me to the door at the very end.

Without knocking, she pushes it open, then steps aside, gesturing me inside a huge corner office. *Whoever said size doesn't matter obviously hasn't been in here.* Despite the grey gloom of the day, the stark space is suffused in light. An atrium terrace runs the length of one side with rain currently lashing against the glass. An industrial looking partner's desk sits almost front and centre of the room framed by an almost panoramic view of the city beyond. To the left, several oversized canvases hang against the bare wall, the bold splashes of colour almost a shock to my retinas. A plush geometric-patterned rug denotes a seating area, though nothing about it looks casual. A console table sits behind it, some stylishly placed *objet d'art* definitely not picked up at Ikea. The charcoal fabric of the high-end Knoll sofa and a pair of matching chairs is perfect complement to the clouds that seem to be hanging just beyond the windows.

"May I take your coat?" The woman's voice brings me back to the moment and the fact that she's stepped into the room behind me.

"Oh. Yes. Thank you."

"Would you like something to drink? A tea or coffee?"

"No, thank you." Even if I could go for a straight vodka about now.

In response, she inclines her head. "Mr Beckett will be with you shortly." She smiles blandly before closing the door behind her.

No way am I sitting. I'm not sure why, but nothing about this feels right. As I place my purse and laptop next to the sofa, it also occurs to me that I haven't seen Luke. *Is that a good omen or a bad one?* I wonder. But as he knew I had a meeting, I guess that means he's hiding from me. I'm not sure how that makes—

"Sorry to have kept you waiting."

At the sound of *the* Beckett's voice, my blood turns to ice water.

"You," I growl as I turn. The man has the audacity—the gall—to lean in and kiss my cheek as if the whole scene in the car never happened. "No!" And hell no, as I place my hand in the centre of his chest and turn my head. "I have no idea what this is about," I add quickly, turning and gathering my things, my frozen blood heated now by a million degrees. "And I really don't care."

"Don't you?"

My angry gaze meets his sardonic one, and I notice today's suit is a navy blue one worn with a matching baby blue shirt. A tan belt and tan brogues complete the ensemble.

The devil does Monday morning.

"I don't care to discuss what happened on Friday." I aim for an imperious tone and hope that I carry it off.

"I can see how the evening may have left you feeling out of sorts, but I assure you, it has nothing to do with today's meeting."

His words are even, his tone oh, so reasonable, even if it's all bullshit as he drops his jacket to a chair facing the wall of glass.

"I have nothing to say to you about any of it," I mutter, flinging my purse over my arm and pivoting to face the door. I realise the wall of glass is now opaque. But it doesn't matter because I have a pretty good idea of where the opening was. "If anyone, anyone *else* in this company is seriously interested in E-Volve, they can call me." Hell, I'll even take the janitor's call over this face to face.

"I'm afraid that's not going to happen."

"I'm sure you don't speak for everyone. Maybe I'll just drop Mark Jones an email." I push on the door, but it doesn't budge.

"You either speak with me this morning or discount JBW as a partner." That steel in his tone? That's new. "The choice is yours."

"Fine," I throw over my shoulder. "You aren't E-Volve's only option."

"Aren't we?"

"Open the damn door," I grate out as steam begins to build between my ears.

"It isn't locked. You just need to know how to touch it."

I make a noise through my nose that would best be described firstly as derisory and second as inelegant when I whip around to face him. "Is this funny to you? I just need to touch it to make it open. And then what? Walk away?"

Urgh, too much, Ols. Don't let him see you're riled.

Leaning against the desk, Beckett crosses his long legs at the ankle, and makes a show of folding his arms over his chest. But his expression? That remains as blank as a mask. A handsome mask, but a mask all the same.

"You mean Friday evening. If you'll just give me a moment to explain."

"What makes you think I want to hear whatever sorry excuse you're about to make?"

"I wasn't about to excuse myself," he answers as though the idea was ridiculous. "But I could explain. Or you could leave."

To Have and Hate

"I like that second one." I turn back to the glass wall, pressing my hand over it.

"A brave choice for someone with so few resources."

This time, my head turns almost like a turret on a tank, and if I could, I'd blow off that man's head.

"What do you know about my resources?"

"I know E-Volve has advanced solely due to your personal finances, that you're paying for everything from the software to the salaries, and that your capital is rapidly drying up."

"That has got nothing to do with you." My words are as hot as my burning cheeks. How dare he go snooping, but more than that, how dare he make me feel like a fool. "That is a serious invasion of my privacy, morally reprehensible, and—"

"Not quite as bad as ensuring E-Volve won't gain finance."

If it's possible for words alone to stop a person's heart, I think that's what just happened. I turn slowly, pressing my back against the glass in case my legs give out.

"You would do that?"

His shoulder lifts and falls, his expression penetrating. "I thought you understood. The man who'd have Satan on his side would stop at nothing to get what he wants."

"And you want E-Volve?"

"You mistake me, Olivia. It's you I want."

9

BECKETT

Her response surprises me. I'm not often surprised, but a sudden peal of genuine laughter is not what I'd anticipated.

"Oh boy," she murmurs, touching a finger to the outer corners of her eyes. "Excuse me for saying so, but it didn't look like that on Friday night."

"Friday night was unfortunate." It was a mistake. And it was everything.

"You're telling me."

"The snide tone is unnecessary, Olivia. As is your attitude."

"Oh, you haven't begun to see my attitude." She folds her arms across her chest, but at least she hasn't left.

"The way I see it, your troubles extend beyond my rejection—"

"Oh, you are just a *prince*."

"—and a little heavy petting on the backseat of a car." She mutters something under her breath. Uncomplimentary, no doubt. "You need money," I continue, "and I can help you with that."

"You'd really stop me from getting finance?" she asks, my meaning finally sinking in. She pushes away from the glass then seems to think better of it, pressing the backs of her shoulders against it again. "Why? Why pick on me?"

"I'm not sure I have anything to do with your difficulties," I lie.

"What difficulties? What are you talking about?"

"I shouldn't need to point out that you're here because of the introduction facilitated by your friend." Olivia glowers over at me. Quite cute, really. Red cheeks and eyes gimlet green. "Do I need to mention his name? Or should we just call him the bad penny?"

"If he's the bad penny, what does that make you?"

"You can't insult me, Olivia."

"Maybe I'd enjoy trying."

"What most people don't understand is that offence exists not within the insult but within any reaction to it." Her expression clouds at my words. "Most people find difficulty with the concept, not because it's terribly far-reaching or beyond the understanding of most, but rather because they're too emotional to see the beauty in this. To put it bluntly, your opinion is so irrelevant, I can't be bothered to take offence."

I'd meant this in general, but Olivia takes it as a personal slight. She's like a struck match and not just in her colouring.

"If I'm so *irrelevant*, why am I here? What do you want with me?" She throws out an arm, though I sense she'd rather be throwing it around my neck. *To choke me.*

"I have a business proposition for you." Nothing to do with the rear seats of cars. *Yet.*

"I'm not sure I understand."

Of course you don't. And that's the way I'd like to keep it for now.

"You work here?" She attempts to turn her question into an assertion by adding, "I mean, you obviously do."

"Yes, though some would object to the validity of your assumption."

Do I appear in this office regularly? Not really.

Am I employed by the company? Somewhat.

Are my investments sound? Absolutely. I've made the partners, my investors, and myself very rich in the process. In all fairness, I've made all parties wealthier, not necessarily wealthy. People in this business aren't exactly the rags-to-riches sorts. This isn't The National Lottery.

"So why weren't you there for my pitch?"

"Who says I wasn't?" I see in her eyes the moment the realisation hits her.

"*You!* You were there—in the doorway!"

"A happy accident following a not so happy one. I see your knees are healing nicely."

"Don't you stare at my knees," she declares, pulling at her skirt as though the whole thing had suddenly become transparent. "How dare you call me in here to play with me?"

"I never play games where money is concerned." Though this is not really true. Venture capital can be a little like playing poker. Experience and a sound strategy will serve you well, skill will get you so far, but there's always an element of luck involved. "I can assure you I'm not playing with you."

"What was Friday night?"

So we're getting to the heart of things. *The Romans were right. A fickle and a changeful thing is a woman ever.* Friday evening was unexpected, tempting, and nothing I can afford to think about right now.

"We'll get to that soon enough."

"No, I think we'll get to that now," she says, finally pushing off from the glass wall. "What were you doing there?" she demands, pointing her finger at the office floor with her eyes narrowed to glittering slits. Her purse begins to slide from her shoulder, and she hitches it higher, advancing like a villager in need of a pitchfork.

"Must we keep going around this? I heard your pitch, and while I applaud your passion, frankly, I'm not interested in E-Volve."

"Your loss," she retorts, batting off the barb. But not before it stings her.

"Not at the moment, it isn't. It's yours. Your redundancies to effect. Your leases to break. Worst-case scenario? Creditors chasing you. Best? A return to the States with your tail between your legs."

"You know nothing about my business and even less about me."

"I know this business is all about connections. As I also understand that, without Luke, you might've waited months or not have been invited beyond this threshold at all."

"There are other companies. Other ways to finance."

"I've asked around, spoke to the companies you've approached. You didn't have many takers. Why don't you just admit that this was your one great hope."

"A hope you've stolen from me."

"Perhaps you should look closer to home when apportioning blame."

"My pitch was not the issue here," she almost growls, jabbing her finger in the air in my direction. I want to bite it, but I can't afford to accede to whims currently.

"Your pitch was . . . cute."

"It was not cute. It was smart and professional. It was on point!"

"Tell me, do you have a thing for tattoos?"

"It was sexy!" she almost yells, ignoring my question. But she's right. It was a good pitch. And she made it sexy with her confidence and delivery. The way she had her audience in the palm of her hand. *And in the way her skirt fell to her knees, revealing nothing yet promising everything.*

On reflection, I hope the latter was just my take on things.

"It was . . ." I reach up and run a considering hand over my jawline. "Of the moment."

She accepts my condescension like a slap, recovering quickly. "Like that even means anything."

"It was Instagram worthy. All sparkle and no substance."

"You . . . *fucker*." By her harsh fricative, I deduce she'd tried very hard not to curse. Another sign of her impulsiveness.

"Tell me, how is Luke adapting to his news of impending fatherhood?"

"How would I know?" she hurls back at me, her eyes skating away, perhaps unsure if she should come closer to cause me harm or cut her losses and run.

"He hasn't yet made it to the office this morning, or else I'd call him in to ask."

"I don't care."

"And if he *were* here, we could also ask him where I got your financials from."

"What?" Her gaze narrows, as though testing my veracity. "He wouldn't . . . He didn't."

"One could argue it's his job. Due diligence, perhaps. A friend selling you out or trying to gain access to your underwear. Or the behaviour of a jilted, jealous would-be lover. It might be any of these."

She takes two steps, dropping a battered leather satchel and her purse to the console table. Her palm press into the wood as she shakes her head, muttering words not meant for my ears, but I hear her distrust and confusion anyway. As her head comes up, and she turns, she mirrors my stance. With her bottom pressed against the console table, she folds her arms across her chest, she effects a relaxed demeanour. She's a sea of calm, but for the way the toe of her shoe itches to tap.

"You're saying Luke is the reason JBW won't be investing in E-Volve?"

This isn't strictly true, but for the purposes of today, I neither confirm nor deny.

"That's the million-dollar question, isn't it? Or pound sterling in this case."

"I didn't ask for that level of investment. I don't need that much money right now."

To Have and Hate

"I disagree. If you want to attract the big players, a million-pound cash injection right now is the least you'll need. While your dating anecdotes were childishly charming, your marketing requires work. I'd also suggest recruiting an information architect, along with a user experience designer. Your interface requires work. It could be more professional. You need a cushion and to start thinking bigger. That is, if you want to catch the bigger fish."

"Why? So you can commit me to the poorhouse?"

"How Dickensian. And I suppose that casts me in the role of Compeyson?"

"If the top hat fits," she sneers. It doesn't last long. Not in the face of my smile. A genuine smile that seems to have thrown her. But what can I say? I'm oddly charmed that she's familiar with *Great Expectations*, though I can't see her rotting away in a wedding dress somehow.

"It's strange that particular character should come up in our conversation."

"This whole day is strange," she mutters. "Mercury must be in retrograde or something."

Now it's my turn to sneer. "Don't tell me you believe in such rubbish."

"Talk to the hand," she replies, "because the universe isn't listening. Not to people like you, anyway."

"People like me who are trying to invest in your company?"

"But you just said—"

"I've said a lot of things, Olivia. Most of which seem to have gone over your head."

"I think I'm beginning to get motion sickness. You trip me," she says, beginning to check things off her fingers. "You get me all riled up in the back seat of your fancy car, you tell me my pitch was no good, that JBW won't invest in me, and then you start throwing around a lot of zeros."

For the first time since I'd entered my office, I trust myself to push away from the desk. Since leaving her sprawled across the leather back seat with her summery dress around her hips and her creamy lace underwear on display, I've thought of little else. The scent of her skin, and the feel of her heated centre, and the noises she made, which seem to now play on a loop in my head. I've imagined the dozen ways I'd take her—a bed, a wall, over a table, her mouth and her pussy wet and open for me.

As I stalk across the room, I get a kick out of the widening of her gaze, the way her fight or flight instincts kick in, and how she strives to conceal them. She stands her ground and even elevates her chin, offering it to me like a prize fighter ready for another blow.

Naturally, she seems confused as I take her hand and lead her to the sofa. But it's that or lifting her to sit on the table and wrapping those soft thighs around my hips. Bigger things are at play right now. And good things come to those who wait, as well as being all the sweeter for the delay.

"JBW isn't going to invest in E-Volve," I say. Taking my place on the sofa next to her, I twist my body to face her while keeping a good twelve inches between us. She stares ahead, though I can tell it's taking some effort to sit still as I appreciate her profile. The upward curl of her lashes as she blinks. The slope of her nose and the shape of her lips that make her appear to be perpetually pouting. Or perhaps that's just around me. "But the B in JBW will."

"Beckett," she answers flatly as if my name is the worst of insults as her head turns my way.

"Yes."

"Isn't that, like, a conflict of interest?"

"No. It's strategy."

"Something tells me that I shouldn't believe a word you say." She sighs heavily, and her breasts rise and fall, evoking a memory from Friday. *In my hands, ripe and full, her cleavage heaving with her sighs under my chin.*

"A million pounds," I snap, beginning to lose my temper. This whole exercise is beginning to feel like herding cats. And I'm not entirely sure it's all her fault.

"A million." She turns to face me fully now, one foot hooking behind her calf. *A calf that was supple and satin soft to my touch.*

"To begin with."

"What for?" she asks, not bothering to conceal her suspicion. *Clever girl.* "I mean, what do you want?"

"I have a business proposition."

"Which is what?" Her tone is . . . uncomplimentary.

"What? Why? Which? At least that's some variance over *well*," I drawl, referencing her discomfort at the dinner table Friday evening. "Perhaps if you'd just close your mouth for a moment and listen, you might find out."

"*Well*, excuse me for feeling a little pissed at being blindsided. I'm entitled."

"Sadly, yes. But I blame that on your status as a millennial."

"That's it. I'm out of here." She jumps to her feet and begins to gather her bags. Her movements are jerky while her mouth moves with unspoken insults.

"Do you know Mark Jones and Luke are related?"

"Don't know, don't care." She throws the strap of her purse over her shoulder, grasping the handle of the satchel tight.

"Mark is his stepfather and close to retirement."

"So?" Her arm tautens with the weight of the bag as she slides it from the table.

"I want this company. The controlling stake."

"What has this got to do with me?"

"Everything and nothing, I suppose. It depends on the choices you make in the next few minutes. Because I want this company, Olivia, and you're going to help me get it. By marrying me."

I suppose I shouldn't be surprised by her response again, yet I am as she bursts out laughing again.

10

OLIVIA

"Are you high?" He doesn't answer unless you count the way he glowers at me. "I'd need more than a million-pounds to persuade me to marry you."

"How much?" he answers baldly.

"Double your net worth. Hell—triple it!"

"You obviously don't know what I'm worth." He relaxes against the sofa, his arms casually propped along its back. I find myself wondering how a smile could look so cruel. "Financially," he adds as I open my mouth to deliver my exact (non-numerical) answer.

"Like you have a high opinion of me," I retort instead. "Let's just call it even."

"You mistake me. I wouldn't be offering to marry you if I didn't esteem you."

"Your flattery is unnecessary." Even that delivered in the vein of Mr Darcy, the extra brooding addition.

She is tolerable but not handsome enough to tempt me

. . . so I climbed out of the car and left her with her panties on display.

"You made it quite clear on Friday evening exactly how little you think of me."

My skin prickles with awareness as his gaze suddenly slides over me. I'd like to say it's with a sense of revulsion or disgust from the recognition that he's blatantly playing with me, but it's not. Damn his haughty manner and looks and damn my reaction to them even more.

"So this is what's important to you? You're feeling spurned."

"You can't put a price on people," I reply, choosing not to answer his assumption. Choosing not to give him the satisfaction of an answer either.

"Have you thought or considered any other reasons as to why I left you when I did?"

"I haven't wasted my time on that night, or you." Even if my currently spotless home disputes those words. He smiles as though silently calling me on my bullshit, and my mouth opens without my permission to make good on my lie. "You're a prick." And with that, I turn on my heel and stride for the glass door. *Please let me find how to open it.*

I hear his footsteps immediately behind me, their echo filling my chest with a tightness I don't recognise. *An excitement. A thrill.* My own feet move faster across the expansive shiny floor, my heart and stomach a mass of jangling sensations as I reach the opaque glass where my approximation of the opening is concealed. But Beckett's hand reaches the glass before my outstretched one does.

"Liar." He lowers his head, his whisper a hot taunt in my ear.

His cologne today is more citrus than spice; a clean, crisp scent that seems to prove my olfactory system is linked to the bunch of nerve endings between my legs. Or maybe it's his voice, or the pheromones he's throwing out at such close proximity. Whatever it is, it's inconvenient.

"Let me out."

"I'm not keeping you here." There's a hint of a chuckle in his statement. "It's not my fault you can't work out how to use a door."

"This isn't a door. It's more like a portal to hell."

"You have a flair for the dramatic, Olivia." His tone is low and velvety. "But you weren't acting on Friday evening. Admit it."

"Go to hell."

"I thought we were already there."

His body hovers close to mine without actually touching, yet I feel the power restrained in him anyway. My eyes fall to where his hand presses against the glass, his long fingers splayed. A strong wrist under a French cuff with the added embellishment of a silver cufflink. I have the mad idea to bite him there over the dusting of sandy hair and tan skin. To press my teeth there. To leave my mark.

Of course, I don't. I might get rabies or something.

A soft gust of breath coasts my ear, a bloom of heated anticipation bursting in my core as a response. I can't explain my body's reaction. My head and my senses at war. I don't even like him, so how come I'm so turned on as my breath clouds then evaporates against the cool glass. Silence trickles between us, building heat and need.

"You were so wet." His whisper is the bedroom kind and without taunt or harsh inflection. And that feeling inside me? It doesn't burst but floods. "Admit it. You wanted me to fuck you right there on the back seat."

"Does that turn you on?" I twist my head and am met by those startling eyes, flecks of amber dancing like fire. *Or maybe the souls of the damned.* "Did it get you hot to leave me there? Is that your kink?" I say, Reggie's words coming back to me as I turn to face him.

In the face of my taunting questions, Beckett just smirks.

"That's really bothering you, isn't it? Don't worry, sweetheart. You are irresistible." His gaze falls over me and everywhere it touches, it burns. "Well, almost."

"I stand by my previous statement." I burn. God, do I burn. "You are a prick."

"I'm the prick who'd put money on you being wet right now. Wet for me."

To Have and Hate

"No, you're the prick who might have found out on both occasions if you were anyone but you."

"Perhaps I decided one night would never be enough."

"So you propose?" I reply with a disbelieving snort.

"Perhaps I couldn't trust myself with you." His hand lifts from the glass, the back of his knuckle ghosting my brow, my cheek, my jaw. And like a fool, I allow him.

"Haven't we already established that flattery will get you absolutely nowhere with me?"

"Come now, I don't think that's true. You were certainly open to a little adoration on Friday night."

"Exactly. I might've put out. So why push me away only to then ask me to marry you?"

"The two things are separate. Our marriage would be a business proposition with all details laid out in a contract."

"You have problems." Instead of pushing him away, my insults seem to be having the opposite effect. And why am I allowing him to take my laptop bag out of my hand?

"There are many forms of gratification, Olivia."

"Meaning you get your kicks out of tormenting women?" I ask saccharine sweet.

"Don't do that," he says, his fierce brows now pinched. "Don't pretend to be something you're not." His words sting like a reprimand, but I don't have the chance to retort as his index finger tips my chin, his eyes searching every inch of my face. "What happened that night has nothing to do with my offer. But make no mistake, I did want to fuck you. I still do."

The fire inside me changes in that instant. I can't make sense of it, but I'm no less angry. And then in the most bizarre of moments, he dips his head and slides his lips against mine. And even more bizarre, I let him.

I have officially lost my mind. But if it hadn't left my skull already, I think the heat in his kiss would've melted it down anyway. His lips are soft yet masterful. No tentative swipes or delicate presses here. I shiver as his finger loops under the strap of my purse and slips it from my shoulder like underwear sliding off my hips. Lord knows as it hits the floor, I wish it was.

"I still hate you," I whisper into his kiss.

His chuckle is low and rough as he rasps, "I'm counting on it." His kiss becomes deeper, wetter, as his hand curls around my hip.

"Don't you dare stop," I whisper as I coil my fingers around his lapels as though to prevent just that. He makes a sound of masculine contentment, his hand sliding down to the curve of my ass.

"Delicious." The rasp is more growl than word, but I don't know which of us made it. Not that it matters as I push my hands over the broad contours of his chest, around to his back, mirroring his position but using both hands instead. Greedy and grasping, I knead the taut flesh as he presses his hard length into me. Desire burns in my veins, along with a strange kind of one-upmanship and a need to be naked under him. *So confusing.* God, I want to win. And it could be that exact thing that prompts me to suck his bottom lip into my mouth, releasing it before sinking my teeth into the plump flesh.

A low rumble rises from the depths of his chest, his body vibrating with restraint as he tightens his one-handed grip on my ass and presses his free hand to the glass. One minute, we're lost in the moment, and the next, he's pulling back, though his hands are still anchored to my ass. The door raps against his knuckles as his amber gaze stares down at me, sort of dazed.

"If that's how you kiss when you hate me, I can't wait to see what being married to me will do to you." His words are rough, and a pulse hammers in his neck. I find both gratifying.

"Don't make me feel bad for kissing a crazy man." I pat his chest as though in consolation. As though that wasn't just the kiss of my life.

"Don't mistake lunacy for ruthlessness."

"Honey, I *loathe* you. It won't get any better than this. Do you need to call a doctor? I really do think you should up those..."

His smile stops me in my tracks. That isn't a smile of wickedness, or maybe it is. Yep, that's it. The man has levelled up.

He steps back, raising his chin imperiously, straightening to his six-feet-whatever frame. If this were a horror movie, this would be the point Bela Lugosi would swirl his cape, and the musical score would swell to a dramatic crescendo. Maybe he'd do me a solid and turn into a bat before disappearing into the night.

A girl can wish.

But no, Beckett wouldn't fly away. Not with those levels of satisfaction settling around him. And not as a gnawing sense of awareness creeps from the base of my spine.

"What did you do . . .?"

If he answers, I don't hear it. Not as I turn my head over my shoulder to see the whole wall has returned to transparency and isn't offering a lot in the way of discretion. I can see clear out into the rest of the suite of offices, which also means they can see *in*. And while people seem to be carrying on with their daily tasks, I know just moments ago, they were frozen like figures in Pompeii with their eyes fixed on us. *Hands mauling ass, lips fused.* How do I know? Because one person is still looking.

Luke. He stands frozen as a sea of activity swirls around him.

"You set me up," I growl.

"That all depends on what you're referring to."

"All of this! From Friday—from the beginning—right until now." I just wish I knew what this was all about. I stand unmoving because I don't want to give in to the urge to punch him. And I so desperately want to, evidenced by my clenched fists at my side. But I've already drawn enough attention to myself for one day.

"Did I plan to be in the exact place Friday for you to fall over my shoe? Or perhaps you think I'm somehow responsible for the pregnancy of the hapless Luke's girlfriend? Let me assure you, if I had gotten the girl pregnant, she wouldn't be trying to pin it on him."

"What's that supposed to mean?"

"He may be the boss's stepson, but scheming middle-class girls don't settle for upper middle-class boys when there's wealthier prey within reach."

"Not everyone is interested in money."

"No? My mistake. But if you're not in my office for money, it can only mean one thing." His gaze rakes over me again, slow and heavy lidded.

"I came because I was looking for investors." Not sex. Not with you, my tone says.

"And our kiss?"

"You came on to me—I take no responsibility for that."

"Olivia," he chastises playfully. "We must all play our parts. Your part was to be in my office today because I required you to be here. And because you need something that I have. You need to get your hands on some of the filthy stuff."

I open a mouth filled with a million denials until I decide he's not speaking about what just happened. But I'm done. Done for the day. Done with him.

"There are other ways to get money," I retort, bending to gather my things once again, causing him to step back.

Because no man wants to be headbutted in the nuts.

"Everyone has their price."

"There isn't enough money in the world to persuade me to marry you."

11

BECKETT

I LIFT the corner of my phone to check for messages again before casting my gaze on the cool interior of the restaurant, content we aren't sitting out on the roof terrace this evening. Clouds hang low over the city, dank and humid, and London's inhabitants are desperate for the reprieve a little thunder will bring.

She'll come around.
She hasn't any real choice in the matter.
I just wish she'd bloody well hurry up.

Money and business aside, she's interested. That night in the car, we might've already fucked if not for my need of her elsewhere. The attraction was mutual, even if she's crying wolf right now.

Too much is at stake for me. But she's interested, definitely interested. Maybe not in marrying me, but she will be. It's just a matter of time. And time is something she doesn't have the benefit of, according to my enquiries.

"Your conversation today is riveting, Alexander." I glance up from the remains of my dinner that has yet to be cleared from the table. "I thought that would get your attention," Harrison, my supposed friend, adds quite happily. "Aren't you going to give me the patented Beckett steely gaze and tell me first naming you is naughty? Verboten? Worthy of a kicking?" As well as his usual Tom Ford suit, the fucker is wearing a shit eating grin. "What are you going to do about it, hm?"

"Turn the other cheek?" I suggest, uninterested in the conversation because my mind has remained on a certain woman who I'm disinclined to talk to him about. To mention her would be a mistake because if I've learned one thing since entering this strange sort of friendship circle, it is to never discuss the woman you've an interest in fucking. I might as well just hand them the chain to yank. Strangely, it's okay to discuss the women you've already fucked, but I think that's because no one enjoys the thought of double dipping. Well, I certainly don't.

So it goes without saying it would be foolish of me to speak with him about the woman I'm going to marry, for convenience or otherwise.

"Last time I called you Alexander," Griffin says, arriving at the table and sliding into the seat opposite me, "you didn't turn the other cheek. You nearly fucking burst it." As though to support his words, he prods the area in question, his tone aggrieved.

"It was your nose, not your cheek."

"It was my fucking cheek. I should know because it led to a trip to the emergency room."

In my defence, it was an accident. I caught him with my elbow, though I did feel like punching him at the time.

Harry drains his drink, his shoulders moving with a deep chuckle. "Where you nobbled one of the nurses in a side room."

"A junior doctor, actually," Griffin replies with a grin. "She was from Prague."

"So he did you a favour, really. Besides, you tried to cuddle him. You know he doesn't like that demonstrative shit."

"So he nearly broke my fucking cheekbone because I wanted to show him a bit of drunken love?"

"You're late." I slide Griffin a disapproving glare, though, as usual, it's wasted on him.

"Yeah, I got chatting to a couple of girls outside." A collective groan goes up at the table. "What?" he exclaims, struggling to hold back his grin. "What's the problem?"

"Come on, spit it out," Harry says. "There's always a story with you." Nothing is ever simple where Griffin is concerned.

"I can't help that I have an interesting sex life."

"Like the dominatrix you met on the Waterloo line?"

"What about her?" He grins rather idiotically, sliding a cold chip from my abandoned plate.

"We know you made an appointment," Harry says. "No woman is going to admit to beating businessmen for money on public transport, for fuck's sake."

"Shows what you know. Anyway, what would you know? When was the last time *you* rode public transport?"

"You're just a voyeur."

"Among other things," he replies a touch defensively.

"I've never paid for it," Harry grumbles.

"I didn't pay her for sex. I paid her for the experience. It's brain sex, not actual fucking. No body contact unless you're touching yourself."

"Or deep-throating her rubber strap-on," Harry sneers.

"Fuck, you. It's no different to seeing a therapist. Besides, I only had a couple of sessions."

"Because you *realised* there was no fucking."

"You were telling us about the girl you met outside," I interject before the pair's arguing escalates.

"Girls, plural," Griffin corrects with a gleam. "They were coming out of the tube station."

Harry groans as he folds his arms across his chest. "You did not pick up two girls on the tube."

"First, we were coming out of the station, and second, it was just one girl I was interested in. The one who was crying. The other one had a face for radio."

"Ever the gentleman," I remark with a sigh.

"I know I'm an aresehole. I'm also a sucker for tears. They're just so pretty when they cry."

"It's his fetish," Harry remarks, turning to me. "Born of an exposure because they always cry when he whips out his dick."

"Cry with happiness," the other man quips.

"Get to the point of why you're late. She was crying, and apparently, you like puffy eyes and red faces."

"Yes, she was upset, God love her. She'd just been dumped."

"So you thought you'd offer to be her rebound fuck?"

"A very particular kind, if I'm lucky." And by the grin, I'd say he thinks he is lucky. Or that he plans on getting lucky. "You should've heard her, crying on her friend's shoulder. *I can't believe he dumped me!*" he intones in a terrible falsetto. "*The bastard dumped me right after I let him shag my arse!*"

This is, sadly, beginning to make sense as Griff carries on.

"*Well, babe,* her mate says, *that's why. You gave him what he wanted and now that he's had it, he's gone.* The other girl, the prettier one of the two, looks up at her friend all wet lashes and big brown eyes, and says, *that wasn't what he wanted, though. He wanted ATM.*"

Harry sits forward in his chair, muttering something unintelligible.

"*He wanted to go to the cash machine?*" Griffin continues. "*No,* she replies, *he wanted me to eat his arse—ATM? But I told him, no way, but you can bum me instead.*"

"Whoever said romance is dead has obviously never met you." I chuckle begrudgingly. He really does get himself into the most awkward scrapes. "You paint such an eloquent picture with words, Griff. Perhaps, you should've gone into the arts instead of law." Griffin is a barrister, Queens Counsel, no less. Harrison, meanwhile, deals in art.

"Get off your high horse," he crows. "Was that a smile I just saw you crack? What's with that?" Before I realise what he's doing, the bastard leans across the table, pressing the back of his hand to my forehead. "Are you running a temperature or something?"

"I didn't know you cared. Sadly, for you, your very obvious homoerotic overtures aren't really my thing."

"Piss off," he retorts baldly. "You boarding schoolboy types are the ones who like a bit of bumming."

I slide my phone from the table, my gaze drawn to the screen. "I thought that was more your style." *Still nothing.* I leave it face up on the banquette next to my thigh.

"It's not gay if you're into bumming girls."

"I thought the saying went more like *it's not gay as long as your balls don't touch?*" Harry helpfully supplies, raising his glass to indicate to the passing waitress that he'd like another. "Not that I'd know anything about that kind of stuff, situational homosexuality or the other kind."

"Are you watching porn?" Harry demands.

I glance around the restaurant rather than give Harry the satisfaction of an answer. *By glancing at my phone again.*

"You're very preoccupied tonight," he continues. "You keep looking at that thing so it's either porn or you're on a promise."

"It's business," I (unfortunately) snap.

"Not true. You've got knickers sticky over something, if I know you."

"It'll be money," Griffin offers, helping himself to another chip. "Some deal he's brewing, which means there's some poor fucker somewhere waiting for him to pounce."

I'd like to pounce. And when the time is right, I will.

And the best part? Olivia won't go down without a fight.

12

OLIVIA

Everyone has their price. Bah!

There is nothing on this earth that would persuade me to contact that man.

I don't care about the depths of delicious depravity.

Or what the press of his lips silently promised.

I don't care how the bulge beneath his belt hailed a penis trifecta of stamina, length, and girth.

Even if—no, especially because—I can't get any of the finance fuckers in town to take my calls. Whether because of his influence in the industry or some other Machiavellian scheme of his, I don't know. But what I do know is I will not bow down to that rich, beautiful autocratic devil in a three-piece suit.

I am not for sale!

"Is your laptop insured?"

"Sorry?" Pushing the unwelcome thought away, I glance up from the email I'm crafting at the sound of Jorge's voice, only for my gaze to slick down again when something on the screen catches my attention. Seems my email has been infiltrated by my angry thoughts; my speculative email turned to a hate-filled rant. I hit delete and look up once more. "I'm sorry, what did you say?"

"I asked if your laptop is insured because the way you're hammering those keys, it's not going to last very long."

"I suppose I am a little crabby this morning."

"Crabby isn't the half of it," Jorge mutters, turning back to his own workstation with a cup of coffee in one hand and a chocolate biscuit in the other. Crumbs trail down the front of his shirt, suggesting he'd stuffed one in his mouth while waiting for the kettle to boil.

"Where's my coffee? You know the rules. Whoever goes to the kitchen—"

"Or the corner shop," Miranda, our twenty-one-year-old marketing expert pipes up, pulling a biro pen from her messy blond topknot. Wearing Sass & Bide jeans and a sleeveless shirt with a Peter Pan collar, she's effortlessly stylish as always. She makes me feel ancient, despite there being only a few years between us.

"I asked," Jorge says in his sad Eeyore tone. Actually, Eeyore has a little more personality than Jorge. For someone who's resume promised *creativity* and *flair* in the field of development, Jorge is very staid in both personality and appearance. The most exotic thing about him is his name, and I'm not sure where that comes from because he's anything but Mediterranean looking. Today's ensemble is much like any other day except for his daring choice of double denim; a long-sleeved shirt buttoned to the neck and skinny jeans that have gone a little baggy at the knee. Over these, he wears a brown knitted cardigan with square pockets and large buttons that look like old-fashioned leather soccer balls.

"I asked," he repeats as Miranda scoffs. "No one answered."

"That's because when you can't be arsed to make anyone else a cuppa, you more or less whisper," retorts Heather, Miranda's younger cousin who's interning with us this summer—for free, supposedly. She has little love for Jorge, and even less like for him, and can often be found rolling her eyes and complaining that his un-ironic grandpa chic gives her migraines.

"Well, you didn't ask if I wanted anything from Subway when you went yesterday."

"Because you gave Miranda the stinkeye last time we had Subway for lunch."

"Because she said something uncouth," Jorge replies quite primly.

"Me?" Mir pipes up. "I only said I couldn't remember the last time I hasdsix inches so close to my mouth."

"And," Heather adds, warming to her theme, "you didn't get me what I asked for when you went to the Co-Op on Tuesday."

"I'm not picking up bloody tampons!"

"They aren't bloody. Not beforehand." Jorge appears to be turning a funny colour at her response. "Anyway, periods aren't catching, you know." Heather stands, pressing her palms against the surface of her Ikea desk, her silver tutu springing around her colt-like legs and drawing up the knotted hem of a white slogan T-shirt which reads:

Girls just want to have fun
damental rights.

She's not the only fashion parody in this office. She wants to work in PR, following studying for a degree in social media. Which is earned by three years spent scrolling through Instagram, I think.

"I don't get paid to shop for your feminine hygiene products," he mutters.

"Well, I don't get paid at all," she retorts, which isn't strictly true. She wanted to get a little experience and was willing to intern three days a week just for that. *The experience.* It was the only reason I said she could—even the accountant said I couldn't afford to take on anyone else—yet she's now getting a hundred quid a week, off the books, so basically out of my pocket, plus her travel expenses. And I know for a fact she travels in with Miranda in the Mini Cooper her parents bought her for her twenty-first birthday. But Mir is worth her weight in gold, so I don't make a fuss.

"Guys, guys!" Heedless, the trio continue to argue like a bunch of grade school kids. So I do what my mom would've done and bang my empty coffee cup on my desk. Unfortunately, it's not completely empty, so my white blouse is now doused with cold coffee. "Mother fuck," I whisper viciously.

"Oh, no!" Heather immediately jumps to her feet. "Quick, give me your top. I'll get the stain out before it sets."

"I'm not stripping," I protest as she begins to untuck the hem from the back of my skirt. "I've only got on my bra underneath," I continue, wriggling away from her woman-handling. *I really wasn't cut out to have employees. Or plants. Or pets.*

"Heather, leave Olivia alone, for goodness' sake."

"Oh, sorry. Did I, like, miss a social cue there?" The young girl's fingers loosen, her anxious gaze flicking back and forth between her cousin and me.

"Generally, people don't strip to the waist at work."

"Unless it's blokes on a building site," Miranda offers with a kind smile. "Then it's fair. Stuff the patriarchy." She half-heartedly fists the air.

"No," I reply, reaching for my purse because I don't want to get into another one of the 'gender discrimination in the workplace' conversations. "Let's just stuff our faces with pastry-archy instead, yeah?" I pull out a twenty-pound note and hand it to Heather. "Do you want to do a bakery run? You can get yourself a peach melba?"

Heather perks up immediately and snatches the twenty from my hand. "Vanilla slice, Jorge?" she asks sweetly, without even a hint of teasing. He nods, and Miranda asks for a skinny cappuccino as she eyes her empty *cup of crappy*, as she likes to call the instant stuff, before sending a pointed glance my way. Apparently, Mir's last start-up office had a European bean-to-cup coffee machine and croissants delivered every morning from a nearby patisserie. Meanwhile, I offer Nescafé and the occasional greasy treat from Greggs, which is, let's face it, only a bakery if you squint. But little does she know she's just lucky I have enough in the bank for this month's salary run.

Next month however...

Heather trots off without asking me what I'd like to order because I'm always on the latest detox to hit the Internet. That's the official line, anyway. The back channels will tell you I prefer to save my pennies for a bottle of wine at the weekend.

We all have our vices.

I head to our gender-neutral bathroom in a building that I'm pretty sure was once an East End slum. I'd opted to rent office space in the vibrant enclave of Hoxton for a number of reasons, but none of them are relevant right now. Particularly as we're at the less desirable end where there seems to be a definite demarcation line for the gentrification of the suburb to end.

This end of Hoxton is less Café Society and more greasy spoon.

The warehouse-sized windows, bare brick walls, and old timber floors were quite seductive selling points. Now I see them as another sticking point because they're impossible to heat in the winter and like a sauna at just a hint of sun.

I succeed in taking the coffee stain from *café au lait* to sludge before I give up and resign myself to an afternoon of follow-up emails and pestering, begging phone calls. It's been ten days since I stormed out of JBW's offices, and since then, I haven't had one bite as far as interest goes. I have until the end of next month before I lose everything. I have no collateral to borrow against, and no one to borrow from. I could ask my family, but I know what would happen before I even do. The Spanish Inquisition has nothing on my grandmother, Elsie, who is my stalwart supporter. But as far as she's concerned, her darling granddaughter is the toast of London town. A businesswoman on the rise. There's no way I can disappoint her. Confiding in her is out of the question.

I have a mom, too, but she's more interested in the ranch in the San Fernando Valley that she bought after her divorce. *Not her divorce from my father. He split before I was two.* There, she's quite content rescuing all manner of four-legged creatures. Which, as she likes to tell me, are far more reliable than the creatures with two.

"How are things going with you today?" I ask as I pass Miranda's desk once more.

"Yeah, pretty good. I've got a journalist at the *Standard* interested in doing a piece for us, and I'm waiting on a call back from the *Evening News*."

"Newspapers?" She nods happily, and I try to return her enthusiasm, but it's hard. Articles in these would be awesome but not if we're going to go bust before we can capitalise on the exposure.

"Wow. That's . . . well done." I lean my hip against the side of her desk as she taps her notebook point by point, giving me a rundown of her plans.

"I've loaded a new post to the blog this morning: Best Places to Meet Guys in London. The hits we're getting already are fucking awesome!" Her gaze slides to Jorge, who doesn't approve of profanity, as she adds in a little glance that I like to call *fuck you, too*.

"What kind of things have you got on there?"

"Honestly? Mainly trawling bars." As my expression twists, she adds "It's not that bad, though, hear me out."

"Go on. Dazzle me." I can't help but smile at her enthusiasm.

"So, I've made a special mention of that hipster place in Shoreditch. You know, the one that has the slider plates you love?"

"And the cinema on the roof?"

"That's the one. Well, I was thinking we could hit them up for a speed dating night. It'd be good for a laugh, as well as a bit of media attention."

"Isn't speed dating a bit passé?"

"The word passé is passé," she deadpans. "Speed dating is

having a revival. It's totally retro now. And I'm going to get a celeb involved. I was thinking about one of the guys from *Lust Island*." At my blank stare, she sighs and rolls her eyes. "Do you even own a TV?"

"I do. I just don't watch it very much." And never to watch reality TV. The only reason I know what program she's talking about is because it's pretty much all she and Heather have done over the past few weeks.

Can you believe Gav cheated on Cher? What about the new arrivals? But she's his ex! Darcy's a total hottie, but I want Aimee to win 'cause she's a normal girl.

I'm not sure about normal. As far as I can tell, the contestants are buffed, bleached, and Botoxed to within an inch of their lives. Besides, can anyone who signs up to live under the scrutiny of around-the-clock filming be normal?

"Well, I've reached out to their agent and am waiting for her to get back to me with the fees. Don't look so stressed. It's all just in the inception stages at the minute."

"So the blog post as it stands?" I bring the conversation back. Mir is like a squirrel on speed with explanations and timelines.

"Just recommendations. Like that place with the massive ball pool, though I always find the kid's places smell like funky cheese. But they have singles evenings, apparently."

"Where you can touch all the balls you want?"

"Even the blue ones."

"You're bad," I reply with a snicker.

"You set it up for me," she retorts, miming a tennis shot. "And then there's the Samba place that has beginner's lessons and any number of Latin men with snake-like hips."

"They'd also have broken toes if they partnered with me," Heather quips.

I smile Heather's way and note the pastry boxes. "Anything else?" I ask, turning back.

"Yeah, a rec for the place that serves drinks from smoking cauldrons." I look back blankly. "You remember the Alchemist's

To Have and Hate

Haven? I wanted you to come with me a couple of Fridays ago for cocktails and eye candy city gents."

"Eww, yes. I remember."

"Come on," she scoffs. "You can't fool me. Suit porn and drinks bought for you by pretty and eager boys is *every girl's* favourite Friday night."

"I'm not a fan of the type."

"A well-tailored suit is to women what lingerie is to men," she intones.

I lean down as I lower my voice, flicking my eyes across the room to Jorge. "I'd rather date a cardigan than a suit."

"That's blasphemy."

"It's also a blatant lie," Satan's voice interjects. When I look up, the fiend has appeared in all his suited glory.

Beckett.

The man with one name.

The devil I've been trying so hard not to think about.

His lips quirk in something that resembles a smile. "How are you, Olivia?"

13

BECKETT

I REALLY THOUGHT she would have cracked before now. And after the incident in the office, and the minor altercation I'd had with Luke after she'd left, word has certainly gotten around. According to my PA, Olivia has been painted a little like Mata Hari within the glass walls of JBW. Adding to the fuel, the number of silly girls who still insist on making eyes at me have taken the hapless Luke to their collective feathery, maternal bosom. Staff gossip, lines are drawn, and people get painted in ways that are perhaps unfair.

So why hasn't she come around?

Extreme stubbornness, I assume.

It seems it's time to raise the stakes.

"What are you doing here?" It's not a polite enquiry but rather a demand.

"I found him wandering around downstairs." The young girl in the tulle skirt, pink hair, and two cake boxes tied with matching coloured string almost vibrates on the spot with a need to share. *Me! Me! Ask me!* "He didn't know how to use the lift," she adds with happy gleam.

"It's rather antiquated," I murmur in my defence.

"Ols takes the stairs," the young girl says a touch conspiratorially. "She's frightened of—"

"Thanks, Heather. Do you want to go and put the kettle on?"

"Not really," she answers, her smile falling immediately.

"How about we try that again?" Olivia says in a tone that's meant to convey she has this under control. "Heather?"

"Yes, Ols?"

"Go and put the kettle on."

"But I got Mir a skinny cap already." She points a black-painted nail at the cardboard cup she's just placed on the desk *Ols* is standing next to. "If you wanted a coffee, wouldn't you have said before I left?"

"Heather." This time, her temper is a little more frayed.

"Yes, boss," the girl answers with an unhappy twist to her mouth before slinking off.

"What a charming girl," I observe blandly.

"Heather has a problem interpreting non-verbal language," Olivia says defensively.

"She appears to have a problem with the verbal type of language also." She'd last less than a day in my office before leaving in a probable flood of recriminations and tears. "But a charming girl, nonetheless. Without her, I might never have found your offices." My gaze scans the space. The brick walls, the large dome-shaped windows that look at least a year overdue cleaning. "And . . . where is your office?"

"You're looking at it." She inclines her head to indicate a nondescript desk, neat in appearance. "Are your minions off today?" she asks. "Only, I didn't hear the crack of thunder as you arrived. Or get a whiff of brimstone."

"I thought we might speak in private," I reply, ignoring her ridiculousness.

"Kind of looks like you thought wrong."

"Beckett, can I make you a cuppa?" the young girl calls from somewhere beyond. As I open my mouth to reply in the affirmative because I'd suffer a cup of poison just to get under Olivia's skin, she answers for me.

"He's not staying."

"Aren't I?"

"No, you're not. I see you're already on a first-name basis with my intern." She folds her arms as she glares at me. "Or was it second? I can't seem to recall."

"Yes, because I'm here specifically to infiltrate your staff and steal all your secrets." Both of our gazes fall to the girl sitting at the desk Olivia leans against, her head moving back and forth between us as if she's at the finals of Wimbledon.

"You could go out onto the roof," the girl offers, noticing she's been caught.

"What a helpful suggestion. Thank you . . ."

"Miranda," she obligingly supplies.

"It's nice to meet you, Miranda. I'm Beckett, a friend of Olivia's." I pull out a business card from my jacket, something I wouldn't ordinarily do, but the occasion calls for it. "If you're ever looking for an interesting challenge, work wise, please give my PA a call."

"Hey, stop that," Olivia protests, trying to swipe the card out of my hand. "You can't poach my staff!"

"It's a free market economy," I reply smoothly, sliding the card into her employee's hand.

"JBW. The venture capitalists?" Her gaze rises from the card before darting between Olivia and myself all over again, all kinds of ideas sliding through her gaze. "You should take him next door for a coffee," she adds quickly.

"I'm not taking him anywhere," Olivia mutters, glowering at me.

"'Course you are. You two obviously have *a lot* to talk about."

The conversation between the two is mostly unspoken and like a battle of silent wills, which makes me wonder if the staff here are privy to how close the business is to collapse. No, I decide. She's too stubborn. She's not protecting them out of the goodness of her heart but rather out of obstinacy. If she was as nice as she claims, wouldn't she fall on her sword to protect their jobs?

"Fine," Olivia eventually mutters, making her way over to her desk as though en route to the guillotine. I stifle a smile as her assistant does the same, adding a lift of her brows and a slight shrug. "But I'm only doing this to get you to leave," she complains as she stomps past me.

I follow her out of the office and down two flights of stone stairs, her feet tapping out an angry tattoo as she pushes open the door at the ground floor, not bothering to see if I'm following.

This is a less than salubrious part of Hoxton. Down at heel, I suppose. She ignores the old-fashioned looking coffee shop next door where I pause expectantly, then lengthen my strides to catch up with her when she doesn't stop.

"You can't outwalk me, you know."

"I wasn't trying to," she mutters. "Don't all the rats follow the Pied Piper to the river?"

She doesn't need a pipe; the sway of her hips is enticement enough.

"Down, down to a watery grave," she continues happily.

"Rats swim, you know." Olivia slides me an unimpressed look. "They also bite."

"And I bite back."

"A mercy killing?'

"For one of us, at least," she retorts.

"I doubt there would be many to mourn me." Just my investors, I suppose. "But you should definitely marry me first. Think of the money."

"I think that's what they call living off immoral earnings." Her gaze cuts my way again, her cheeks pink and her eyes blazing. It's easy to see what she thinks of my proposition. "Stop looking at me like that," she mutters, looking away again.

"You think marrying me would be tantamount to

prostitution? If that's the case, half the wealth of England would be in the hands of the immoral."

Oligarchs and their streetwalkers, earls and their tricks, high-flying businesswomen and their male escorts. Money and sex make the world go around, just as they say.

"Just... stop talking," she mutters as we approach a bakery on a corner advertising takeaway coffee. She strides straight past the plate glass window.

"You really weren't joking, were you? I'm sure there are easier ways to murder me. It's quite a walk to the river. I imagine those shoes must pinch."

Her heels are electric blue, pointed at the toe, and sharp at the heel. They can't be comfortable for a lengthy stroll, but I'm not complaining. I'm not the one wearing them, but I am the one who gets to appreciate the sight of her in them. The way they force her back ramrod straight and the effect they have on her smooth calves. The way, as they hammer against the pavement, they demand your attention and leave you wondering what she'd look like wearing them and little else.

I also appreciate how they make her a little taller, bringing her under my chin. Her skirt swishes against her bare legs as she strides. Floral and diaphanous, the fabric falls from a thin blue belt, the colour matching her footwear. She wears a white shirt with girlish puffed sleeves and a scooped neckline, the soft cotton betraying the rise and fall of her breasts with each step. As always, she looks very pretty. She doesn't exactly move with grace but rather determination, and there's something about the set of her expression that makes me want her all the more.

We pass a dozen shopfronts with faded and worn signages. There appears to be a distinct lack of shoppers about, though one or two miscreants looking to either commit thievery or perhaps score linger. I had wondered if she was leading me somewhere a little nicer, but now I see her point is the opposite as she begins to slow, pushing on the door of what appears to be a café.

Not like any café I've been inside in a long time.

To Have and Hate

The red paint on the doorframe is faded and peeling in parts, the overwhelmingly pungent scent of fried vegetable oil almost assailing. Inside, a handwritten menu is tacked to the wall, offering the great British staples; a full English breakfast—a heart attack on a plate—plus burgers, and other things, all delivered with chips. *Hence the smell.*

"Tea?" Olivia asks as she reaches the glass counter, the likes of which I seem to remember are usually found in a butcher shop. All manner of sad-looking sandwiches sweat it out in plastic wrap as a singular fly swarms around, trying his luck. "Or would you like a coffee?" She drops a handful of coins against the glass.

"You can wipe that evil look off your face and order me a black coffee, preferably in a takeaway cup."

She has the audacity to chuckle. "You're not worried about the state of our environment?"

I glance around pointedly. "I'm concerned about the state of the environment I'm currently in. I'm also concerned for the state of my constitution. And try not to slip anything untoward in my cup," I add over my shoulder as an afterthought.

"The temptation is great," she calls back, causing me to turn at her tone. "But, according to my friend at the pharmacy, she can only legally offer me laxatives. No cyanide."

I shake my head before giving one of the plastic-covered tables a cursory glance and pulling out a rickety-looking chair. Olivia follows me presently, sliding a reasonably clean-looking mug my way.

"Your conscience might not worry about landfill, but mine does." She ignores me as she pours tea from a stainless-steel teapot into a cup balanced on a thick saucer. She then sets about doctoring her tea with milk from a tiny white jug until it's the approximate shade of the thick brown stockings I recall my nanny used to wear as part of her uniform.

"I see you've embraced the great British tradition," I murmur, turning my mug of blackness around until the handle is in the right spot. Or I might be looking for signs that she's already doctored this one.

"Tea is mostly Indian, isn't it? And Sri Lankan? It's nothing to do with the British, really."

"The taking of tea is a British tradition."

"The taking of anything is a British tradition," she mutters almost under her breath. "Just ask any of the colonies."

I sigh as though bored. "You want to talk about history?"

"Your fault," she grumbles, bringing the steaming cup to her lips. Because you started it."

"I was making polite conversation." She grumbles something behind her cup I don't quite hear. "Besides, your grandmother is British, isn't she?"

She smiles as though she can't help it. "Very. Tea probably runs through her veins. It's because of her that I drink it."

"You were indoctrinated at a young age, I take it."

"When I was a little girl, maybe five or six. It started as a treat, a cup of tea in one of her delicate flowery cups, along with a biscuit or two. A very English biscuit," she adds with a fond smile. "Yet always out of a packet. A bourbon or a couple of chocolate fingers. Sometimes, she'd serve afternoon tea; Darjeeling and delicate sandwiches with the crusts cut off, and little cakes she made just for my visits. But mostly it was just like this." She tilts her cup a little to show me the brick-coloured beverage. "Builder's tea, she calls it. Strong enough to stand your spoon in."

"She sounds quite the character."

"She wouldn't say the same about you."

"There aren't many who would."

"She'd definitely make short work of you."

"Are you trying to charm or annoy me? It's hard to tell."

Her body shoulders vibrate with her scoff. "I'm telling you how it is. She's got a will of steel, my gran."

I don't think she's ever sounded anything other than American up until now. "You must be very fond of her."

"I am. She's the bomb." And then very American again.

As she returns to her tea, I peel the bottom of my mug from the floral plastic tablecloth and take a tentative sip, scalding my tongue with the acrid taste of very hot instant coffee. Olivia chuckles at my grimace. "You didn't need to use poison, apparently."

"It can't be that bad."

"You only brought me here to make me uncomfortable."

"Not true," she murmurs unconvincingly, her gaze flicking to the yellowing ceiling and the matching walls. "So." Her gaze returns to me.

"Here we are."

"I guess you're here to say *I told you so*." When I don't answer, Olivia ads, "Or maybe to appeal to my better nature."

"Do you have one of those?"

"Probably not where you're concerned. Come on, fess up. Why are you here?"

"Because, as much as it pains me, and as much as you don't seem to believe me, I need your help."

"Not this again," she murmurs despondently. "Why me? I'm sure there are dozens of women who'd marry you for a few months." This doesn't remotely sound like a compliment. My thoughts are confirmed as she adds, "If you paid them enough."

"I'm sure there are. You included."

"What did I ever do to you? Apart from falling over your foot and giving you a little snark?"

"You were already in trouble before you fell over my foot."

"So that's it? I fall, and I'm it for you? Easy prey. Like a gazelle who stumbled and became lunch for the lion."

"I knew as you stared up at me that you weren't as nice as they made you out to be. A nice girl with a vaguely interesting business."

"What?" At this, her expression slackens, firming quickly as she sits forward in her seat. "*Vaguely* interesting? And who said I was nice?"

"I seem to remember you saying as much."

"*They*, Beckett. Who are they?" she demands, her green eyes suddenly furious. "And how'd you know about my gran?"

"I sat in on a meeting. Luke took us through the pitch you emailed. The partners decided it wasn't of interest, but Luke, to give him his full due, fought to get you an in-house pitch at the next meeting. It was Mark, his stepfather, who explained that Luke had gone to university with you. That you were a *nice* girl. I suppose we were to infer from that what we would."

"Infer what? That because I'm nice, he should do me a favour and take my meeting?"

"I'm not quite sure that's how it went. It became obvious Luke had some kind of romantic interest in you. I'm sure you can work it out."

"You're saying Mark Jones decided to throw me a bone . . . so Luke could bone me? No, sorry, that's not believable. That a bunch of rich suits would take a meeting in order to get the boss's son laid?"

"You'd be surprised how cruel people in this business can be. But as it was, other than Mark, no other senior partners were present for your pitch."

"Seriously?"

"I'm next in seniority. I didn't attend in an official capacity."

"I was never a serious option?"

"For Luke, you were," I say softly, hating the vulnerability in her tone.

"That . . . shit! How—how dare he! He really painted that kind of picture of me? That I was withholding sexual favours in order to get a meeting, as though I'm some scheming courtesan?"

"I'm sure it wasn't explained as explicitly as all that. But in a nutshell, I'd say you have a good grasp on how it went."

"I really never had any chance," she whispers, dazed. But then her head comes up, her gaze steely and hard. "They weren't really saying I was nice. What they were calling me was a whore. But when I'd tripped, you decided I wasn't nice anyway."

"You were . . . unexpected." *Desirable. Bright. Passionate.*

To Have and Hate

"You can't expect someone to be civil when they're injured. I tripped—I skinned my knee. I was in a hurry, and I was obviously a bitch to you."

"You didn't have time to sugarcoat your response. What I saw was the real you, and that's what I want. I want the real Olivia to help me while also helping herself."

"But you're mistaken. That isn't me—neither of those are me. I wouldn't fuck anyone for financial gain. I'm trying to keep my business from sinking because people rely on me. I was late and anxious, and you judged me from an encounter that was no longer than a few seconds."

"That's all it takes." *And you're hungry enough to help me with this.*

"You have a very high opinion of yourself." She leans back in her chair, crossing one smooth leg over the other.

"And you're sick and tired of hustling. You want your life back."

"I don't know how you know all this, but yes, that's true. But it doesn't make me a bad person to want to spend twenty pounds on sushi for lunch instead of making do with polystyrene containers of ramen. Sure, I want my bank balance to look like it did so I can buy a four-hundred-pound pair of shoes for no good reason other than I want to. But this isn't just about me. I have employees who rely on me."

"Even if you're tired of the responsibility?" She shrugs uncomfortably. "Olivia, I can help you with all that. I'm here to revise my offer. Whatever money you've sunk into E-Volve, I'll reimburse you, direct into your bank. In fact, I'll give you more. I'll also give you the capital you need to take the company all the way to your exit plan. And I'll help you get it to that stage. You can't lose. Think about it, your capital plus a viable business to walk away with, debt free."

"All for just a twenty percent commission, right?"

"I'm not offering you financing in the usual form, you know that. I won't expect you to pay me back my investment. In fact, I won't take a penny from you. Not in commission or stake or interest. I'll help you get this company where it needs to be, and then I'll sign away my rights to all of it as part of a prenuptial agreement, where I'll set aside the monies to invest on your behalf. A new career direction for you, as it were. I'll make you a very wealthy woman."

"I don't understand why you would do this."

"Several reasons." Mine to reveal. "First and foremost, I want to own JBW, as I've said."

"I also don't understand how I can help, not that I'm saying I am helping or that I'm in, but what could I possibly do? I have no connection to any of this."

"Mark Jones, Luke's stepfather, is convinced I'm not the right man for the job and refuses to allow me to buy a controlling stake. He's of the opinion that I'm too much of a loose cannon, despite my uncanny ability to make the wealthy wealthier. He thinks this is just a passing phase for me and that my background and personal wealth will someday lead to my losing interest. Make me complacent. Which, quite frankly, is ridiculous, and merely a reflection of his opinion on my private life."

"What's wrong with your private life? Are you a coke-head or something?"

That had to be a stab in the dark. Mere coincidence.

"What do you think?"

"I'm not sure if you've noticed, but I don't know what the hell to think." The latter she almost hisses as she leans forward in her chair.

"My private life is my own. It doesn't affect my flair for business."

"What on earth would marrying me change?"

"First, I wondered if giving you a little background to your pitch might fuel your choices. Societal privilege and all that." I wave my hand as though all this is above me when the truth is, nothing is above or below me when in the way of getting what I want.

"If you think I'm going to marry you out of some kind of desire for revenge, you really don't know me at all."

"It's part of the appeal, though, isn't it? Truthfully." Her gaze roams over me as if I'm the lowest creature she's ever seen. But her anger will undoubtably kick in. That is to say, the anger reserves not directed at me but rather at those who have the unmitigated gall to keep her from her goal. Anger at those suffering from the illusion that they're somehow superior. At least we have that in common. "Do try to stop glowering at me. Those looks may be effective on others. I, however, am becoming inured to your repertoire of narrowed glances. A word of advice; the more you use them, the more the effect diminishes."

This doesn't stop her from continuing to glare at me over the rim of her teacup.

"There really is nothing—*nothing*—appealing in the notion of marrying you," she murmurs.

"With the exception of solvency, saving your company, sushi, and expensive footwear. Along with a little payback. Not to mention the opportunity to harness your potential plus a little cultivation to help you become a business powerhouse. The kind of woman other women look up to."

"No woman would look up to someone who became successful by selling herself."

"I'm not buying you. I just need to obtain a little of your time and cooperation."

"In exchange for a piece of my soul."

Such melodrama. But then, she'll need to be a good actress to go through with this.

"You'll get so much more in return."

"Maybe I'll just take my chances."

"On failure or bankruptcy? That's all that's left for you. London is more than a little incestuous. I'm sorry to say the town criers have already begun to call out."

"I've no idea what you're talking about."

"Vicious gossip. The fact that half of my office saw us kissing.

The general opinion that something was quite obviously going on between you and Luke prior to the fact. For whatever reason and whatever form."

"There's nothing going on between us. It wasn't like that," she protests hotly. "He has a pregnant girlfriend. You know that, and they will too, soon enough."

"If I know, it's only because I have your word for it. Meanwhile, Luke hasn't mentioned it to his parents. All is quiet on that front. So you were caught kissing me following your actions after your pitch meeting. Actions that were remarked upon."

"What are you talking about, actions?" she asks, suddenly sitting bolt-straight. Perhaps the recollection is as uncomfortable as the realisation.

"Tactile touches, longing looks, that sort of thing. Add to that the rumours that will no doubt begin to filter down after you were subsequently caught kissing one of his superiors." Eyes wide, I feign a little shock.

"Well, you aren't superior to him in any way, shape, or form," she retorts. "Seems to me you're both cut from the same cloth."

If that's the case, the cut of my cloth comes from Savile Row, and his is one of an inferior quality, picked up from some East End outdoor market somewhere.

She refuses to meet my gaze, despising me for all things, it seems. But no one ever said business was easy or life was fair. And I'll do what I must to get her to help me in this. No one else will do.

"How is business?" I ask evenly. "Do you have meetings or other pitches lined up?"

"You know I haven't," she answers with the kind of dangerous quiet that comes before a storm. "And now I know why."

"Perhaps the next few days will see this work in your favour. You might end up having no end of people willing to see you." Her gaze lifts but not her head. "Men in particular." I allow the implication to hover in the air between us.

To Have and Hate

"My God, I hate you."

"Some would say your honesty is a perfect basis for marriage. And most marriages turn to hate at some point anyway." This I know. The same way wine turns to vinegar.

"Is that a personal observation?" I don't answer her sickly-sweet enquiry. "How about you stop trying to sell me on this, telling me what my problems are and how you can fix them. How about you tell me what you'd get out of this arrangement?"

I almost answer *you*. Ridiculous, really. But also, partly true.

"In short, the illusion of having settled down. The appearance of a stable personal life. And the ultimate chance to get my hands on ownership of JBW business."

"Settling down with his stepson's *nice* girlfriend who, for all intents and purposes, has since been painted as anything but nice? Surely, that's not going to help you."

"It has no bearing."

"Don't you think you'd be better served to set your laser-sharp sights on someone less tainted?"

"Where would the fun be in that? Besides, I would be doing Mark a favour, in his mind, by preventing his son from making a mistake with a woman willing to ingratiate herself to any man who'll help."

She blinks heavily, and I get the impression she's throttling me in her mind.

"So the word at JBW is that I'll do anything to get my hands on money. Great. Just great. I cannot see how marrying me will help you. And you know what? It occurs to me that marrying you isn't going to help *my* reputation either. People will still remark *first Luke and now you*, which, in reality, is a little like choosing death by the devil or the deep blue sea. Not that anyone will say that, of course. They'll say I've married you for your money. How can that be flattering to you?"

"I think you'll be surprised what people say. Firstly, you're a pretty girl, when you're not scowling, not to mention very engaging. You're a good actress, so you'll have no problem winning people over. Also, no one has ever seen me smitten by anyone or anything." Except money. "They'll buy the fact that we're in love, especially once we've done the rounds by touring a few dinners and social functions."

"Why do you keep saying that? That I'm a good actress? That I pretend?"

"Intuition."

"You are so wrong. I can't mask who I am so what you see is what you get. And that's why I can't pretend to like you. Because I *don't*. Don't you get it? I'm mean to you because you deserve it. Because I don't like you."

The lady doth protest too much? She doesn't need to like me, not in that sense. I know she desires success above all things. Just as I know she wants me. And that's enough.

"I'm sure people will delight in the almost karmic play of things. That I deserve being tied to a girl who'll trample on my heart."

"You haven't got a heart. If you did, you wouldn't be making me do this."

I sigh heavily. "There's that flair for the dramatic again. No one is making you do anything. You have free will; you can do what you wish."

"Behold," she declares, sending me another of her choice looks. "I send you out as a sheep amidst the wolves."

"What's it to be, Olivia?" I ask, paraphrasing the rest of the dramatically delivered Bible verse. "Will you choose to be as wise as a serpent or remain as innocent as a dove?"

14

OLIVIA

He left me with a sleek-looking business card in my hand and my choices ringing through my head.

Would I be as meek as a lamb and give in to my fate?

Or be as wise as a serpent and slither away? Or would I be the kind of snake Luke had been? Or the kind that is driven to retaliate. To strike.

As for the dove metaphor, I'm not feeling very peaceful at all, though I kind of wish I had wings because then I'd fly off someplace where these troubles couldn't follow.

Another week passes, and the payroll run is complete. An electricity bill sits in the kitchen unopened, waiting for me. I have three missed calls from my accountant, five more politely sterile *no thanks* from other finance options, and twice as many more refusing to take my calls. I've spent hours wondering if I led Luke on. If there was something I did or said that would make him see me as unworthy. Disposable, even. The hours I've spent having conversations with him in my head I will never get back. But I've decided there is no way this can be explained away. There is no reason for what he's done. In short, I'm never speaking to him again.

But that doesn't help my options, which are few.

I am up shit creek and paddling with my arms against the current.

And the worst of the situation isn't Luke's betrayal, but the sense that I've frittered it all away somehow. My share of my grandfather's life's work. His and Gran's hopes and dreams for me. I have a business that I've fucked up, despite my best intentions and hours of hard work, and only one very unappealing option to fix things. Maybe if I'd worked harder or smarter or taken more advice I might not be in this situation.

Was it pure hubris that will leave me with nothing?

And I've no one to talk things over with. I can't call Reggie and tell her what has happened with Luke and Beckett and their fucked-up plans. I can't tell her because I know she'd say the same thing I'd say if our roles were reversed.

It's not worth it. Cut your losses and walk away.

But that's because we're both good friends who want the best for the other. But it's a little different when you're living in your own skin and wondering if retaining the moral high ground is worth losing the roof over your head.

I think I have to say yes.

Though not to becoming homeless. Yes to the other thing.

I sit on my bed with my back pressed against the headboard as I scroll through my phone, not truly paying much attention to anything on my social media feeds. I flip over to the E-Volve app, not because I'm looking for a hookup but because it's mine. The one thing I own in my life. I grew this from a tiny seed of an idea where I wanted to find my best friend a date after she'd discovered her boyfriend had been cheating on her. It was a project, and that's all. A project that's grown and grown until it's depleted my resources and left me on the verge of homelessness. Not that I'll ever truly be homeless. I know my mom will always take me in like one of her strays. Reggie would make space on her sofa for me in a heartbeat. And then there's Gran. She'd move heaven and earth to make sure I'm okay. But I'm nearly twenty-seven, and I can't keep expecting people to clean up after me.

A fragment of our conversation in the coffee shop comes floating back to me.

"Tell me more about this grandmother of yours," he'd said.

"Why? Because she's a neutral topic or because you pretending to listen to me would make me less of a bitch?"

"Because I asked you," he'd griped right back at me. So I did.

"She's originally from Yorkshire but has lived in the States since she was seventeen. She followed a G.I. home after the war, against the wishes of her parents and all that kind of thing."

"She must be very brave," he'd asserted.

"She says it's what love does to a person. That it makes you foolish, not brave. But he wasn't a good husband, and the marriage didn't last long. He was, however, good enough to die so she didn't have to divorce him."

"Sporting of him."

I'd wrapped my hands around my teacup, finding I was fighting a smile. While I was aware he was up to no good, it just felt nice to talk about my favourite person for a while.

"And your mother?"

"Divorced."

"There's a kind of symmetry, then." His murmur was bland. *"Three generations of women who didn't find love the first time around."*

"I count only two." My response wasn't as bland and came with a pointed look. *"As I'm not divorced, the symmetry lends itself only to two."*

"I assume both found happiness afterwards?"

"My gran did. My mom tried."

"Presumably they weren't made wealthy when their husbands removed themselves."

"My grandmother was because he adored her. The only thing that could've torn him away was death. He left Gran well provided for. He left us all well provided for." We fell quiet for a beat before I spoke again. *"Removed themselves is an odd choice of words."*

"Not really. If we do this, our divorce won't be an emotionally

fraught affair. We'll both be going into this with our eyes open and a timeline. When it ends, there will be no recriminations. We'll just remove each other from our lives. It's not like we belong to the same circles. The loss of your inheritance needn't be common knowledge. You would come out of this marriage in a matter of a few months in a position so much stronger."

"*I don't remember telling you about my inheritance,*" I'd replied coolly.

"*You didn't need to. The fact is, you need help, and I can give it to you. There's no shame in acknowledging that.*"

"*You're wrong,*" I'd snapped angrily. "*There's no shame in failure. But in selling yourself out? Well, that's another matter.*"

"*You're being far too puritanical about this,*" he'd insisted. "*What would have happened if I'd stayed in the car? If I'd taken your hand and led you into the house? Into my bed?*"

"*I expect we would've had sex,*" I answered simply. "*But I wouldn't have committed myself to you for six months. For cash.*"

"*Not for cash,*" he replied hotly, "*for our mutual benefit.*"

Would one of those mutual benefits be sex?

But now? Now, I'm not so sure about anything.

From across the room, Beckett's business card sings to me. A low murmur, a whisper of temptation, promising all could be well.

Six months to give my business the chance it deserves.

Six months to make a success of myself.

Six months of tying myself to the devil's representative here on earth.

Swinging my legs off the bed, I make my way over to my dresser, pick up the card, and throw my back against the mattress once more. I hold both phone and card above my head as I press in the digits.

Sure, it'd be better to send him a text, but that's not how being a grown-up works. Besides, he'd just call back. *Probably to gloat.*

My heart beats like the hooves of a runaway stallion as I wait for the call to connect.

"Beckett." One word bitten out as if he doesn't have time to take my call.

"It's Olivia. Olivia Welland," I add, just in case he proposes marriage to virtual strangers on the regular.

"I was beginning to think you wouldn't call." His tone turns softer, almost kinder, but certainly curious.

"Were you? Really?" I think his tone is a ruse and that he's played me like a fiddle. That maybe I've even allowed him to. *More stupidity on my part.*

"I thought perhaps I'd overestimated you."

"Your backhanded compliments are unnecessary. I find myself, as my grandmother would say, on the bones of my arse. And without recourse."

The bark of his laughter is startling. "Your grandmother has inspired you to a decision?"

"She's pragmatic," I say with a sigh. And I'm trying to be.

"Am I to take this as you calling to say you've come around to logic?" Despite his words, his tone holds a note of hesitancy. I find it helps.

"I'm not sure any of this is logical. All I know is I don't want to lose my company, and as much as I'd like to blame you or Luke for putting me in this position, I've concluded the fault lies with me." And that the problems were always there. I should've prepared better. Sought sound advice and followed a different path. Not been full of such reckless confidence.

"There's no need to sound as though you're about to face the firing squad. For what it's worth, I think you're doing the right thing. I want to say the grown-up thing, but I don't want to make you cross."

"That's a first." I almost laugh as I flick his business card across the room. It spins like a helicoptering maple seed.

"What is it they say? Happy wife, happy life?"

"Now you're just being mean."

"Where are you, Olivia?"

"At home. Why?"

"Give me your address and I'll send a car over for you."

"I'm not going to your house," I say a little panicked.

"I'm in the office," he replies smoothly.

"On Sunday? I thought you lot didn't work very hard?"

"I get paid for what I know, not for what I do. Yet here I am. Doing."

"Couldn't we *do* this tomorrow, then? Mondays are so boring as it is. It'd give the devil something to look forward to. A nice pound of Olivia flesh?"

"As tempting as that sounds, do you really want to go over the particulars with an audience milling around?"

My mind goes back to the things he said, and I imagine an office full of admin staff holding grudges and wielding pitchforks.

"We could meet somewhere public," I reply, ignoring the implications in his words.

"You don't trust me." There's that amusement again. "Or perhaps you don't trust yourself."

"I'm pretty sure I can manage to restrain my base urges where you're concerned."

"You mean you can restrain yourself from murdering me."

"I'll certainly try my best."

"If you're disinclined to come over to the office this afternoon, we could do dinner this evening."

After last time? Ah, hell no. "Can't. I'm busy tonight."

"Tomorrow is no good for me, and I'm flying to New York," he answers crisply. "In short, I won't be around for a week. Is that going to complicate things for you? Your cash flow, I mean."

I sigh. This is embarrassing. The last time I was beholden to anyone was when I was at college. *And having family pay my bills isn't the same.*

"Olivia," he says sharply. "If you find it difficult to be in the same room as me already, I'm not sure this arrangement will work."

"Fine," I answer quietly, blowing out another breath. I strain to keep my eyes wide open and glued to a spot on the ceiling. If I can do this, I won't cry.

I. *Won't. Cry.*

"Then you'd better give me your address."

I consider not getting changed and turning up in his sleek and shiny office in a pair of boyfriend jeans and an old T-shirt. But in a fit of panic, I begin to wonder if he'll change his mind at the sight of schlepy Sunday Olivia.

"Ridiculous," I mutter as coat hangers screech against the rail of my tiny closet. "I'm not going to become a Stepford wife. Just a pretend one for a while."

I eventually settle for a pair of fitted black pants that end a little above the ankle with a matching top. A sleeveless shirt, this too is slightly cropped and sitting just at the waist. Sure, it's black, but it's the kind of outfit that would be fine for a stylish brunch. Or the day I sign my life away. I forego heels in favour of a pair of jewelled sandals and leave down my hair. Then tie it up again. Then settle on tying the front up while leaving the back loose. *So stressful.*

At the appointed time, the buzzer sounds. With my face pressed against the glass of my third story window, I can just make out the shape of a somewhat familiar black Mercedes. With a feeling that's part trepidation, part disbelief, I grab my purse and sunglasses before heading downstairs when what I really want to do is climb into my wardrobe and stay there.

The journey into the city is quick, quicker than I'd like, for sure. I try not to think about the last time I was in the back of this car. *Because, awkward.* Thankfully, it isn't long before I'm deposited outside the towering building.

A security guard sits behind the reception desk, though he lumbers his way to the front door to open it.

"Mr Beckett is waiting for you," he informs me, his delivery monotone.

Is that his usual tone, or is he deliberately trying to keep his voice from betraying any inflection? Judgment? What does it matter? I've made my decision, so I suppose I'd just better get used to it and try not to feel like someone has whipped out a Sharpie and scrawled the word *ho* across my chest.

"Let her cover the mark as she will. The pang of it will always be in her heart."

"Pardon?" the security guard asks, bemused.

I give my head a shake. "Nothing. I was just thinking out loud."

I sign in and am escorted to the elevator, the uniformed guard using his key card to select a floor. My eyes are on my shoes as the doors close, my stomach staying on ground level as the rest of me hurtles toward the devil I don't really know. The devil who has promised to save me.

Kind of.

I must be mad.

"Olivia."

As the doors slide open, Beckett is there to greet me. For a moment, I'm taken aback. What do you know? Weekend Beckett wears jeans and a fine knit sweater that clings to all the good parts of him.

"You look beautiful," he adds as though this is our usual exchange as his hand slides to the curve of my waist as he pulls me in for a perfunctory kiss on the cheek.

What isn't so casual is my reaction as my shirt parts slightly from my pants and his thumb lightly skims my skin. Under the sensation and the pressure of his fingertips, my nipples immediately harden, and a deep pulse beats between my legs. *Just once, but so hard.* And I claim no responsibility for the things running through my head.

Skin to skin.

What kind of experience would that be with him?

Hard and unforgiving?
Torturously slow as it builds to a peak?
All of those things.

As Beckett pulls back, I get the sense he knows he's taken a liberty, albeit accidentally, but my body's reaction is the same. And it's that reaction he's extremely aware of.

Just remember why you're here, I caution myself. He's not the only one who can be a snake.

"Shall we?" He indicates that I should walk ahead before he falls in step with me. "You're not usually so quiet."

"It's Sunday. You can't annoy me today."

"Is that a dare?"

My hair whips around as I turn to face him. "Can we just get this over with?"

"Without the thrust and parry?" When I don't bite, he gives an almost imperceptible nod of his head.

Once in his office, he offers me a drink, an actual drink. I refuse, though watch appreciatively as he bends to a concealed fridge (jeans *so* suit him) and pulls out a beer for himself and a water for me.

"In case you change your mind," he says, depositing a glass along with an imported bottle of still water. "You're sure I can't get you something stronger?"

"Positive, thanks." I purse my lips, reminding myself of the half bottle of cheap Chardonnay cooling in my fridge. A reward to myself after this.

Beckett takes a seat opposite me this time, dropping a manila folder to the low table between us and taking a deep pull on his beer. Knees bent, his feet are planted wide, and I notice the designer tennis shoes he's wearing.

"Olivia."

At the sound of his voice, my head pops up. The warmth in his gaze seems to have lifted by degrees. But it doesn't make me feel easier.

"I'm fine," I murmur. I find myself reaching out to twist the cap off the bottle, pouring a little of the liquid into my glass. "Seems I am thirsty after all." Bringing the glass to my knee, I cup it in both hands, my fingers dancing nervously against it.

"Shall we?" He reaches for the folder, flipping the cover open with the pad of his thumb. "I've had my lawyer draft a prenuptial agreement, as discussed."

"Wait a minute." Water sloshes in the glass as I put it down. "You had this pulled together already?"

"Of course."

"But you didn't know—you couldn't have known I was going to say yes. I only just decided an hour ago!"

"Olivia. I earn a lot of money. More money than most people will spend in a lifetime. And I earn that money by using my instincts."

"But—"

"You're an intelligent woman. You aren't one of those people who life happens to. You make life happen for you."

"Didn't we talk about flattery already?" My words hit the air sharper than I'd intended.

"Fine. Yes, I had it drawn up without knowing what you'd decide. Given your choices, I made an educated guess, and here you are. Is that okay for you? Does it make you feel a little happier? A little more content?"

"Not really." I shrug. I should've left it at the compliment.

We go through the agreement point by point as Beckett explains the legal jargon in layman's terms. It turns out, he has a law degree, though he suggests I take it to my own counsel for confirmation. I nod rapidly at his suggestion and wonder if I have a couple of hundred free on my credit card. But unless the credit card balance fairies have visited, I'll be spending a night with my cheap half bottle of wine, a pad and a pen, and Professor Google.

But the bottom line? I walk away from this marriage exactly as he promised; I'll own E-Volve free and clear, and I'll have a very healthy bank balance and some investments made on my behalf for the future.

"So, that concludes the legalities for the minute." Cuffing his wrist, Beckett pushes the sleeves of his sweater up his forearm once, then again, highlighting the play of tendons and muscles there. *It shouldn't feel like I'm watching porn, and yet . . .* As an encore, he pushes back his elbows, stretching the muscles in his shoulders as his sweater moulds to his flat stomach and chest. He stands, and suddenly, his crotch is at eye level. Yes, okay, so there's a coffee table between us, but it doesn't stop my mind from going back to that night in the car. The smell of leather and cologne. Taut sighs in the tight space. The feel of his hands on my thighs, and the rock-hard bulge between his legs as I'd worked myself over him.

You were wet. I bet you're wet now.

"You're sure I can't get you anything stronger?" I'm about to demand a bottle of wine and a straw, when he adds, "You look like you need a little fornication."

"I beg your pardon?" I exclaim, springing to my feet. "How dare you! Just because you may have copped a feel or two doesn't mean you can make these assumptions about me. I'm not desperate!"

By the end of my angry little speech, I've watched his expression change and morph through a range of things. So much so I find myself playing the exchange back in my head.

"Positively Freudian." His smile leaks through his words.

"What is? What are you talking about?" My own tone is a little less vinegary than just moments ago, because what the hell just happened?

"I think we'll blame this one on him." He turns back to the concealed fridge. "I expect you're ready for a wine now. Pinot Grigio?" he asks, already walking away. Walking away with his shoulders shaking.

"*Ohhh* Lord." I drop to my butt on the sofa, my face in my hands and my elbows on my knees. "Fortification, not fornication."

"That was the general suggestion." The glass connects with

the tabletop, but I still can't look at him. "That said, I'm all for fornication. We'd just need to sync our diaries quickly."

My head comes up so quick, my hair knots around my face. "What are you talking about?"

"Fornication is out of wedlock, and we'll be married within the week."

I snort. Actually snort. "This might be my first marriage, but I'm pretty sure it takes more than a few days to arrange a wedding, no matter how secretive."

"We're not getting married in secret, Olivia. We might elope, but I need people to know."

"That's what I meant. *Sheesh*. But aren't there legalities we have to abide by? When Miranda's older sister got married, there were bands or something to post."

"Banns," he corrects. "Yes, these have to be read out in church three weeks in a row. In advance of objections."

I wonder if this bride objects she'll get to keep her company. Maybe just in a daydream world.

"But it's irrelevant, given we're not going to be married in the UK."

"We're not?" I grab my wine and take a sip or six. Every time he says anything to do with marriage, my stomach knots. I mean, I know that's what I'm here to talk about—what I've agreed to, but it doesn't feel real. *Until he mentions it, at least.*

"We'll go to New York. A prenup in the UK isn't worth the paper it's written on."

"Okay." Sure, why not!

"We'll go to the courthouse."

"I need to have a look at my diary."

"I'm going tomorrow, and you'll come with me."

"Yeah, I don't think so," I half laugh.

"It's hardly like you're run off your feet."

"Hey, you're the one with the easy job," I protest. He was the one who said he gets paid for what he knows, not what he does. Well, that's not the case for me. I get paid for none of that stuff!

To Have and Hate

"Besides, you're a hair's breadth from going under. The quicker we marry, the quicker you'll have the money to fix it."

"I still have shit to do!"

"And don't swear. It's beneath you."

"*Ohhhh*." The noise is a hundred syllables long. "Do you think this is the nineteen fifties? That marrying me means you get some dominion over me?"

"I'm well aware of the year. I'm also aware that you are the junior partner in this venture. So yes, to a certain extent, you are mine to direct."

"It's not too late for me to change my mind," I mutter mulishly.

"That's true. But you're not an idiot. And if you think you were busy before, well, you weren't. You will need to learn to recognise that for the next six months your time isn't as important as mine. Sacrifices will have to be made."

"I'm not about that whole *sacrifice life*." My answer is delivered on an unpleasant chuckle. "I don't kill spiders, and I'm vegetarian," I add with a good measure of teenage style provocation as I stretch my legs out under the coffee table. Beckett's eyes follow the motion.

"Tomorrow, you'll come to New York with me. We'll return Friday and spread the good tidings to all concerned."

"Will you tell your family?"

"I have no family."

"Everyone has a family, Beckett. Even if it's just Uncle Satan."

"My parents are dead, and I'm an only child. The remaining members of my family aren't a part of my life," he utters brusquely. "What about you? Will you inform your grandmother?"

"God, no, she's ninety-two. I don't want to kill her."

"Good. Less complications."

"Although," I add as a thought occurs to me, "she'll be flying to the UK at the end of the summer." This is her annual pilgrimage, and every summer, she says she won't be around to make the trip the following year. This has been going on so long, I think the family have stopped listening to her. "No," I decide, "I won't tell her." Because she'll want to meet him, and then she'll want to know why I married a man I can't stand.

"I suppose now is as good a time as any to go through the contract."

"Didn't we just do that?"

"That was the prenuptial agreement; what you'll take from the marriage once it's dissolved."

"And what I won't." Like my dignity.

"Exactly. The contract is a little more complex than that. As I've said, you should seek legal counsel," he murmurs, passing over a single sheet of paper.

"What's this?" I look but don't touch, my spidey senses going into hyperdrive.

"A non-disclosure agreement. I'm presuming you haven't spoken with anyone about what we discussed."

"Like I'd tell anyone about this shit." Beckett's brows pinch. "Look, I curse on occasion, so get used to it. And no, I haven't told anyone because I don't want anyone to know."

I snatch the paper from between his fingertips and the pen he holds out next before scribbling my signature on the applicable line.

"There. Happy now?"

Without answering, he slides two more pieces of paper out of the folder.

"I'll give you a few moments to look it over."

"No one does business on Sunday," I grumble without heat. But as he stands again, I don't look up from the table as I separate the pages, one has CONTRACT across the top, and the second one PRENUPTIAL AGREEMENT.

I pick up the first and begin scanning the terms.

A six-month term dissolved by mutual agreement.

No-fault divorce to be processed in the state of New York

"Why New York? I haven't even agreed to go there yet."

To Have and Hate

"The UK has the unfortunate requirement of divorce proceedings not beginning until twelve months after the date of marriage. And there's currently no such thing as a no-fault divorce."

"Pretty sure whatever goes wrong will be your fault anyway," I mutter, returning to the paperwork.

Half a million deposited into my personal bank account and the same amount into the company account within forty-eight hours of a legal marriage . . . further to point something or other.

Wow. He really wasn't kidding.

Further monies deposited into the business account at monthly increments for the period of six months, totalling the amount of . . . That's a lot of zeros, and it will more than keep my baby afloat.

Beckett to be appointed to the company board. A board we currently don't have, by the way.

A number of new hires listed, candidates to be vetted by him or his representative. Sure, these I need to take the business to the next level, apparently.

I flip the first page over, picking up my wine glass, when the last three points almost make me drop it.

Monogamy for the length of the term.

Cohabitation a prerequisite of the agreement for the full term.

The marriage is to be consummated with forty-eight hours of a legal marriage or all terms to become null and void.

I find myself blinking rapidly, my mind empty of all other thoughts.

Live with him.

Have sex with him?

Once? Twice? Every night? Once or twice every night?

"Well, you're not storming out of the place, so that's promising." He's suddenly sitting across from me again. "The final two points, or three?"

I nod, mumbling something about marriage being created for monogamy. But isn't it also meant to be for love?

"I'm sure marriage means many different things to many

different people. For some, it's for financial gain, insurance coverage, and tax breaks. For others, it's cultural requirement, a tenant of a religion even. Some marry for stability or prestige. But not all marriages work on the basis of fidelity. Ours will."

His gaze is fiery, his language one of absolutes. I will be his and his alone. Something dark and exquisite breaks open inside me—a sudden ache, a need, a requirement for him to fill—but I can't admit to any of that.

"You want me to whore myself to you?" My question is reasonable. Well, maybe my tone is.

"That's not what this is," Beckett answers carefully.

"No? I guess I must've misunderstood." Picking up the papers, I lick my finger and begin flicking the edges angrily as though I can't remember where the words lurk. Words tantamount to money for sex. *Sex with him.* My heart is beating so fast I feel like I've run a marathon, my body and my head at war with the words I'd just read. "Ah, here," I bite out. "The marriage is to be consummated—"

"I'm aware of what it says," he replies in a similar tone. "But if you'd let me explain."

"There is nothing to explain here. You want me to have sex with you!"

"Forgive me if I'm wrong, but you're here in part because you feel the same."

"You know shit!"

"I know your understanding is tragically parochial."

"My understanding is just fine." Context is everything. Fancy ass words just need googling.

"I thought you would've been a little more adult about this." He spreads his hands out across his thighs, sliding them towards his knees. It's not a sexual thing, but my insides clench anyway. Why is that?

Because you're attention starved.

Because of what happened in the car.

Because no one ever wanted to buy you before, though you've been discarded plenty.

"Fine." There. I reined it all in. I didn't shout, swear, hit the roof, or jump on him. Even if there isn't anything *fine* about his stipulations. "Go ahead. You tell me how this isn't good old-fashioned prostitution."

"We need to live together to make things believable."

We're moving on from sex to cohabitation. So, basically, this explanation is taking the scenic route.

"You could move into my place," I offer, testing the waters. Though for what, I don't know.

"I could, in theory. How many bedrooms do you have?"

"One." The word comes out strangled, and the corner of his mouth twitches as though he's trying not to smile.

The two of us bumping around a space built for one would be a disaster of epic proportions. We'd end up hate fucking because sex would definitely happen, one way or another. *Oh dear, you appear to have tripped and driven yourself inside my body while I was unloading the dishwasher. Accidents happen, what!*

"I have several more bedrooms," Beckett adds in a cool tone. "Do you still want me to move in with you, or would you prefer to live somewhere where you'll also have your own space?"

"Ha." I sound like one of the Muppets. One of the squeaky ones. "You wouldn't move in with me anyway. You're just trying to play nice."

His expression is wry as he agrees with a slight incline of his head. "Do I get points for at least looking like I would?"

I don't condescend to answer. I'm not finding him cute. Annoying, yes. And maybe one or two other things.

Sex. He wants to have sex with me. Can we get to that discussion point before I explode and make a mess all over his nice furniture?

"Married people live together."

"Not all married people," I protest.

"Newlyweds do."

"Not those in the armed forces."

"Are you thinking of enlisting? No? Then don't be ridiculous. I have lots of space and several spare bedrooms. You won't even need to see me in private. Unless you want to."

"Which is the perfect segue into the next point. You want to fuck me," I state bluntly. "And you felt the need to put it in a contract."

15

OLIVIA

"I *so* don't have anything nice to say to you right now. You brought me here under false pretences."

"I don't believe that's true," Beckett retorts smoothly.

"You lied to me about this whole thing," I almost yell, trying very hard not to get emotional or overwrought. But how can I not be emotional when it feels like my life is unravelling? "You never once mentioned that we would have to have sex."

"Did you think we had to have sex in my car? Did I coerce you or lie to you then?"

"I'm not talking about that, not now. I'm talking about this." I stab the paper on the table in front. "Have you added this clause just because you want to fuck me?"

He leans back in his chair, his expression a study of calm. If this image of him was hanging in a gallery, the little card next to it would read: Man Not Giving a Fuck.

"The answer to that is complicated," he offers eventually.

"Then I really don't understand. *You* climbed out of the car. We would've already had sex if not for you!"

"Don't do this," he says softly.

"What? I should just let you do it to me? Let you fuck me? Fuck me over, every chance you get?"

"There really is no need for profanity." He sighs as though this topic bores him. "I'm not sure what you want me to say."

"I want the truth. Those things you said about Luke—were they true?"

"Yes."

"So if I pick up my phone and call him, he'll tell me the same?"

"I'd assumed you would've already had that conversation with him." His reaction kind of throws me for a loop. Cool and calm and definitely calculated. "I'd also expect him to add a little creative spin."

"What about dinner that night, when you just appeared behind me?"

"A happy coincidence," he replies with a sigh. "I wasn't following you. This hasn't been some grand master plan. You really do seem to overestimate me."

"I'm not sure that's true. I just . . . I just don't know what to think." Except I'm running out of options and beginning to doubt myself.

"Do you want me to tell you I find you attractive? Because I do."

"That's not what I'm asking. I don't want adulation, and I don't want lies. I have this whole ridiculous argument running though my head right now. Which came first?" I laugh, but there's no joy in tit. "Like the chicken and the egg. Do you want me because of what happened in the car, but only with your boundaries and provisos and addendums and stuff? Or was the dry humping some crazy audition or an interview? A test drive for your plans?"

"You're painting all sorts of unsavoury images."

"Tell me which it is!" I demand.

"Does it really matter?"

"To me it does. It matters a hell of a lot."

"I want to fuck you," he states baldly, almost knocking me from my chair. "I wanted you then, and I want you now. Does that make you happy? Soothe you? And yes, I want it all in a contract because I refuse to give you an excuse to back out."

"I'm not going to back out," I answer, because what choice do I have? The same choices as I had before. It's either marry him or lose everything, with or without the added fucking. And the fucking? That I feel very conflicted about.

"Wanting you is aside from everything else. I need your help, Olivia. You were in the right place at the right time or, perhaps, the wrong time. But whichever way you choose to view it, it became obvious we could each help the other. Right wrongs and be all the better for the experience."

"I don't want revenge."

"The best kind of revenge is success. Your achievements will never be at the mercy of men like Luke and his stepfather again."

"Don't try to pretend you're some advanced altruistic being." He doesn't even flinch. "My God," I moan, pressing my hands to my head. "I can't believe I let you touch me like that!"

"And I can't believe I got out of the car, but I never do anything without an exit plan."

My head comes up fast, my mouth falling open. "You seemed to exit the door pretty well. In fact, you seemed to do it very efficiently."

"It doesn't mean I wasn't tempted. Sorely tempted."

"Is it because you just want someone to control?"

He barks out a laugh that seems to surprise us both. "Because you're such a docile flower. So biddable."

"Okay, someone beholden to you?"

"Someone who fights me at every step? Someone who can be quite ridiculous? Look, we're going around in circles, and I have a lot to do before we leave for New York."

"I've already told you, I'm busy tomorrow."

"Then you will need to follow another day. Tuesday or Wednesday." The cracks in his composure are highlighted by the tension in his jaw and the way his eyes begin to flame. "Just pick a fucking day, Olivia."

"The twelfth of never," I mutter, my gaze skating away.

"You want me," he suddenly grates out. "And I want you."

"Want to own me."

"Why does this have to be so difficult? We both need this marriage, no matter how temporary, to work. Let's look at this practically and discuss the very valid reasons for an annulment, which would ruin both of our plans." He sits forward suddenly, poised to tick the points off his left hand. "Bigamy. Incest. Age of consent issues. Idiocy—"

"That's it!" I throw up my hands. "You can't marry me because I *must* be crazy to even consider marrying you." Crazy desperate, for sure.

"Coercion," he continues without even a pause. "Fraud and non-consummation of the marriage."

"Non-consummation of the fake marriage," I repeat. "Did I get that right?"

"It isn't a fake marriage. It's a temporary one, but with the same commitments and the same legal pitfalls. Make no mistake, you won't be allowed to back out of this. There are consequences should you say yes, then try to renege on this deal."

"Is it a deal or is it a marriage?"

"Both."

"What kind of consequences are we talking here?"

"I urge you to seek the help of your legal team, but in brief, you'll lose everything. Seek an annulment or divorce or walk out before the end of the term, and you lose it all."

"What about if you end it?"

"There's a penalty clause. You'll receive an obscene payout, but don't count on that happening. I need six months of your time and acting skills. I want this company, Olivia, and I'm willing to do what it takes."

"Including me," I mutter unhappily. "What difference does it make if we don't, you know, have sex? If only the two of us know, who's going to pick fault?"

"I will," he states bluntly. "And you will. And we'll probably kill each other in the interim without it because we both need to get this out of our system."

Listening to him, looking at his expression, it's like he thinks sex between us is some kind of virus. Something debilitating, something he needs to sweat out of his system.

"Like it or not, what happened in the car wasn't all one-sided. I didn't force you to respond. You enjoyed it as much as I did. The proof was in those breathy little noises you made and the way you rubbed yourself against me."

His eyes were like fire as I slid myself over the hard length of him, his upward thrusts making my insides clench violently.

I shake my head and the sensory memories away, and as I look back at him, I realise he probably just read every pornographic thought I just had.

"In fact," he says slowly, softly, temptingly. "I'm almost certain the only thing keeping us from tearing the other's clothes off right now is this." He rests his hand on the low table between us.

"I'm pretty sure I can resist you."

With what can only be described as a look of pure incitement, he wraps his hands around the top of the table, sliding it along the rug.

16

BECKETT

I promised myself I wouldn't do this. I promised myself when she called that I'd bring her here but not touch her. Arguing with myself that I should wait until the deal is sealed, the ink is dry on the contract, and the wedding license is in my hand. Yet here I am, pushing the coffee table across the floor, my gaze unmoving from hers.

Not even as she gasps as the table drags across the rug.

Not as she reaches for her glass before it falls.

Not as my empty bottle of Pilsner teeters, then clatters against the floor.

Not as her gaze returns to mine full of challenge.

"So you've moved an obstacle. A physical thing. Big whoop. You'll note I've yet to jump your bones..."

Her words trail off, her eyes widening as she tips her head, watching me as I stand. But I don't move toward her yet. Instead, I feed my hand over my shoulder and grip a fistful of my thin sweater, yanking it up and over my head. I drop it to the floor without a word. We don't need words because the truth is in the fresh bloom of her cheeks and the way her teeth dig into her bottom lip. It's in the heat of her gaze before she lowers her lashes, hiding it. The truth is in the rasp of my breath as I run my hand down my chest and the ridges of my stomach.

"What are you doing?" Her voice wavers. Is it nervousness or need?

"What was it you called me?"

"I've called you lots of things. And most of them uncomplimentary." The sentiment is the same, but her tone is less strident. It lacks conviction and strength as though the air around us has absorbed the need to fight this.

"You said I was an incitement. A provocation. I suppose I'm living up to the way you've painted me."

"You moved the table, but you haven't made your point. Put your sweater back on."

As she lifts the glass to her lips, there's a tremor in her hand. I swiftly reach for it as her hand retracts, depositing it fuck knows where as I pull her up swiftly by her other hand. It all happens so fast she doesn't have time to protest. And I realise she won't as our bodies collide, and she gasps.

She tilts her head, her lips parted as though gifting me prior consent and her eyelids flutter closed. *Like the little girl who doesn't want to admit to herself and instead chooses to hide.*

"Open your eyes," I whisper, pulling her body into mine, pulling her heat and softness against where I'm aching and hard. My God, I need to be inside her, to possess her completely, if only for a little while.

Her lashes flicker open, and I get such a visceral reaction seeing the dark depths of those bedroom eyes, the want and the need, right before our lips finally meet. This was never going to be tentative. We kiss as we live, grasping, possessive, our tongues tangling and our teeth clashing.

"You need some sense fucked into you." My hand slides into her hair, my mouth skimming her neck and biting the soft flesh there.

"*Ha.*" Her answer is a soft breath.

"By someone who knows what they're doing," I growl as a white-hot need pulses through me.

"Better add that job to the list of your new hires." With the taunt, she slides her hand between us, cupping my balls.

"Make no mistake," I rasp, grabbing her hand and pulling it away. My balls throb, missing the contact immediately as I bring her hand to my mouth. I kiss her palm. Bite her fingertip. "When this finally happens, there will be no recovering from it." With a growl I can't restrain, I take her face in my hands as I proceed to kiss the hell out of her.

Breath ragged, my words are as husky as my kisses are wet. The scent of her is addictive, her skin as smooth as silk. I can't wait to taste her—to really taste her. And don't ask me how I know, but when the time finally comes, I know she'll taste this good *everywhere.*

"Beckett." A whisper. An enticement. *Her incitement.* "We could do it now."

"Do it?" I repeat. "You want to have sex?"

"*Yes,*" she whispers almost breathlessly.

"Would it be fucking or making love?"

"Stop talking."

"And make my mouth more useful? Sorry, sweetheart, you're not wriggling out of our contract. Not when we're so close."

"What if I say I can't wait that long," she half moans as I lower her against the sofa. As I cover her with my body, something pulses low in my belly, my hands itching to strip her out of her clothes. She feels so small under me, and I wonder if I'm crushing her, but as she wraps her legs around my thighs, the heat of her pussy through her trousers steals the rest of my thoughts.

"I won't beg," she murmurs, moulding her mouth to mine. Her whispers are as sweet as her breath, her lips shiny and pink.

"I could make you."

"I'd like to see you try."

I chuckle darkly, because we both would. I bite off a curse as she arches under me. "Let's table that for later. Waiting is character building."

"Waiting sucks." Truer words were never spoken when I want her lips around my cock and my fingers inside her. "Let's call a truce," she murmurs, her hand sliding down my chest to toy with the buckle of my belt. "The next thirty minutes, no speaking. No calling names. Just a little old-fashioned f-fornication."

"I don't trust you." And by that I mean I don't trust myself as I tuck my elbow between her body and the back of the sofa, freeing both hands to touch her.

"I'll be good," she purrs.

"Oh, I don't doubt it." Sliding my hands under her blouse, I push it up her body. Her bra is little more than lacy cobwebs, her nipples pink and hard and begging for my mouth as I press my fingers into her bra cups. I promptly forget the rest of my thoughts at the breathtaking sight before me. Round and full and creamy, her nipples are a dusky kind of pink. I slide my thumbs across their tight pebbling and her breath hitches, bringing my attention to her face again. Her red-brown hair splayed across the sofa, her cheeks are flushed, and her gaze as dark as coal. She looks otherworldly, like a nymph escaped from an enchanted forest to torture me.

I shake my head, coming back to myself before swapping my thumbs for my tongue. She inhales in a sharp breath as I suck her nipple into my mouth.

"Oh, God."

She makes me feel like the Almighty as I use the threat of my teeth and the rasp of the bristles from my chin. I grind against her so hard she moans. Then, to my profound surprise and delight, she grabs my arse and begins rocking into me as a means to get herself off.

This, *she*, is the hottest thing I have ever seen. Pressing her pussy against me, she undulates and writhes, releasing tremulous breath after breath. I haven't been this turned on in such a long time.

"You're so fucking delicious," I rasp, pressing my lips to her neck.

"Bad man," she whimpers, "you said a swear."

"You have no idea just how bad I can be. But you're going to find out."

"What a shame you'll only get one shot. So much pressure for a wedding night."

My responding laughter is a touch cruel. "You keep telling yourself that, sweetheart. Once I've had you, you'll be crying out for my touch."

"Promises, promises . . ." The retort dies on her lips as I drive my hard cock against her as she begins to fall apart.

"Next time you come," I whisper, pressing my mouth to her neck, "we'll be married, and I won't stop at just one."

17

OLIVIA

You're so fucking delicious.

Monday morning, and his words are still echoing in my ear as I reach for my coffee and I notice the tremble in my hand. Who knew Beckett saved his cursing for the bedroom? That he'd be such an effective dirty talker?

I can't believe I got myself into that position. And I can't believe how good his body felt over mine. The weight of him, the fire in his eyes.

Next time you come, we'll be married. I won't stop at just one.

Orgasm, he meant. Not that he himself...

His words were both a dare and a promise, and the husky timbre of his tone a guarantee. And my whimpers weren't by choice as he rocked himself into me. *Hard.*

"No comment?" he'd taunted, once he'd gotten me off.

"None," I replied, my voice reed thin. It was probably a good thing I was so into the moment because it stopped me from voicing the words running through my head.

Yes. Please. Give it to me.

I can feel the shape and weight of your cock.

I agree. I will be destroyed.

And I will die with a smile on my face.

Because it's been far too long since I've felt anything like this.

My body pulsed with aftershocks as he'd pressed his lips over my nipple, his teeth. My hips bucked into him, my whole body crying out to be filled.

"So fucking sensitive. Do you think you could come like this? Just like this?"

The truth at that moment? Yes, I think I could, the strings of this new orgasm tied tightly to the first. But I wasn't telling him. He wanted to tease me. Make me tell him my secrets and beg for his dick. And I probably would have, despite my earlier protests.

Beckett kissed me so hard, feeding me his tongue as he would his cock. Grasping my hair at the base of my skull, he exposed my neck to his teeth. I felt so utterly owned and had never been with someone who made me feel like he did. Made me crave the marks of his passion without fear of wearing them afterwards.

"Come to New York, Olivia." His deep command had curled around my ear as he tightened his grip, the base of my skull pounding in time with the beat between my legs. *"Say yes and I'll let you come, right here, right now. Say you will."*

"I don't need you for that," I'd purred.

His deep ripple of laughter reverberated through me, adding just another level of torture, and another as he'd pulled my hands up over my head.

Pinned under him. Pinned by him. He watched me squirm like a thing in heat, all the while giving me only what he wanted to give. And oh, how I wanted it all. I wanted to feel him inside me, to ride him like a fucking horse named Beckett. I wanted it right there on that couch, not in New York. Not when we were married. I wanted it illicit and hard. My hair in his hands and his body pressed to mine.

"Come with me tomorrow. Let me destroy your pretty little pussy."

"Let me touch you," I'd whispered, my insides pulsing at the beautiful savagery painted by his words. *Let me taste.* His eyes were all pupil as his hand tightened on my wrist, restraining

which of us I, it was hard to tell. *"It's only fair I get to see what I'll get in the deal,"* I taunted. *"See what I'm marrying."*

My cheeks heat at the implication. Like I was marrying him for his dick.

But his smile was a lesson in pure wickedness as he loosened his grip, and I'd crawled over him, all crumpled and coming apart at the seams, running my hands and my mouth all over his body in a fit of desperation. On my knees between his splayed thighs, I could hear my own rapid breaths. I'd reached for the opening of his jeans when a sharp crack, like a knock against glass, had sounded through the space. I'd jumped three feet in the air, or so it felt.

Under me, Beckett cursed then groaned. I looked down and realised I'd caught him in the crotch with my knee.

"Hey, boss lady."

Again, I almost jump three feet in the air, this time at the sound of Miranda's voice, almost spilling my coffee. Because, of course I wasn't going to pack up and fly off to New York just because Beckett promised me orgasms. So instead of lying in his bed, today I'm in the office. *Yay.*

It's not that I wasn't tempted, especially after the interruption. We were so close. I could practically see the shape of him through his jeans. Before I'd kneed him in the crotch, of course

I hope I haven't broken it.

"What's up?" Miranda angles her head like an inquisitive terrier, and I give myself a little shake. *It's Monday morning. Get your mind out of his jeans and into your workday.*

"Nothing," I reply, clearing my throat and giving the scarf around my neck a little tug. "Why, is something up with you?" A sunny summer in London may not be guaranteed, but of course, today of all days, the sun *has* got his hat on. Meaning *I* couldn't put on a turtleneck. Not without drawing comment.

Yes, okay, so I have a damned hickey the size of a planet on my neck.

Damn Beckett and his sexy talk. Who would've thought under

those expensive threads and that very proper demeanour was a sexual deviant waiting to be unleashed? Well, me. I guessed, didn't I? That first night in the car. It was probably the reason I offered myself up like a platter yesterday. And now he knows what kind of sex noises I make. And he'll fucking gloat, I know he will, because my behaviour totally flies in the face of everything I've said.

At least I kept my clothes on. Though I'm kind of surprised they didn't disintegrate in the heat of the moment. But I'm very glad they didn't because when I'd eventually calmed my hammering heart and righted my clothing, and Beckett was no longer purple, I'd noticed the team of cleaners standing on the other side of the glass wall. There were at least six of them, all mouths agog. One of them seemed to be missing a mop which was lying on the floor. I dread to think how long they might've been standing there, and how much more they might have seen.

Hey, but at least I didn't burst into flames for my immorality, even if I go pink every time I think about it. And then I turn red because every time I think about *it*, I think about *him*, and then I wind up replaying the things he said.

Let me destroy you.

Let me destroy a very particular part of you.

A very particular, unmentionable part.

I so suck at dirty talk. I hope he's not expecting it. Despite what I'd said, I only curse when the occasion calls for it. Like when I'm annoyed. So basically, whenever I'm with Beckett, I guess.

"You're doing it again."

"What?" My attention snaps to Miranda again. Her elbow planted on the desk, she balances her cheek in her hand. "You're very spacey this morning."

"I just have a lot on my mind," I reply quickly, my words running together and making almost one word of the sentence.

"It hasn't got anything to do with the reason you've come to work dressed like one of the Pink Ladies, is it?"

"What?" I feel my expression scrunch. What is she talking about? But then she plucks at an invisible scarf around her own neck.

Damn.

"It's a little Rizzo. You know, like from *Grease*? Are you wearing it for the same thing? I'm not judging," she continues with an air of triviality, "but we all know what's going on under that thing."

"It suits my outfit," I protest a little too hotly, even if I'd thought the look was more Girl Scout than teenage tearaway. "I was aiming for Roman Holiday." I glance down at my ankle-length pants and sleeveless blouse. "This is Saint Laurent, you know. Vintage!" Still sounds better than secondhand.

"It's well dodgy," sniggers Heather. "It's like, twenty-six degrees out there."

"The question is," Miranda says, turning to her cousin, making me a topic of conversation rather than a participant. Remind me just who is the boss in here again? "The question is, who gave the boss-babe a hickey."

"No one gave me a hickey! I'm pleased Jorge isn't in the office right now, or he'd be making very serious noises about sexual harassment in the workplace."

"He'd love a little sexual harassment, if you ask me," Heather pipes up. "He could probably do with a bit."

"Enough of that." Pointing a finger at the young girl, I feel like a decrepit old killjoy and the morality police all rolled into one. "No one wants to be sexually harassed." Because that's how you end up with an expensive lawsuit.

"It's true, though," Heather grumbles.

When I was growing up, we had a little terrier called Fred. The thing used to bark constantly and for no reason, and when Mom told him off, he'd slink back to his basket, but always with one last little bark or growl as he climbed in. That's what Heather is like. She just *has* to have the last word.

"He'd love a little bit of touchy-feely harassment. Especially if it was from you."

"Heather," I almost cry. "Can we just leave it? It's not fair to Jorge, and quite frankly, I'm not comfortable having this conversation."

"Look, we all know what the fancy scarf is for," she says. "Jorge knows, too. And because he has, like, a mega crush on you, he's taken a half day to deal with his little bit of heartbreak."

I just don't have the energy for this.

"I don't think that's true," I bluster, even if what Heather says rings somewhat true. I guess I've just been ignoring it, but I'd hate to upset him. I mean, what happens if he throws a bug in the system? Though I guess this is mild-mannered Jorge we're talking about. Ruination is probably more my style.

"It is true, but sod him," Miranda asserts. "Dish the dirt. Who gave you the hickey? Was it that hot piece of manliness who was here last week? The venture capitalist?"

"No comment." I wiggle my mouse and my laptop springs to life.

"That suit," Heather adds with a dreamy sigh. "He was throwing out mega levels of BDE."

I don't want to ask. Really, I don't. But I also don't like feeling as if I'm missing out or behind. *FOMO is truly a thing.*

"Okay." I lean back in my chair. "I'll bite. What does BDE stand for?"

"Seriously?" Mir replies.

"Yes," I answer witheringly, then decide I must be hanging around with Beckett too much. And that's not going to improve over the next six months. "I've never heard the acronym before."

"Big. Dick. Energy." Heather answers in a deep bass, punctuating each word with a thrust of her hips.

"You were checking out his . . . package?" I don't think I like the sound of that. Either as her boss or as his soon-to-be wife. *Shoot me now. I don't want to be the jealous type. I don't even want to be his wife!*

"BDE isn't about dick size," Miranda cuts in. "It's more like an aura. A presence. A life force."

"It's an attitude or the energy you give out," Heather argues. "And you don't have to have a dick to have BDE, it's totally non-gendered. You've got a BDE, boss-babe," she adds in a lighter tone. "But that aside, I bet he really does."

"Really does what?"

"Have a mega dong." She drops her shoulder and swings her arm as though imitating an elephant's trunk.

"Don't expect me to answer that because I don't know," I say quickly. Strictly speaking, this is true. He might've used a prosthetic—that might've been an eggplant I was riding yesterday afternoon. But I don't think so.

"Hmm. What do you reckon, Heather?" Miranda asks in a playful tone.

"I reckon mega dong is the name of your favourite vibrator."

"That's enough, both of you. Just settle down. I've got a whole heap of work to do before my flight."

So I might not have jumped when he clicked his fingers. I am, however, flying out tomorrow morning. Alone. And as I received my ticket by courier earlier, I know I'm going business class. This sweetens the slightly bitter pill, making it grapefruit bitter rather than anything gross and medicinal.

"I hope your mum gets well soon," Heather adds sincerely.

I nod and fix a sad expression on my face. *Don't think about the free champagne.* And yes, it's all for effect. There's nothing wrong with my mom as far as I know. I'm just covering my ass and telling lies.

Just think of the money that will be in your account by the end of the week, I tell myself. *And try not to think of his very obvious BD, less of the E.*

Marrying for money. Lots of women marry for money. Men too, I reason with myself as I stare at the darkened ceiling of my bedroom. My suitcase stands packed at the end of my bed, my clothes laid out for my early morning, but still I can't sleep. Instead, the shadows from the trees in the garden dance like wraiths against the ceiling while I do what I do best lately. I overthink.

The world is full of women being bankrolled by their spouses for all different reasons. I won't be the first. I will, however, be joining their ranks. But what I can't seem to get my head around is why does getting married for sex sound so much seedier? Maybe I'm looking at this wrong. Maybe I should think of it as a perk. *Especially after yesterday.*

So many conflicting thoughts and feelings.

I agreed to have sex with him and tell myself it's because I have no choice—that I'll do whatever it takes to save my business. To save face. But in the dark, quiet moments, I can admit the truth to myself. And when I think about the deal I've made with the devil, my skin starts to tingle and my core aches emptily. I want him so badly no matter how many protestations I make.

Everyone has a price. My price? It's complicated.

I'm cranky and tired as I get to Gatwick at an unearthly hour the next morning, but perk right up again as I'm ushered into the business class cabin, allocated my lovely seat-cum-bed pod and handed my first glass of champagne. There really is nothing to complain about when travelling in style. And it's odd that I can manage to sleep while hurtling through the sky at eight hundred miles an hour, but I can't travel in a lift without feeling sick.

I've packed for three weeks, but as we'll only be there three days, I've probably overdone things. But Beckett didn't happen to mention what kinds of functions, if any, I'll be expected to attend apart from our courthouse wedding, for which I've packed a summer dress. *It might be my something old.*

After a mostly sleepless night, I've come to a few conclusions. Decisions, I suppose. Ways to deal.

Number 1:
I've decided to think of this next six months as a part-time job that I've taken on in order to help my business. Which isn't a bad analogy as far as these things go. I'll gain some much-needed business acumen from Beckett while adding a little extra money to my pocket. I'll be to Beckett what Heather is to me. Sort of. And I've chosen to focus on the plus points and let the rest take care of itself.

My business will benefit.

I'll make it a roaring success. The only kind of revenge I'm interested in.

I'll be able to eat proper food.

I'll grow. Personally, business wise, and probably a little wider, too. *See food above.*

I've already accepted that Beckett is going to be a pain in my ass. It's not as though I'm not expecting that. *Your time isn't as important as mine. Sacrifices will have to be made.* What a prick. But if luxury travel is the kind of sacrifice I'll be forced to endure, then I think I'll be able to cope for six months without killing him.

It'll be like having a super hot, cranky, demanding boss.

Number 2:
I've decided on the separation of sex and our marriage, a little like the separation of church and state. I've agreed, by signing his paperwork, that I'll submit to his will on the point of consummating this thing, but that's all I'll give. After that? Who knows. Maybe we'll hump like bunnies, or maybe once will be enough for us both. *Don't laugh.*

Number 3:
And perhaps the most important decision of all. I've decided that, because he brings out the worst in me again and again, I'm going to try a little reverse psychology. From now on, I'm going to turn my murderous frown upside down and kill him with kindness. With polite enquiries and soothing words. With smiles and shit. I'm just not going to let him get under my skin anymore.

And he'll hate it, I think gleefully.

I might be resigned to my fate, but I'm not going down without a fight.

Or maybe I'm not going down until he's gone down first.

Maybe he's not the only one with parts to be destroyed.

With a small yet smug kind of smile, I settle into my flight. I'll watch a few movies, drink a few more glasses of champagne, and maybe take a nap before we're due to touch down.

18

OLIVIA

I SUFFER the usual pains after landing. Immigration queues. Bags lifted from the conveyor belts at the baggage claim, leaving passengers to play hide and seek with their belongings. You've got to love JFK. The hustle, the bustle, the rude people.

Just like London.

What I'm unprepared for is the sight of a familiar steely gaze as I push out of the baggage hall.

Damn. I thought he'd send a driver. I haven't yet pulled out my game face.

"I was considering sending a search party," he begins in a tone dripping with boredom. It's the kind of tone that makes me want to slap the back of his head.

"I wish you would have. It might have saved me from arguing with an unpleasant Indian lady who insisted my case was hers."

"I see you won," he answers, moving adroitly to one side before taking my suitcase out of my hand. *Manners maketh the man-devil and all that.* He leans down to kiss my cheek, his lips landing on my neck just below my ear, and his breath is a puff of warm air that makes me shiver. I half expect him to put his hands on me, to turn me to face him as he kisses me properly. But whatever drove him to react to me like he did inside of his office seems to have burned away as he straightens and begins striding towards the exit.

"It was either that or get married in a sari." I jog a couple of steps in order to keep up with him.

"This is why you should never travel with anything but carry-on luggage." I note he ignores my remark, his body language unchanged as he chooses not to react.

"Spoken just like a man."

"A man left waiting far too long."

Outside, the arrival of Beckett's car is timed to perfection as if the universe wouldn't dare to offer him anything less. My bags are stowed in the trunk, passenger doors close with a satisfying *clunk*, and I find the air a cool respite to the summer heat. And then we're on our way into the city.

"How is your trip so far?" Check me out, being all civil and polite and stuff.

"Busy. Fruitful. Warm."

"That's good."

"How was your flight?" Check him and his pleasantries out. Time to turn up the niceness.

"*Ah-mazing*," I reply, all wide smiles.

"Really?"

I giggle. "*Raleigh*? Like the city?" Because, seriously. That's what it sounded like he just said.

"What's going on?" He shoots me a sideways glance.

"What do you mean?" Pleasure bubbles up inside me. This is *so* easy!

"You're . . . happy. It's unusual."

"If you knew me, you'd realise it's only unusual around you." My reply is sunny, yet his body reacts as though bitten, stiffening as though I'd pressed my teeth around his wrist. It's a flickering response and usual service resumed almost immediately.

"I'm not sure how I feel about this version of you," he murmurs, reaching into the inside pocket of his suit jacket.

"Well, you'd better get used to it," I sort of sing, fixing a smile

To Have and Hate

back onto my face. Because I'm going to win this happiness thing. I'm going to kill him with kindness, even if I die doing it myself. "I'm happy. Just happy."

"You didn't take something to help you travel, did you?"

"Like, happy pills?"

He shakes his head as though realising how ridiculous that sounds. "Well, if you don't mind, I have a few messages to catch up on." While unfailingly polite, his reply is not without a coating of ice. And as for my caring, it would be a shame if I did because he does it anyway.

Feeling oddly disappointed and thoroughly dismissed, I turn my head to the passenger window to watch the city crawl by. The last time I visited New York, I was a kid, and it had been a family trip. We visited some distant relatives upstate, and I think we came to see some show off Broadway. The one distinct memory I have is standing on the sidewalk, one of my small hands in a grown-up's while my other was flat to my ear, reacting to the street noise. Vibrant and frenetic might be cool when you're old enough to appreciate it, but when you're knee high to those around you, it's not so much fun.

Traffic. People. Lights. Noise.

Cracking open the window, I'm instantly overwhelmed by the sounds and smells. It's almost as though I remember, but I can't see how that could be. A mouth-watering aroma of garlic on one corner giving way to something vile on the next. The noise and the traffic, they all serve to distract me from why I'm really here.

"I'm going to drop you off at the hotel. Do you think you might be ready to leave by three?"

No take a little time to recuperate from your flight, Olivia. Or have a nap and I'll see you this evening for dinner.

I look down at my own phone, check the time, and shrug. "Sure. Where are we going?"

"To take care of the reason for your visit."

Well, damn.

It goes without saying that Beckett wouldn't stay anywhere but the very best, but this hotel? It's another level fancy. A liveried doorman and a red carpeted path herald the tone from the car. I take the man's hand with the sense of being very much out of time and place as I step from the car and look up. Among the glass and steel, the building stands like a sentinel of the old-world order.

We're staying at the St. Regis.

As I turn, I realise Beckett hasn't moved from the car. I place my hand on the top of the door, preventing the doorman from closing it.

"You're not going to make me go in there by myself, are you?" My voice is a little shrill in the darkened interior.

"I have a meeting," he answers in that oh, so cultured voice I'd like to throat punch out of him.

"Yeah, but—"

"Olivia, I really don't have time for this. Your key to the room is waiting at the desk. Surely, that isn't beyond you." I'm almost surprised when icicles don't suddenly sprout in the air. Though I feel my brows pinch, I swallow the retort balanced on the edge of my tongue. *It starts with* f *and ends in* it.

"Thank you, *Beckett*. My mistake, but I thought we'd have some points to discuss before we take care of the reason for my visit." I'm surprised my jaw doesn't crack in the effort to keep my words reasonably calm.

"My lawyer is waiting for you inside." His eyes move back to the screen of his phone, and I'm effectively dismissed.

Without another word, I straighten like an automaton, then silently applaud myself for managing to close the door with a satisfying *thunk*. No slamming doors on my watch.

"I'm so sorry!" I almost stumble into the doorman who catches me by the elbow.

"Excuse me, ma'am."

To Have and Hate

"No, that was totally my fault. I should watch where I'm going. And sorry about stealing your job with the whole door shutting thing." *Shut up. Just shut up.* "Thank you again. I'm just . . . just going to go in now."

He smiles sympathetically. Oh, fuck. I've just turned into Julia Roberts. This is my *Pretty Woman* moment just without the skanky dress and thigh-high boots. I glance down, you know, just in case, and I'm actually relieved when I realise I'm still wearing yoga pants, a slouchy cardigan, and a pair of battered slip-on Vans.

Oh my God. I'm about to step into the world of the rich and fabulous wearing a striped T-shirt that makes me look like an onion seller.

Pushing the ridiculousness away, I climb the few short steps, the opening lines of the movie playing out in my head.

What's your dream?

This? This isn't it.

I cross the Italianate marble lobby, trying very hard not to marvel at the frescoed ceiling and the gleaming chandelier hanging above my head.

Pretend this is no big deal. Like you visit these places all the time. You know, when you're vacationing at the Cap d'Antibes with your good friend J-Lo and—wait. The Cap is in France, not Italy. Okay, like when you're on Lake Como with George Clooney and Amal—

And . . . I've just realised I don't know what name the room is booked under. Beckett. Is that his first name or last?

"I . . . have a room booked . . . under the name *Beckett?*" Please say I have a room booked under that name.

"Yes, of course, Mrs Beckett." There isn't even a ripple of amusement in the receptionist's expression as he dips his head, hammers something out on the keyboard, and passes me my key. "Mr Braunstein is waiting for you in the library."

"Mr Who?" And why?

"Mr Braunstein. Ali will show you the way."

The library is the kind of place you'd expect to find in a

neoclassical building such as this. Expensive-looking books kept behind glass and wooden panelling. With a domed ceiling and chandelier, the room is set up with several small tables covered with damask tablecloths instead of worn-looking leather chairs filled with curmudgeonly old men. And there is a man in here, one with thinning grey hair and a sombre suit. As I draw closer, he stands to greet me, his blue shirt straining a little over his girth. Save for the outfit and the absence of whiskers, he looks like a scruffy Santa Claus between gigs.

"Ms Welland, I presume?"

"Yes." I reach for confident Olivia as I take the man's outstretched hand.

"Braunstein," he says, then waits for me to sit before doing so himself. "Thank you for making time to meet me so soon after your flight. Can I get you a drink? A coffee perhaps before we begin?"

"No, thank you." I rub my lips together, not sure where to start. "Mr Bernstein, before we begin what?"

"Braunstein," he corrects kindly. "Mr Beckett didn't mention we'd be meeting today?"

"No. It must have slipped his mind."

He makes a noise that's not quite a surprise. "Mr Beckett never forgets anything. No matter. I have the pre-marital agreement paperwork here. I believe you've had your own counsel look at this?"

"Yes." I nod. Professor Google helped me with my copy.

"As I've said to Beckett, I would've preferred at least a month's notice, but I understand this has been a bit of a whirlwind courtship."

"Some would call it that." I applaud him for playing his part in what he undoubtably knows is a charade. *After all, he's holding the paperwork.* His smile confirms this, pushing a nondescript folder across the table. When I open it, the terms of our agreement sit on top of the files again.

Money. Monogamy. Cohabitation. Consummation. My cheeks

heat as I read through the now familiar terms. I try not to think of the man across from me having read this stuff as I give it a cursory look. Underneath is our prenup. I scan through it once again, this time without my online legal counsel.

Except as otherwise provided below, both parties waive the following rights:
To share in each other's estates upon their death.
To spousal maintenance, both temporary and permanent.
To share in the increase in value during the marriage of the separate property of the parties.
To share in the pension, profit sharing, or other retirement accounts of the other.

Same as before. I keep what's mine, including what he's giving me, and he retains his assets once we divorce.

"Where do I sign?"

And just like that, I'm one step closer to selling myself.

Everyone has a price, but my price is not my worth.

As the elevator spirits me upwards, I try not to think of the journey but the destination, and I don't mean which floor I'll be exiting on.

A viable business. Food other than ramen. No disgrace. Actually, scratch that last one. I might not ever need to tell Gran I lost my money, but I think I'll always look back on this experience and feel a little shame. But the honest addendum is that I've chosen this outcome. I may have all kinds of conflicting feelings, and I may end up spending thousands in therapy, but the choice is mine. I need to remember that.

The elevator doors open, and I step out, not into a hall, but a small lobby with grey tiles and tactile wall coverings. A padded bench sits against the wall along with a mirror and an Art Deco-esque looking credenza. And only one door.

I swipe my key card and step into a suite that is the epitome of another world. In fact, I think I just found the actual physical place where 'the other half lives'.

Standing on the threshold of a lounge that's so stylish, I almost don't want to step inside for fear of making it less so. My gaze is immediately drawn to a set of French doors leading to a stone walled terrace with an expansive view of Central Park beyond—and from way above tree height! So much blue and green, the city beyond shimmering on the horizon. Sumptuous drapes hang from original ornate coving, falling to the parquet floor in pristine pleats, and soft furnishings that look so inviting. The whole place is just dazzling.

The suite is more like an apartment, a home away from home. *If your home is worth millions, I suppose.* There's a formal dining room with seating for a dozen, a small kitchen, and two bedrooms, each on opposite corners of the suite. As I discover my case set in the smaller of the two, I don't know whether this makes me feel more nervous or less. Sure, he's giving me the illusion of space, but as I stand in the master bedroom staring at the snowy-white bed, trepidation washes through my stomach.

Will I be sleeping here? Or only . . .

Something that resembles a thrill very quickly follows the trepidation.

I back out of the larger room, feeling like an intruder, and make my way to the other. Equally sumptuous, there's something haven-like about the calm space. A velvet sofa is tucked into the corner, a vase of pale peonies on the end table, lushly blooming yet so delicate.

I unfasten the clasps on my suitcase, open it wide, and pull out the outfit I've packed for today. No wedding dress for me. No veil or flowers. My something old is a dress from my closet from what Reggie liked to tease was my *Great Gatsby* stage. Following the release of the movie remake with Leo D and Carey Mulligan, I became a little obsessed with clothing from that period. It was short-lived as there are only so many cloche hats and drop-waist dresses you can wear before people start staring.

This dress is glorious, and I think I wore it once for a wedding, ironically. Peach silk overlaid with intricate beadwork and a ruffled hem, it's more fancy than fancy-dress, and it cost me almost a week's rent when I bought it in a little boutique in Camden.

I have a shiny barrette for my hair and a purse that's definitely of the period, the treasure *borrowed* indefinitely from my gran for prom, in what seem like a lifetime ago. I make a mental note to take off my phone cover to be sure I can fit it inside. Then I hang up my dress, throw my cardigan across the back of the sofa, and chastise myself for a ridiculous thought.

Something old and something borrowed.

This isn't that kind of wedding. There's no need for sentimentality.

But as I drop my cardigan, I notice a box placed on the velvet bench at the end of the bed, wrapped in blue ribbon.

My bedroom, my box, right?

I rapidly untie the bow, unravelling it from the shoe-sized box which might contain anything. But, *quelle surpris*, it actually contains a pair of shoes. There's also a card, so no need to guess who these are from. Though if I find the previous occupant of this suite left a pair of Olivia-sized shoes behind by mistake, then too bad. Finders keepers!

I pull out the card and read it.

Olivia,
I hope you'll enjoy this four-hundred-pound pair of shoes, purchased for you for no good reason other than I wanted to. And just because I can.
Your turn soon.
Beckett.

. . .

Despite our earlier exchanges, I find myself smiling as I recall the conversation including those same words.

It doesn't make me a bad person to want nice things.

Maybe he's trying to remind me. Or maybe it's a gift for the pure sake of gifting. Whatever it is, I'm not going to read into it too deeply. But I am strangely touched all the same.

And something else I know? These shoes cost way more than £400. I saw them in Selfridges two weeks ago. Okay, coveted them. But two weeks ago, I would no more have been able to buy a pair of shoes as frivolous as these as I would have booked a night in a hotel like this. But in a few short hours, I'll be able to buy all the ridiculous footwear I want.

No more nagging sense of dread at what will become. No more avoiding calls from the accountant. No more scrimping and scraping to get by or worrying about where my next month's rent will come from. No facing the team to tell them I can't pay them anymore. I can breathe easy. Buy the fucking shoes.

Meantime, I'll just have to learn to live with myself.

As I glance down at the shoe in my hand and run my fingers over the kid-soft leather and frivolous ribbon, I think:

I can and I will.

19

OLIVIA

Forty-five minutes later, and fifteen minutes before I decide to go down to the lobby to meet Beckett—because there's no sense in him coming to me—I hear one of the outer doors open and his deep voice calling my name. "Olivia, are you ready?"

"Nearly," I call back, smiling ridiculously to myself. *It seems I was wrong. Maybe the mountain sometimes does move for Mohammed.* "I'm in the bedroom." Turning back to the floor-length mirror, I continue fixing my hair.

"You're in the wrong one." His deep voice pulls my attention to where he stands in the doorway.

"Sorry?"

"The bed in this room is smaller." His gaze slides in the bed's direction, my own following. I swallow.

He's saying we're going to need a big bed.

For wedding night acrobatics or for something else?

Maybe he wriggles in his sleep, or snores, or maybe he even—

In a blink, he's behind me, his hands resting against the curves of my hips. Always so handsome and proper in a suit, there's just something about the shadow of scruff on his jaw that lifts the whole effect. Something that deepens the suggestion of rakishness. When he presses his lips against my cheek, something yearning and slick bursts inside me.

"I am calm," I whisper to our reflections. *Even though I appear to be pulling a face.* "I'm mostly calm." I might be calmer if he wasn't touching me. I might be calmer once we've done the dirty deed. As it is, just having him near feels all kinds of illicit and just not enough.

"I didn't say anything." His earnest gaze meets mine in the mirror.

"My bag was already in this room when I got here," I babble, changing the subject. "I didn't want to presume."

"You didn't want to presume I'd want you in my bed?" One delusory eyebrow lifts. "On the night of our wedding?"

"Fake wedding."

"Real wedding," he corrects with a squeeze of my hips. "Real wedding night. That was the deal."

That sounds so wrong. Why can't he just say fucking?

I turn in his arms, feeling all sorts of fluttery, but he doesn't release me.

"All I'm trying to say is I don't know what to expect. My bag was in here, so I thought you wanted—"

"What I want is you. In here, in that bed behind you, in the other bed, against the chair. Did you see the dining table?" I nod dumbly, my lashes fluttering, though not for effect. "I want you there, too. Bent over the end or spread out against the wood like a feast while I sit between your legs and eat you like the glutton you make me."

"I didn't make you anything," I whisper, rolling in my lips as all my plans for good behaviour fly out of my head.

"Did you like the shoes?" I nod, refusing to give him the satisfaction of looking down at my feet. "Good, because I'd like to fuck you in those, too."

My heart begins to race at the pictures painted by his words. As if I can see it all before me. My body begins to tingle as it anticipates the path his lips will take, the ways he'll touch me, take me. But if there's one thing I know it's that I won't be passive. I think I might need this as much as he does, though for different reasons.

"I wanted you in the back of the car on the way here from the airport, with or without the driver watching. Because, my darling Olivia," he growls, his words such a visceral kind of compliment, "I just want you. Why do you think I didn't follow you into the hotel?"

And things were going so well...

"Probably because you had Mr Braunstein waiting."

"I would have kept him waiting downstairs all day, and his billable rate is fifteen hundred dollars an hour."

"All day? You're sure you'd need all that time?"

"Don't start," he replies in that languid, taunting tone of his. "In fact, why don't you go on. Make your assumptions and your little jokes. We'll see who can't walk tomorrow morning."

"Hmm, these shoes are a little high," I say, ducking my head as though to look down at them. Really, I'm just hiding my smile. When was the last time anyone made me feel like this? Their focus. Their absolute desire. Probably never.

"We'd better get going." His hands slide from my body with a slow kind of reluctance, his trailing fingers not quite interlacing with my left hand.

"Let me just get my purse," I murmur, moving towards the sofa.

"Don't forget your flowers."

"Sorry?" I turn, though my gaze immediately follows his to the side table.

"I'm assuming those are for you."

"What? How—you ordered me flowers?" I almost squeak. That is so unexpected. And a little ... un-Beckett-like, maybe? *But the shoes*, my mind whispers. Maybe I haven't seen all sides of him. Like the physical parts of him I'm yet to see but that already promise so much. *I'm so banking on more than just viewing tonight.*

"Too sentimental?" he asks evenly.

"No. Flowers are always a treat." Lifting them from the small vase, I admire the lush greenery. Their unusual colour—not quite cream and not quite pink—is the perfect complement to my dress. Bringing the petals to my nose, I inhale their fragrance. When I look up to express my thanks properly, Beckett has already gone.

Something old. *My dress.*

Something new. My shoes. My flowers.

Something borrowed. *My purse.*

Something blue . . . Spying the ribbon wrapped around the shoe box, I grab it quickly, wrapping it around the base of my bouquet.

My wedding, my way. Right?

As we reach the Office of the City Clerk, I stare up at the imposing building. I'm not sure what I was expecting, but I'm pretty sure it wasn't arriving in a chauffeur-driven Bentley. My surprise is almost visceral as Beckett takes my hand at the bottom of the stone steps. I almost ask if we're acting already but sense the question wouldn't be appropriate.

"Wait!" I call out, pulling him back before he begins to climb. "Don't glare at me," I sort of hiss. "This is important."

"What is it?" he asks, that fierce expression hardening, his grip on my hand tightening.

"Do you have a name? I mean, you must have because your lawyer called you *Mr* Beckett, meaning Beckett isn't your given name. What if they ask me in there?" I gesture to the building, aware my quiet tone might have passed into the realms of mildly hysteric.

"Of course I have a name," he replies tersely.

"Then why don't I know it?"

"Perhaps you didn't ask."

"I so did ask!" Apparently, I've turned into a Minnie Mouse.

To Have and Hate

"You said *it's just Beckett*." I affect a deep and proper tone, a vague approximation of him. So why is he smiling?

"My name is Alexander. And if you call me anything but Beckett, I'll divorce you before the forty-eight hours are up."

"Alexander. That's a good name," I reply as he begins to climb the steps again.

"Thank you, but I had nothing to do with it."

"Can I call you Alex?" I ask, wrapping my free hand around his upper arm. A thrill courses through me as the solid muscle tenses beneath my fingertips.

"No."

"What about Al? Xander? How about Ali?"

As we reach the entrance, he finally answers. "You may call me none of those things. Unless you want to make me very cross." His arched brow matches his tone perfectly.

"Oh, I'm sensing leverage."

"And I'm thinking about ways to shut you up."

"There was nothing about that in—"

Suddenly, I find myself pulled against the hard bulk of his body and being kissed very thoroughly. It's exactly the kind of kiss you imagine you'll receive on your wedding day. Maybe not in front of the congregation but later, when everyone is drunk, happy, and high on love, so no one notices when the groom steals you away for a little passion. While it might not have happened in the setting I've imagined, the effect of this kiss is just the same. It steals my breath and my thoughts and almost the power in my legs. Which could be why I'm feeding my hands under his jacket and pulling him closer. His lips taste of heat and need, and *God*, what I wouldn't give to be alone with—

The harsh sound of a jeering catcall followed by a wolf whistle pierces my attention. Beckett's head lifts, his fiery gaze sort of hazy and his full lips a little kiss swollen and pink.

"I think we attracted an audience," I whisper, our lips just a hair's breadth apart.

"They're just jealous because they aren't the one kissing you." And with that, he pulls me to his chest.

Be still my pitter-pattering heart.

"That might have been one of the nicest things you've ever said to me." And I'm pretty sure the look I'm giving him can only be described as sappy. I was toying with the idea of asking him if he'd like to call a truce today. Maybe he's had the same idea?

"That's not true," he says as he turns, sliding his arm across my back. "I told you earlier that you look very beautiful."

"When?" I scoff and almost trip as he stops quite suddenly again, pulling me back.

"In the bedroom before we left."

"No, you didn't." Because *that* I would've remembered. *Like how I remember he told me I looked beautiful in his office. Before I kneed him in the nuts.* Compliments absolutely fly in the face of our usual interactions, so of course I remember.

His expression clouds, and were I not standing so close, I might've missed the almost imperceptible shake of his head. His countenance suddenly clears, and he takes my face in both of his hands.

"You look so lovely, Olivia. You're like a creature from another realm, almost otherworldly. Far too beautiful to be true." The kiss that would perfect this moment never comes as his hands slide across my shoulders. "Now, let's get married."

Inside, a sign directs us to the Marriage Bureau. The interior is quietly genteel with marble floors, Art Deco crown mouldings, and bronze accents. Strangely, the place appears almost empty. *I thought courthouse wedding were massively popular, and we'd have to wait for hours.* As we walk the long hallway, a couple appear before us, walking towards us hand in hand. They're so happy it's almost as though they're floating an inch or two above the marble floor. Their joy is infectious, and it's hard not to smile at them even though they only have eyes for each other. What's not so cool is when they stop right in front of us and start making out.

"They must be in honeymoon mode already," I whisper as we make our way around them.

"Someone ought to get a hose," Beckett comments blithely.

"Do we take a ticket or not?" I ask as I spot a machine, the kind you'd expect to find in a DMV.

"Not," he replies, sliding his free hand into the inner pocket of his jacket and pulling out his phone. "We're here," he murmurs, ending the call almost as quickly as he started it.

"Did you check the times?" I point at the signage demoting the business hours. We're five minutes away from the office closing. *Did I get gussied up for nothing?*

"Do you have your passport?"

"Of course."

"Then let's take a seat at the counter."

"The closed counter?"

"Trust me, it won't be for long."

The words are barely out of his mouth when a man on the other side of the counter bustles up.

"Mr Beckett, I assume."

"Ah, wonderful. Mr Smith." The pair shake hands before the newcomer extends the welcome to me.

"Ms Welland," he says by way of greeting, shaking my hand vigorously as he beams. "Thank you both so much for your patience. I have your paperwork here and your judicial waiver." He waggles said paperwork before setting it down. "Now, if I can get you both to read through the documentation and sign in the appropriate sections, we can get to the fun bit."

The forms are basic, though I'm surprised to see my details already filled out. *Name. Date of birth. Address.* No one asked me for this stuff! Other than these, there are a few other things that jump out at me.

Beckett, at thirty-nine, is twelve years older than me, and a few years older than he looks.

He was married and divorced eight years ago.

His name? Alexander William Beckett III

"You look good for an old man," I whisper, resolutely keeping my gaze on the form.

"And you're angling to be pulled over my knee, *young* lady."

Unfortunately, he doesn't keep his voice to a murmur as he answers. I'm not sure who's more embarrassed—the clerk or me.

Forms are signed and passports are produced before we're led down the hall by our new best friend, who has slipped on his suit jacket and is regaling us with the details of a recent refurbishment, including the addition of stylish new restrooms. *Nothing says* wedding *like the talk of washrooms!*

"How did you get them to marry us after hours?" I whisper, wrapping my hand around Beckett's bicep, who happens to still be holding my hand. *If we're only playing, I'm going to make the most of it,* I think squeezing the muscle.

Oh, a little flex!

"I find you can fix most problems by throwing a little money at them. Though on this occasion, it's more a case of who you know rather than *what*."

"Friends in high places?"

"Something like that."

We enter the west chapel, though the room isn't very chapel-like at all. It's a modern space; the walls painted a pale shade of apricot and the light fixtures a modern take on Art Deco. A lectern stands at the far end of the room, our companion taking pride of place behind it with a wide smile. *As far as civil servant positions go, he must have a great job,* I think to myself. All the happiness and none of the heartache. Well, except for the admin.

The ceremony is short. Actually, that might be an understatement—a couple of minutes tops, words going by in a blur, our so-called solemn declarations.

Love. Honour. Cherish. Keep the bonds of matrimony. I follow the vows as dictated to me, feeling nothing before Beckett does the same.

"I, Alexander," he begins gravely, "take you, Olivia, to be my spouse."

I'm not going to cry.

Maybe I have hay fever, judging by the telltale prickling of my nose.

"To have and to hold from this day forward."

Nope, I'm not crying. Not as he looks lovingly into my eyes, the big faker.

"For better for worse, for richer for poorer, in sickness and in health."

I'm not crying.

Absolutely not as he squeezes my hand.

Not as he smiles the kind of smile I've never seen on him.

"To love, honour, and cherish."

Nope, definitely not crying.

I think it's just raining. Yes—indoors.

"From this day forward..."

For the next few months.

Yep, that'll do it. Waterworks be gone!

It's then that I notice the ring. It looks so tiny and so shiny as he picks it up from the lectern. And before I can say *I do* or *don't*, he's sliding it onto my finger, and I'm looking down at it in bedazzlement.

"By the powers vested in me by the laws of the State of New York..."

Oh my God. I just got married.

I think I'm going to throw up.

20

BECKETT

"He was right about the restrooms."

Olivia looks sheepish in the extreme as she appears in the hall. I jump up from my seat, and in a few long strides, I'm in front of her.

"Are you okay?" Is it jet lag? Is she ill? Or does she just feel sick at the thought of being tied to me?

"Yeah." She nods, a lock of hair falling across her face. I find myself sliding it from her cheek with my index finger, curling it around her ear. Apparently, that also makes her feel ill by her expression, so I drop my hands to my side.

"I wasn't ill. I didn't vomit," she qualifies unnecessarily. "I don't know what came over me. First with the crying and then rushing out of the chapel."

"You aren't the first to succumb to its pastel charms, according to our friendly officiant." His name already long forgotten. The analogy of the organ grinder and the monkey springs to mind. "Besides, it's not every day you hitch yourself to one of Satan's relations." This, at least, gets her to smile. "Before I drag you to meet dear old Uncle S, I believe there is some paperwork to sign."

Outside once again with our wedding license tucked into my jacket pocket, I'm out of sorts and at a complete loss of what to do

To Have and Hate

next. It's a feeling I'm unfamiliar with. A feeling I don't appreciate.

"Have you eaten at all?" I turn to Olivia who still looks quite wan.

"On the plane, maybe? Oh! I had some fruit back at the hotel."

Damn. "That wasn't very sensible, was it?" I find myself snapping.

"Excuse me, but between meeting your lawyer and getting ready for our wedding, what was I supposed to do? Order roast beef and Yorkshire pudding to go?"

"I didn't mean it like that. I just meant—"

"I know what you meant." She sniffs and I notice her nose is quite pink. "I think you'll find the word you're looking for starts with an *s* and ends in a *y*."

I find myself stifling a smile. What is it about her that makes it so much fun to goad her? She turns her head as though to look down the street, but I catch her gaze sliding to me.

"Snippily? Sublimely?" She purses her lips, fighting a smile. "Sinuously? Spontaneously." On the last one, I pull her against me, and whisper hotly in her ear, "I'm all out of words."

"Remind me not to play Scrabble with you," she grumbles, though I hear her smile anyway.

"What a selfish prick I am," I admit, causing her to pull away just a little, her expression censorious. "I just promised to honour and cherish you, yet I can't even offer you a sandwich."

"I could really go for a sandwich. Or a burger," she offers with a fervent gleam. "I won't even hold the rest against you. I don't remember you offering me any honouring before."

"I—" I am *not* going to apologise. For whatever seems to be bothering me. "I thought you said you were a vegetarian?"

"I am," she answers, hopping from the top step to the one below. "I just didn't say I was a good one."

A bark of laughter breaks free from my chest, and I'm not the only one startled. "Get back up here," I insist, pulling on her hand.

"What for?" Despite her complaint, she allows me to tug her to the top step where she takes my face in her hands. "Did I tell you that you look rakishly handsome today?" Her expression is perfect, her face far too beautiful. With her pink nose and her glistening eyes, I find it's an earthy kind of beauty, the human kind. Raw and sensual. Real.

"You did not. Please feel free to tell me so," I murmur, sliding my phone from my jacket.

"I just did!" Her gaze snaps left to where I hold my phone aloft. "What are you doing?"

"Say *just married*!" I answer, taking the shot.

"Are you feeling okay?" A pinch of confusion settles between her brows.

"Perfectly." I look up from the image. Her ring catching the light, the dapple of freckles revealed from under her makeup as, eyes open, she smiles into the kiss I'd delivered. *Perfectly wonderful.* "Why do you ask?"

"You're sure you're not getting sentimental?" She tries and fails to curtail a saucy grin.

"That would be you," I reply, sliding my phone away as I take her hand. "Do you always cry at weddings or just your own?"

"I don't know. You'll have to ask me next time I get married." My footsteps falter on the step, though I recover without swearing. Or glaring. Or generally being an arse. If she notices my misstep, she doesn't remark. "Did *you* cry the first time you got married?" Her tone is more inquisitive than needling, though I wondered how long it would take her before she asked about it.

"No. I very wisely saved my tears until later."

"I'm sorry," she offers softly, her free hand touching my shoulder from where she stands on the step behind.

"I was devastated. She took the dog."

"You!" The comforting gesture becomes a swat, and as I reach the pavement, I turn swiftly and place my hands on her hips.

"No New Yorker worth their salt would go to dinner at this hour. How about something a little more relaxed?"

"How about a hotdog?" she suggests with the kind of excited shimmy that speaks of an insatiable appetite. Something I'm looking forward to discovering. But a long strip of lips, tits, and arseholes is not much of a wedding feast.

"I've got a better idea." Then I kiss her, just once, a stealthy stolen moment as a yellow cab's horn blares, and someone yells profanities from the other side of the street.

"You've gotta love New York City," she says, beaming up at me.

"Damn, that reminds me. I meant to get us a couple of T-shirts from inside." Slogan T-shirts that were quite charming. *I got hitched in NYC,* I believe they read. I turn as our car pulls up and Olivia giggles behind me.

"From the place selling plastic flowers, elastic wedding rings, and aluminum bow ties?"

"I'm almost certain that word has a couple of *i*'s in it. Alumin-i-um?" I murmur, curtailing a smile.

"I can't help that you can't say it properly," she taunts as I open the door for her. "You're just, like, an alien. An Englishman in New York."

"We're not going to a karaoke bar," I answer in a withering tone. As I begin to close the door behind her, she holds out her hand like a stop sign.

"Hey, Beckett? I'm really pleased you didn't get me an elastic ring." She glances down at her hand to where the Cartier band sparkles. "It was so unexpected. Can I . . . can I just say no one has ever given me anything so beautiful? The stones are just so shiny."

I'm struck by the moment, by her expression, and by the sheer delight she exudes. Those stones have nothing on her beauty. Nothing on her vivacity.

"Don't mention it." My voice, when I eventually find it, is little more than a low rumble. "But you should know, diamonds don't truly shine. They reflect."

I close the door on her wavering expression, unable to give her anymore.

While not a venue that screams wedding or romance, I direct the driver to the Polo Bar behind the flagship store on Fifth Avenue. Given Olivia's request for a heartier fare, and the fact that it's nearer cocktail hour rather than dinner, I think it will do the trick.

There is one annoying moment when we're stopped by what I assume is a recent recruit to the door denizen team, but the issue is smoothed out easily enough.

"You know Ralph Lauren?" Olivia asks, suddenly a wide-eyed ingenue.

"His son, actually. He's out of town and said I could make use of his table. Not that the place will be busy at this hour. Often, there's a celebrity or two in the dining room, but I expect most people are still on afternoon tea. If you prefer, we could join the ritual, given your love for the stuff, though this place has a decent cocktail menu." Personally, I'd happily take her back to the hotel and start the real business of celebrating. Given she hasn't eaten and that I plan on more than a quick fuck, an early dinner seems like a reasonable plan.

"No one celebrates with tea," Olivia replies quite rightly as we descend to the subterranean dining room. Fucking would be much a more appropriate celebration, not to mention more fun. Cocktails and food is a distant second best. "Except maybe my gran."

"Are we celebrating?" I taunt a little as we follow the now embarrassed employee. Dressed in the ubiquitous uniform, like a Ralph Lauren branded mannequin, she leads us to our designated table.

"Celebrating, commiserating." Olivia gives an airy wave of her hand as though the difference is of no consequence. "There's a fine line between the two."

"You mean like there is between love and hate?"

"Thank you," she murmurs as she slides into the tan leather banquette facing the rest of the room. Thankfully, our table is a little less communal than the rest. I don't care to find my fellow diners at my elbow. "Exactly," Olivia adds, throwing me. *Ah. Our conversation. Love, hate, and the difference.* "Just because we're married doesn't mean things have to change."

"Meaning you intend to keep on despising me."

"I wouldn't say despise exactly," she demurs, trying hard to hide her grin. "But if you're ever run down by a bus, they should check the steering wheel for my fingerprints."

My deep burst of laughter reverberates through the space.

We settle into an amiable dinner; a ribeye for me and a burger for her, while enjoying champagne and a cocktail or two. Olivia then decides it's a good idea for us to order the other a cocktail.

"After all, *husband*, a good wife is supposed to know all the things her man likes."

"After tonight, I think you'll be a little closer to grasping that."

"That's what *he* said." She sniggers, but I don't respond as I catch the attention of one of the waitstaff. "He'll have . . ." She runs her finger down the cocktail menu. "A highflyer, I think."

"And for you, a blackberry cobbler." I close the menu and notice Olivia's smirk. "Care to share what's amusing you?"

"I thought for sure you'd order me a jockey club and make some joke about being ridden well later."

"A gentleman would never utter such a thing."

"That makes you either a liar or wrong."

"How so?'

"Because I've heard you say much naughtier things."

"Naughty? I don't think I've ever been called such a thing. At least, not since I was out of short trousers. Remind me, what did I say?"

"Ha! Good try, but no. Not in a million years. Not unless you want me to burst into flames for such wickedness."

"You've thrown down the gauntlet now. You know what that means," I add suggestively.

"I've thrown and stomped on it—trashed it! So, not happening!" she says all flushed and giggly.

I like this version of Olivia. A little unguarded and suggestive. Truthfully, I like the combative Olivia just as well, but a little champagne buzz suits her. I wasn't at all sure how today would play out, given the circumstances of our union. Hell, given the circumstances of our last meeting when the tension between us in my office resulted in her knee in my crotch and my balls in my throat. Not to mention earning us a cleaning crew audience. If at all possible, I'd prefer for us to get to the point of nakedness without any injury this time, and if that means a little champagne-aided relaxation, I'm all for that.

Our drinks arrive, and we both decide we prefer what we ordered for the other. I'm more than happy to let her fly high tonight even if she does tease me mercilessly for not removing the blackberry garnish from my glass.

We talk about everything and nothing. Or nothing important, I should say. Despite our teasing, she accuses me of being reticent, which is the least of it.

"We're doing this the wrong way around," she murmurs softly. Her eyes glitter in the ambient light as she stares at the contents of her glass.

"Is there a prescribed way to do these things?"

"Well, yeah." She scoffs. "People tend to get to know each other first. You know, before getting married."

"Not always. What about arranged marriages? Besides, I tend to believe we should make our own rules. But feel free to tell me all your secrets."

"There's not much to tell."

"I don't believe that. Tell me about school," I demand, suddenly curious.

"I have a degree in communications." She shrugs like the topic doesn't interest her.

"Is the degree for talking?"

"Yeah, very funny. I'm laughing so hard, just on the inside."

"I remember when you used to get a degree in an actual subject like science, humanities, or the arts."

"*So old*," she taunts. "I bet you don't even use a calculator. You have an abacus, right?"

"I'm much more holistic in my approach. I take off my shoes and use my fingers and toes."

"What happens when you get to the bigger numbers?"

"I make everyone in the office take off theirs."

As she laughs, I come to realise this is my new favourite sound. At least until tonight when my body will be over hers.

"You find that amusing?" I quirk a brow as though to suggest she's laughing at my very existence.

"Yeah," she replies on the breath of a sigh. "But that's okay because it was always in my plan to marry an older man." If possible, my brow arches higher. "You know, so I can watch him die and stuff."

Plates are cleared away, and more cocktails are served.

"What were you like growing up?" she asks, planting her elbow on the table and cupping her pink cheek in her hand. Her expression is so animated, though that could be the champagne.

"Lonely," I reply in a moment of honesty that surprises me. "Mostly. My parents were older and not really interested in child rearing. I went to boarding school quite young and thankfully things improved."

"Boarding school was an improvement?" she repeats tenderly. But there really is no reason for her sympathy unless it makes her feel better. "I can't imagine what that must've been like."

"I imagine the exact opposite of your perfect childhood."

"I wouldn't say my childhood was perfect."

"I don't believe it wasn't an idyllic experience."

The way she conducts business says there's an innocence

about her. And innocence is the result of a lack of exposure to the real world. "I'm sure yours was a halcyon experience full of trips to the ice-cream store, teddy bears, and cuddles on demand." Because who could resist hugging her? *Having her.* There's just something about this woman. Something utterly enticing. Something I can't help but want to own. I'm sure my childhood sounds like a Dickensian novel in comparison, but I need to remember that, despite the way she's looking at me, she's here because I gave her no other choice.

"Not so. I come from a broken home. My dad left when I was very young. I barely remember him."

"Daddy issues?" I ask with a gleam, hating myself as I do so.

"You wish." She picks up her glass, pensive for a beat. "My grandfather was a father figure for me. He owned a chain of drug stores until he retired. He was the best kind of man. Loyal and honest, he taught me the value of hard work. It's to him that I owe E-Volve—his passing gave me the capital." She makes a noise that can only be described as disparaging. "I guess I didn't pay enough attention to the advice he gave, or maybe I wouldn't have fucked it all up." She takes a deep swallow, but I refuse to allow her to become maudlin.

"I'm sure I don't need to tell you that three out of every four start-ups fail. Are you saying seventy-five percent of all start-up owners are losers?"

"No, it's just—"

"It's just life. Sometimes the cards are stacked for failure." Her expression hardens. For some reason I'm sure she's thinking about Luke. *Good.* "But failure is not final. What's important is having the courage to continue, no matter what else."

"I don't want to talk about it anymore." Her words fall in a rush, determined to steer the conversation elsewhere. *Also good.* "Where did you go to college? University, I mean."

"Oxford."

"Naturally," she deadpans. "Why'd I even ask?"

"Because I intrigue you," I supply.

To Have and Hate

"Annoy me, Mr Fancy-pants law degree."

"Jurisprudence," I correct before adding, "I'm suddenly very interested in your fancy pants. Pants meaning lingerie in my neck of the woods. I wonder, are you a lace or a silk kind of girl?"

"Cotton. Big ones." She makes a comical charade of hiking the elastic waistband over her breasts.

"My favourite."

"Pervert." She laughs.

"Perhaps I just like the reveal. Remember, I've already seen your underwear." *Felt your heat.*

Her eyes darken as she watches the path of my thumb over my bottom lip. "Play fair," she whispers.

My answer? "Never."

"You haven't asked me where I went to school."

"You were at UCL."

"Stalker, much?" She narrows her eyes suspiciously. "I see you've done your homework."

"Would you expect anything else?"

"Back to you." Her tone turns forthright, her hands now clasped together at the edge of the table. "So you went to the kind of swanky-ass school that's so special they can't call a law degree a law degree."

I stifle a sigh. "The topic of lingerie is so much more appealing than our schooling."

"I'm not sure big old granny panties count as lingerie," she mumbles quickly. "But yes, moving on. So Oxford, huh?"

"I suppose some people would say Oxford sounds quite pretentious."

"I suppose some people were trying to be polite," she deadpans.

"There's no need to be on my behalf."

"Ah, yeah. I forgot you can't be insulted. My opinion is so irrelevant, as I recall, you can't even be bothered to take offence." I smile wryly in response as she reaches for her glass. "You're not even going to defend yourself? Oh, I don't know, say, apologise?"

"My, you are emotional."

"It's kind of hard not to be when you're so personal."

"The issue was that you were determined to take it personally. If you hadn't been so ready to be offended, you would've heard what I actually said. Which is that I choose not to become emotionally invested in people's opinions of me. Their words have no power; therefore, their opinions are insignificant. It's a thought process."

"I'm pretty sure that's *not* what you said."

I smile again, which absolutely ruffles her feathers. "You should try it sometime." I reach for her hand as she sets the glass down. "A diamond doesn't lose its value due to a lack of admiration." My thumb rubs over the sparkling stones I'd slipped onto her slender finger just a little while ago. "Value your own worth, Olivia, for it is great."

Because, or maybe despite my honesty, I'd wager the words tumbling from her mouth are delivered without a lot of thought.

"You mean try not to take offence when my spouse tells me they think I'm a grouchy ass?"

"Your spouse would never cast such aspersions on your delectable arse. In fact, your spouse has some definite designs on the area in question." Very much so, in fact.

"My spouse had better remove his head from his own ass. Because there isn't enough money in the world for him to buy access to the area in question."

"Don't do that." The bite in my tone is immediate. "Don't make this out to be something it's not. Something sordid and soiled."

"I-I think I have a pretty good handle on what this is." Her gaze slides away, her expression not quite pensive, but maybe preparing what she has to say. "I came to the truth, my truth, after a lot of soul searching and a lot of time spent in my own head. Could I do this? And what would it say about me if I did?" I don't speak but rather wait for her answers. "You're looking at me like I'm a bug stuck under a glass."

"Am I? I suppose I'm just trying to work out what conclusion you came to." While wondering if she'll change her mind when we get to the bedroom. *No,* I think. *She's come this far.*

"I decided it doesn't have to be black and white. Life is full of grey areas and lurking shadows. I decided that everyone does have a price—everyone."

"Just as the moon orbits the Earth, and the Earth reacts likewise to the sun's gravitational pull, I'm sure more worthy truths will never be put into words."

"What I also decided is that while you may have found my price, my price isn't my worth."

"Congratulations." I raise my glass and toast the strength in her words. "As the aphorism goes; everyone wants to be a diamond, but few are willing to accept the cut."

Olivia is a prize I will never deserve.

Deserve? No.

Have? Certainly.

"Would you like dessert?" I ask in a careless tone. "Or are you ready to go back to the hotel?"

21

OLIVIA

THE CAR JOURNEY back to the hotel is tense. Or maybe that's just me. And maybe tense isn't the right word for the way I feel. I'm not exactly nervous but more excited. Jumpy and a little on edge.

Or maybe I just want to jump on him.

We don't speak, and I don't dare open my mouth for fear of where it might end. And I don't mean with words but in actions. In destinations. In the places I want to test and taste. Don't ask me why or how. I still don't fully understand how I can be here today under these conditions and still want him like this.

"This car has a privacy screen," Beckett murmurs as though reading my thoughts. His hand reaches out, his fingers entwining with my own.

"Don't even think about it," I whisper back, turning to the darkened passenger window.

"Why not? You obviously were." Strange how I can hear the smirk in his words without even having to look. "There might be some symmetry in it," he suggests. Or dares.

I turn back to face him again. "You want the first time this happens to be in the back of a car? Maybe Reggie was right. Maybe you do have a fetish."

"I'm just teasing," he protests.

To Have and Hate

"Such a boy."

He reaches out to cup my cheek, bringing my face closer to his as he whispers, "This man *is* going to fuck you in a car sometime soon." My insides begin to pulse in response to the image his declaration paints. "And you're going to beg me to make it happen."

"Don't build your hopes up too high," I whisper back as I slowly pull away. The push and pull, the taunt and the challenge —it's like our foreplay. "The contract said consummation. In my mind, that happens just once."

"We'll see," he purrs smugly as I turn back to my evening view.

"Fun Olivia fact for you." I rub my lips together nervously as, a little later, we make our way to the elevator. I don't know what's making me more nervous; being in the tight scary space with Beckett or what will follow afterwards. "I hate these things. Elevators, I mean." I bury my nose in my bouquet as if I could hide from him.

"I know." The doors open, and he takes my hands as we step into the empty compartment. "Heather told me the day I turned up in your office."

"Heather." I pull an unhappy face in an effort to fight my smile. "Don't laugh. Her social media skills are vast. Plus, she doesn't cost me a lot of money, payroll-wise."

"I wouldn't presume to make fun of your talent management skills," he replies, tugging me closer and wrapping his hands loosely around my waist. It's like we're already familiar with the ebb and flow of the other's body. Sure, the cocktails have helped, but it seems more than that, almost as though it's on a cellular level.

"Says the man who wants the veto on all new hires."

"I just want to help you get the best out of E-Volve. It certainly has nothing to do with a lack of faith in you."

Somehow, I don't believe him despite the apparent sincerity in his words. After what happened with JBW, let's just say my confidence has been rocked. It's like I no longer trust myself sometimes. Take what's happening now as I lean into him, pressing my cheek to his chest. When you dine with the devil, aren't you supposed to take a long spoon? I should be maintaining a distance, not leaning on him.

"Heather tells me you take the stairs every day. Sensible, if you ask me. The lift looks like a death trap."

"It's not so bad. And climbing the stairs up three floors isn't too bad. Plus, it's good for the glutes." As he slides his hand down to the muscle mass in question, he makes a noise which kind of suggests he agrees. "It's even better when you do it in heels."

"Yes," he almost groans. "Yes, it is."

"I didn't thank you for the shoes." *I'm going to fuck you in them.* I push away the memory of his words. "You have good taste."

"You know what would make them look better?" I angle my head to better see him. "If they were around my shoulders." His words and his expression render me speechless for a beat, but as the doors slide open to our floor, we step out.

"One moment, please." Key card produced, Beckett suddenly bends and sweeps me up into his arms.

"What are you doing?" I might even squeal a little, then laugh as I notice the card now clenched between his teeth.

"I would've thought that was obvious," I think he says, and I almost ask him why. This isn't supposed to be a real wedding night experience. *Is it?* We're not supposed to feel swept away by giddiness and passion, so why is my heart galloping like the hooves of a runaway stallion?

"Would you mind?" Again, I *think* that's what he says. I take the card from between his teeth, and he lowers me a little so I can reach the keypad. Before I can do so, the door clicks and swings open, and we're met by a man in a pale grey suit. About my age, he looks completely unperturbed by our arrival, which is more than I can say for my reaction.

"Allow me." He pulls the door wide, and Beckett angles me,

legs first, through the doorway into the suite. "On behalf of the St. Regis, may I offer you our congratulations, Mr and Mrs Beckett."

Oh, that sounds so strange.

"Thank you," we seem to answer in unison. Beckett's tone is solemn while mine is more a hysterical giggle.

"I don't think we'll be needing any assistance this evening, will we, darling?" Beckett's gaze sparkles with challenge and the unspoken. *Are we going to need his help while I fuck you?* I can't find the words to answer either of them, so instead, I shake my head.

"Then I'll just wish you a good evening." And with the sincerest of smiles, he removes himself from the room.

"Why was there a man here?" I squeak as I'm lifted sharply into the air, Beckett adjusting his grip under me. "Put me down! My legs work perfectly fine, as well you know."

"The butler," he answers succinctly. "Your legs are more than fine, but allow me to play my manly part and carry you over the threshold."

"This isn't even—" *a proper marriage,* I almost say as his gaze dares me "—a proper threshold!" I say instead, throwing my arm out somewhere behind us. "We already passed that."

"One down, many more to go?"

"Thresholds?"

"Boundaries, Olivia. I plan on encouraging you to cross all kinds of boundaries tonight." My heart beats so loud I can literally hear the whooshing in my ears. Or maybe that's the sound of my dress as Beckett lowers my feet to the bedroom floor.

There's a champagne bucket on the table with a telltale golden wrapping protruding from it. Two silver stemmed flutes stand beside it along with a silver dish of delicate offerings. Tiny macarons, swirls of rich, dark chocolate, and raspberries, along with an embossed card offering us the hotel's congratulations.

"Do you think they thought we might get the munchies?" My laughter is a nervous gurgle that's not quite carefree enough to be classified as a giggle as I place my bouquet on the nightstand. "Or maybe we'd need a sugar boost." I bite my lip against the rest of that sentence. *In between fucking.*

"Something's missing." As Beckett comes up behind me, the heat of his presence almost burns.

"I can't think what." *A balloon display? Banners that read "enjoy your first married people sexy-times"?*

"Condoms." He pauses a beat, his arms sliding from my shoulders to my wrists. "Do I need to call concierge?"

I shake my head in the tiniest of motions. I'm on the pill. "Not on my account, unless—"

"You're safe with me, I promise." He kisses my cheek then steps away.

As safe as I would be sharing a cage with a tiger. Even though it may go against everything I think of him, in this instance, I believe him. I also believe he'd sell his grandma to get his hands on JBW, but at heart, Beckett remains a gentleman.

Or maybe I'm deluded.

No more conversation. No more dancing around this thing that both terrifies and titillates in equal measure as I turn to face him. We stand a couple of feet apart, the dust motes dancing in the rays of the setting sun between us. While he's always so powerfully handsome, the light seems to gild him, turning him into something less reachable. *Not that unreachable ever stopped me.*

My tongue darts out to wet my bottom lip because my whole existence suddenly feels parched as I take my first tentative step towards him. Beckett's eyes dip to my mouth, then farther still, his lazy perusal of my body igniting every nerve ending.

"I like that you wore a tie." If my hand shakes, it's because I'm nervous as I slide it down the strip of blue silk in my approximation of alluring. *Is this what he'll expect? Sexual confidence? Bedroom voices and purrs?*

"You like my tie, do you?"

"Yeah. I might've thought about strangling you with it once or twice."

His chest moves with a soft sounding laugh before he replies, "Only once or twice?"

"Ten or twelve times."

"Why, Olivia. That sounds kinky."

My stomach dips unpleasantly. "It's—I'm not. I don't want you to think that because of the app, because it's not about hookups. It's about finding love." Love. The other four-letter word that has no place between us right now.

"I thought it was about making money."

"Yeah, that, too." I keep my eyes on his chest as I speak. "I just don't want you to get the wrong idea."

"You have no clue what I'm thinking."

I tip onto my toes to brush my lips across his jawline, concealing my embarrassment. "Just don't expect me to be something I'm not."

His brows draw together, a question perched on his lips, but instead of asking, he turns his head, and our lips meet in a kiss. A soft, lingering brush that leads to another. A wet slide. A tight gasp. I've never been kissed this slowly, this tenderly, as he holds my face in his hands, his mouth almost savouring.

"Don't stop." I won't let him, not as my hands slide across his chest and shoulders, pushing his jacket until it drops to the floor. The tenor of our kiss changes, like a stone gathering speed down a hill. His lips demand fiercely, his hands greedy and grasping as he feeds me his tongue. He tastes of fruit from his earlier cocktail, his cheeks bringing with them the heady scent of his cologne. But under it all is the scent of man. Of male. Of Beckett himself.

Need builds in my veins, every cell in my body seeming to cry out for more. More touch. More taste. More Beckett as I suck on his tongue as though it's a substitute for his cock. The thought is jolting—and a truth. I want him in my mouth as much as I've wanted anything. As his body bucks against mine, I wonder if I've said that out loud because with it comes a sound of such deep, masculine need, like he's read my thoughts. His body vibrates with something that feels almost dangerous as he walks me backwards into the room.

"Turn around," he demands, his voice all gravel and bass. Every inch of me aches for his touch as I turn. "We're going to do this my way. Take our time. Don't worry, you'll enjoy it," he adds with just an edge of taunt as he brushes my hair over my shoulder.

His fingertips slide a tantalising tease against my sensitive nape. I shiver as he gathers the strands, almost as though he's about to tie my hair back. Instead, I find my eyes rolling closed, my neck extending to the left as he presses a soft kiss against the curve there. One kiss becomes two, two becomes a sense of delirium, every press and caress seems so intentional. As though he's been thinking about this. Anticipating. Planning and preparing. Deciding ahead that he'll tighten his grip at this very moment to pull move me how he will. This isn't like the car or his office. There's no frenetic motion or desperation, just time and desire and my bending to his will.

"Do you remember what I said about the table?" He purrs his words directly into my ear. I try not to give in to a whole-body shiver as I make to nod my understanding, finding I can't. Not with my hair twisted tight in his fist. The realisation turns to sensation, washing over every inch of me.

"What was that?" His grip tightens. "I didn't quite hear you."

"Yes." I sound like I've been running, my breathing ragged. "Yes, I remember."

"I think we'll start in here." *A kiss.* "If you have any objections." *His free hand slides around my body, cupping my breast.* "You should say so now because something tells me when I taste you." *A press of his teeth. The way he tortures my aching nipple.* "I'm going to want to make your sweet pussy my home."

The dirty deliciousness of his words ignites a desire that instantly needs acknowledgment, his teasing attentions making it almost impossible to remain passive. But as I try to move, his grip tightens, the frustration and need layering and building until I feel I could crawl out of my own skin.

"Take off your dress, darling. Would you do that for me?"

I nod, not trusting myself to speak. What he's asking for seems more than the sum of his words as he lowers himself to the mattress in front of me, a picture of manly confidence and ease.

My fingers tremble as they reach for the zipper. It feels too much to strip while he watches, too personal, like I'm exposing more than just skin. But the zipper eventually stops, and I slide off one shoulder strap and then the other. The gauzy fabric falls and gathers at the curve of my hips. I shimmy a little because it seems less seductive to just shove it down. As I do, I notice how his eyes are mostly pupils and glued to the rise of my breasts. I shimmy again as I shake the dress loose, the fabric whispering against the backs of my legs. As I step from the pool of apricot silk, his gaze falls to the creamy lace between my legs.

Not sure what to do, I begin to bend to pick up my dress when Beckett's hands clasp my hips, pulling me backward to where he sits. He's so hard and so warm under me, the metal of his belt a cold contrast against my spine

"You enjoyed teasing me, didn't you? Enjoyed me watching before you thought to fold away your clothes like a good little girl."

"It's been a while since I was a girl," I whisper as his hands slide over my skin as though seeking confirmation. Finding it in the curve of my breasts and the weight of them as he takes them in his hands. In the hardened peak of my nipples the gauzy cream lace.

He doesn't speak anymore. He doesn't need to as his hands touch me in ways that make me feel treasured, his lips follow with their praise. My bra comes loose, his touch rough and tender in equal measure. The pads of his fingers. The drag of his blunt nails. My needy sigh as I turn, and he brings me between his splayed legs, his tongue sweeping yet barely brushing my nipples.

"Please," I whimper, pressing my body against his mouth. His hands slide to my elbows, pulling them behind me. The position changes the experience in that instant. I feel and I see everything. The dark intent in his eyes as his soft breath blows over me. The pulse pounding in his neck and the echo of it deep between my legs.

My skin feels electrified as his mouth meets my breast, his teeth biting the curve. I cry out on a long, stuttering exhale, my nipples aching and hard, my skin singing out for more of this kind of torturous tease. The kind of rough relief only Beckett can give. Finally, he pulls the tight bud into his mouth, flicking, teasing, circling with his tongue.

"Your skin is like moonlight," he whispers, his voice rasping and raw as his fingers slide my panties over my hips. I wrap my arms around his neck, feeling like I need the assistance to stay upright. "Your freckles are a constellation." His words are almost pondering as his hand trails across my collarbone, his eyes following. "A constellation I want to cover in cum."

My reaction is visceral, my body jerking, the noise expelled from my chest a sharp vowel sound as I see exactly that in my mind's eye—Beckett over me as milky ribbons splash my chest.

Immediately, and by some unspoken agreement, we begin to strip him out of his clothes. Tie pulled wide. Cufflinks discarded on the floor. His custom-made cotton mistreated as the fabric is yanked from his body. My greedy hands run over his stomach and chest, the muscles reacting as I trail my nails over the warm ridges and crests, until my fingers reach the buckle of his belt, but only getting so far. *Damn.*

Flipping us over, Beckett lays me across the bed, adroitly inserting himself between my legs. His mouth teases and nuzzles, sucking on the inside of my thighs, before I'm rudely cleaved, his hands sliding my knee higher to expose me. His tongue, arrow sharp, parts my flesh. I cry out at the contact, my hips bucking from the bed as the man over me just whispers, "Yes, that's it, my darling."

The heat of his words and his exhale blow across me, and I shiver, anticipation dialling my senses sky-high. With a swipe of his tongue, I almost levitate from the bed, but he avoids where I need him. Long swipes and shallow circles, dipping inside, his tongue arcing higher before starting again.

My body is a wire strung so tight it's bound to snap, my hips chasing the cruel devotion of his lips and tongue. I reach for his head, intent on his hair, when he bands my wrists with his hands, pressing them to the mattress. His rough reprimanding *tsk* vibrates deliciously.

"I've lost my place now. I'll have to start again."

"*Oh.*" I hear myself whisper, swapping my thrusting hips for a soft cry as he starts the process all over again, his tongue seductively narrowing, drawing maddeningly close to my clit before moving away again. I whimper, on the verge of tears, when he licks my thigh, adding to the torment.

"Beckett, please." My words are a plea for release, a cry for clemency.

"Please what?" He doesn't even stop, doesn't lift his head.

"I need you to..."

"What is it that's not working for you?" It's not a serious question. It's a smug one that makes me want to scream. Not that I'd give him the satisfaction. *Yet.*

"Please. You know what I need."

"Hmm." A non-committal agreement as his breath blows over me again. "You're as soft as silk here."

My body shakes. He is a villain. The worst of men. But oh, my God, he should give up finance and do this for a living.

Just this. Just for me. And I'll pay him however he sees fit.

Because it's. Just. That. Good.

"Oh, God. Please." My thighs begin to shake.

"You do like that word, don't you? Please what? Please where? Please...?"

"Just. Suck on me. Lick me there. Touch me."

And with a growl, he finally does, engulfing my clit with his lips. He sucks it. Kisses it. Makes out with my pussy until I'm writhing beneath him, thrashing wildly. He feeds his hands under me, drawing my hips up and my pussy to his face as he inhales me, sucking and swirling, flicking and repeating again and again until I'm tipped over the edge into ecstasy. Light, heat, and the sensation of where his tongue meets my climax, my body rising to meet them both.

And when I finally come back to myself, he smiles up at me from between my legs with a hint of mercilessness.

"Oh, God," I whisper, unable to manage much else. But he just licks me slowly, working me with the full flat of his tongue. I begin to twist from under him. "Beckett, please. It's too much."

"No, darling. We're only getting started."

22

BECKETT

I NEED YOU.

Were words better than this ever spoken? If so, I don't remember them.

I love the way she cries out as I lick and tease her, trying to close her legs even as she presses her hand to the back of my head to draw me nearer. I knew it would be good. I just didn't realise the magnitude. And I have so many plans. So many ideas. One night won't be enough. Who knows, six months may not be so.

I push the thought from my head as I stand and begin to strip. Trousers, shoes, all of it, as she watches with those otherworldly eyes.

"Don't," I whisper as she begins to cover herself. *To lower her leg.* "If you get to watch, then I do, too. This," I assert, taking my aching cock into my hand. "This is what you've done to me. The question is, what are you going to do about it?" I slide my hand up to the fat crown, twisting it just the right amount.

"I could think of one or two things," she whispers, her eyes as dark as sin.

"You're staring." My abs tighten in anticipation as I slide the pre-cum from the tip over my shaft to lessen the drag. *Teasing myself, tormenting her.*

"It's hard not to." By the small crease of her brow, she'd preferred not to have said so, which just makes my smile wider, makes something dark and sweet bloom in my chest. "I'm so conflicted," she mutters, covering her face with her hands. And she then actually growls.

"There's no shame in wanting."

"It's not that," she answers suddenly, her face appearing again. "Part of me wishes that *that* part of you wasn't quite as perfect as the rest. Physically perfect, at least," she adds as though annoyed with herself.

"I'm . . . sorry to disappoint?" Only, I'm not sorry at all. "But I don't think you're close enough to judge."

"What?"

"You should come closer. You're too far away to find fault."

"Really?" The word is more giggle than anything else. She probably thinks I'm crazy.

"Yes, an odd-looking freckle or a slight bend to the left?" For the record, I have no such impediments. And while this isn't the most erotic invitation I've ever tendered, Olivia is a different kind of girl.

Lashes lowered, she moves toward me, her hand reaching out and brushing softly against my thigh. Higher her hand moves until her thumb meets the crest of my hip bone. She makes small circles there as she studies me, so close to where I need her touch.

"Damn." Her eyes lift, their depths lustrous.

"Did you find a fault?" The muscles in my thighs are pulled taut, and my balls are aching. She's so close, her soft breath blowing over me. I just want to grab the hair on the back of her head and—

"It's not really any smaller up close."

"I feel like I ought to apologise." Is sex supposed to be funny?

Before I can say another word, she presses her mouth to my crown, her lips like the brush of petals. I groan, the feel of her lips and the soft brush of her hair causes my abs to flex and my thighs to tighten. I suck in a breath, my hands falling away at her touch because she's holding my shaft, tonguing my glans and slit, and my legs are trembling, my head fit to explode at the intensity of the feeling.

"You're not the only one who can tease," she whispers, looking up at me with a wicked smile. I'm sorely tempted to wrap my hands in her hair and show her exactly what her threats do to me. But instead, I press her shoulder, pushing her flat against the bed.

She's so fucking perfect. And I am so ready for this.

"I'm going to fuck you." I grunt as my cock meets where she's wet. "Tell me you want this, too."

"Yes. Yes, I do."

"Tell me you need this."

"I need you." Try as I might to harden my heart to her words, I've never wanted to be inside someone as much as I do Olivia. Inside her head and her body, I'm picking her apart only to put her back together again. My skin feels like it's on fire as I wrap my hand behind her knee and slide her leg higher up the bed.

Her soft sigh is an invitation, her languid gaze a provocation, but everything drops away as I exhale slowly and thrust inside.

"*Yes.*" My grunt is a counterpoint to her cry as our bodies collide. The heat and pulse of her are unravelling as I fight the urge to thrust, to rut and fuck, need flooding my veins, hot and frantic. It's almost as if I can't believe we're here—finally. Is the feeling in my chest relief? Whatever it is, I'm greedy for it as I kiss her, sharing the taste of her from my tongue. As I withdraw, we both give a taut moan, her thighs pressing my hips as though to hang on to the sensation.

"Oh, God," she whimpers as I begin building an easy rhythm, lost in the tide of her body pulling me in. Slow and deep, our pace is punctuated with sucking and greedy kisses. She cries out as I go deep and whimpers when I deliver shallow thrusts, hungry for it all.

I wonder if she can feel me shaking like it's my first time.

I wonder if her heart is playing the same tune as mine.

I wonder what she's thinking and then worry she sees it all.

Her hips follow mine as I pull out, her moan a monument to her frustration. But as I slip my arm under her thighs, she's quick to get onto her knees for me. Our pleasure ricochets around the room as I sink into once more, angling her pelvis to hit that not so cerebral pleasure centre.

"You take my cock so well." She's so hot and tight, and the angle is so much deeper this way, as the city lights turn her skin to pure moonbeams.

She whispers my name on an exhale, her tone part plea and part ecstasy.

"I know, sweetheart." I grunt, my follow-up exhaled in a rush. "It's so fucking good." I knew. I just knew it would be. But nothing could've prepared me for this.

She turns her head, sinking her teeth into my arm, unleashing a flood of something hot and sweet into my veins.

"Harder," I demand, pressing my mouth to her shoulder to deliver a kiss, then a lick. I pull back on her hips, and slam in, my body punishing hers again and again until there is nothing but this. Wild and frenetic movement steal my thoughts. There are no recriminations. No push and pull. Nothing else exists outside of this room.

"Yes! Beckett, I want you to come inside me."

I react to her words as though lashed by a live wire. My hands grasping her freckled shoulders, I begin to fuck her as though I mean to be inside her in my entirety—as though I mean to break her apart.

This is real. This is happening. And it is terrifying.

Every inch of my skin feels pierced by a million hot pins, the

To Have and Hate

feeling building and twisting as it shoots through my extremities, white hot and intense. As I bury my mouth against her salt-slick skin, I pray to the heavens I'll survive this.

23

OLIVIA

I WAKE TO AN EMPTY BED, which is fine. I'm not freaking out.

I'm not!

Because Beckett looks like the kind of man who runs marathons before most people have wiped the drool from their cheek. Myself, I'm more a caffeine and carbs morning person. The closest I get to the gym is by wearing a T-shirt and leggings that are Adidas by Stella McCartney.

The empty bed allows me to stretch languorously and count my sucking bruises while delighting in each one of the accompanying aches. I worked muscles I didn't think I possessed. Last night was . . . wonderful. Incredible. All kind of intense. I'm pretty sure I could make a list of superlatives, and it still wouldn't cover the experience.

I was so right, I think quite smugly to myself. A man couldn't possibly be as self-controlled as Beckett without becoming a little freaky in the dark. And let me tell you, his energy is pretty freaky. To put it another way, last night, Beckett persuaded me to try this thing—the kind of thing that's still making me blush six hours later—but it turns out, he was right. There are two kinds of women in this world. Those who like it, and those who have never tried it.

To Have and Hate

After a final stretch, I pull myself up from the bed and—

"Oh, my God!" I see red—splotches of red all over the white bed linens. With my hand over my thundering heart, I try to reason with myself that there's not so much blood that I could've killed him. Unless it was death by a thousand cuts, and I've finished him off in the bathroom. Which, funnily enough, was something I did do last night. Finished him. In the bathroom.

On my knees.

In the shower.

He moaned a lot but I'm sure I didn't murder him.

I don't think.

It's then I notice the tiny seeds. The red splodges are actually squashed raspberries. The rest of the room? It looks like a bomb detonated here.

A puddle of champagne stains the wood of the nightstand, and the glass bottle lies on its side. *Don't ask. I'll never tell.*

One of the glasses has been separated from its stem, and the other lies abandoned on the velvet sofa. Macaron crumbs appear to be embedded into the carpet while Beckett's clothes and wet towels are lying everywhere. My beautiful bouquet lies squashed and abandoned after it became one of his props last night, when he used it to caress every inch of my skin.

I am out of here before housekeeping arrives!

Tiptoeing over the debris, I make my way to the bathroom and tie back my bird's nest hair. I brush my teeth then cover my nakedness, courtesy of the hotel branded plush robe. As I make my way into the lounge, I hear Beckett's deep tones coming from the dining room.

I shuffle my way in, my gait impeded by the hotel slippers. A weird quirk, I know, but I don't like walking barefoot on hotel carpet. The man of the hour, rather the man of many, *many* hours, sits at the head of the table, his phone glued to his ear. Which reminds me . . . I shuffle out of the room again, grabbing my phone and charger. As usual, the thing is dead, but I'll use one of the outlets in the dining room.

As I enter this time, Beckett is ending his call.

"You look bright-eyed and bushy-tailed this morning." My voice has a sandpapery rasp to it. *Interesting.*

"I had a few calls to make," he replies, glancing up.

"You could've done those in your pyjamas."

"Except I don't own any."

"Whatever will you do if you're taken ill and are rushed into hospital?"

"That sounded very insincere. Have you been making plans?"

"No." I bite back my smile. "Not yet at least. Though I did wake this morning and think I might have murdered you already."

"The raspberries," he murmurs with a sexy little smile. A new smile for a repertoire unveiled just last night. "They were fun while they lasted."

And they lasted longer than the chocolate but made just as much mess.

"Good morning."

I pivot—mostly shock—at the cheery female voice. This time, the butler is woman, judging by her uniform. It's so weird finding a hotel employee in your room, especially while you're wearing nothing but a smile, slippers, and a robe. Good thing I didn't think to ambush him naked this morning. *As if!*

"May I bring you some breakfast or a coffee, Mrs Beckett?"

Her appearance might be weird but not quite as weird as that form of address. My mouth works but no sound comes out, though I manage to clasp the gaping robe as the belt untwists.

"Fruit and perhaps a yogurt," Beckett answers on my behalf, checking my expression for a reaction.

"And coffee, please."

"How do you take it?"

I send Beckett a glare because if he says *very well*, I might really murder him. "Black, please." Because it's the kind of morning a girl needs a kick-start.

We're mostly quiet as our lady butler serves breakfast, sticking to quiet murmurs of *please* and *thank you* and other quiet banalities. Once we're alone again, Beckett reaches across the table to snag a strawberry from my plate. He pops it in his mouth with an inciting grin.

"Are they good?" I ask, a juicy blueberry poised between my fingertips.

He licks his lips as he answers. "Mmm. Very sweet."

"Good?" Then it's his turn to ask as I press the blueberry between my lips.

I nod obligingly, swallow, then take a sip of my coffee to wash the acidity away. I follow it with a spoon of yogurt, my tastebuds not yet awake enough to handle any kind of complication, and oh-so so sexily miss my mouth.

"Dammit." I have yogurt pretty much sliding down my cleavage. Grabbing my napkin from my knee (as though every one of my breakfasts is served with starched linen napery) I lift it, when I realise Beckett is moving. He leans across the table and rubs the smudge with the pad of his thumb. Leaning back again, he slides it into his mouth.

"You missed a bit."

Oh, I'm aware. A great seductress I make, huh?

"With a mouth this size," I mutter, "you have to ask yourself how."

"Your mouth is perfect." His smile is one of supreme satisfaction, and suddenly, neither of us are thinking about yogurt right now. It really is no wonder my pink cheeks have drawn his thumb. It brushes the path of my cheek, chucking my chin before dipping down to where the cotton robe has gaped again. "In fact, you're pretty damn perfect everywhere."

As his hand slides inside, I find myself leaning closer, his fingers teasing the curve of my breast as he takes the weight into his hand.

"What do you want to do today?" I ignore the smug tilt of his lips because I'm almost certain he'd like to spend the day the same way as I do right now.

"I had an idea," I begin carefully, desperate to keep my sighs to a minimum.

"I'm all ears," he purrs.

And I'm all nerve endings and sensation. "I—" Oh *yeah*. Just like that. "Thought we might take a little time to guarantee the error for consummation m-margin last night was nil."

"That *is* an idea." His thumb and finger tug my nipple, turning it into a tight, aching bud.

"Just to be sure."

"I agree. We should make sure this marriage is consummated very . . . very . . . thoroughly."

I close the last few inches of space between us, pressing my mouth to his. He tastes of coffee and mint and like a dozen other things I need. I fight to keep the contact between us, his teasing lips almost as provocative as his half-smile, the faint scrape of his stubble doing funny things to my insides.

"You're such a tease," I whisper, barely noticing how the robe is now almost open to my navel, one breast full in his hand.

"So do something about it," he coaxes, sliding the cotton from my shoulder. "Come closer."

"Why? Are you going to make good on what you said would happen at this table?"

"That all depends on how badly you want it."

"Bad enough to ask," I answer truthfully, my insides igniting with the expectation.

"Bad enough to know there are people just beyond the door? How good are you at keeping quiet?"

"I . . . think I can wait. I'm not into the whole being watched thing." I find myself leaning back, severing the connection between us. The idea of being caught just leaves me cold.

"Chicken," he whispers, leaning back, his arms now passive against the arms of his chair.

"If you ever owned chickens, you'd know that isn't an insult."

In response, the ass starts making poultry noises. "Chickens are smart, inquisitive, and friendly. Not to mention a little bloodthirsty."

"What about that margin for error?" he taunts. "There's a perfectly good table here for our use."

"I'm sure there will be other dining tables," I answer, which, by the hardening of his expression, he seems to take as there will be other men.

I suddenly feel like a bitch, but wasn't he the one who drew up our timeline?

Oh, God. This is going to be a long six months.

Before I can apologise, which I hadn't planned on anyway, or before he can do his masterful thing and spurn me or whatever, my phone springs to life at the other end of the room with a buzz that tells me it now has a little charge. *A little is better than nothing.* I slip out of my chair because the moment is awkward. Also, I have a business to run, and I barely looked at my phone yesterday.

"Olivia, come back to breakfast," his darkness demands. "You didn't finish your yogurt."

"I'll just get my phone." And be the rude colonial scrolling through her email at the breakfast table.

"I need to talk to you about something first."

"Sure." *Okay, Dad. I promise to pay attention to your* we-need-to-talk *talk*. I unplug the charger from the socket, accidentally swiping the dark screen of my phone.

Why do I have a million notifications?

OMG! THAT'S MR BDE?!?! This from Heather via our company group chat, followed by a volley of messages from Miranda.

BOSS LADY, YOU GOT HITCHED?
WHEN?
HOW?

And I have messages—lots of them, their arrival like party streamers fluttering down my screen.

WTF Ols. This from Luke.

W00T! Another from Heather, along with **BRING ME BACK SUM OF DAT WEDDING CAKE.**

Girl, we need to talk! This from Reggie.

My levels of confusion are great.

"I don't understand," I murmur, my sense of bewilderment deepening as I input my security code. "How could they possibly know?" Confusion turns to horror as my phone suddenly chimes in my hand, displaying a message from my gran.

Olivia, kindly explain what you mean by your Instagram post.

I swipe the icon, diving straight in.

One new post and one new profile image, though the pictures are the same.

A sparkling ring on a hand, cradling a handsome face.

Flushed cheeks, eyes open, whisky and green.

A kiss that is part smile and one-hundred percent genuine.

And words to go along with the post:

> **Wish me congratulations.**
> **Beckett asked, and I said yes.**
> **Guess who just took a trip to the courthouse?**

The post even has the use of appropriate hashtags, the last one a company creation we've tried to make popular.

> **#OlsandBecks #EngagedForOnlyADay #NewlyWeds**
> **#HePutARingOnIt**
> **#ISaidYes #WeLoveNYC #WeAreLove**
> **#FindYourPersonEVolve**

The post has had over nine hundred likes already. But even with the distant possibility of this being the result of some post-sex

To Have and Hate

induced wave of euphoria or memory blackout, I know I'm not responsible for this.

How? Because of the post's perfect grammar.

It turns out Beckett posts as he speaks, even when he's pretending to be me.

24

BECKETT

"Go away!" The bedroom door shakes as, from the other side, another projectile bounces off it. "I'm not speaking to you!"

"Clearly, you are. Yelling is a form of communication. "Also, you're also behaving like a child," I retort while wondering if there's perhaps another way to handle this as I slide my hands into my pockets and lean my shoulder against the doorframe.

"Go fuck yourself"

That's what? Eight times she's suggested I do so. Perhaps more if I include the minutes she spent ranting over breakfast. Rather than engage, I'd decided to shower and give her a little time to cool down. And here we are.

"An unruly teenager," I amend, which I'm sure doesn't make either of us feel better. Myself for thinking it because of the whole age gap thing, and her for . . . whichever of the million offences I'm currently guilty of.

"Well, guess what? I don't care what you think. You're not my dad, and you don't have the rights to my cell phone. You're morally fucking bankrupt, and right now, I hate you."

"Olivia, please." I can't remember the last time I actually asked for something. I usually just demand. Except for last night when she'd . . . I shake my head because now is not the time to be thinking these things. Sex with her clouds my judgment, obviously. I sigh, pressing my head against the frame now. "It was going to come out sooner or later. You know that. I was just ripping off the Elastoplast, the Band-Aid. Whatever you want to call it."

"You had no right. No right to invade my privacy, and no right to force my hand."

"Would it help if I said I've just spoken to your grandmother?"

"What?"

I spring back from the door as it opens. "Oh, there you are." And oh, what have you been doing in there to cause your hair to stand up like that? I don't ask. Mainly because I like my testicles where they are.

"What did you just say?"

"I spoke with your grandmother. Elsie. A charming lady."

I'm known within the city for my instincts. The choices I make are from the gut, and the confidence in my actions and my investments is unwavering. I pride myself on my judge of character, and my first impressions are usually the correct ones.

What I don't understand is how I could've been so far off when it came to Olivia.

A fickle and a changeful thing is a woman? Looking down at her right now, I'd suggest the Romans didn't understand the half of it. She calls me the devil, yet she looks positively demonic.

"I'm sensing you're not happy I spoke with her." Because the looks she's throwing my way? It's like she's Medusa's more annoyed and spikier sister.

"Oh, whatever makes you say that?" But she's not really asking me a question, I realise, as she opens her mouth to speak again. "I mean, why should I object? What could possibly bother me about you railroading through my fucking life?"

"Olivia—"

"I'm not finished," she snaps. "It's my turn to speak because I think I must've missed something on the contract. I don't remember reading anywhere that you were going to treat me like a chattel!" As she speaks, both tone and volume rise, eventually reaching the kind of ear-splitting rant that could only be categorised as *fishwife*.

"Clearly, I overstepped, but my actions were all in good faith."

"Good faith? Good faith! You are despicable. Your moral compass swings so wildly I'm surprised your head isn't spinning! You're selfish and egotistical, and you don't have a thought for anyone or anything. I mean, what kind of man would blackmail a woman into marrying him?" At this, she finally stops, seemingly shocked by her own words.

"Blackmail is such an unpleasant word. I know who I am, and I accept what I am capable of. I don't look at others when at fault. Denial is a near cousin of rationalisation, Olivia. But if it helps you sleep at night..."

I leave her at her bedroom doorway, and I'd be lying if I said her stunned expression does nothing for me.

"Please explain how you've gotten me into this."

Later, Olivia appears in the lounge where I'm working on my laptop. She looks more or less the same as she does usually. A little paler, perhaps. A little tired, despite her perfectly applied makeup. Dressed casually, she's tied her hair back in a ponytail. But these are all smaller observations, the larger being that the fight has left her.

"What do you want, Olivia?" I ask tersely, my fingers continuing to fly over the keyboard.

"I want to talk about this. About what you did and about what I said."

I pause and lift my head, but I don't look at her. It wasn't supposed to be like this. How I feel is complicated. "Let's not rehash things."

"We need to clear the air. If we're going to spend six months together, we can't go on like this. You need to accept you were wrong, just as I need to apologise for saying those things."

"I was wrong?"

"Is that such a novel concept?"

I shrug, opening my mouth to speak when she cuts me off.

"Don't say it." She holds up a forestalling hand, her tone resolute. "Whatever you were about to say, just don't. And I am sorry because neither of us buy into the things I said. This is a business arrangement, first and foremost. I need to keep sight of that. Be less emotional."

But it's the emotion I crave, I think but don't say. The push and the pull, the sniping arguments. The picture I posted yesterday with my face in her hand, our kiss and our smile. Have I ever kissed a woman while feeling such overwhelming happiness, no matter how temporary?

"But you shouldn't have gone into my phone." She pauses, her gaze sliding to the sofa before she commits to moving to it. "My phone is my business. You wouldn't like me using yours."

I lean forward and grab it from the coffee table, pitching it to land on the sofa next to her curled, bare feet.

"Help yourself."

"I don't want it," she says, glancing at the thing as though it were contaminated. "Besides, the difference is that you've given me permission. I did no such thing."

I sigh heavily, my fingers poised on the keyboard. "If it makes you feel any better, I didn't invade your privacy. Whatever you think of me, that was never my intention." It was a mad thought, though, for one moment during the small hours when the sun was barely a smudge on the horizon. "I couldn't sleep." Though I'm sure I've never felt as exhausted or as sated. "You were lying next to me, and my arm was curled around your waist."

"No wonder you couldn't sleep." Her smile is small, her attempt at humour almost a win. "Sounds uncomfortable. I'm told I wriggle in my sleep."

For a reason I don't quite understand, I'm unwilling to

examine how she knows this or explain how it was, in fact, the opposite of uncomfortable. Or discuss how my lack of sleep seemed to stem from contentment. I'm not a religious man, but I can see the appeal of giving over your life to a deity. Just as I could see myself spending my days worshipping at the altar of Olivia. Fucking her was a divine experience, but this isn't necessarily what I can't bring myself to say. It's more that I felt content for the first time in a long while, just lying there with my arm around her and our fingers entwined.

"Go on," she prompts softly, bringing me back to the moment.

"I couldn't sleep." My brows lower. "So I stretched out and brought my phone from the nightstand. Only it wasn't mine. I didn't realise until the screen was already open, and I was already staring at your Instagram account."

"And you'd sent me our wedding photograph earlier."

"Yes," I agree. Between fucking, and touching, and drinking champagne, she'd asked me why I'd taken it.

"Proof that it had happened," she repeats with an odd twist to her lips. And, yes, that's how I'd sold it to her. "And if it isn't on Insta, it didn't really happen."

And I needed it to have happened. Needed for this to be as public as possible and for there to have been furore back home. Gossip and speculation. Something to later spin.

"According to your demographic, yes."

"My demographic? You were the one who posted *all* the hashtags! All that was missing was 'hashtag blessed'." She pulls a face that I can only describe as belligerent.

"If it helps, I also posted it to my social media accounts."

"You have that sort of stuff? I didn't know you even knew what a hashtag was."

"I'm not dead, Olivia." Apparently, the prospect of being so seems appealing to her, so I choose to refrain from explaining how my accounts are business related and run by my assistant. "We hadn't discussed how we were going to broadcast our union, and an announcement in *The Times* didn't seem appropriate."

"None of this excuses what you did."

"Even if I thought I was helping? Even though your website has received thousands of hits already. Hits that will, no doubt, convert into new membership subscriptions. Not to mention the possibility of attracting media attention. E-Volve's owner finds love with the coldest man in England?"

"None of that even comes close to being an apology," she mutters, examining her fingernails now.

"I make it a point never to apologise. We've talked about this."

"How on earth do you keep friends?"

"I keep associates. That's all I need."

"Not true. Word on the street is that you need a wife. And to use your phrase against you; happy wife, happy life. Now who's pouting?"

"This is not a pout," I answer. "This is a calculation."

"Oh, God, no. What else!" She brings her hands to her face as she mutters something unintelligible—a profanity, no doubt—before opening her hands to ask, "Do I really want to know?"

"I suppose that all depends on if you want advance notice of your grandmother's visit."

25

OLIVIA

"How are you this morning?"

Yesterday had begun so well, so full of promise, but then had rapidly gone nowhere. Bad enough that Beckett saw fit to post our personal business on my Instagram account and then tell me he thought he was doing me a favour, but he'd also decided to invite my gran to spend the following day with us.

Hmph. My mistake. She's spending the day with me because he 'has business to attend to'. *My ass.*

"I've been better," I eventually answer from my position on the sofa, hotel magazine in hand.

It's not that I don't love my gran because I absolutely do. She is the most awesome person on the planet. But what I'm not looking forward to is having to lie to her. And her calling me out on it. The woman has an uncanny knack for sniffing out the truth. She says it's a mother's instinct, but my own mom never noticed half as much. And getting married for money isn't quite the same as being caught eating candy before dinnertime.

"You're not still pouting, are you?" My shoulders stiffen at his tone, but I bite back my retort. "I already explained I arranged it because I thought you'd like to see her."

"How about we make a deal," I say, turning to him as I

imagine knocking off his head. You know, just because I might decide he'd like it. Or deserve it. "How about you stop doing things you think I'll like and ask me what I'd like instead?"

"There's no point talking to you when you're pouting."

"I'm not pouting. I'm pissed off!" My response earns me a glower.

"You know, Olivia, you really should try to see things on the bright side. We'll return to London, and everyone will already know. The gossip will be over, and by the time you go into your office following the weekend, there will be barely a ripple of scandal."

"Shows what you know." Miranda and Heather will have conniptions the minute I walk through the door. "We need to come up with a story," I say, swinging my legs down.

"I don't follow."

"People will ask how we met, how we fell in love. And what possessed us to get married within a few days of meeting."

"Weeks," he corrects. "I should imagine people will infer we fell in love. As for the rest, who's going to ask?"

"My friends!" I jump up from the sofa, throwing the magazine down. "The people I work with. My grandmother! Don't you understand that? She's going to walk in here and know instantly that there's no way I married you in a whirlwind of love. Her bullshit meter is like nothing else. She's ninety-two, Beckett. She's been around a long fucking time. And she's not even a little bit senile."

"You're worried I won't be able to convince a senior citizen of my devotion to you?"

"She won't be watching you. She'll be watching me."

"And you can't pretend to be enamoured for a few hours?"

"I don't even like you at the best of times." I throw my hands up in frustration. "And it just gets worse when you open your mouth."

"That's not what you said on our wedding night," he replies

archly. "And the best of times would be when, I wonder? When I have you *in* my mouth?"

"Stop. Please think carefully before you speak."

My God, the man should only be permitted to use his mouth to get me off.

"Oh, I am thinking very carefully. Very, very carefully. Especially after what happened at breakfast yesterday."

"Nothing happened at breakfast." I feel myself frown.

"That's exactly my point. Nothing happened in the afternoon or the evening, either."

"I told you I had jet lag," I offer half-heartedly, which isn't exactly true.

After Beckett left yesterday morning for whatever dark overlording he'd had on his planner, I went sightseeing. Foregoing the use of the Bentley and the driver, which apparently is one of the perks of staying in this suite. It might've been nice if Beckett had explained this before the butler (the butler; just crazy talk!) was forced to explain how it worked. Anyway, I went walking, avoiding the usual tourist spots, and ended up in the West Village. I found a café, Merriweather's. If you need a recommendation for *the* best coffee, this place was light and bright and the ambience welcoming, so I'd pulled out my laptop and lost myself in a little work. By the time I got back to the hotel, I was beat. And asleep before Beckett resurfaced from whatever he'd been up to.

So no sexy times. No extra consummation. And yes, this was also in part because of the bad mood I was in following his self-appointment to the head of my personal social media.

"We could do something about it," he suggests, stepping closer. Though stepping isn't the right description for the way he moves across the room. This morning, he's all about the swagger. "Make up for lost opportunities."

"Nope." I place both hands on his chest as he reaches me. As tempting as he always is, especially dressed so properly for the office in navy pants today, white shirt open at the collar and rolled at the sleeves, I'm not in the mood. To clarify, I'm in *a* mood but not *the* mood. "I'm due at the airport in an hour."

"A quickie?" he suggests, all charm and persuasion and divine smelling cologne.

"I think we'd make better use of our time coming up with a backstory. A meet-cute thing."

"A meet what?"

"Like they have in the movies. The scenario that brings two potential lovers to cross paths. They meet, it's cute, and it develops into a romance."

"So that would be what, for us?" In an alarmingly tender gesture, he lifts my hands from his chest, bringing them to his mouth where he places a kiss against the backs of both of my hands.

"For us? Well, I fell over your foot. That could be cute, I suppose."

"Not with the way you were glaring at me," he replies, one brow raised.

"Hush. That could totally work. I fell at your feet, and you just fell for me." The man looks seriously disturbed at the prospect. "Pretend, Beckett, just for pretend. But what else?"

"What do you mean? Isn't that enough?"

"How did we come to be in New York at the same time?"

"Does it really matter?"

"The devil is in the details. Didn't your uncle Satan teach you anything? We met, and I fell over your foot into abject dislike? That was the story before I got on the flight." Minus all the other things we're not talking about. "Because as far as Miranda and Heather are concerned, I think you're an a— unpleasant individual. Oh, and I also told my friend Reggie what happened in the car."

Beckett chuckles. Trust that little nugget of information to have entertained him rather than embarrass him.

"Which reminds me," I add, "I really need to give Reggie a

call. Thanks to my social media guru." My tone is snarky to the max.

"That must've been an interesting conversation. About the car, I mean."

"Not as interesting as the next one is going to be, so let's work on this." I pull my hands from his.

"You must admit, it is a little funny. Almost farcical." He surprises me when he puts his hands on my shoulders and I try not to shiver as a sensory memory shimmers across my skin. With a spin, he turns me to face the other way. "You're very tense," he murmurs, beginning to knead my shoulders.

"I wonder why that is?" I'm surprised the words are whole, given their delivery though gritted teeth. *I mean, really?*

"What did your friend say about the car incident? Might it help with the explanation?"

"She said you were probably kinky."

"Are she and I acquainted?" I pull my elbow back and nudge him in the ribs. "I'm kidding."

"She said maybe your kink is withholding the D."

"The—ah. Got it. Under the right circumstances," he replies kind of airily, "it can be fun." He pauses. "You're wrong, you know. Some men do enjoy the chase."

"What's that—Ow!" I turn my head to glare at him, my shoulder hot and smarting. "That hurt."

"Because you're all knotted. You should book a massage while we're here."

"Let me get this over with Gran first," I grumble, my shoulders relaxing almost involuntarily. "Oh, that's better. Yeah, that's good." Beckett's hands work their way down my spine, my once taut muscles almost liquifying.

"I've got it!" He turns me quite abruptly to face him. "You fell, you hated me, then I chased you and tried to help you with your company. Then we met at the airport, and I was determined to win you over, so I made sure we sat together on the flight. Eight hours in close confines—you couldn't fail to be bowled over."

"From abject dislike to hey, let's get hitched?"

"Unless you've got a better idea," he retorts, his brows pinching.

"You don't understand. My gran could've worked for the CIA."

"Stop being so negative, Olivia. She's your grandmother. Just smile and let her be happy for you."

But even if I can get her to that point, I'll still feel crappy because her happiness will be built on lies.

"So your flight was good?"

"Very nice. Smooth," Gran adds, tightening her cardigan. My grandmother isn't a slave to old lady fashion. She might like her knitwear, but she's pretty hip. How many ninety-two-year-olds have Instagram accounts? *It's for the local chapter of her horticultural society, but still.* Her red hair has long since turned white, and she wears it in a classic short bob. She's not so steady on the old pins, as she likes to say, so she's recently given up heels for flats. Today's pair are cherry red. She wears a pair of silver-grey pants and a scarf to compliment her startling blue eyes because, as she likes to say, a scarf will hide a multitude of sins.

And don't I know it.

"The tea was awful," she says, reaching out to pat my hand, "but they served a nice butty." A sandwich, for those unfamiliar with the Yorkshire dialect, which clings stubbornly, interspersed with a more American flair.

"How's the business, love?"

"Yeah, it's going great." Or at least it will do now.

"Lots of people lining up to sign up for this app thingy, then?"

"Our numbers are growing steadily."

"Lots of people falling in love?"

"That's the plan. Or part of it, at least."

"Is that where you found your fella, is it?"

"No, not online. We met through work." Conversation

between us isn't usually so stilted. So circuitous. Blunt in the extreme is more my grandma's style.

"It's a nice car, is this." Her gaze roams the buttery leather interior before she adjusts her purse on her lap, leading up to her interrogation, I realise. "Have you told your mother yet?"

"I called and left a message. It'll probably take her a week to realise I've left one."

"Maybe you should just bark at her. Aye, like Lassie. *Little Livvie is up the duff, woof!*"

My heart sinks. "It's not . . . I'm not—"

"You're not in the family way, love?" Her tone is soft, her eyes almost penetrating. "Because that would be okay."

"I promise." I shake my head, which feels like the opposite thing I should be doing.

"Because you don't have to get married for that these days." I look down at her hand over mine, spotted and papery with time. "You don't ever have to be beholden to a man. You've got a bit of cash in the bank and more coming to you when I shuffle off this mortal coil—"

"Gran, please. Don't say that."

"I'm not immortal." She says this like she doesn't mean it. Like *come on, death. I dare you to have a go.* Sensible money would be on her.

"Your mum would be okay with that, too. Even if she couldn't say it." My mom is someone very special but not great with people. Her mouth purses when I offer nothing. "So it's a whirlwind romance, is it?" *Sceptical. That sounded sceptical.* "Are you going to tell me where you met this rich bugger, then?"

"I thought we'd wait until we get to the hotel. Beckett booked us an early afternoon tea."

She sniffs, unimpressed. "I hope he's not ugly."

"What? Gran, why would you say that?"

"Well, he seems to have gone to a lot of trouble and expense. I just wonder if he's overcompensating for summat."

"He's not overcompensating for *something*. Or for anything.

I'm sure you'll love him." If he gets strep throat or some other illness that prevents him from talking.

We'd agreed that he'd join us for an early dinner. That it might be best if we spent as little time together as possible, at least while she's here. Bad enough that I must lie to her at all without the added pressure of needing to curb my reactions to Beckett.

"What's his name again?"

"Beckett," I say for the fourth time. She's not dotty. Just playing the old lady game today. Hell, if I get to ninety-two, I'll play it, too.

Once at the hotel, we make our way into the Astor Court, the St Regis' home of fine dining. *Apparently*. With cream walls, gold accents, and Romanesque frescos, the place isn't exactly understated.

"My word! That's enough to put you off your dinner," she announces rather loudly as we pass a large mural. "Look at the face he's pulling." Despite my best efforts, she slows to a stop. "He looks like he's got wind—he's proper grimacing. I hope that's not prophetic."

"Come on." I link her hand over my forearm, hoping to encourage her to move along. "Maybe you should switch your hearing aid on."

"What?"

"I said—"

"I heard what you said, I was just teasing, love."

"The food here is great," I say enthusiastically. "Let's order a tea, or maybe a sherry."

"Oh, now you're talking." And thankfully, she begins to move on from the mural.

I'd ordered our afternoon tea prior to her arrival, mainly to avoid her seeing the prices on the menu. People of her generation are generally known for their frugal ways, born from the necessity of having to make every penny count. Gran is reasonably wealthy, but that hasn't changed anything. Add to that, Yorkshire folk are renowned for their thrifty ways. Legend has it, at least, according to her, that copper wire was invented by two Yorkshiremen fighting over a penny.

In her world, clothes are bought for quality and durability, patched and mended when the need arises, before being repurposed when a garment reaches the end of its life. Zippers are saved in a container, and squares of fabric allocated to the *cupboard under the sink* to be used as dusters and all manner of things. Old vegetables become soup, fruits are preserved, and dishes are always hand washed. A cardigan is donned rather than the heat switched on, and heaven forbid you squeeze the toothpaste wrong.

"It's lovely, is this," Gran murmurs, her eyes darting around the airy space. "And this is a lovely spread." She points at the delicate cake stand and the tiny offerings decorating the plate. "I'll never eat it all, unless you want me to pull the same faces as that fella in the picture. You should ask them for a dog bag."

"But you're flying back tonight, aren't you?"

"Yes, this is just a quick visit. Your fella said he'd book me a room, but I like to sleep in my own bed. It's only an hour by aeroplane," she says softly. "I've been on longer bus rides than that."

"I'm sure."

"So why don't we just get to it, lass. You tell me why you've married this fella. This fella I know nothing about."

"What's to tell?" I feed my finger through the delicate handle on my cup and raise it to my mouth. "We fell in love." As a sudden afterthought, I add, "Really quickly."

"I'll say."

"Where did you meet him?"

"In London. At work."

"He doesn't work for you, does he?"

I laugh. It sounds unpleasant, and before I can bite the words back, I find myself saying, "I'd probably kill him."

Gran makes a noise. That noise—you know the one that says

interesting without having to use the word. "Married for nought but a couple of days, and you already want to kill him?"

"It's not like that."

"Darling, it's exactly like that," a deep and familiar voice says from behind me.

Beckett.

I turn my head, but he's already bending to kiss my cheek. "Hello, darling."

26

BECKETT

"What are you doing here? I mean, I thought you were going to meet us for an early dinner?" Olivia fixes a smile on her face, but I'm sure both Elsie and I saw what was under it. "You said you were busy."

"I thought I'd surprise you." As I smile down at her, she looks like she'd happily throttle me. "I've been looking forward to meeting the person who means the most to you, darling."

"I thought that was supposed to be you," her grandmother offers without conviction.

"I wouldn't presume." I hold out a hand to Elsie, the generationally appropriate thing to do. I must say, for someone who sounds like she might make a good CIA interrogator, her appearance is very unassuming. Which, I suppose, would be the point. She's roughly Olivia's size, though with the inevitable age-related rounding, and though her eyes are blue rather than Olivia's mossy green, they have the same kind of intensity. "It's nice to meet you, Elsie. May I call you Elsie?"

"That's my name," she answers prosaically, allowing me to take her hand. I pull out a seat between the pair and order a coffee. "Well, he's a handsome devil, I'll give you that." Elsie's statement is somewhat begrudging and not at all directed at me.

"He's definitely something," Olivia mutters as she eyes a tiny chocolate tart on the cake stand. "I told you she was a good judge of character." As punishment for the devil quip, and just because making her cross seems to have become my life's work, I beat her to the chocolatey morsel and pop it into my mouth.

"I'm starving." I widen my eyes in provocation. "You didn't mind, did you?"

"Of course not. What's mine is yours and all that."

Elsie sets off laughing, not at all fooled by her granddaughter's tone. *But then, who would be?* "A word of advice for you. Never come between Livvie and something she wants, lad. Not if you want to keep your pretty looks."

"Gran!"

"Tell the truth and shame the devil, love. You looked like you could have had his fingers off."

"I was not going to bite his finger. Beckett is quite welcome to help himself to anything he wants." The old lady begins chuckling again. "Ew, Gran. Stop it. Not like that."

"I'm not too old that I don't remember what marriage is for. Well, one of the things it's good for."

"Companionship?" I offer blandly.

"Nookie, lad. Nookie." She leans over, laying her small hand over mine. "You're a fair old size." Olivia makes a noise as though she's in pain as I find myself chuckling. I feel like a prize bull being viewed for stud as she takes stock of my appearance. "Don't mind me. When you get to my age, you say what you mean because if you wait, you might not ever get to say it. I speak as I find."

"As it should be," I agree.

"How about we speak a little less about the joys of the marital bed?" Olivia mutters.

"Oh, the joys, is it?" Elsie shoots me a wink. "That sounds promising."

Leaning in a little closer, I murmur, "A gentleman never tells."

"You'll have to speak up, lad. I'm a bit deaf. Come a little closer and—"

"Gran, really? Don't, Beckett." Olivia's attention swings my way, suddenly flustered. "Before you know it, she'll wheedle out all your secrets."

"*All* my secrets?" Olivia flushes as I slide her a provocative glance.

"I'm only interested in the juicy ones, not where the bodies are buried." Her gran then adds, "Where else is an old lady supposed to get her entertainment from with a grandchild as bossy as this one?"

"Don't start on that old lady business." Olivia scoffs, folding her arms. "I'm tenacious, and I get it from you."

"You're more obstinate," I offer unhelpfully.

"And *you* are going to keep her on her toes." Her hand taps mine before retracting. But that was just to sweeten me up. "How old are you, Buckett?"

"It's Beckett," Olivia mutters. But I'm sure she already knows.

"The right side of forty. There are a dozen years between Olivia and myself. That's what you're really asking, isn't it?" We watch each other carefully, like two cats prowling around the same territory.

"And what do you get out of this marriage, then? Apart from a pretty girl on your arm."

"I can get a pretty girl to drape over my arm any day. Anywhere. There is, however, only one Olivia. She's not just a pretty face, as I'm sure you don't need me to tell you."

"Well, there's no one quite as headstrong. And when she's in a strop, she throws things about. Have you found that out yet?"

"As a gentleman, I couldn't possibly comment." I don't bother trying to hide my smile.

"So, the fella is all right for cash," she says, addressing Olivia now, "but then you're not exactly poor yourself. And he's good looking, and you fight a lot, which has its obvious benefits." Olivia looks about to protest again when Elsie sends her an icy

To Have and Hate

look. "You're not pregnant, and a week ago, you'd never mentioned him. And now you're married. What am I missing?"

"Nothing. You're not missing anything. It's just . . . it's just been a bit of a whirlwind." Olivia's hand shakes as she slides her hair from her face.

"Yes. So you said," Elsie answers in a flat tone. "But a whirlwind just chucks people about, love. Shakes them from their normal, everyday living. It might be exciting while it's happening, but it never lasts long. And all it leaves behind is a trail of devastation. So let's not call this a whirlwind, eh?" With barely a breath taken, she turns to me.

"You're divorced, I take it?"

"Yes."

"What about children?"

"I don't have any."

"Do you want them?"

"Gran, stop! I don't even know if I want them. I can't even keep a potted palm alive."

"Bugger plants! I'm talking about your future here. By the time you decide you want little ones, he could be really old. I had your mum late in life, but your grandpa was the same age. What if you don't want to have children for another dozen years? He'll be in his seventies by the time they're grown."

"Urgh! Please, stop."

"It's okay, Olivia. Your grandmother is concerned, as is understandable. Our marriage has come as a surprise."

"A bloody shock," she corrects, adjusting the scarf around her neck. "I'm just saying the things that need to be said. I speak as I find. Didn't I already say that?"

"Truthfully, Elsie, this is my fault. I made the announcement on Instagram, and Olivia was very cross. But I couldn't help myself. Look at her." We both turn our attentions to the other side of the table. "What man wouldn't want to shout from the hilltops how happy he is?"

"She is bonny," she agrees. "And you looked very happy in

your instagran post," she adds begrudgingly. No one corrects her. "You've just not got the best track record when it comes to lads, and I worry about you."

"There really is no need to."

"But it comes with the territory," I offer. "There can be no love without concern."

Elsie nods, reluctantly agreeing. "But why so quickly? Act in haste, repent at leisure, so the saying goes."

"You said you never regretted marrying your first husband, Gran. You said it was all part of life's grand plan for you. Well, I won't, I don't regret marrying Beckett because he's good for me. Really good."

I'd be lying if I said Olivia's words didn't affect me. So much so, as I stare at her, I find I need to remind myself why we married in the first place. Why *she* is my wife. Yes, I saw her as an opportunity, a beautiful opportunity, but I also saw a little of myself in her. Because Olivia is ruthlessly determined. However, it doesn't come from the same place. I'm addicted to making money. She just wants to look after the people around her. And she's afraid of disappointing her family.

I also thought she was a good actress, that certain facets of her personality were fake, but she's no more fake than I am underprivileged. She's genuine. Real. We're all flawed. We're all scarred, and I'm the first to admit to being a less than perfect human. But Olivia is someone who deserves good things, and I'm not good for her. The cards are weighted in my favour in that sense. Which is a pity. *For her, at least.*

"We fell in love," I add. "And I simply couldn't bear the thought of her belonging to someone else. As I reach across the table for Olivia's hand, both women seem stunned.

"Well, Livvie," Elsie eventually says. "You're a grown woman, and you've made your choice. I will say that I often thought it'd be a very particular kind of man you'd need."

"What's that supposed to mean?"

"It means this one will keep you on your toes. I don't know

what you're smiling about," she adds as her gaze glides my way. "It works both ways." She looks me up then down, seemingly unimpressed. "You won't have it easy." She turns back to Olivia as though this finalises things. "All right, give me a look at the ring." Olivia dutifully lifts her hand. "That's a bobby dazzler, is that!"

At least that seemed positive.

"Beckett has good taste," Olivia offers, still looking down at the ring.

"Of course he does. He married you, didn't he?"

The atmosphere improves from here. There are no pointed questions or snide remarks, though whether the introduction of another glass of sherry is the reason or a genuine truce, it's hard to tell. I'm persuaded to eat while the pair finish their tiny sandwiches and try very hard not to laugh when my champagne risotto is delivered and Elsie immediately complains to the waiter that there appears to be a candy wrapper in it, which is actually gold leaf. When the waiter returns with a plate sans gold leaf, she takes one look at it and sniffs before declaring it looks like rice pudding.

Talk turns to what we're doing in New York. *Work*. Where I'm from. *London; that godforsaken heathen town*. She tells us that, in her opinion, living in Maine is almost as good as living in Yorkshire.

"God's country," she declares the place.

And for holidays? "There's nowhere better than Whitby. You can keep your tropical beaches and your palm trees. Give me a bit of cold sand between my toes at Scarborough or a bit of dramatic headland like in Whitby. Fish and chips and a half pint of ale. You can keep your cocktails with umbrellas and bits of fruit floating in it. Yorkshire will do for me."

After her grandmother's declaration, Olivia leans in. "One of your ancestors is buried in Whitby?" I frown, and for a minute, I think she might be being serious. *Silly me*. "Dracula is buried in a church in the town."

"I'll have to visit next time I'm up that way." Which is probably never, because—

"That would be lovely!" Elsie declares. "I'm back to the UK next month, and I always have a right hard time persuading Livvie to come with me. We can all go together. I'll even buy the fish and chips."

So, it looks like I have a family engagement to get out of next month.

After the food is cleared away, Olivia takes her grandmother to the suite to change her shoes while I wait downstairs, then we make our way out to the car together. I have a meeting, and the pair have decided a wander around Bloomingdale's is in order.

"He must be worth a fortune." I hear their approach before I actually see them.

"Gran, hush."

"Why? Do you think he doesn't already know?"

"It's just not polite conversation."

"What have I said to you, my girl? One of the perks of being old is being able to speak my mind."

"Quite right," I answer, as the pair walk past the deep armchair I'm sitting in.

"There you are," Elsie answers as though they had been looking for me. "You're not a criminal, are you?"

"No. The amounts I'm paid, however..."

"Criminal," she answers prosaically.

"The amounts may seem so."

"Well, where there's muck, there's brass. And that'll do for me. Now, let's go shop till we drop, shall we?" The pair turn, and I dutifully follow. "Or shop until we need to stop for a cuppa, at least."

"Yeah, Gran. Whatever you want."

To Have and Hate

At the airport, we watch as Elsie is escorted through security by the very helpful airport staff; the other travellers making way for the airline-issued wheelchair.

"I know she's tired, but she's perfectly capable of making it onto the plane herself. She's just working the system."

"She's very sprightly for someone of her age."

"It's in the genes. Her mother lived well into her hundreds."

When the last of the waving is done, and Elsie disappears into the bowels of the airport, Olivia sighs, slumping her shoulders. Then she turns, feeding her fingers into my lapels as she bumps her head against my sternum.

"I hate lying to her," she groans.

"But you love her very much, and you're trying to protect her." Her head lifts from my chest with a frown. "And lying is such a harsh word. Isn't it more the case that you're being selective with the truth? Keeping a secret from her."

"I'm not sure she'd see any difference."

"Well, she's not going to find out, is she? So the point is irrelevant."

We begin making our way back to the car when Olivia's hand wraps around my arm.

"I bet when you planned on dragging me to New York for your wicked plans, you didn't expect visiting relatives."

"My plans were thoroughly non-wicked." She shoots me a sceptical glance at my reply. "Or only partially wicked. But, no, I didn't exactly expect visitors. I like her." I glance down and catch her quizzical look. "It's easy to see who you take after."

"There's a terrifying thought."

"You'd rather take after someone else. Your mother, perhaps?"

"No. I love my mom, but she and I don't always see eye to eye."

"Another headstrong redhead like yourself?"

"That's such a cliché. But no. Mom has dark hair like my grandfather."

"And that's how you got a mixture of the two, I suppose." We both come to a halt as I find I'm running my hands through the silky strands of her red-brown hair.

"Why are you trying to make me feel better?"

"Do I have to have an ulterior motive?"

"And what did Gran say to you when she took you to one side before she left?"

"Ah." I feel my expression lighten. "She gave me a few words of marital advice."

"God." Her shoulders slump. 'Do I need to know?'

"Your call," I reply, my eyes scanning for the arrival of the car.

"Go on. Hit me with it."

"She said to take you dancing." I glance back at her. "That you like to dance."

"I do not! Well, not especially."

"My mistake. She said women like to dance."

"A *huge* generalisation. Way to drag us back under the man, gran."

"Funny, that's sort of what she said. Dancing is a vertical expression—"

"Of a horizontal desire," Olivia finishes. "Urgh. No one likes to hear that their grandmother used to have sex. She still goes dancing, you know. I am so going to need brain bleach when we get back to the hotel."

"How about a drink instead?"

"Deal," she answers as our car arrives. "But we might need to make it more than one, for purely analgesic effects."

"Of course." I open the passenger door, and Olivia slides in.

"Were there any other words of wisdom she had to offer?"

"No, nothing." She shrugs as I close the door. We may hide things from the people we love, but it seems entirely possible for us to also hide things from ourselves as I refuse to acknowledge her grandmother's other words of advice.

You can be right, or you can be happy. It's up to you to choose.

27

BECKETT

"Favourite colour?"

"I don't have one."

"What? I don't believe you." Olivia slaps her hand against the top of the sticky-looking bar.

We didn't make it back to the hotel. Instead, we stopped off at a sports bar on the Upper East Side, of all places, for *wings and beers*. Olivia seemed quite animated at the prospect, though changed her mind about ordering wings almost as soon as we took a seat at the bar. Call me suspicious, but I feel like she's somehow trying to test me. *Test my patience*. Perhaps as a way of paying me back for the social media post and her grandmother's visit. Lord knows, both of those were out of my usual pattern of doing things. The post? Spontaneous. And Elsie's visit? A result of that spontaneity, a bind I'd got myself into. But also a way of making our marriage less of a secret. More official. If her grandmother knew, Olivia would be forced into the role of doting wife. And fooling her grandmother was a perfect trial run for my ultimate goal of fooling those in London. Or so I'm telling myself.

Regardless of my reasons for being in this bar tonight, and regardless of the lack of interest I have in the ball game playing out on the screen above our heads, I find I'm happy to spend a couple of hours perched here with Olivia. How could I not?

"That's not possible," she insists. "Everyone has a favourite colour, even if they don't examine the concept. Everyone has a colour they gravitate towards. Pick one, and don't say black."

"Why would I say black?"

"I don't know." Her expression slightly comedic, her shoulders rise to her ears as she pushes her palms face-up in the air. "Maybe because it matches the colour of your soul?" Her hands slap the bar as she begins to cackle, and for an encore of ridiculousness she sticks out her tongue while attempting to cross her eyes unsuccessfully. "Did I do it?"

"What?" I try to frown though I expect it isn't very convincing, given I can't curtail my smile.

"Make my eyes go like that?" she asks, her index fingers crossed, still laughing. It's fair to say buzzed was a couple of beers ago. *For us both.*

"The question should be, why would you want to?" I hide my smile behind my bottle of beer, the brand recommended by Olivia. I'm not a beer drinker usually and can't say I'll even remember the brand as I've peeled the label off. This is a sign of sexual repression, according to the amateur psychologist to my left—her hair a little wild, her cheeks a little pink, and her mouth a little too tempting to ignore.

So I don't.

She almost hums, her fingers pressed against her lips as I pull back from the sweet, lingering kiss that lacks the intensity I seek. "A PDA?" she questions, all taunting tone. "I'll allow it."

"I wasn't asking." I take a swallow of my warming beer, then call the bartender over and order a couple of whiskey chasers from a bottle behind the bar that's caught my eye.

"Because it's easier to ask for forgiveness than permission?" Her tone is a playful reproach as she watches the bartender pour. But that doesn't suit me.

My hand on the back of her chair, I turn her to face me, my

To Have and Hate

legs bracketing hers. "I never apologise." As I lean a little closer, she moves to meet me, my mouth pressed to her ear. "And the only pleas for clemency you'll hear tonight will be your own."

"You think?" Her breath whispers across my neck, leaving the sense of being kissed there. And the heat of her so close yet so unavailable to my touch burning.

"I do. Because when I'm buried so deep inside you, you won't remember where you end and where I begin."

We separate as a cheer goes up in response to the game; not the one we're playing but the one on the screen.

"Here's to us." I raise my glass, Olivia reacting likewise. "May we get what we want but never what we deserve."

We return to our conversation, or rather her quest to psychoanalyse me by the use of a colour chart, but we're both aware of a simmering anticipation. The unspoken expectations of what tonight will bring.

A little while later, Olivia excuses herself, hopping down from the stool. I watch her weave her way through the bar, observing the eyes of other men following her in a way that's almost instinctual as she disappears from view. I wait. And I think. And argue with myself. But then I follow her anyway.

"My God! You frightened me." Her eyes are all pupils as I grasp her shoulders and push her back into the bathroom. It's not as bad as it sounds; less aggressive. More assertive, buoyed on by the way she bites her lips as she struggles to curtail her smile.

"What happens if—"

If the walls fall down? The roof blows clean off, or the world implodes? We won't realise. Not as her fingers curl in my shirt and our mouths come together in the only impact we're aware of right now. Our kiss is a fight. A battle for the upper hand.

"What are we doing?" Fire runs riot through my veins at the sound of her breathless words, at the taste of her.

"What's on the table?" My hands feed from her ribs to her breasts as my mouth finds her neck, delivering rasping, biting kisses. A quick fuck in a grubby bathroom stall isn't my style.

That's not to say I'm a stranger to the experience, but it's been a while. Another decade. Another life, and another kind of existence, driven by another kind of high.

"Be reasonable, Beckett." Yet she still tips back her head, whimpering as I make good on the access to more of her skin.

"I want to fuck you."

She trembles at my dark whisper, at the press of my teeth against her skin.

"What if someone walks in?"

'That's a distinct possibility. Care to find out?"

Beneath my fingertips, I feel her wavering, her decision solidifying as she breaks our contact, resting her back against the tiled wall opposite. For the first time I pay a little attention to our surroundings. White tile. Harsh lighting. And I wouldn't exactly describe the place as clean.

"That sounds like a dare," she murmurs. Actually, no. She taunts. "The answer is no, by the way. I don't want to find out."

"Then why are we here?"

Another roar from the bar patrons, a clink of glasses, footsteps and other muted sounds. She licks her lips as though preparing.

"Because I opened the door, and you pushed me in, then started mauling me." I look pointedly down at my creased shirt, then run my hand down it. "And then you told me you wanted to fuck me."

"I do. But you're right. Not here." I grab her hand, and with the other, pull open the door.

The bar tab settled, we make our way out to the car. As the muggy air hits me, followed by a gust of something fetid, I realise what led me to follow her to the bathroom and why I feel like I'm listing suddenly.

"Fuck." I throw my head back against the headrest as the car interior begins to spin. "Beer. I should never drink beer."

"Baby." Olivia scoffs. But she doesn't understand. She wouldn't. Her knowledge of me is only surface deep.

To Have and Hate

"Hey, Benny."

"No, no bennies. Not—" Fuck. I crack open an eyelid to find Olivia staring at me, the wash of orange street-lighting lending her a demonically confused air. "What? What are you looking at?"

"Bennies, as in amphetamines?" Her incredulity is almost sobering. "Did you think I was offering? Beckett, the driver's name is Benny. I was having a conversation with him about the best place to get something to eat. Turns out, I should've ordered those wings. I could really go for a hotdog." So beer makes my head swim and gives Olivia the munchies. *Fuck. I'm usually more aware of my limits than this.*

"No Bennies, no Charlie, and no hot dogs. All that shit is bad for you." The driver hits a pothole in the road, causing our bodies to collide. I wrap my arm around her and tell myself it's because of the bump in the road, then sigh as I realise she's looking at me like I've grown another head. *I'm not getting into this. Not now. Not ever, if I can help it.* "We'll get to the hotel, and the butler will order you something. To eat," I qualify. Because once upon a time, I might've sent him out for another kind of takeaway.

"Beckett, it's gone two. The butler won't be waiting around for us like a mom."

I snort. My mother wasn't the kind to wait up. But that is irrelevant. I might have issues but not of the Oedipus kind.

"Room service," I grate out. "It's available all night. As is the butler." As it should be for the price I'm paying.

"Excuse my husband." Turning to the driver, she places the kind of heavy emphasis on the title that suggests she finds the term distasteful. "He was born with a silver spoon in his mouth." Hand on my chest, she pushes herself upright.

"That's true," I agree gruffly.

"And a stick up his ass."

This is just her way—at least, it's her way with me, I remind myself. She's sweet on the surface, but with me, she's everything else. Haughty. And naughty.

"What are you smiling about?"

"You like me."

Or she likes my cock.

"You think?" And she likes goading me. "No, seriously. What are you smiling about?"

"I'm thinking about what I'm going to eat when we get back to the hotel."

You can be right, or you can be happy. Her grandmother's words echo in my head. I can be happy that I'm right about her wanting me. How about that, Elsie?

"And you are delusional," she grumbles, digging me with her elbow. "And you can't hold your liquor."

"My tolerance is shot." Because that's what addiction will do to you, and I'm not just talking about alcohol. "But I'm still going to make a meal out of you."

Despite her assumption, I'm not feeling so drunk as we get to the hotel.

"Where's the key card?" Olivia asks, turning to face me.

"In my pocket."

"Do you want to give it to me?"

"Always," I purr. "Call me conventional, but I'd prefer to get you inside first." I press my hands against the doorframe and rock into her as she searches my pockets for the key. "Left a little. Yeah, just there."

"You're determined to make this difficult for me, are you?" she grumbles, but I can hear the amusement in her tone. I love that she gets this. Gets me. Fucking serves it right back.

"I don't know about easy, but you're making something really hard for me."

"That I can tell."

"You're also making me easy." Easily aroused. Easily pleased when she simply looks at me.

"You're something all right." She turns in the tight space between my chest and the door, mumbling as she swipes the card, complaining when the red light won't change to green. It could be something to do with the way I'm pressing kisses down her neck or slipping my hand under her blouse. I could become addicted to these curves.

"A little help here?"

"For you, anything." As she holds the card up, I take it from between her fingertips, then turn her head to kiss her. Soft and slow, our mouths work in unison, and when she whimpers against my mouth, something inside me tightens desperately. The tenor changes in that instant. Our bodies pressed together, I kiss her hard, suck on her tongue, and begin to whisper all the dirty things I want to do to her.

"Beckett." My name is her prayer, my hand between her legs our communion.

"You should be wearing a skirt," I growl into her neck. "Like the one with the blue belt."

"You remember that?"

"I remember everything. I wanted to gather it in my fingers. Slide my hands up your soft thighs and into your underwear. Touch you. Taste you. Wear your scent like a cologne." And now that I have, I'm not sure I'll ever be sated.

"Take me to bed," she whispers, pushing herself into my hand.

"No, not this time." I want her here, up against the door, my fingers on her throat, tangled in her hair. Sliding into her arse.

"You are so . . ."

"Desperate to be inside you." As though the point needs proving, I take her hand in mine and press the flat of her palm against my cock. "This is what you've done to me." What merely thinking of you does to me.

Her shoulders tense, and she snaps the card out of my hand. With one determined swipe, the light changes, and we're inside.

"Do you want another drink?" Olivia pivots then takes two steps backwards. And two more again as she notices me following. Stalking. Making my way to her with a clear intent.

"I thought I made myself clear. What I want is you."

"But I thought we'd already met the terms of this thing. Sealed the deal. Consummated our union."

"Fucked, Olivia. We've fucked." She comes to a stop as she collides with the back of the sofa, my eyes boring down on hers. "Tell me you don't want this."

"I didn't say that," she almost purrs.

"Name your price, darling." Her soft expression hardens, and I realise what I've just said. In truth, I wouldn't hesitate to offer her material possessions to get between her legs, if she were that sort of person. But that isn't Olivia. "Tell me to get on my knees and beg. To suck on your pussy until swollen and shiny, until your legs are shaking so hard, you can't stand." She shakes her head slowly. "I thought you didn't like telling lies." I slide off my jacket, dropping it to the sofa before moving to unfasten my cufflinks. *One, two.* They both hit the floor. "Fuck the terms of our agreement. I know you want this as much as I do. Tell me the truth. Admit you want me to fuck you."

Her gaze falls to my chest as I begin to loosen my shirt buttons before she seems to come back to herself with a jolt. "You have a very high opinion of yourself. What I really want right now is a drink." Squeezing from between me and the sofa, she makes her way over to the bar. So, of course, I follow her.

She reaches for a bottle of brandy, sloshing a couple of fingers into a crystal tumbler. I find myself smiling, especially when I notice the tremor in her hand. She throws the dark liquid back then grimaces as she clasps the glass to her chest.

"Urgh!" She shivers. "That was no better the second time."

"Do you think we could beat last time?"

"What?"

"Do you think we could best our wedding night? You must admit, whatever else we are, we're exceptionally compatible in that sense. I'm not trying to take all the credit here. A second time." I close my eyes for a beat, assailed by the memories. The sound of her soft moans and the feel of her skin under me. *What would it be like to have access to her body every night?* "A third. For the entire six months. Or for as long as we both see fit."

"We'd probably angry fuck each other to death."

My eyes spring open to find her staring at me. *Daring me.* "But what a way to go."

"I set that up for you, and it flew right past your head."

Her eyes are dark as I step closer. "How so?"

"You were supposed to say we'd go out with a bang. You know you want to smile."

And I do, giving into the rueful offering as I take the glass from her hand. I set it back on the drinks cabinet in a deliberate motion before taking her hips in my hands. I can't resist pressing my lips to her hairline to inhale the scent of my new addiction. "Say yes, Olivia."

More plea than persuasion, I slide my mouth across the skin where her neck and shoulder meet. Her breath hitches as I flick my tongue across that elegant arc. Her exhalation is stuttering as I trail my fingers south, seeking the button of her tight jeans. A flick of the button and a pull on the zipper, I begin wiggling the denim over her hips.

"The quicker these come off, the quicker I get my mouth on you."

"What has gotten into you?"

"Just you. You've gotten into me. Your sweet smell and your sharp wit. You're in my head all of the time, and I can't get you out." Crowding her against the wall, my palm slides down her flat stomach before I breach the waistband of her underwear. She gasps as my fingertips find her wet, her whole body beginning to tremble as I cup her and draw her earlobe into my mouth.

"You don't mean it. You just want me to give in." Her voice is barely a whisper, her chest rising and falling with tight little breaths as I begin to love on her clit. Pet it. Circle it. Tease. Paint it with her own arousal before loving it a little more. "You've just had a little too much to drink, and it's making you be nice to me."

"Come sit on my face, and I'll show you exactly how *nice* I can be."

"You can't—"

"Come and rub your sweet pussy on me like that night in the car. Fuck being nice, Olivia, come and be bad for me."

She makes no protest as I strip her from her jeans and heels, turning her and sliding my hands up the sides of her body to grasp the hem of her blouse. I yank it over her head, her palms falling flat against the wall as she pushes herself into my hands. *Underwear next.* I divest her of her bra and kiss my way down her spine to relieve her of her tiny thong . . . then I make her giggle as I help her slip her heels back on.

"There's a method to my madness," I murmur, biting the round flesh of her arse.

"*Ohhh.* I'm sure there is."

I don't reply to her taunting tone, not as the moonlight hits her just right. She's all satin and temptation, her hair like midnight in the shadows. I slide my hand around her waist, slipping it between her legs.

"You're so wet for me," I whisper, and even I can hear the treasure in that. The awe in my tone. "I think I could take you right here. Your hands on the wall, bent at the waist while I fuck you again and again."

The shadows we'd make.

The shapes I'd bend her in.

The way she'd take me inside her body, the way she'd cry for me.

"You like the sound of that, darling? Standing for me. Taking me—taking all of me." Gripping her chin in my fingers, I twist her head, bringing her lips to mine. It's a kiss that's mean and biting, all tongue and teeth as her hands come off the wall, twisting behind her as she scrambles for my belt.

"Yes . . . Yes. Do it."

"I can't wait for you to beg me to come." I lick the seam of her pretty mouth. "Beg me to make it stop."

As I release her head, she whimpers, rolling her lips in as

though to mute the sound. If I wasn't completely sober before, I am now. Her reaction . . . it's everything. My hand on her breasts, her back pressed to my chest, her desperation chasing my touch as she fucks the air, her gasps all vowel and no sound.

The muscles in my abs tense with raw need as I press her against the wall again, pulling on her hips as I drop to my heels like a penitent. In an instant, I'm sliding the flat of my tongue through her slickness as I worship at the altar of her pussy. The room is filled with the sound of her sweet gasps and cries, and the way she rocks back against me, the sounds she makes, drives me to fucking distraction. I growl into the very centre of her, unable to get deep enough, to feel deep enough, to have enough.

The experience is raw and it's overwhelming as one word repeats over and over inside my head.

Mine. Mine. Mine.

28

OLIVIA

Oh. My. God. Drunk Beckett is another level of demandingly sexy.

"Don't come," he rasps, his voice thick with need. "Not yet."

My hands splayed across the wall, my ass in his face. I'm wearing nothing but my shoes because he wants me to, and I am *loving* this. Why is it I despise being bossed around by him, but I thrive on his bedroom commands?

Is it the novelty?

Is it him?

"Ohhh..."

So I like being bossed around by the man I tell myself I can't stand?

"Spread your legs. Wider."

"Oh, God!" And, apparently, I also like having my ass spanked. And squeezed. Manhandled like it no longer belongs to me.

"You're so fucking sexy." His words burn though me like a meteor shower. My palms pushed against the wall, I lock my knees as I cry out, desperate to keep upright. "I wish you could see how wet you are for me. How pink and pretty."

My insides begin to pulse, my whole body now trembling. I've never had anyone go down on me like this. *Standing. From behind.* It feels so dirty. I've never experienced this kind of intensity—never needed the release of orgasm so hard as Beckett eats me like a starving man at a feast. I can't process a thing as my orgasm begins to crawl through my insides, gathering and building until I'm fit to burst.

"I can feel you," he growls. "I can feel you coming on my tongue."

The dual sensations of his words and his tongue push me over the edge. It's all too much—his touch is too much—and I try to move away, but his fingers spear inside me, pinning me in place. My orgasm twists, heightens, and threatens to wash me away.

"Please, it's too much," I whimper between panting breaths. Before I can process what's happening, Beckett stands. He turns me to deliver a savage kiss, a kiss of possession. My back flat against the wall, I'm like a butterfly pinned as he pulls my knee over his hip, and his fingers slip between my legs again.

"No more, please." I can taste myself on his tongue, hear how wet I am. "I need you inside."

"You want me to fuck you?" his deep voice rasps.

"Yes." More than anything. "I can't come again," I whisper, my fingers digging into his shoulders. "Not like this."

I know in that second that I shouldn't have spoken, not as he blinks, his dark eyes staring down at me in a dare. Not as he swaps the pad of his finger for the rasp of his thumbnail.

I cry out. I am pure electricity. And I am coming again. And again.

Then I'm limp, lying across him as Beckett lifts me as though I weigh nothing. My arms slide around his neck and my legs around his hips as we kiss. The surface of the dining room table is a shock, but not quite as shocking as when he grasps the backs of my knees, spreading me as though I were a magazine.

"Remember this place?"

"How could I forget." I roll in my lips together because I'm not sure I have the energy to laugh. "I ate my breakfast here this morning."

His eyes narrow. "I seem to remember wanting to eat something else here." My body jolts, and I moan as he draws his finger through my wetness, my pussy reactive and overstimulated.

"Don't tease." My tone lacks conviction, and as I run the backs of my fingers up my body, his eyes are dark and avaricious. "It's not nice."

"I never claim to be anything I'm not." What is it about this man that makes me want to goad him? And what is it about him that makes him serve it right back? It's like we're a perfect warring pair. "And you, my darling, are so much more than *nice.*"

My thoughts drain away as he splays his hand over my stomach, his thumb slipping between my folds.

"You're so much more when I'm touching you. Kissing you." His words are soft, his gaze glued to where I'm shamelessly spread. *Even the cool air is a brush too much.* I groan as he slides two fingers deep inside, the intrusion so slick and sublime as I throb around him.

"God, oh. *Yes!*" My soft words become a hiss, a hiss that counters his masculine grunt as he unleashes his cock with his free hand, deliberately taunting me by sliding it through my wetness.

His forehead touches mine, our lips just a whisper apart, and it's then I realise that it's taking him some effort to execute his tease. And that I'm not the only one suffering.

I wrap my hands around his neck, pressing my mouth to his ear. "That feels so *nice*," I whisper, pressing my teeth to his lobe and relishing his groan. "You're so nice to me. In fact, I think this whole commanding thing is an act."

His wicked grin falters, his eyes turning dark as he glides the fat head of his cock against me once more. He exhales. I inhale. Then we both watch as he breaches my wetness.

"Fuck me, that is a sight to behold." He grunts, watching my body accept his, my back bowing in a silent urge for him to thrust. I tighten my hands on his biceps as though I could keep him—to hold the unravelling sensation of being filled so beautifully. Then he starts to move, slowly at first, my whimpers turning to cries, cries that become louder and more desperate as he picks up the pace. Sliding from tip to base, he switches to shallow movements, small jabs and punches of his hips until I'm writhing beneath him, desperate to come again.

Beckett splays his hand across my collarbone, sliding down to my chest. "I can feel your heart beating." His eyes are so dark and his expression fierce, our mouths meeting on the up thrust, all jagged breath and teeth. I cross my legs behind him as though to keep him there, keep him inside me as my orgasm springs to life at his powerful thrusts. Everything inside me draws tight, my spine arching as a wave of pleasure rushes though me, heat and sensation spreading through my body so quickly, I feel I could surely burst.

"God. Oh, God. I'm—"

I'm unable to process the waves of pleasure pulsing through me, the rush of sensation and heat overwhelming.

"That's it, darling," he grunts. "That's it. Come for me."

Seconds later, he tautens, his expression becoming almost pained. His body follows the rhythms of my own and we are rendered a twitching, pulsing mess.

29

BECKETT

Light pierces.

Air conditioning hums.

Soft furnishings are plush under my cheek.

I blink and take in my surroundings.

At least I'm not in an alley somewhere, though I do feel like someone wearing steel-capped boots has spent the evening tap-dancing on my skull. Also, something appears to have died in my mouth, something spiky and angry. It feels like it chose my throat for its death throes, maybe in an attempt to suffocate me.

I pull myself up, hands on either side of my thundering head to discover I'm not in bed, but on the sofa in the hotel suite. Stark bollock naked, and I reek of booze from my very pores. Worse, this splitting head and aching throat are familiar. It's how I feel after a night spent vomiting.

Addiction. A body remembers and will purge the results of the brain's idiocy, given half the chance. It's always the brain that's at fault, those fucking neurotransmitters chasing the high of that dopamine release.

And what goes up must come crashing down.

In other words, I wake feeling the way only an addict can understand.

To Have and Hate

An addict who has slipped.

An addict who hates his own weaknesses, even after so many years of abstinence, because there's no such thing as a former addict.

I lurch to my feet and make my way into the bathroom, the bathroom farthest from the master suite where Olivia presumably still sleeps. I don't even look at myself in the mirror, not yet ready to view the damage. The disgrace. Not yet ready to face myself. Instead, I switch on the shower and step immediately under the scalding stream. I press my hands against the tile, letting the water crash down on the back of my head and my neck, easing the knots in my shoulders and spine.

What the fuck happened?

Being in bars, pubs, clubs, and restaurants, being around wine, beer and all kinds of liquor—indulging even, it's never been an issue before. Alcohol was never my drug of choice to begin with; cocaine was my king. Booze was only ever to lengthen the buzz. But since getting clean, moderation has served me. The only difference between last night and countless others was the company.

Was it the combination that pushed me over the edge? Between booze and Olivia, I know which is the stronger bigger stimulant. The high I craved was the one found between her legs.

Everything in moderation. Restraint and self-control are key. A state of mind I can't seem to embody when I'm near Olivia.

I straighten, pushing the thought from my head and the stream of water from my face. I reach for the shampoo. I've mixed my vices since recovery. Drank and fucked. Fucked and drank. But never used. I've never needed to.

I get the high I need these days by making money. It's not the same kind of high, but at least it's an acceptable one. A high that drives me to fill my pockets, not empty them for the benefit of my dealer. Making money is an honest drug, one that's acceptable in polite circles. One that keeps me out of prison. *Out of a grave.* So I drank a little too much and I fucked. What was the difference?

Olivia. Only Olivia.

My absolute desire for her was in the sensation of need crawling out of my skin, and once inside her, my pleasure centres lit up like a fucking pinball machine. Olivia was a hit coursing through my bloodstream.

Jesus Christ.

I soap, I rinse, water serving as absolution, my sins sluiced away and swirling around my feet.

I towel off, the mirror too foggy to view the damage, then wrap the thing around my waist as I make my way to the master suite. Maybe I should've come here first and checked that she was okay. But no. The only person I've ever harmed while off my face is myself.

I stand in the open doorway. Why does it feel like I've spent so much time watching her from this position? *That can't be true, can it?* She lies on her side, her hair fanned out against the pillows, her back to me. Her bare shoulder rises and falls with the slow, easy rhythm of her breath. I'm not sure how long I stand there, just watching. And torturing myself. But I eventually move towards the dressing room without giving in to the need to crawl between her legs again.

A couple of hours later, Olivia appears in the dining room, one side of her face wearing the creases from her pillow. Otherwise, she looks perfect; fresh faced with just a hint of recently well fucked, courtesy of her messy hair and the way her cheeks and lips are rubbed pink.

"Good morning." I barely look up from my phone at her address. Still, it's odd that I can detect so many details in just one glance.

"Yes, it was. At least, when I woke." At daybreak. Aching. Shaking. Forcing myself first into the shower and then into the gym to punish myself on the treadmill. To purge, to seek distractions and endorphins elsewhere.

She takes her seat, the same one as yesterday, the same seat that puts her breasts in reach of my fingers, her lips just as accessible. But I won't think of those things. I might not be drunk, but it seems I'm still craving. I reach for my coffee cup gratified by the fact that there isn't even a tremor in my hand. The rest of me, though? I'm trembling with need just from having her near.

"What?" There's a terseness to my tone that I can't help. I don't want to blame her for my reactions last night, but a body can only take so much self-loathing.

She doesn't answer, but I can almost feel her frowning. And why wouldn't she? Last night, she enjoyed the company of a man who is more beast this morning. And beasts need keeping on a leash because they are prone to giving in to their baser selves without warning.

"Are you okay?" she asks softly.

"I'm perfectly fine," I reply, my tone clipped.

"You don't look fine."

I'm acceptable. Satisfactory. Well enough. And I am a liar, because I am none of those things. "Thank you for your observation," I eventually manage.

"Are you . . . hungover?"

If only it were that simple. There wouldn't be this level of hatred to myself.

"I'm gonna guess that's a . . . *yes?*" I still don't answer her. "I mean, we didn't have a lot to drink. Champagne and a couple of shots, but—"

"If you're quite finished hypothesising, perhaps you'd like to pack."

"But our flight isn't until tomorrow."

"I brought our return forward." Because if I can't avoid Olivia, I can at least return us to our normal lives where we'll both have other distractions. Other habits to feed. "We're booked on a flight this afternoon."

"But I thought..."

"Everything I came here for has been achieved. There's no reason to linger."

"So I guess the honeymoon is over."

"If by honeymoon, you mean the fucking, then yes, I believe it is." For self-preservation if nothing else. If I keep saying it out loud, maybe I can convince myself.

I hear the sharp inhalation preceding her tirade when we're interrupted by the butler. The same one as yesterday; young and bright and female.

"Good Morning, Mrs Beckett. May I serve you breakfast?"

"No, thank you," my wife replies, rising stiffly from her chair. "I find I've lost my appetite."

I watch her leave the room, wishing I could say the same.

30

OLIVIA

We fly out the same afternoon. The first-class cabin, not business class this time, but there's no joy or excitement in the experience. I don't avail myself to the use of the spa or the private suite prior to boarding. I just stay away from him. A spot of duty-free shopping, a coffee from Starbucks, a bookstore to pick up a couple of magazines. And then it's boarding time, where I see the cabin lends itself to feuding couples, providing each a little pod of luxury. We don't even have to look at the other, never mind talk.

At least if we'd been travelling economy, we'd be forced into the same space.

I spend the whole eight-hour flight going over yesterday. How the day had gone from bad to good to even better in the evening. Sure, there was no letup in how we responded to the other; the thrust and parry of our interactions, the jibes and complaints. But by the time we'd hit the bar last night, I'd really begun to feel I was gaining a better understanding of Beckett. Maybe even liking him a little. Then later, the sex was phenomenal. Raw and sensual, and about as far away as can be from the man at the breakfast table this morning.

A man so cold my ass was almost frostbitten from just sitting next to him.

I don't know what happened, and I don't know what to think. But think I do. Overthink, even. I can't help it—isn't that what we women do? But I may have taken this to extreme levels. You know, thinking for almost the *whole* eight-hour journey. But what the heck. Two hours into the flight, my questions have turned to anger, and by the time we've been airborne for four hours, I'm ready to cut a bitch. A bitch named Beckett, more specifically, who appears to have thrown himself into work for the whole flight. What kind of a person doesn't take a few minutes to eat or relax? He's paid for the luxury of having a space and a bed comfortable enough to sleep for a few hours, but he doesn't even take advantage of that. He waves off the offer of champagne as we board, then the afternoon tea (tiny sandwiches and cakes served with a choice of infusions, Assam for me, along with an accompanying Kir Royal). He even refuses dinner. What the hell is the point of paying for first class if you're only going to stare at your laptop?

"What is it you want, Olivia?" Over the divider between his pod and mine, Beckett glances my way, a line formed between his brows.

"I beg your pardon?" I ask sweetly. Are you talking to me, or are you planning on swallowing my fist?

"I'm having trouble concentrating thanks to the heavy weight of your glares and I have work to do. Spit it out, whatever it is."

"You have nothing I want," I reply icily.

"Once again, you and I both know that's not true." There's so much suggestion in his tone and his barely-there smile is so wickedly suggestive.

I shouldn't want to touch him. I shouldn't be tempted one little bit, yet here I am. *Just call me Tempted McTemperson.* I exhale a breath, pushing away the urge to slap him. Then kiss him. Then sit on his face. I must be glutton for punishment, but then again,

I've never been one who responded well to being told *no* to anything.

"You keep deluding yourself." I turn my back on him. Because unlike him, I haven't imposed a moratorium on flying fun. My pod has been made into a bed already and covered with snowy white sheets. Well, they were snowy white. Now they're a little less so. *Maybe I should've taken the time to wear the cashmere jammies. No matter, I'm sure my sheets would still be scattered with stains and crumbs.*

On second thought, I decide I do have something to say to him, but as I turn to deliver a verbal dressing down, I realise he's pulled up the screen between us, essentially cutting me off.

That rat bastard. The absolute—

"More champagne, Ms Welland?" I look up into the owner of the deep voice.

"Yes. Why not." I grasp my glass from the mini table and hold it out as I look up into the dark-haired and sultrily sexily Spanish-accented member of the flight crew. "Thank you, Roberto." *According to his name badge.* Roberto with the lashes like an emu and a smile like sunshine. A smile I find myself returning.

I'm not smiling as the screen between us comes down again.

"I'm not sure Roberto can satisfy your needs," Beckett murmurs smoothly.

"What would you know about my needs?"

"A little more than I knew about them last week. Do try not to flirt with every handsome face that passes your way. You'll recall you're Mrs Beckett now."

"How could I forget?" I imagine I won't be able to. At least until the six months is up, and maybe not even then. *Probably not ever.* Needless to say, we barely speak for the rest of the journey.

My needs.

I tried not to guess the meaning behind his words, but it was hard not to. Did he mean financial needs—the money I'd needed for E-Volve to succeed? Or was he referring to the purely physical? What happens between us when we touch? And if it was that, then I'm also learning about my needs along with him because my body has never responded to anyone like it has to his touch. That knowledge doesn't warm me one little bit. Not as we arrive at his Georgian period mansion house where he leaves me in the entry hall.

Yep, as our cases are carried in by the driver, Beckett turns to face me as he pauses at the still open door.

"I have some business to attend to."

"What? But it's gone midnight?" I want to bite back the words the minute they're in the air. Better that I look like I don't care. But I do care because he's leaving me here. In his house. Without even showing me where stuff is. Where am I supposed to sleep? If he thinks I'm sleeping in his bed, he is wrong on so many levels.

"Not everywhere in the world is currently heading for bed." He sounds tired. It would be so much easier to argue with him if he didn't. Actually, it would be easier if he wasn't already closing the door behind him. "Make yourself at home."

I'm left looking at the oak door as it closes behind him.

I'm not sure how long I stand just staring. But how do you make yourself at home when you're clearly not. Go exploring, I suppose. Or if you don't have the heart to explore, at least find where the kettle and teabags are.

My shoes squeak against the marble floor as I make my way deeper into the house. A grand staircase leads to the upper floors, the ceiling above a vaulted cupola and a delicately gilded ceiling rose. There's a tiny *no thanks* or, as others call it, a small elevator, set in an alcove next to the stairs. Italian marble leads to oak floors and large windows, the doors to each room twice the width of those in my tiny apartment.

A drawing room to the left, a parlour to the right, a library opening to a large office with a Bauhaus desk in oak. A billiards room with table covered in sandy baize, not the usual green, and a bar in the corner with matching high stools covered in an Oriental embroidered silk. Each room has original features; fireplaces and plasterwork, pale painted linenfold panelling.

To Have and Hate

Tasteful artwork hangs on walls, stylish furniture and oriental rugs tie together the chic colour scheme. There isn't a thing out of place. Not a magazine or a stray mug. No shoes discarded or clothes draped over chairs. It's hard to believe anyone lives here at all. Despite the obvious history of the place, each room smells new. It's hard to describe. Maybe the smell of new furnishings? The palace-like proportions are far too big for one man, though I expect he has staff onsite somewhere.

I eventually find the kitchen, which is dark, sleek, and vaguely masculine, though I give up on the kettle after five minutes of opening each and every handle-less cabinet. Three silver pendant lights hang over a central island, floor-to-ceiling units cover two of the walls, the other two made entirely of glass, revealing nothing but darkness beyond. There is nothing sitting on any of the countertops. Not a toaster or an appliance or even a fruit bowl. The only things discernible as kitchen-ish are the sink, the double oven, and a stove top with a teppanyaki style grill, none of which look like they've ever been used. It's a shame because this is a kitchen for entertaining. I find the fridge eventually, for what it's worth, a large industrial-sized thing camouflaged by cabinetry. Sadly, it only contains a couple of wrinkled lemons and some fancy-looking cheese wearing a furry coat.

Does the devil's offspring not eat?

I'm going to have to bring my kettle. My toaster. And I foresee a visit to the grocery store in my not too distant future.

Turning the lights off again, I make my way back along the hallway. Ignoring the tiny elevator, I begin dragging my suitcase up the staircase, each bump echoing through the cavernous space. There are five bedrooms, each with their own bathroom, a massive media room with a TV the people three boroughs away could probably watch through the windows, and a tiny half kitchen void of snacks. *What hell is this? No popcorn or soda pop to keep a girl company when she's reduced to watching trashy TV?*

It feels weirder to open the doors to the rooms upstairs. Like

I'm intruding, even if he did tell me to make myself at home. Home. Ha! I think it might take me at least five and a half of our married months to get used to the layout of the place.

Two of the bedrooms are decorated in blues, and two in green. I don't pay much attention to anything in the next one, but it's easy to tell it belongs to Beckett because it's the only one that doesn't smell like the rest of the house. *New and unused.* Instead, it smells like him. Of his cologne. Of . . . I don't know. Beckett pheromones?

I stand at the doorway, but don't go in. Then decide I'm being a wuss.

His bedroom appears to have been originally three rooms: there's a central area housing a huge bed in pale linens. To the right, is a living area with a sofa and a TV, and at the other end, a dressing room that Mariah Carey would envy. A huge master bath lies beyond; black marble with white veins, a basin more like a trough, a bath you would almost swim in, and a shower you could definitely party in. *You get the picture.* Everything is on a grand and expensive scale. And makes me think of two things.

1. If I didn't know better, I'd think he was compensating for something, given the size of the master suite.
2. A million is pocket change to him.

I wheel my suitcase into a bedroom at the other end of the floor. One of the blue rooms. This one is just as lovely as the others but a little less grand with low ceilings, understated touches, a chair and a small writing desk, plus a bathroom off to the side.

I unpack my case, piling my laundry onto the chair before pulling out my wash bag and helping myself to a hot shower. I climb into fresh pyjamas and slide myself into bed. Then get out again, unplugging my phone from the socket before searching for a suitable podcast.

To Have and Hate

Ten minutes later, I'm out of bed and wandering around the place.

I didn't lock the front door. Was I supposed to?

I don't want to be murdered in my bed.

I go down and check. It's an electronic lock. Automatic. My worries are unnecessary here.

I'd kill for a cup of tea but settle for a glass of water, which I bring with me on my second inspection round. This one is a little more thorough.

Hey, I'm just making myself at home!

The bar is filled with high-end liquor, and spiral stairs next to the elevator lead down to a basement. *I'm not investigating down there. Nope, not in the dark and after midnight.* I slam a few coloured balls around the billiard table with my hand, spilling a little water on the baize. *Oops!*

To the library next, which is filled with all kinds of books from ancient-looking, leather-bound tomes to a battered Jilly Cooper romp. I tilt my head, reading the spines until I get a crick in my neck.

There's a TV in the less formal of the two lounges, concealed behind a cabinet. Expensive looking art hangs from the walls but there are no family photographs on display. I eventually make my way upstairs to do the very thing I've been avoiding. The thing I'm drawn to.

Snooping. I'm dying to snoop in Beckett's bedroom.

I turn on the light and step into the huge room, running my hand along his bed as I travel, the linens super soft under my fingertips. I poke around the two nightstands; he sleeps on the left, evidenced by the reading material stacked on one end. No Jilly Cooper, sadly. Boring business books and one on Turkey. *The country, not the feathery thing.* The contents of the drawers are likewise. Boring, though I steel myself for the box of condoms I'm sure I'll find but don't.

Why does that feel sort of gratifying?

I flip on the wall-mounted TV, wondering what it is he

watches. *Ugh, the news. How uninteresting.* Then I pull throw pillows from the sofa to see what treasures this might yield. *Nada. Nothing. Not even a penny.*

Not satisfied yet, I continue my snooping in his dressing room, where his suits appear to be colour coded and the pockets empty. A couple of Tom Ford, more that are bespoke, a Gucci in grey, a Paul Smith number in blue. Handmade shirts and leather oxfords and brogues, Armani sneakers and Gucci loafers. Balenciaga jeans, and all manner of designer T-shirts. This room is like the menswear department in Harrods.

Leaving everything as it should be, I make my way into the bathroom, and pull off the lids and sniff at least six of his bottles of cologne. Stopping at the one that smells most like him, I squirt a little on my wrist, then I stick a finger in his moisturiser—*okay, aftershave balm*—and slather it on the back of my hand. I open the cabinets and poke around the contents. *Towels, all exceedingly fluffy and white and in all sizes. Unopened bottles of products stocked behind the opened bottles.*

I flip off the light and stalk back into the bedroom, annoyed. Why has my snooping yielded no information? If someone were to dig around my home, I'm sure they'd learn so much about me. My kitchen might not be full of food, but it is full of cookbooks, and there's always a bar of chocolate stashed somewhere, and a half full bottle of wine in the fridge. I read the type of books where the heroine always gets her man, or the detective collars his serial killer, because I like my endings to be happy, and my bathroom would reveal the kind of analgesic I take for period pain. And my bedside cabinet? I dread to think. Pink dicks and purple pricks. Plastic ones, obviously. Not that I'm obsessed or anything, but a girl has to have options, especially when she's been single for a while.

Fists on my hips, I turn and survey the room. Other than the clothes hanging in his vast and tidy closets, it could well have been a hotel room. There's nothing personal about the house at all. It's beautiful, for sure. And worth tens of millions, and I dare say the same for its contents. Turn of the century antiques and contemporary artworks. But who is the man behind the tastes? Who is Alexander Beckett?

Just the man I'm tied to for the next six months. *Minus three days.* God, has it only been three days? The Botox I'll need by the time this experience is over. I'll age a dozen years at least.

I move back to his huge bed pressing my palms on it. It's a big bed. *For a big man.* Because the Alexander Beckett I know, I understand only physically. I know it takes two of my hands to span one of his biceps and how the ladder of his abdominals reacts to even the slightest caress. I've become familiar with at least a dozen variations of his smile, from the icy twist of his lips that tells me his patience is wearing thin, to the sardonic smirk he wears when he imagines he's winning. I know the way his gaze darkens when he's turned on, and I'm familiar with the low, guttural growl he makes as he comes.

I dip my head to the mattress, trying to ignore the heavy pull between my legs.

"I'm so screwed," I whisper. *The things I know about Beckett are the things I want to study more*, I think as I inhale the scent of recently laundered linens. If you're going to stalk, you may as well cover all the bases.

For a split second, I consider what it would be like to be married to Beckett properly. To sleep with him in this bed. I mean, I'd probably commit mariticide, but I expect I'd be acquitted on the grounds of extreme provocation or something. The jury would understand, I'm sure. But what would it be like to crawl into bed with him every night? His long arms slung around my waist. My head nestled in the dip between his chest and bicep. But then, maybe the bed is a ruse. Maybe he doesn't sleep but hangs upside down like a bat in his creepy basement or maybe he has a silk-lined coffin down there. It's hard to tell how he sleeps—if he sleeps. I've twice gone to bed with him yet woken alone.

Lifting my arms, I stretch. Then, like a child, I give in to the impulse to lean back and flop into the middle of the bed. I giggle as my body bounces, the mattress yielding under me before I wriggle into the middle. My head is suddenly buried under an avalanche of pillows. For a moment, I feel like I'm being suffocated and, in my panic, begin flipping the things from my face and the bed.

What the hell am I doing here? Not here, in this house, which is crazy enough, but here on his bed? Sniffing his sheets and rattling his drawers for evidence of who he is? This isn't like any kind of jet lag I've ever experienced.

"I am seriously losing it," I whisper at the ceiling as I close my eyes and rest my forearm over my face. The scent of Beckett's cologne on my wrist awakens some sort of sensory memory. *Beckett's whispers hot in my ear, his body over mine and blocking out the light.* Along with the snapshot, heat floods my veins. I shouldn't want him, but it doesn't alter the fact I do. How is it that just the scent of him triggers a wave of need so great that I'm sliding my hand over the satiny front of my pyjamas?

The honeymoon is over. His words echo in my ear, and I find myself answering. "Maybe for you."

I slide my hands between my legs, cupping myself as I squeeze my thighs together, my sigh a quiet, stuttering thing. I know I shouldn't, but the badness calls to me as I add a little pressure with my palm.

His bed. My orgasm.

"Yes." My whisper echoes in the air as I loosen my thighs and slip my hand under the waistband of my pyjamas. As I coat my clit in my own arousal, I recall the feel of his fingers trailing from my ankle to my thigh. His breath against my shoulder as he'd taken my hips in his hands. I've never felt so possessed, so thoroughly owned as I do when I'm with him. But from now on, it looks as if I'll be relying on memories as I begin to circle and pet, my fingers picking up their well-practised rhythm. I dig my heels into the bed and arch my hips, the recollection of his words an echo in my ear.

Spread your legs.
I can't wait to fuck you.
Let me destroy your pretty little pussy.
"Oh, God, yes!"

Something, an awareness, maybe, causes me to turn my head. My hand springs from my pyjama pants like I'd, well, like I'd been caught touching myself.

Because I have.

Beckett stands at the doorway, a hungry longing in his eyes.

With a groan that's probably closer to a whimper, I roll onto my side away from the sight of him.

31

BECKETT

"Don't stop."

The words come without thought but, *fuck*, I mean them. I drop my T-shirt to the floor, and in a half dozen steps, the bed is dipping under my weight. Whatever I did to deserve a welcome like this, I'm not certain. After today, I probably deserve to never touch her again. But we don't always get what we deserve. It's often the opposite, and that's certainly true as I lay my hand on the curve of her hip.

She was touching herself. In my bed.

"Pretend I'm not here, unless . . ." Unless the reason she's lying on my bed touching herself is because she was imagining the opposite.

Is she wearing my aftershave?

At the realisation, the confirmation, a fiery thrill courses through my bloodstream. Unless . . . unless this is some kind of *fuck you* gesture after my ridiculous declaration. And if that's the case, not only do I deserve it, but I'll take my punishment because the sight of her owning her own pleasure was like nothing else on this earth.

"Olivia." Her name is an appeal for mercy. A plea for her to continue with my punishment.

To Have and Hate

"Go away." She presses her face deeper into the bedding, curling herself into an even tighter ball.

"I can't, darling. You're in my bed."

"Like you need to remind me," she almost groans.

But, Christ, the sight of her as I'd entered the room. Midnight satin in a sea of stark linens. Someone should paint her like this to preserve the image for posterity. I'd have to blind the artist afterward, of course. Because no one should see her like this but me.

"I'm sorry," I whisper, my hand tightening on her hip as though my touch could convey the truth of it. I lashed out and punished her because I couldn't punish myself enough. *I can never punish myself enough.* The ninety minutes I'd just spent in the gym is the usual precursor to the spiral of self-loathing.

"I thought you didn't ever apologise."

I don't. Yet I have. But not for the reasons she's thinking. "Darling, scratch that. I'm not sorry. How can I be sorry for this? For finding you here."

"Just go. Away. Far away."

"I can't. You're in my bed. In my bed, touching yourself." Under my hand, she flinches. It doesn't stop me bringing my bare feet up onto the mattress and curling myself behind her. "Watching you get yourself off was like a glimpse of the forbidden. A peek at the heavens."

"Fine, so you got you got your peek. Please leave and let me end this."

Desire radiates from my chest, manifesting itself in a growl.

"Not like that." Her denial is immediate. "I meant leave me so I can die from my humiliation."

"Stop. Stop pretending to be embarrassed," I demand, steel lacing my words. "You know you did this to punish me."

"What?" She turns her head over her shoulder, offering me her angry profile. But I can work with angry over embarrassed. Twist it into something that works for both of us.

"I deserve this." I press her hip, encouraging her onto her back. "This punishment."

"You deserve a lot of things." Her words are a puff of indignant air. "And none of them very pleasant."

"So you'll torture me." My gaze flits over her, her nipples pebbling under the satin. I bunch my hand in her pyjama top as though it might stop her from moving away.

"It wasn't—" Her lashes almost flutter as she slowly comes to realise what this looks like from my side of the bed. Did she expect me to reject her? Fuck. Yes, she did. I've been nothing but a bastard to her since we last fucked.

"You left me here. Alone." There's a husky quality to her words, something teasing almost.

"I did." Because I'm stupid, apparently.

"What was I supposed to do?"

"Of course, when I was supposed to be here, touching you." I slide my thumb along the sliver of skin exposed between her pyjamas. "Feasting on you."

"Yes."

"I left you no option but to touch yourself."

"I don't need your permission." An arched brow and a husky defiance. "And stop looking at me like that."

"Stop looking at you like I want you? Like I'd sell my soul to be inside you?" Her eyes track the movement of my fingers as I outline my erection through the thin fabric of my shorts. I lay my forehead against hers. "Show me." I kiss her, just one tempting slide of my lips as I take her hand and slide it back between her legs. "Please."

"But you're wrong," she whispers, her back arching into our joint touch. "You don't deserve this." Her statement ends on a needful sigh as I curl my fingers around hers, pushing them against her pussy.

"I don't deserve you," I whisper, kissing my way across her jaw as I slide my hand from hers. "I don't deserve a taste of your silken skin." I engulf her nipple over the satin, her body bowing with a sigh. My eyes follow the movement of her hand as it slides under the elastic waistband, and I tighten my lips to a sharp tug, my cock as hard as steel as she sighs her surrender.

As she touches herself, I make short work of the buttons of her pyjama top, spreading the sides open like the pages of a book. I can't take my eyes off her as she lies here in my bed, half undressed and playing with herself. Not to be left out, my part in the proceedings a hum of dirty whispers.

That's it, darling. Fuck your fingers.
See how hard you're making me? How desperate you make me?
Punish me, darling.

Until she isn't playing anymore, arching from the mattress. Her movements are fast and her breathing erratic until she cries out, her eyes wide and unseeing. And she is glorious in her undoing.

Before any more awkwardness sets in, I tell her so, wrapping my arm around her waist as she turns to her side.

"I never want to hear you mention this ever again," she murmurs.

"Is it okay if I think about it? Actually, I'm not asking permission because I don't think I could stop myself."

"Stop it," she whispers, but without ferocity this time as I tighten my hold.

"I should've known this would be where Goldilocks chose to sleep." At her questioning glance, I add, "I mean having you here in my bed feels just right."

"So you want to sweet talk me now?" There's no real bite in her response as she yawns deeply, almost nestling into the pillow under her head. There's a pause, and I wonder for a moment if she's already succumbed when she lifts her head. "Where did you go?"

"I had some work to do, like I said. But I also worked out." Worked off some of this energy and none of the self-hatred.

"That's not really what I meant." Thoughts seem to flicker and fade across her face. "Though you did just leave me standing in your hallway, so an explanation would be good. What I'm asking is where Beckett went, the Beckett I met in New York. Because when I woke up yesterday, the man I'd married, the man who'd arranged for my grandmother to fly in to see me. He'd gone."

"I thought you weren't pleased about my part in that. In fact, I remember there were things thrown."

"I wasn't pleased how you handled it." She doesn't react to my teasing, my attempt to lighten the act that annoyed her so. As she turns to face me, my eyes dip to her chest before she pulls the sides of her pyjama top closed. "I was so happy to see her. I speak to her every week, but the last time we were together was over a year ago. You made that possible." Her candour is surprising, it's almost a compliment, but I try not to react. "We had a good day together, and then you turned up at the restaurant, and you were *nice* to her even though she wasn't particularly friendly to you, which made me think maybe I'd misunderstood you. Maybe misunderstood isn't the right word, but maybe I was seeing your layers, a little depth because there had to be more to you than just the man who enjoys bossing me around. Then we hung out at the bar, and it was fun. You laughed at my jokes and even cracked a few of your own. It was like you were revealing yourself piece by piece. If I put all the Beckett snapshots together, I'd somehow know you, and the puzzle would be solved."

"Maybe it's a puzzle that isn't worth solving."

Her expression clouds, perhaps missing the intent of my words. "Are you punishing me?"

"No." I find I can't hold her gaze. I thought I was done with guilt.

"That's what it feels like," she says softly. "Like you've revealed too much of yourself, the human side of you, and that it's become my fault, somehow."

She's right, and she's wrong. And if I don't answer her, how will we get through the next six months?

"There's a gym in the basement accessed by the second staircase in the hall. You can access it from outside, too."

"Okay," she answers slowly.

But it isn't okay, and she doesn't really get this at all. How could she? Who works out when most people are sleeping?

"After the bar, I woke early. I wake early every day. I don't sleep a great deal. It's one of the residual effects of addiction." I give her a moment to let that settle in. Or maybe the moment is for me. My weakness is something I should be reminded of from time to time. "Cocaine," I admit, answering her unspoken question. The financial district stimulant of choice. City boys do love their Class A drugs, and this one is A for acceptable in the circles I move. "Don't worry. I no longer indulge. I haven't for a long time."

"Well, that's kind of obvious."

"Is it?" My eyebrows lift. I wasn't expecting attitude. *And confusion, perhaps?* Addiction usually elicits sympathy or morbid fascination. Not that I make it a habit of sharing this information. I'm not what you'd ordinarily call the sharing type.

"Well, you're not exactly mellow."

"You've never dabbled?" This much is obvious without the shake of her head. "Not even at university?" Another denial. "You spent a year in a central London university, and you never . . . ?" How the fuck is that possible, Olivia the innocent? "Don't I feel like the degenerate seducer all of a sudden."

"Hardly," she answers defensively. But I do suddenly feel very old.

"Coke doesn't mellow you out. Quite the opposite," I add almost in a whisper, brushing the strands of her hair from her shoulder. "Not that it matters because I don't do it anymore. I also don't drink. No more than a few glasses. Because when I do, it can bring back all the not so pleasant reminders of addiction. The sweats and the shakes, the fear and the self-loathing. And that's what happened after the night at the bar."

It's not the whole truth, but she doesn't need to hear the rest as she offers her sympathy, not in words, but in the warm hand she splays across my chest.

And the rest? I'm no stranger to obsession. Money. Work. Exercise. But what I'm not ready to admit is my new addiction is her. I came to an understanding while on the treadmill, my legs working like pistons as I'd fought to exhaust this weakness from my system. It's called a habit for a reason. And the only way to avoid it is to remove the source of the addiction. I can't do that right now. I need her to get my hands on JBW, which means I capitulate. I give in. And later, I'll go cold turkey. When the ink is dry on the contract, I'll remove her from my life in exchange for an equilibrium.

Until then, I'll gorge on her.

"So." I peel her hand from my chest, bringing the backs of her fingers to my lips. "I can usually remove myself from society when I feel the way that I did. I should've insisted on travelling back alone."

"I'm not how sure that would've helped."

"It might have been more pleasant. For you, at least."

"I'm guessing for you, too. You're not exactly an open book, are you?" she adds by way of explanation. "But I appreciate you telling me the truth."

Not the whole truth but enough. Enough to make me uncomfortable, but whether for being secretive or telling her anything, it's hard to tell.

"And I guess if I look really hard, maybe get out a magnifying glass or something, that kind of sounds like an apology for the way you've treated me."

"I'm certain I've already said I never apologise." God knows how, but I manage to curtail my burgeoning smile.

"Well, I make two tonight."

"I retracted the earlier apology. That doesn't count."

"Ah, so you admit it," she says with a smile. "You apologised at least once tonight. That's not never."

With a growl, I take her wrists in my hands, pressing them into the mattress as I roll over her, my knees bracketing hers. "I *never* apologise."

"Except when you do." A puff of sweet breath catches me on the cheek as she tries to blow strands of hair from her face. "A little help here?"

"I never apologise, and I never help."

"Sorry. I forgot, oh dark and awful overlord."

"That has a certain ring to it. From now on, I think you can refer to me as just that."

"And you can kiss my ass," she replies with a snort.

"I thought you'd never ask," I reply, burying my mouth against her neck.

"I thought the honeymoon was over."

"It seems I was a touch premature," I cut off any smart-arsed reply with a glance of my lips against hers. A bare brush but a welcome one, judging by the small moan she makes. A small moan that lengthens as I lower my body, my chest brushing hers.

"Beckett?" Her voice pulls at my attention, the soft curl in my name causing me to lift my head. The dark moss of her eyes is a perfect complement to her flushed cheeks. "We're attracted to each other." she whispers. "This isn't just about business."

I glance down the space between our bodies, my cock hanging hard and heavy behind the thin material of my shorts. "Does that look like business to you?" I ask, as my gaze returns to hers.

"It looks like it means business." She bites her lip, fighting a smile. "Whatever else this is, do you think we might be friends?"

"Olivia." Beautiful, tempting Olivia. "You should make it a personal rule to only be friends with people who are worthy of you."

"You're saying you're unworthy?" It's not a taunt or a snarky response, but a genuine question. And one I wish I didn't feel compelled to answer.

"Of friendship, yes."

Of you, most definitely.

32

OLIVIA

"Oh my God! I can't believe you snuck off to New York to get married, and you didn't even tell us!"

"Holy heck, Heather!" I reply with a wince. "If there's life on Mars, they heard that squeal. Ouch, my ears."

"Actually, there isn't life on Mars," Jorge mutters coming up behind me, not waiting for me to step into the office. "It's been proven it can't be sustained there. It's too cold, there's no water, and there's too much UV radiation. Plus, the issue with the soil."

He takes off his denim jacket and loops it over the Ikea coat stand without looking around. Which thankfully means he's completely oblivious to Heather pretending to hang herself through boredom, Miranda's pitying look, and my perplexed one.

"Not the right nutrients," he adds. "It's all barren wasteland. And the pressure is enough to make a person shrivel up."

"Sounds a bit like your sex life," the younger girl mutters, not quite under her breath.

"Heather!" Miranda gasps, but Jorge just ignores her. In fact, he ignores us all as he trudges off to the tiny kitchen to flick the kettle on. I know this, not because I can see through walls, but because the man is a creature of habit, if he's nothing else.

"He didn't even say good morning to the boss lady, never

mind offer her congratulations." With that, Heather takes two tutu-clad steps in my direction and throws her arms around my neck. "I am so happy for you!" She plants a big smacking kiss on my cheek before falling back on her heels. Her body seems almost to vibrate with excitement.

"Did you have a good time?" Mir asks carefully.

I was dreading this. I'm not a great liar at the best of times, and despite Beckett's assumptions, I'm a terrible actress. I foresee a whole lot of screw-ups over the next six months. *I can only try to meet my part of this arrangement.*

"Of course, she had a good time," Heather crows. "She was whisked off to mother-fluffin' NYC for a bit of nookie and ended up married! Did he propose in Central Park? Times Square? Where? Tell me where!"

"Do you think it would be okay if I just took my jacket off first?"

"Yes, but then you have to tell us all about it," Heather demands as I deposit my laptop bag on my desk and hang up my Burberry trench, while trying to tune Heather out.

". . . How he proposed. What he said when he asked you, and what you said in response. It's all just so exciting," she says with a little twirl.

She'd be so upset if she knew the real story.

What he said: A mutually beneficial agreement. You'll lose your business if you don't.

Where he proposed: He didn't. He just harangued.

What he did: Got me so amped in the back of his car, I had to know what he was like between the sheets. And now that I do, I'm well and truly screwed.

Well. And. Truly. For the next six months, at least.

My cheeks begin to burn as I think of last night, despite telling myself I would never ever think of it again. I'm pretty sure Beckett has done the opposite, pinning it to the front of his. In fact, I'm certain he was thinking of it this morning while I dressed for work.

This is like an erotic reverse striptease, he'd murmured, all dark eyed, lounging grace from his position on the bed. He was probably thinking of it when I brushed my hair, and then later when—

"He's such a hottie." Heather's words snag my attention. "And that whole captain of industry vibe he's got going on." As I turn my head, she's fanning her face.

"Do you have any plans to work today?" Damn. She looks back at me like I've slapped her. *Acting failure number one, I guess: the euphoric bride let down.* "Ignore me," I say with a tired sigh. "I've spent all weekend moving into Beckett's house." His *big enough to be a hotel* house. Not that I've really moved much at all. A few clothes. Some small kitchen appliances. A box of Yorkshire tea.

"It's your house now, too." Mir sends me a quizzical glance. Or it might be a concerned one. Maybe hanging out with Beckett seems to have made me an expert on all his scowls to the detriment of everything else.

"Yes, I know. I'm just exhausted because I insisted on doing it myself."

"By yourself? Whatever for?"

To stay out of his way, maybe? Because of last night and the day before and the day before that. Honestly, I feel like I'm suffering from whiplash. Just when I thought we were beginning to get along, he pulls out Dr Hyde again. And sure, we talked about it, but that doesn't mean I understand him. Does he really think he's unworthy of being my friend, or was that some kind of warning?

I realise I'm being studied. "Sorry, what were we talking about?"

"I asked why you moved out of your flat into the house by yourself."

I wave away her concerned glance. "I only packed a couple of suitcases. For now, I mean."

And ran over the place with a vacuum. And a mop. And a bucket of bleach. Cleaning soothes me.

"Was New York amazing?" Heather asks, all starry-eyed.

"It's pretty cool."

"What did you get up to while you were there?"

"She got married and went on honeymoon," Mir says with a cackle. "What did you think she got up to?"

"Okay, enough," I say as Jorge comes back into the office space. "Tell me what I've missed while I've been gone."

"Well." Mir sits straight, her body almost vibrating with the need to spill. "There has been a twelve-percent rise in our membership numbers over the weekend."

"Awesome! Do we have any idea of the reason behind that?"

Her eyes positively sparkle as she says, "I'm getting to that. I also heard back from the *Lust Island* guys, and I have three of them interested in coming along to our retro speed dating night."

"What were their fees again?" Just because I now have money in the bank doesn't mean I'm going to become profligate.

"Free." Miranda gives a careless shrug. "It seems they just want to hang with the cool, new hookup app on the block."

"But that's not what we are," I say carefully. "That's not our ethos." Relationships, not casual hookups.

"Don't be judgey. Sometimes casual leads to more."

"Hmm. I'm not sure I believe that."

"You and the new hubs weren't exactly seeing each other seriously last week, as far as I can tell. There were lots of sparks flying and buckets of chemistry, but you weren't doing the whole dating thing, were you?"

"Ours was more a whirlwind affair." That's all I'm offering, despite Gran's analogies. And I do so in my boss voice, hoping to end the conversation. Notice there's no mention of love in that explanation? No love. Nope. But maybe a little like. He can be sweet when he wants to be. Our wedding, my beautiful ring, the shoes and flowers, and his compliments. Equally, he can be an annoying, irritating ass. But strangely, when he's behaving like this, it's almost as though he doesn't have any choice, which is ridiculous because we all get to choose our behaviour. Except when we don't, like when I'm throwing things around under that red swirl of angry mist. But at least I apologise afterwards. And that's something Beckett likes to wholeheartedly reject. *Even if I've heard him say it.*

So like. I can manage to *like* him, just about. And mostly when we're in bed and my pleasure centres are lighting up like the Vegas Strip. *Even if he doesn't think we can be friends.*

"Just to confirm." Mir's voice brings my attention back to the current moment. "We're not going to get concerned about that kind of thing, right? Publicity first, bums on seats second. Or rather monthly payments deducted from our subscriber's bank accounts."

"Fine. But if the *Lust Island* lot are doing it for free, don't offer them membership as a sweetener."

"Why not? Think of what their profiles will bring."

"Yeah, they're like, modern day poets," Heather offers up.

"Okay, I'll bite," I say, turning her way.

"What about the iconic phrase 'No pizza before Ibiza'?" she says, mispronouncing the place.

"Poet Laureate worthy, for sure."

"Weight Watchers worthy, at least. Actually, I think one of them got a gig representing Weight Watchers with that slogan."

"I'm just not sure they're the right look for us." It's not that I have anything against reality TV celebs. In fact, I think they must have a pretty awful existence, their moment in the sun lasting about as long as it takes for *Lust Island* to be aired on TV.

Check me out, being all highbrow and selective, and worrying about the long-term effects of partner associations. Before the weekend, we were nearly bankrupt. The only thing long about the business then related to our list of creditors.

"Well, I do have another idea. Did you happen to look at your Insta feed over the weekend?"

"I imagine she was very, very busy." Heather sniggers. "Being banged and boffed and bent in funny shapes."

"Heather, come on!" Give me a break.

"Oops," she mutters, turning a little red in the cheeks.

I definitely need to work on the whole authority thing. Maybe Beckett will rub off on me. *Yep, so not going to suggest that to him.* "I saw your messages." Which reminds me, I still need to call Reggie.

"I hope you don't mind, but I shared your post to the E-Volve account." As she speaks, I pull out my phone, flicking over to the account. "See how much love that post got?"

"Yeah." I look up, confused by the numbers. "But how?" Our following isn't huge. We've been trying to harness the potential of the platform with limited success for months.

"Because, boss lady, the post went viral. It was in the weekend newspapers and all over the net! Oh, the spin I've spun! Move over Tinder, E-Volve owner finds love in her own algorithm!"

"But that's not true. That's not how it happened."

"Yeah, but it was reported, so I just ran with it."

Beckett is going to flip his lid when he finds out he's been linked to an internet dating app, touted as a customer of E-Volve.

I suddenly experience a very malicious wave of glee.

"And guess what?" she adds, brimming with eagerness. "We've had a phone call from *Hiya* magazine. They want to interview the happy couple!"

That sounds like it's going to be an interesting conversation to convey . . .

33

BECKETT

My phone rings, and Harry's number flashes up on the screen. I swipe it, silencing his call again, only for it to chime with a message in a group conversation we've had going for at least a year.

Harrison: Alexander, would you care to refute the scurrilous accusations that have reached my ear concerning your wedded status?

Not particularly, I text back.

Harrison: This isn't your fucking press office I'm speaking to. Why haven't you picked up your phone?

Because I've been busy. Very busy.

But not busy with fucking my wife sadly, who appears to want to be anywhere that I am not. I suppose I can't blame her, not after the way I've treated her due to my own fucked-up head. If only it were a case of making a note in my diary to remind me to behave more appropriately. I'm going to try anyway while trying not to twist myself into knots over her. It's a fine line, a delicate tightrope I find myself balancing. I want her badly, crave her company and her touch, yet she offers me friendship when she should be running from me.

And speaking of friends, mine are reprobates.

Harrison: Answer the fucking question.

Unbunch your knickers. I've simply been too busy to speak.

Harrison: Did you get married in NY this week?

In a word, yes.

Harrison: I'm calling you now. You'd better pick up the fucking phone this time.

Not convenient. In a meeting.

Harrison: You've got me worried now. Very worried.

What's to stress over? I'm a big boy. I can take care of myself.

Griffin: What my learned friend is trying to assess is if you were in possession of your full faculties when you decided to tie yourself to a woman. You know, for life.

Affirmative.

Griffin: Impossible. Any man who marries has already handed over his balls at the very least. But the question remains, did you marry a nice young lady you met in a crack den?

Crack was never my poison. Fuckers.

Griffin: So you didn't propose to a nice young lady you've been doing speedballs with in New York?

Relax. I haven't relapsed. When you meet her, you'll understand.

Griffin: Mail order bride from the Eastern Bloc?

Griffin: Some Russian oligarch's ugly (but richer than sin) daughter?

Griffin: An AI sexbot?

None of the above, I reply.

Griffin: Then please explain.

Griffin: C'est à dire.

Griffin: What do you mean?

Griffin: Please.

Griffin: Explain.

Are you taking Adderall? Had a big night and an even bigger morning?

Griffin: Negatory. But come on, she must be at least a little bit defective if she married you.

Harrison: Congratulations, Beckett. @Griffin, grow the fuck up.

Thank you. @Griffin, fuck you still.

Harrison: @Griffin . . .

Griffin: Okay! Congratulations, fucker. Also, congrats also to me. The pool of pussy just got bigger.

With a bit of luck, you'll drown in it.

Griffin: Ha, funny. You know what else is also funny? Not once in this exchange did you mention love.

34

BECKETT

IN THE WEEKS following our return to London, I discover dozens of things about Olivia. She invariably starts her day with a cup of tea the colour of brickwork and ends it in a glass of white wine after dinner without much thought to quality or palate. Her taste in fashion is eclectic and her beauty regime fascinating, and I'm especially fond of watching as she lotions her skin nightly with a product she describes as *body butter*. It certainly makes me want to gorge. She likes to sleep in short pyjamas but invariably wakes up naked, though upon reflection, that might be my doing following her nightly basting. She sleeps like the dead and is just as difficult to rouse in the morning, though I have learned one or two tricks to assist. She likes to cook almost as much as she likes to eat, which are two things I find utterly fascinating to watch. She has a favourite daytime perfume that's citrus based and another for evenings that smells like secrets and night blooming jasmine. She's not a devotee of jewellery beyond her wedding ring, which I imagine she wears for appearances, and a pair of earrings, often hoops. Another thing I've gathered is she could do with a decent watch because she's always bloody late.

Then there are the other facts and facets that I'd somehow utterly overlooked as a possibility. She has a temper that shakes the walls, but thankfully, a very long fuse. She's kind to a fault and not only invariably manages to find a few pounds in her purse to press into the hands of the homeless, but she also stops to speak with them. She's a terrible actress, which came as quite a surprise—since when has my judgement been so off?—and the word she'd insisted described her personality perfectly all those weeks ago. *Nice?* It doesn't come close to doing her justice. There are a thousand others much more suitable, but the one I find suits her best is *beguiling*. And the strangest thing is that she doesn't even realise I'm under her spell. I'm sure she thinks I follow her around just to annoy her, and that I turn up at her office to entice her to lunch because I have nothing else better to do.

"Why are you here again?" she'd asked yesterday when I'd turned up at her desk. Again. *Y"ou're only supposed to show up for board meetings."*

"I've come to see how the new team members are working out." I'd leaned closer, adding in a whisper as I'd pulled her in to kiss her cheek. *"While playing the part of the doting husband, of course."* What I kept to myself is the fact that I want to dote on her. That I find it hard to stay away from her.

I have been spellbound by the woman I'd bullied into marrying me. This I'll admit. I also counsel myself that it cannot last. My infatuation will run its course before the six months is out. It must.

Maddening. That's another suitable Olivia descriptor, and one most appropriate when speaking of her timekeeping.

In one hour, we're due at the home of Mark Jones. An invitation issued under the guise of 'getting to know my gorgeous new wife'. His words, and my absolute irritation. It's an invitation wrapped in a pretty bow to hide the fact that the old bastard is nosy. He trades knowledge like currency and likes to think he has a finger on the pulse of what happens in this city. But it doesn't matter what he thinks, not when this invitation will take me a step closer to my ultimate goal.

Ownership of JBW.

I twist my wrist, glancing down at my watch—a Rolex, not the Patek Phillippe, because there's no need to remind Jones that I'm wealthier than he is—while wondering for the tenth time where the fuck Olivia has gotten to. The car has been on standby for hours to pick her up, and my calls to her phone have gone unanswered, and now are going straight to her message bank, but as the front door *clicks* open, I find I'm propelled out into the reception hall.

"Honey, I'm home," she whispers, her black dress almost invisible, absorbed by the same coloured door that dwarfs her frame.

"You're late."

"Jesus, Beckett!" Hand on her chest, she spins to face me. Her eyes widen briefly before narrowing. "You scared the crap out of me."

"You do know we have a dinner to attend in under an hour?"

"*Yes . . .*" The woman is a terrible, terrible liar. It's perplexing how I could've gotten her personality so wrong. "I knew we had an important dinner to go to *this week*. I just forgot it was today. Or maybe I just forgot what day it is today."

"Fascinating," I drawl, slipping my free hand into my trouser pocket, the other gripped tightly on my whisky glass. "Perhaps if you looked at your phone occassionally, you'd notice your calendar. You might also have seen my texts." Not to mention my calls.

"It died on me in the bar." She gives a careless shrug. "Mir and I went to the place we're holding the speed dating event to brainstorm and have another look at the place, I guess."

My chest rises and falls with a terse, irritated sigh. "You went to work dressed like that?"

She glances down at her black dress. It's more like a long T-shirt that gently skims her curves before ending at her calves. A pair of pink glittery Converse peek out from underneath. She looks more like an art student than a businesswoman. Young but not quite innocent.

She looks up from her shoes, eyes wide now. "You don't think this is dinner appropriate?"

"I don't think that outfit is office appropriate. In fact, I don't think it's any kind of appropriate."

She immediately fires from mildly amused and happy to bait me to seriously pissed off. "Did they teach you how to be an insulting dipshit at boarding school? Or maybe that's where guys of your ilk go to get the stick surgically shoved up their—"

"As charming as this conversation is, we're due at the Jones' in fifty-five minutes now." I make a show of looking at my watch.

"I ate tapas at the bar with Mir." She whirls around, dropping her huge blue purse to the hall table as she begins to tug at the strands of hair that have fallen from her high bun. It's a style that's more haphazard than elegant, and one hundred percent her. If I throw in the adjectives *raw* and *sensual*.

In the mirror, her breasts rise with the motion of her arms, the soft cotton moulding to her like a second skin. It evokes the image of her rising from the bathtub last night, the water clinging to her like silk. The effect was fleeting but so enticing.

"I don't think I feel like dinner now," she murmurs.

Yet I'm ravenous. For a feast named Olivia.

"I don't particularly care for what you do or don't *feel like*." *Except for how she feels under my fingers. How she feels under me.* As I step out behind her, my reflection is tense. Eyes dark, my jaw flexes against the temptation of her. But it's a look that could be interpreted many ways. "You know how important tonight is to me. I expect you to do your part and play the dutiful, love-struck little wife."

"You know what I think?" She turns to face me, her hands grasping the table edge behind her. *Another action that pushes out her breasts.* "I don't think this is about me being late." She reaches up, her hand cupping my cheek. Her thumb presses my bottom lip, her own exaggeratedly jutting. "You're always so pouty, Beckett."

"And you're always so late."

"But you don't care. Not really. You care more about this dress." I quirk a brow, an action contradictory to my surprise. Her hand falls away, and she pulls at the scooped neckline with that same thumb, revealing a little more of that constellation of freckles and creamy skin.

"Remember your position in this partnership, Olivia."

"How could I forget?" she purrs, her words ending in a playful curl. "Would you tell a junior partner how to dress?"

"I would if they were doing so inappropriately."

"You don't like it?" She leans back again and stretches out her foot, running it along my inside leg.

"You're playing with fire."

"I just want you to admit you don't like my dress."

"You're right. I don't."

"You want me to get rid of it." Something twists in the pit of my gut because that wasn't a statement. It was an invitation. "Don't you." And those words? A dare.

"Take it off. Strip." My words are all command, my grip on the situation tenuous.

"Oh, I'm sure your fancy boarding school taught you better manners than that."

"Take off the dress, Olivia." My voice sounds deeper. Rougher. The air between us filled with the energy of this push and pull. "Take it off. Before I do it for you. Before I rip it from you."

"Well, if you put it like that . . ." She pushes from the table, her movements unhurried and indolent. Until she crosses her arms over her body and prepares to pull.

"Slowly, darling. Don't rush."

"I thought we were in a hurry?" Even as she speaks, she's uncrossing her arms and trying to hide her damn smirk.

"But you want to make me suffer, don't you?" I watch as she places her hands on her thighs and begins to draw the cotton up her body in small increments. Slowly, so slowly, the action like a rising curtain on opening night. *With ten times the anticipation for the reveal.*

Lithe legs, the triangle of black lace. The flare of her hips and the dip of her waist before the round fullness of her breasts are revealed, encased in a matching bra. Her expression is triumphant as she holds out her arm, dropping the dress to the floor. She pluck the glass from my hand and saunters off in the direction of the kitchen.

Of course, I follow her. Follow that swaying arse and those violin hips, adjusting my aching cock as she opens the fridge door without any real intention. A fridge now filled with groceries where before it was bare. I push away the thought that the appliance is somehow a metaphor. Before and after Olivia; a life that was empty, then full. *Then empty again, when the time comes.*

"I thought you weren't hungry." I wrap my arms around her, my words pressed into her satin soft neck.

"A girl has appetites," she answers, rolling her head to the side to give me better access to her neck.

"You're maddening."

"It's only what you deserve."

I don't deserve her. Not her taunts nor her kisses. But she is worthy of my worship. I wonder if she ever notices the strength of need in my kisses. If she knows I feel like my arms can never hold her tight enough. That I can't seem to be inside her long enough or fuck her hard enough.

That I'm not enough.

The fridge door swings shut, and she turns to me, her intention in the hand she slides down my chest. I lean down, and there's little grace or finesse as our mouths meet. No slow curtain rising as she strips me from my tie, our kisses as unruly as her fingers are uncooperative as they attack my shirt buttons. Unhooking her bra, I pull it from her arms, unable to resist the lure of her nipples. Savouring her low groan, I use my grip on her hair to open her more fully to my touch.

"I thought we were late." Her voice is all bedroom and gravel as she slides my half-unbuttoned shirt over my shoulders.

"We are. And I'm going to punish you for it."

"Oh, goody."

I can't help the low chuckle that escapes from my throat as I grab her arse and curve her into my embrace. Her heat almost sears me through the thin lace, our kiss turning wild and possessive. Her fingers slice between us. Tug at my belt. My zipper. My cock is suddenly in her hand.

"You're so hard," she whispers, sending my desire soaring and my will freefalling. "I want you to give it to me. Give me it hard."

Without cognisance, I spin her and push her down against the countertop, spreading her satiny thighs wide, opening her to my touch. My jaw is like granite as I reach down and fill her with my fingers, her pleasure sticky and sweet as I bring them to my lips.

"You taste like heaven." And feel like an addiction.

Lips kiss-plump and eyes dark, she turns her head over her shoulder, silently begging me.

I line up and bury myself to the hilt with a curse, the contact like that first line euphoria running through my system. One singular crystalline hit. Olivia's body bows beneath me, shuddering as I withdraw. With the next thrust, I grind against her, twisting her face to meet mine for a savage kiss. Her body throbs around me, making my head fucking spin. With each thrust, I pull her hips back, aware in the deep recesses of my brain of the sharp marble edge against her hips, yet completely overtaken with this need to crawl inside her.

"You drive me insane, you and your fucking dress. Look but don't touch."

"Touch, please touch," she rasps, bringing my hand to her breast, crying out as I squeeze and thrust again. Shivering as I feed my hand between her legs, my fingers finding her clit, slippery and swollen. Her body begins to jerk under me, her hot walls tightening around my cock in pulsing bursts as I fight to keep us both upright. "You're going to come for me, aren't you." An order, not a question, her answer a jumble of words as her body begs me to make it so. "You're going to come so hard you'll need my arms to hold you up as you pulse around me, coating my fingers and my cock."

She chokes back a strangled cry, her entire body trembling and pulsing and bowing as her orgasm hits, and her whole body stiffening as she cries out my name.

Every inch of my skin is prickling and hot, and I don't think I'll ever get enough of this sensation. Not as I twist my head to the windows, the sight of our reflection turning us into one deviant entity. I suck in a breath as I wrap her in my arms because I'm coming, and coming hard, the tight muscles of her pussy echoing my final thrust.

35

OLIVIA

"Remind me again why we're here?" I stare out of the passenger window of the Mercedes at the house that looks pretty fancy but not nearly as fancy as the one we've just left. We're barely twenty minutes late, but if you'd asked me a half an hour ago how long I'd been lying across the island countertop, I'd have guesstimated three weeks. Because when Beckett fucks, he's all in. Even just for a quickie.

And when Beckett opens up, even just for a moment, it's hard to resist him. It's that lure of a complex puzzle sitting in my lap. And though I don't even like puzzles very much, lacking the patience for them, I so want to get to the bottom of this man. From the bottom to the top, I want to learn all his secrets. I want to take him apart to discover what makes him tick.

"We're here because we were invited. That's the official story. Unofficially, we're here because Mark Jones wouldn't sell me his stake in the company because he thinks I'm too much of a loose cannon, despite me making him wealthier than he's ever been. He equates my background and personal wealth as something that will eventually make me complacent. Which is all bullshit, of course."

"Ah, yes," I answer, adjusting the cuff of my blouse while also wondering if he has knowledge of Beckett's former addiction. I'm sure that would also count as a valid concern. Quick on the heels of this is the stab of something uncomfortable. Disloyalty, maybe?

"Are you all right?" He tips my chin, bringing my gaze to his.

"Yeah, fine. I was just thinking, it's like the guy should've married us himself."

"I'm not sure I follow." A familiar line pulls between Beckett's fearsome brows. I stop myself just in time from reaching out to smooth away the crease.

"I just mean he's as responsible for us being married as the officiant. If it wasn't for him, we might have had our little bit of fun on this very back seat before going our separate ways."

"Do you really think that's what would have happened?" he asks. Grunts? One of those two.

"Well, you like your exit plans, and I had a company that needed rescuing." A company that's thriving these days, thanks to the decisions I found so hard to make. "Maybe we should've brought the guy flowers."

"I sometimes struggle with your strange sense of humour."

"And I sometimes struggle with your lack of one." We smile at each other; his begrudging, mine wide and proud. "Back on the same page now?"

"Equilibrium recovered," he agrees smoothly. "Shall we?"

"Yes, let's go convince some asshole we're in love."

As we step from the car, it's obvious there's a party in full swing behind the front doors. The noise levels aren't that of a sorority shindig or a rave, but something a little more sedate. Music plays and laughter drifts out of the open windows, the scent of cigar smoke passing on a breeze.

"I thought we were here for dinner." I glance down at my clothes. My wedding heels, cigarette pants, and a high-necked shirt with blousy sleeves cinched at the wrist. My hair is piled on top of my head still, though with a little more panache than earlier. I'm not wearing a great deal of makeup because sex with

Beckett leaves me with a weird kind of glow. "I'm so not dressed for a party."

"I didn't realise we'd been invited to one."

"Beckett," I almost hiss, pulling on his hand. "I can't go into a party dressed like this." I fan my hand in front of me, even as the certainty of his response occurs to me.

"You've spent the day wearing the T-shirt dress equivalent of the *Emperor's New Clothes*. I'm pretty sure you can pull off a shirt and pants while making everyone else believe you're dressed in sequins."

"Listen." I pull on Beckett's hand, forcing him to stop again. "I want you to know I'm going to try my very best to sell this marriage tonight, but I have to tell you again—"

"That you're not a great actress?"

"Finally, he listens!" I slide my clutch higher under my arm, my hip cocked immediately.

"Tell me again, did you plan to seduce me in the kitchen earlier as a way to fool our host? Given you're a terrible actress."

"What?" I feel my expression twist. "How does that even make sense? It's not like we had sex in their kitchen."

"We could try it, if you think it might help."

"Ha. *So* funny." And so much snark.

"Come on." He slides his arm around my shoulders, pulling my side into his. "All I was trying to say is you're much more agreeable after sex. Very tactile, and not at all like your usual hedgehog self. I wondered if this had occurred to you earlier."

"Watch it." As quick as a flash, I pull out my clutch and hit him with it square in the stomach. "The spikes are easy to re-employ."

"Spines, darling." He chuckles. "Hedgehogs don't have spikes, they have spines."

"Whatever. The answer is still the same. One false move and I'll be a pain in your ass. But in answer to your question, no, I didn't *plan to seduce you*," I affect a deep tone and add in little air quotes for good measure, "as a way to make up for my lack of acting skills." I don't think. *Did I?* Nope. Not true. "The sad truth of it is, annoying you gets me off."

Beckett's deep burst of laughter is all white teeth and deep baritone. And kind of astounding. "That is probably the most honest thing you've ever said to me."

"I'm honest all of the time."

"A different kind of honesty," he suggests, pressing a kiss to the top of my head. "It makes so much sense. Now, let's get this show on the road. Who knows what or who might be lurking behind those curtains, waiting to catch us out?"

"I'll try my best, but I feel like I'm going to struggle," I grumble as we make our way along a gravelled path with lush green topiary leading the way to the double front doors of the house. "He played me, and that makes me angry. I hate that I hung so much hope on my pitch, yet to him, it was nothing. I was an amusing way to spend an hour, and that's all. A plaything. Well, fuck him and his rich dick privilege." *Not to be confused with big dick energy.* I expect his energy is more pencil dick because anyone who treats another with such disregard must be lacking something.

"Is that how you think of me?" We slow to a stop, and Beckett turns to face me. "Do you think I've used my position? Forced you into yours?"

"Yes." My answer is immediate. "But you've been candid from the beginning." Except for his initial drip feed of information.

I want you to help me get JBW.

I want you to help me get JBW by marrying me.

I want you to help me get JBW by marrying me. And by having sex with me.

"I knew what you wanted." Mostly. "And why. I also knew what you were willing to give in return. You don't knowingly get into bed with the devil and expect him to turn into an angel overnight. But that man. I just can't put it into words how—"

"I understand." Beckett's large hand tightens on my shoulder.

"But what's done is done, and it's brought us here, to this night. This is very important to me, Olivia."

"I know, but—"

"But nothing. I have no love for him, and I don't agree with his methods. He's a weak man, self-indulgent, and full of his own importance. He underestimated you, just as he has underestimated me. Rather than indulge in this impotent kind of fury, remember that you now have what you want. You own it free and clear. You owe him nothing but a little payback, something you can help me serve him."

"By being here tonight."

"By playing your part," he agrees. "And I'll be by your side every step of the way."

"Okay." I nod, no less wronged but maybe a little mollified. "I can do this."

"One more thing. His work and private personas are very different. You might find it hard not to like him. Many do."

"I doubt that," I reply with a snort.

"He's very engaging. A colourful character. A raconteur and a bit of an old roué."

"Speak English, for goodness' sake." I haven't got time to google this shit.

"He's a bit of a libertine, or he was. These days, he's happily married to Luke's mother."

"Oh, God. Is Luke going to be here?"

"I shouldn't imagine so. But then, I didn't expect a party. Would it be a problem if he was?"

Cheeks puffed, I blow out a harsh breath. I haven't seen him since the day in Beckett's office when we were caught kissing. I don't know why he looked so betrayed. It's kind of his fault I was there in the first place. And to think the word I used to describe him was honourable. "I suppose it depends on what he has to say," I eventually reply.

"He won't cause a scene," Beckett responds with a cold kind of certainty.

"Maybe not. He has bigger things to concentrate on than me and my anger." Like a pregnant girlfriend.

"You'd be surprised. Most men would smart over losing you to someone else." In a surprisingly tender gesture, he reaches out, cupping my face with his hand.

"He never had me to begin with." At this, Beckett's gaze darkens, the corner of his mouth kicking up a touch. "If he's in there and tries to speak to me, I'll cut him with the precision of a grande dame at Almack's."

"That sounds brutal."

"Stop smiling. It works in Regency romance novels." And sounds so much more badass than ignoring his calls and deleting his texts and emails. "So, Jones. I guess what you're trying to say is that he's a bit of a man whore, right?"

"I'm not sure he'd approve of the title. Also, I think he's more like an inappropriate great uncle these days. I'm sure he thinks it endears him to those around him."

"Okay, so he's a dirty old man with a colourful past and more money than Croesus, and that little fact makes everything okay? Rich people are so weird." Beckett shrugs carelessly as my gaze slides to the house again; a glass and steel monument to personal wealth. "And if he's as rich as Croesus, I suppose that makes you as rich as ... God?"

But none of that matters, not when I've an axe to grind.

The door is opened by a young girl in a dark skirt and white shirt. She wears her name on a badge denoting the catering company. People mill around the vast open plan space, the overhead lighting glinting off expensively coloured hair. Champagne glasses in hand, women wear this season's Gucci and Valentino, their red soled shoes as high as stilts. Gold shines and bling blings, as men in Italian suits ignore the waitstaff but not the free drinks. I look down at my clothing, more Target than top of the range. *Oh well.*

Before we're more than a few feet into the house, our arrival is announced by our host, his shirt almost unbuttoned to the navel.

Okay, so I'm exaggerating a little, but it's hard to tell exactly where the buttons end because of the pelt of white hair sprouting out.

"Surprise, Beckett, old boy!"

The effect is a sort of scratching needle on vinyl, the whole place seeming to come to a standstill to examine the happy couple. Naturally, Beckett doesn't seem to notice. Or he's playing the part of *male; overflowing with insouciance* very well.

"And, of course, the lovely new Mrs Beckett." Mark Jones appears before me, the back of my hand lifted and pressed to his lips, and I wonder if he ever met the first Mrs Beckett. "How lovely to see you again."

"Mr Jones." I smile, hoping it looks better than it feels as his silvery head rises, his blue eyes shrewd.

"Nonsense. Do call me Mark, my dear." How about I call you something much worse than that, huh? Worse than an old roué, whatever the hell that means.

"What's going on here?" Beckett's tone is all business, as usual. "This is slightly more than a dinner party." But check out the warmer curl to the end as he feigns a sincere sounding note of surprise.

"Yes, well, Rosemary and I decided to throw a little party to extend JBW's felicitations to the happy couple."

"That's so nice of you." Unfortunately, my response is not quite as believable as Beckett's. Over Mark Jones' head, Beckett's brow quirks a fraction.

"Come along now. Let everyone see the happy couple." Like monkeys in a zoo.

"Everyone?" I ask, trying not to respond to the looks thrown our way.

"Staff, associates, the odd investor," Jones responds, not missing the proprietary hand Beckett places on the small of my back. Or the way he smiles down at me with such naked adoration, pressing a small kiss to my hairline. *As though he just couldn't resist.*

Warmth floods my treacherous system, blurring the lines just a little bit more.

"Ah, young love. How delightful." I don't think I imagined the way his eyes just ran over my tits. "Young definitely, but I believe there's quite a gap in your ages, isn't there? You went to university with my stepson, Olivia, I think."

I think you know this without my confirmation, Mark, old buddy, old pal.

"That's right. How is Luke?" The total shit.

"Very well. I'm to be a grandfather soon, though I feel far too young for that title." If that was our cue to soothe his ego, the moment comes and goes unremarked upon.

"Is Luke here tonight?" Beckett enquires.

"No. He had other plans. Young people. Always gadding about, I find." Mark Jones, the home version, is very different from Mark Jones, the city version. But I can roll with it for the evening as junior partner in this plan.

"What a pity." Now *that* sounded sincere. Go me.

"Rosemary, look who I've found."

Up ahead, a group of women all turn at our approach, Mark Jones slinking along to stand next to a very attractive woman of an indeterminable age. Long beige-blond hair, the woman could be Elle Macpherson's doppelganger. Oozing wealth and sophistication, she dangles a glass of red wine from her fingertips. The women standing around her haven't had the same kind of luck with their own plastic surgeons. But they do seem to have a lot of diamonds to compensate for that fact.

"Beckett. How lovely to see you." Not Australian, judging by her very English accent, so not actually *the* Elle, but beautiful in the same timeless way the supermodel has.

"Rosemary." Beckett replies with barely a whisper of warmth in his tone. Is it me or is there a weird vibe between these two? A tension almost, as she stares at him oblivious to how awkward this is. "Allow me to introduce you to my wife, Olivia. Olivia, Rosemary, Mark's wife."

"And Luke's mother," she adds, holding out her hand. Check out the heavy emphasis there.

"It's lovely to meet you. Thank you so much for hosting tonight. It's very kind of you."

"You're welcome." Beautiful and Botoxed to the max, her expression barely alters as she replies.

"You have a beautiful home." Small talk. Ack!

"Thank you." The woman has perfected the art of smiling without actually moving anything. "And congratulations to you both." Without giving up her glass, she steps closer, and with an arm languidly draped over Beckett's shoulder, she kisses both his cheeks before repeating the action with me, bending from the waist and making a point of the disparity in our heights. But, hey, I'm not the one who married a troll. *A rich troll is still a troll.*

"And how is married life treating you both?" she purrs, her gaze pinging back and forth between us.

"Wonderfully," Beckett replies, casting his gaze to mine. "If only I could've found Olivia sooner."

I find myself blushing, my hand suddenly splaying across the flat planes of his torso as Rosemary's eyes track the movement.

"That's right. You two haven't known each other very long," her husband booms.

"I defy anyone to take longer than a few hours to fall in love with Olivia," my husband croons.

"How sweet." Rosemary's strangled expression suggests the opposite, and judging by her figure, sweet isn't something she indulges in. Ever. "But darling, they don't have drinks," she rebukes, affecting a pout.

"We must certainly rectify that!"

And off we trot behind him, my hand in Beckett's as we draw curious looks.

"What was that all about?" I whisper as Jones leads the way.

"What was what?" I send him and his blank expression an eloquent glance. A glance that I hope conveys *don't fuck me about.*

"I get the strange feeling that you and the lady of the house have boned." I feel more than see his chuckle. But I'm not laughing. Inside, I'm burning.

"Your impression couldn't be more wrong."

"Then maybe I'm picking up on the fact that she'd like to. Bone you." Which makes me think I'd happily poke out her eyes before setting fire to her perfect hair.

"Jealous, darling?"

Am I? I shouldn't feel jealous. This is all pretend. If only these twisty feelings weren't real.

"You wish." And the face I pull? It can't be attractive.

"Thank you for the clarification, I think, but I wouldn't fuck her with her husband's dick, let alone my own."

"I'm sensing a story."

"It's not a very interesting one."

"You're sure?" By this point, I'm teasing. Or trying desperately to hide the fact that I'm actually jealous. Jealous of my former friend's mother's almost proprietorial nature toward my husband. My *temporary* husband. "I feel like I'm stuck in a ninety's song; Luke's mom has got it going on."

"It's probably the house," he whispers back. "It's a little dated. And I'm certain that Basquiat is a fake."

"Bas what?"

"The artwork we just passed. Jones has enough money to buy the original. Why settle?" His gaze sweeps over me in a way that makes me feel like treasure. Oh, God. Any more of this public loving and I'll be forced to drag him out to the bushes for another kind.

"And what was with the women Luke's mom was hanging with? Any more plastic surgery and they'd all have had beards."

Beckett almost chokes on his laughter.

Drinks are found, inane chats are had, and I'm introduced to a dozen people, each introduction going smoother than the one before, thanks to my wave of wine-aided bravery. All the while, Beckett never leaves my side. I almost wish I could catalogue the litany of looks and small touches he sends my way as he weaves our tale for the masses. *Something to keep me warm when he's gone.*

"I met Olivia outside of the office. She tripped and literally fell into my arms."

Cue the adoring looks from the womenfolk, accompanied by longing sighs. Pretend. It's just pretend. Don't get sucked into the tales he's spinning.

"We met again on a flight to New York where I persuaded a member of the cabin crew to get her the seat next to mine. Eight hours in her company was all it took for us to fall in love, wasn't it, darling?"

Cue my own adoring look and a love-struck whispered agreement.

"We were so certain this was meant to be, we applied immediately for our marriage license. I wasn't letting her get away."

For the next six months, at least.

"Without even having sex?" I overhear the comment on the way to the bathroom. "I couldn't do it. Not without a free sample of the goods."

"Ah, so that's what you get up to on the weekends," cackles one of city boy's friends. *Someone from JBW rather than an investor, I'd guess.* "I mean, what if she was rubbish in the sack?"

"You're so shallow," one of the girls in the group hisses back. "Have you seen the way he's looking at her? That's love."

"What about chemistry, though?"

"Same thing. You're just jealous. Besides, I bet ninety percent of the women here would marry Beckett, no questions asked." Judging by the looks he's received since we arrived from all manner of age groups, I don't doubt it.

"Yeah, 'cause he's loaded."

"Let me rephrase that; ninety percent of the women here would tap that. Tap that until it fell off, and then they'd pick it up and tap that some more."

Seems I'm in the majority. Not that I want it to fall off. He's got a really pretty—Yes, well. Enough of that.

"There you are." Beckett's gaze is warm and genuine as I find him in the garden, a glass of whisky in his hand. "I've missed you." He pulls me against him, his chest expanding with a sigh of satisfaction beneath my ear.

"Have you really?"

Soft looks and warm words. His finger hooking the back of my pants as he presses his lips to my head. It all feels so genuine that I need to remind myself that none of this is true. We're not sniping and arguing like we usually do. We're just pretending for the benefit of others. But the problem with pretending and with lies is, that after you've been doing it for a while, it's hard not to be seduced by it all yourself.

36

OLIVIA

INVESTMENT IS LIKE MARRIAGE. It shouldn't be entered into unless you want to hold onto it for a long, long time. A toast to the happy couple!

The toast that Mark Jones had insisted upon was strange, especially given the fact that JBW is a venture capitalist company, and by that definition, believe in high risk investments and cashing in on fast returns. Also, as Beckett had pointed out, the man is on his fourth marriage. His *investments* aren't exactly what you'd call long term.

But maybe not so long when you choose to invest in New York State, some bitch whispered from behind us, alluding to the State's preference as a wedding venue for those requiring prenuptial agreements. As I'd attempted to turn to see who'd made the comment, Beckett had tightened his hand on mine, giving an almost imperceptible shake of the head. Haters are gonna hate, his glance said, though maybe not with the same patois.

But we didn't have to fool everyone that night. Just the important ones. And fooled they seemed to have been, thanks in part to Beckett's declarations of love, and my doe-eyed glances, and our tactile touches.

Beckett played his part perfectly.

Me? Like I said, I'm a bad actress.

Case in point: I'd felt a visceral green-eyed fury watching Jones and his wife eye fucking each other because of the hot glances they'd thrown Beckett's way. It was almost as though they'd happily push him to the floor and make him their mattress. Or maybe the slice of prime beef in their sexual sandwich. I was so angry, filled with such vehemence that the moment we were alone, I'd curled my hand around his neck and whispered in his ear, *"When we get through with this tonight, I want you on your knees."*

I deserved some kind of payback. Wanted to assert my own part in this. I'd spent the rest of the night with a smile fixed to my face, my body thrumming with need.

We'd made it barely through the front door when I dropped to *my* knees, blowing more than just his mind while I desperately fought to assert my possession of him. His back pressed against the wall, his pleasure was all mine at the slow drag of my tongue. His eyes squeezing shut as I savoured the taste of him, his body jolting as I worked him into my mouth.

"Harder."

His eyes were as dark as his demand, his intent calling to something inside me, something driving me to respond as his hand tangled in my hair. And then later, when he'd recovered the power in his legs, he'd helped me up and kissed me slow and sweet.

"Where did you come from?" He'd pushed the tangle of hair from my face and smiled as I'd replied,

"Have you forgotten our story already? I fell at your feet, then fell in love."

I realised right then that I might not be pretending anymore.

Since pulling off that state of newly wedded bliss, things between us have changed. Beckett is mellower and almost pleasant to be around. *Almost.* I wake alone in his bed most mornings, but he comes to me soon after, reeking of endorphins and need. His skin is slick from his exertions, and his gaze greedy as he pulls back the covers. The evenings we're home, I cook while he opens a bottle of wine from his climate-controlled cellar. We'll eat in the kitchen before Beckett clears up, which basically means he piles the pots and plates in an orderly fashion before leaving them for the housekeeper to take care of. We usually take our wine to the sofa following; I'll prop my legs in his lap or curl into his side while we watch TV. When it's his turn to choose, it's usually something in black and white or totally obscure, or else some boring documentary, but I don't mind. It's not like we often make it to the end.

Because sofas make for versatile positioning.

I haven't once felt the urge to return to manic cleaning sessions borne of anger and frustration. These emotions seem to have been replaced by a feeling of resignation.

I love him.

I know I'm not supposed to feel the way that I do, but I can't help it. Why couldn't he have stuck to being a pain in my ass? Anyway, it's not always a garden of roses. And when it isn't we can usually find use for the thorns.

I lean back in my very comfortable chair in my very swanky office. On Beckett's suggestion, I'd leased the suite on the fourth floor. I needed more space for the new staff, and this floor had the bonus of a private office. For me! It turns out he was also right about making myself less accessible. I get more work done now because Mir and Heather need to schlep up a flight of stairs if they want my attention. The setup is good for us all, including Beckett, considering he has a habit of turning up unannounced.

Just yesterday, I'd almost dropped the files I was carrying as I'd walked in to find him sitting in this very chair. One ankle crossed over the opposite knee, a very knowing smile played across his mouth, yet didn't quite give in. I wasn't sure if I wanted to eat him up or slap him. Maybe slap him then kiss the sting. But that was the whole point of him choosing to sit in my seat. For the purpose of annoying me.

"*And to what do I owe this pleasure?*" I'd asked.

"*Forgive a besotted husband who can't stay away from his wife.*"

His words were so smooth they might've been rehearsed. And while I would do well to remember that none of this is real, I'd still given in to the glow of pleasure. *I've been shopping.*

"Buy anything interesting? A cruise liner, a small principality? That sort of thing?" I'd turned from dropping the files to the desk as he'd sat up, catching me around my waist and drawing me between his legs.

"*I didn't buy anything for myself.*" His hands slid up my body, a current of electricity chasing his touch. I allowed him to turn me and pull me back onto his lap as he whispered, "*I bought you this.*"

Something delicate dropped in front of me, the slight weight settling between my breasts. I placed my hand over a pendant, though as he fastened the chain, I was filled with the overwhelming sense of being collared like a pet. But as he'd pressed his lips to the nape of my neck, the sensation seemed to change, becoming something much silkier.

"*It's beautiful*, "I'd whispered, staring at the long pendant hanging between my breasts; an infinity sign with two green and two clear stones woven in with the gold.

"*I went with the intention of buying you a watch.*" He huffed an amused chuckle, the brush of his breath making me shiver. "*But then I saw this. Diamonds for a diamond. Because diamonds don't shine, they reflect. And peridot,*" he'd added, "*considered to be lesser stones compared to emeralds, but these are so much closer to the colour of your eyes.*"

Is it any wonder I feel such confusion? I shouldn't feel anything, because this is just pretend. He forced me into this marriage for his own reasons, and yes, the choice was mine to agree or not, but I should still be furious.

But I'm not. I'm in love.

A glance to the top of my desk brings my attention to the

magazine lying there. Leaning forward in my chair, I pull this month's glossy copy of *Hiya* closer. The magazine that contains our centre spread. As it turns out, Beckett hadn't responded the way I thought he would, and was more than happy to invite the features editor and accompanying photographer into his home to sell the world on what a joy we'd found.

"It'll be good for business," he'd decreed privately. *"Good for both our businesses."* Publicity for mine, another layer of deceit for his machinations.

I spread open the glossy pages and look at the photo of us in his perfect kitchen. I'm standing on one side of the island, my back pressed against the cabinets opposite while Beckett's long frame lounges on one of the high stools. There's a bowl of lemons and limes sitting in between us, their vibrant colours a perfect contrast to the dark and sleek tones of the marble countertops and cabinetry. My hands are curled around a cup of coffee and I'm laughing, though not for the camera but rather at something Beckett had said. And he's watching me with that perfect half-smile of his. It's a picture of love and domesticity, with a headline that's a complement to the tales we've been spinning. The tales we'd continued to spin for them.

Love E-Volves: How the finance magnate and the romance start up owner found the algorithm for love.

If only.

My phone begins to vibrate against my desk, so I close the magazine before I get sucked into the article and all it represents for the third time today.

A click denotes a transatlantic call, Reggie's dulcet tones almost a purr. "How goes married life?"

"Oh, just peachy," I reply, my own tone more sing-song.

"Not lime-y?"

"Why, because he's British?" I sort of snort, my gaze turning to the window. Blue skies, fluffy clouds, and chimney pots. It's shaping up to be a beautiful fall.

"Good pun, but no. I'm looking at *Hiya* magazine online. I even paid for a subscription to get my hands on this baby."

"*Ahh.*" I quickly turn my moan into something else. "The limes on the countertop?" Did I even mention the interview to her? Maybe she saw it on one of E-Volve's Instagram stories.

"You didn't tell me Beckett was rich. Or like, mega rich."

"I did. The first time we talked about him." The day I told her about his hot/cold thing in the car. She'd said that the rich get a pass for being weird, as I recall. The second time we discussed Beckett was when I called her to tell her I'd married him. That time I did not get a pass. I got a grilling.

"But babe, there's rich and there's ridiculous. And Beckett is—"

"I know he is., but how am I supposed to tell people?"

"How do you say you're marrying a rich man to your friend?" she repeats. "Your best friend?" Or maybe how do you avoid telling your best friend that your marriage is all business and convenience? "You just say it," she adds simply.

"So I was supposed to say; 'Reggie, I'm marrying a man I just met. I fell into deep, passionate love with him but because he's super rich people are going to say I married him for money and that's going to make me feel like shit."

"No, you were supposed to say; Reggie, I've met the dick I'm gonna ride for the rest of my life." I burst out laughing, the sound echoing through the sparsely decorated room. "No one gets to make you feel bad for making decisions in your own life."

"You are a good friend, but you don't think like other people." The ones full of scepticism. The ones whose doubts will be proven right in a few months.

"Fuck other people. But not really, unless y'all aren't monogamous. But their opinions don't count. All that matters is that *you know* you're far too principled to be that person."

If only she knew. But she won't. Because this is a secret I'll carry to my grave. I suddenly feel like shit for projecting this on her. But at least I don't have friends or family nearby to continually fool. Beckett might not have family, but he does have friends. Friends I've yet to meet. Friends he says that, for my sake, I should avoid meeting. I guess he fears my crappy acting skills. *If only he knew.* But avoiding them is easy given they're grown men with busy schedules. *Single* grown men.

"It's your life, babe. Only you get to live it."

"I know." God, do I know. But it would be good if I could stop fucking it up somehow.

"Sounds like you're having a rough day."

I sigh and tip back my head to stare at the stained ceiling. "I was just thinking that we've been together three months now. This is usually the stage in a relationship that things are falling apart, or else couples are declaring their love."

"So your timeline is accelerated. So what? I knew I loved Josh within a week of meeting him. We moved in together after only a month. You and me? We're just both a little ahead of the curve."

Nope, I'm right on the curve, performance as it should be at this three month mark. I'm just not declaring my love because there's no space for such declarations in our marriage. This isn't the contract I signed. And as far as accelerated goes, Reggie is closer than she understands. Time flies because in less than three months this will be over.

"Anyway, who makes these rules?" Her voice brings me from my melancholy thought back into the moment. "Dumb internet quizzes and *Cosmo* articles. Your relationship will follow its own path, regardless of what so called internet experts say. Now, are you gonna to answer my original question; how's it going? How are *you* doing?" Her words are carefully spoken but sincere.

"I'm good. It's going . . . good. I guess it's just a little overwhelming at times."

"Like when you have to turn on the gold faucet to brush your teeth? But seriously, of course it's overwhelming, relationships are hard. It's like they take on a life of their own and are almost a whole other entity, when before there was only you to think about. Now there's you and there's him and then there's your relationship and a million thoughts about those three things."

A million is right. A million in my bank accounts.

"I'm just in a funk. Don't mind me, Reggie. I'm just having one of those days."

"Oh-oh. Time to stock up on the chocolate?"

"That's probably it."

"I hope he's the kind that'll go out in the middle of the night to buy tampons."

"I'll have to report back to you on that one." He probably has some online concierge service he'd pay to do it for him.

"Can I just say, this magazine spread? You look *hot*. Marriage suits you. Makes you radiant, girl."

"They brought in a stylist." My reply is accompanied by a chuckle as I glance at the magazine cover and the photograph of the Duchess of Cambridge. Now *she* looks radiant.

"No amount of makeup could paint the expression Beckett was wearing while looking at you."

"You think?" Be still, my hopeful little heart.

"Oh, I do. And you can't style the way you were looking at him. I'm calling it the *Beckett effect*."

"He is easy on the eyes."

"No, it's not about how he looks, it's how he makes you feel. The love shining from your face? As clear as the nose on *my* face. And you know I have a nose."

"There's nothing wrong with your nose," I scoff.

"Nothing a good plastic surgeon couldn't fix, you mean. But you tell me I'm not reading that picture right," she dares.

"He makes me feel good." A lot of different kinds of good. "And other times he makes me feel like I could happily murder him."

"Passion." She draws out the word on so many syllables, her tone all bedroomy.

"Sometimes. And other times he just makes me feel . . . " My answer is a sigh as my thumb brushes the stones on my pendant.

"Attraction is supposed to increase and decrease with how they make us feel. We can all appreciate the sight of a rocking hot bod or a handsome face, but the way they make us feel is the key to how much we dig them."

"He makes me want to choke him." Flowers and diamonds and mind-blowing sex, but we're still sticking to our timeline? Really? Okay, so maybe it's just when I overthink that I want to choke him.

Reggie's hoot of laughter vibrates down the line. "Oh, I get that. I do. One of these days I'm going to make Josh wear the toilet seat as a necklace. I might make him wear a big old D on his head."

"I do not need to hear about Josh's D." I snort, then giggle, my friend joining in.

"D for dummy," she splutters through a laugh. "The other D stays where it is. I have use for it! And toilet seat wearing isn't a fantasy, by the way. I'm not into the whole humiliation thing."

"I get it." I find words spilling out of my mouth. "I have this fantasy of helping Beckett on with his tie. We're standing close, and his hands are on my hips. His fingers become almost piercing as I tighten the knot of his tie again and again until my hips are arching, and his eyes are full of panic. And I'm just loving the power."

"Listen to you and your bad self." She chuckles, still not taking me seriously. "That sounds like some hot passion."

I blink, not sure why I've told her that. "I thought it sounded more like homicide."

"No, you were talking about sex. And it sounds like the sex is good."

"He makes me feel worshipped," I almost whisper.

"Oh, that is a good answer. Passion and worship. A good recipe."

Or one for disaster. Because this will end regardless of how I feel. Regardless of how he makes me feel.

"You know what they say," she adds. "You can't have a relationship without fights, but you can make a relationship worth the fight."

"That sounds suspiciously like it came from Pinterest."

"Are you throwing shade, girl?"

37

OLIVIA

"Come on, Ols. It's not meant to be serious. It's just for fun and a bit of publicity."

I glance around the city bar, the velvet lined booths and wingback chairs. One cork lined wall is filled with framed black and white photos which are, on closer inspection, vintage mug shots. The rich patina of the mahogany bar, a smoky mirror behind, etched and aged. The hundred fancy bottles lined up in front of it. The cocktail menu offering liquor-laced cordials and tinctures at prices to make your eyes water.

"This place isn't exactly subtle, is it?" I glance at the staff, the women behind the bar dressed like can-can dancers, the men like bootleggers in collarless shirts and suspenders, along with flat caps and Trilby hats.

"What?" Miranda's gaze follows my own, though seems to see a different space. "It's cool. Sort of intimate. It doesn't look like a knocking shop, if that's what you mean. Besides, you chose the place. And we've hung out here twice since."

I let out a long, nervous breath as I push my hand through my hair. "Tell me I'm panicking over nothing."

"You totally are. This place is the bomb. It's got exactly the look we're going for. It's vibey and the punters are going to love it."

"Vibey," I repeat, looking around the place again. "Not more kind of refined depravity?"

"Retro," she argues. "Someplace you'd expect to find gangsters and their molls hanging out. Pinstriped pants and jackets with wide lapels, feather boas and red painted fingernails holding thin cigarette holders."

"Underworld charm."

"It's a bar, for goodness sakes. It's sexy. The exact kind of place you want to be associated with. We're selling romance here, are we not?" I smile at her use of the majestic plural; we are amused. Very amused. But we are also very nervous. "Just think of how the photographs will look."

"You're right, I'm just stressing."

She's right about the photos, too. The *Evening News* are sending a reporter along tonight, plus a photographer, and they've promised us a feature in their weekend supplement. The more publicity we get, the more members we have, and the more members we have, the easier it'll be to sell E-Volve. The aim of the game. The reason I sold my soul to Beckett and all that.

"What do you want me to do with these?" Heather suddenly appears next to me, a dozen small silver buckets dangling from her hands. She looks like a dairy maid off to do the milking. If dairy maids wore skinny jeans and T-shirts that declares: BRAINS ARE THE NEW TITS.

"Put one on each table," Mir directs. "Then put the cards inside each."

Heather has spent the week printing out fancy prompts that are to go in the buckets, so our guests have somewhere to start. Icebreaker questions, I suppose.

What do you do for fun?
What's on your bucket list?
What do you do to relax?
What's your biggest dream?

Tell me something fascinating about yourself.
And other kinds of scintillating enquiries.

"So, when they come in, I give them each one of these little scoring cards, right?"

"It's maybe better we don't call them scoring cards, Heather. This isn't a game of mini golf."

"But we're giving them each a mini pencil, aren't we?"

"Yeah, one of the branded ones." Mir's idea. I don't know. Maybe she likes mini golf?

"Let's call them feedback cards." After all, that's what they are. Cards with checkboxes to rate their speed dating companions.

- X or ✓ as appropriate.
- Yes I'd like to be contacted by this person again with a view to getting to know them better.
- No thanks.
- I'd like to hear from this person with a view to being friends.
- Or friends with benefits, please don't tell us.

"So they get a little pencil—"

"And as much free booze as they need to loosen them up," Miranda interjects with a cackle.

"No, they get a glass of some drink they're making in honour of the evening." I wave my hand in the vague direction of the bar. "And there's some prosecco after that, and a few bottles of wine; red and white. The last thing we need is a bunch of drunk, horny singles on our hands."

"Speak for yourself," Mir answers. 'That sounds like some of my best work.'

"Anyway, getting back to it. Heather, it's your job to collect the score cards—"

"Feedback cards," she corrects.

"Yes, those. You collect them at the end of the evening and

then we collate the scores, I mean, the information. Then we'll get back to the participants through their membership email."

"And then one or two of the couples will see each other again," Mir exclaims, "they'll have a date at the cinema, then he'll take her for a nice meal, they'll date for a couple of weeks, then shag, and fall in love. And then E-Volve gets in the newspapers again. Bish, bosh, bash!"

"We'll see," I answer.

"You still don't seem very excited for tonight. Come on, chill out." Miranda's arm slides around my elbow. "It's going to be a grand success. People don't take speed dating too seriously. It's just a way to have a laugh and a few drinks, maybe meet some cool people, or get back into the saddle after a breakup. It's just for shits and giggles, Ols. That's all."

"We're not in business for shits and giggles though, are we?" At least I'm not.

"You're just feeling the pressure. First that thing in *Hiya* and now the *Evening News*. But that's what happens when you become half of the hottest power couple in London." I actually groan because I know what's coming next. "Bolivia."

"Wipe that grin off your face. It's such a terrible portmanteau."

"Port man what?"

Which is pretty much what I'd said when I'd told Beckett how we were now being referred to in the office. I'd used explanation *ship* and he'd looked on, confused. I'd tried to explain when he'd smirked and informed me the word I was looking for was a *portmanteau*. Smart ass.

"Bolivia is a portmanteau of Beckett and Olivia, don't you know," I reply loftily.

"Same thing as a ship?" Mir asks, her face still scrunched in consternation.

"Yeah." I give in. "Exactly like that."

"Bolivia isn't that bad. After all, it might've been Olecket."

Strange. That's what Beckett had also said. Not that Olecket wasn't bad, but that it wasn't too bad if you consider Bolivia as the home of llamas, cocaine and civil unrest. He said if you take out the llamas, as a name, it wasn't so random for us. I didn't laugh.

"All done," Heather announces, appearing next to me "Name badges are by the door, profiles and pencils are on the table, ice breakers are in the buckets. What's next?"

"I know," Miranda answers with a gleam. "Let's make an early start on that prosecco."

38

BECKETT

"What are you doing spending Friday night with me?"

I place my phone face down on the table and turn my attention to Harry, sitting across from me.

"I know I'm pretty," he continues "but I would've thought you might prefer to spend Friday evening staring adoringly into the eyes of your new wife?"

"Is that your not-so-subtle way of telling me you're bored with my company?"

"Bored? It's like I'm sitting here by myself. All you've done since you arrived is brood over your phone. You've grunted a few times, your contribution to the conversation less than scintillating, and you've nursed one drink. I've had more fun with statues."

"I don't need to know what you get up to in your gallery. Or what gets up you."

"Funny. Put your fucking phone away," he complains as I reach for it again.

While late to the phenomenon, I've suddenly become obsessed with social media. More specifically, the E-Volve Instagram account. I find I can often discover how Olivia is spending her day and see her smiling face. Though she's not responsible for the running of the account, she features in many of the posts.

Let's face it; I'm my wife's stalker.

"You know, you're pretty shit company all round these days." My gaze slides away from Harry's smug expression, despite the truth in his words. "You won't introduce us to your wife, and we're not allowed to talk about her. If I hadn't seen photographs of you together, I might think she wasn't real."

"My wife is my business," I reply sharply.

Harry grins and reaches for his drink. "Business you're not attending to tonight."

"She has commitments. And a business to run, just as I do." Because as of yesterday, the B in JBW is the majority shareholder of the company, two and a half months ahead of my projected timeline.

"Congratulations once again," he offers, tipping his glass. "Although, it appears to me to be all the more reason you'd be with her right now. You know, celebrating."

But in order to celebrate, I'd have to have shared the news. And I haven't. It's the strangest thing to admit to myself that I'm not content with the expedient play of things. I even went as far as to negotiate a lower bid, thinking perhaps the lawyers could haggle for a few weeks, but no such luck. Maybe the bastard is currently fucking Mrs Jones number five behind the back of number four, because he agreed to a lower price and wouldn't move on a completion date, insisting it be pushed through this month. It all sounds like he's trying to liquidate assets while he has a chance, after refusing to sell me the business for a year.

There was, of course, a sense of triumph in signing the paperwork, in knowing that I'd achieved what I'd set out to do. But now I don't particularly feel like I've won anything. I've mentioned the change of status to no one but Harry, and even that wasn't in the plans. He'd happened to call into the office at the same time Jones had cracked open the champagne to celebrate the company's change of direction— new blood at the helm. *And the doubling of his bank balance, no doubt.*

The bottom line is, the minute the news is out is the minute I lose Olivia.

But *lose* isn't the precise term. I never really *had* her to begin with. Not really. She shares my bed because the sex is good, because I make her feel good. And she shares her meals with me because she's kind and a generous cook. We talk, of course, mostly about work and I've become a sounding board for her. It's been gratifying to see her flourish. Add in a few engagements she's accompanied me to and that's the extent of my *having* her.

Meanwhile, my insomnia these days is filled with less exercise and much more introspection and longing looks. I find myself watching her sleep like some fucking dolt. My head tells me to run this to full term would be dangerous, but my heart and my hands know they can't give her up.

I know I must. That I'm not the one for her. But it doesn't stop the cravings.

"What is it she's up to on a Friday night that's keeping her from you?"

I don't like his insinuation, even though I know he's just poking sore points. Trying to get a rise. But because the bastard seems to have no intention of giving up, I flip over my phone and pass it to him.

"There's a function tonight for E-Volve, speed dating, I believe. The press will be there, that sort of thing."

"Speed dating?" he repeats without looking up from the screen.

"It's for the dating app she owns. She's not taking part, obviously."

"It's at Parman & Co." Looking up once more, he slides my phone back across the table. "That's near here."

"So?"

"We should go." My brows pinch at his suggestion. "You'll get to see your wife and I might even take part. Find myself a pretty little date."

"Don't be ridiculous."

"What's ridiculous about it? We don't all have wives to warm our cold beds."

"So get a fucking electric blanket," I grumble, slipping my phone in my pocket. "Anyway, you've got to subscribe to the app to join the event. Preregister, I should imagine."

"Who says I haven't joined?" he answers, his expression suddenly inscrutable. "Besides, I'm sure you could put in a good word for me. You know, with the wife I've yet to meet."

But he doesn't need to meet her. I prefer to keep her for myself. "No." I can't afford for him to meet her. Not now he knows about the business.

And she doesn't.

"What do you mean *no*?"

"I should've thought that was clear enough, unless there's something wrong with your hearing."

"Fine. Leave your wife at an event full of single men. Rapacious, randy *single men*."

"She's working," I growl.

"But do they know that? These single, rapacious, randy—"

"You're an utter bastard," I murmur, signalling for the cheque.

39

OLIVIA

"If at first you don't succeed, get another drink and try another table. You'll be amazed how much less you care," Mir declares, taking the note from the petite brunette in front of her before shooing her back into the room.

"The men are the ones that move tables," I hiss. "How much prosecco have you had?"

"Just a couple," she protests, glassy eyed. More like a couple of bottles than glasses. And to think I was the one with the nerves. "Give it to me," I demand, taking the folded card from Mir's hand.

"Where's your favourite place to have sex," Heather reads aloud over my shoulder. "That's not as bad as the last one."

"Except she said his answer was *in the bum*." Mir sniggers, rolling her lips together to unsuccessfully mute the sound.

"Who the hell would spike the prompts?" I wonder aloud. Because yes, some utter ass has added a few more prompts to our buckets. So far we've had the 'situational sex' prompt, along with:

What is the weirdest thing you've ever masturbated to?

Have you ever looked at your own butthole in the mirror, and if so, did you like what you saw?

"It isn't someone from E-Volve," Heather says in a serious tone. Thankfully, she isn't off her tits on cheap bubbles like her cousin. "They would've used the same card. It's been sitting on my desk all week." I consider the note in my hand, blue biro scrawled hastily on a piece of paper that appears to have been torn from a notebook.

"My money is on one of the *Lust Island* guys," I say scanning the room for the sight of one of the heavily muscled, darkly tanned, and carefully styled miscreants. They were only supposed to be here for the reception to kiss a few cheeks and shake a few hands. And to be in some publicity shots, of course. Thankfully, these didn't include the signing of some of the attendees boobs, boobs presented eagerly and willingly.

So much for people *e-volving*.

"They did seem to have the sense of humour of fourteen-year-olds," Heather adds. "And to think I was looking forward to meeting them."

"They're hot, though," Mir announces, swaying a little.

"Ew, Mir. One of them is wearing pink pants that don't touch his ankles. He looks like he put his sister's chinos on!"

"*Pssht*," her cousin replies, with a heavy wave of her hand. "They're fashionable."

"Baa!" Heather bleats. "Only sheep follow fashion."

"Miranda, go and sit down, please." I point to an empty booth away from the main event before the two get into this any deeper. "I don't have time to deal with you right now." With an exaggerated pout, she trots off in the direction I'd indicated.

"Our so-called celebs. Have they left?"

"No, I think I saw them go downstairs to the other bar." Heather's expression twists.

"No doubt adding drinks to my tab. Just be sure to stay away from them." I turn over my phone, which is set to the stopwatch app. "The four minutes are up. Do you want to do the honours?" Heather gives an excited little nod, making her way over to the brass gong framed in a carved wooden stand which we've set on the bar. She hits it solidly with the accompanying lollipop sized hammer.

"Gentlemen," she announces following the low shimmering hum, her confident voice carrying just as clear across the room. "Please change your tables."

"I love bashing that," she admits shyly when she returns. "I think we should take it to the office to announce staff meetings and stuff."

"Why not?" I reply, amused.

"Where'd you get it from?"

"It's Beckett's. I've just borrowed it for the night."

"Cool."

"Listen, Heather," I say quickly. "I just wanted to say that I'm so proud of you." I pull her in for a hug because tonight, she's really stepped up to the plate. She'd swapped her jeans, T-shirt and sneakers for a skirt, shirt and ballet flats. She not only looks the part, but she's embodied it, too. "You handled yourself so well when those drunks tried to sneak in earlier."

"Not on my watch," she says, drawing herself taller. "I've got three older brothers. I don't take anyone's shit."

"Good for you."

"Speaking of which," she says. "Do you want to get ready to ring the gong for all change or do you want to chuck that chancer out?" My gaze follows hers to the door where a handsome blond in a blue suit is sneaking in. Not sneaking exactly; men as good looking as him have no need of being furtive.

"You do the gong. I think this has something to do with my husband." Because behind the hottie comes another piece of hotness, all brooding six-foot-two of him.

"What are you doing here?" I ask, unable to keep my delight from my tone.

"We thought you might need a little moral support," Beckett answers, drawing me in for a quick kiss. "I also didn't want you running away with anyone else." His purr is low in my ear.

"Ladies and gents, this is your four-minute marker," calls Heather from deeper in the room.

To Have and Hate

"You're not getting rid of me that easy." I absolutely can't help my tinkling laugh or the bloom of pleasure radiating through my bones. Reggie was right; this is the Beckett effect. Sniping and arguing, or loving words, I'm mad for the man. And I think it might be time I pull up my big girl panties and tell him exactly that.

"I want to introduce you to someone," he murmurs, his expression warm as he pulls on my hand, leading me across the room. "Olivia, this is one of my oldest friends, James Harrison."

My gaze flicks immediately to Beckett. *He's introducing me to his friend? This is a reversal of plans.*

"Olivia. So lovely to meet you at last," says the blond with a genuine smile.

"Harry!" I'm bursting with what this means. It's such a little thing on the surface, but it must mean so much more. "I'm so sorry," I add immediately. "It's just, that's what Beckett always calls you."

"That's perfect." His smile turns kind of breathtaking. I bet he's a hit with the ladies. "All my friends call me Harry, so you should, too."

"You can let go of her now," Beckett grumbles, fairly pulling me away from his friend. "You don't mind if we gatecrash, do you?"

"The photographer doesn't," Harry interjects. As we turn, I realise Beckett and I will also be included in their feature now.

"The couple of the moment," Danielle, the reporter calls giddily. "Our readers will love it!"

"Of course I don't mind," I answer, still smiling as I turn back to the pair. "Actually, do you think you can help me out with Miranda?"

"Why? What's wrong with her?" Beckett asks.

"She's drunk." I roll my eyes as Beckett's narrow.

"While she's getting paid?"

"Technically, she's not. I was just going to give her the day off in exchange for her being here tonight." We'd been planning this event for months and, at that point, I didn't have any spare money to spend on overtime.

"Then she's still getting paid," he contends. "And the girl is drunk at work."

"Listen, we can argue the semantics of it later but help me out here. I've got enough on my hands without dealing with her."

"Point her out and I'll take her to a corner and ply her with coffee," Harry offers.

"Would you? That would be so helpful. That's her. The girl in the blue dress." I point at Mir, currently weaving in and out of the tables. And patting one of the male attendees on the head. *A bald attendee.* And then kissing his pate.

"Consider it done," Harry says, already on the move.

"So, this is a bit of a surprise," I say, turning back to Beckett.

"Is it really? I seem to be unable to stay away from you these days."

"I'm not complaining." With my hands clasped behind my back I find myself twisting left and right as Beckett follows the swish of the hem of my dress. His thumb taps his pouty bottom lip as though contemplating something.

"I know that look." I'm hyper aware of the way his eyes devour me, warmth flooding my body as a consequence.

"Do you indeed."

"You look like you're thinking of doing something, which is lucky because . . ." His eyes widen slightly as I hold out my hand as though in greeting. "Hi. My name is something."

His laughter is deep and pure as he uses my hand to pull me into his broad chest. "You still have a little to learn about negotiating."

"Yeah? And what's that?"

"Never make the first offer," he growls into my skin.

The evening passes quickly and when the speed dating part of the experience is over, the singles get to mingling. The photographer takes some candid shots and Danielle interviews a few attendees vox pop style, before she exchanges a few words with the *Lust Island* guys again. We chat before she leaves, and she promises not to include what has become the comment of the night in response to the prompt cards.

Question: Tell me something fascinating about yourself?
Answer: I don't have a gag reflex.

It's not exactly the evolved romance vibe I was going for. And not exactly the sort of thing you'd expect from a woman named Prudence who is five-foot-tall if she's an inch, a kindergarten teacher who looks like a little angel and sounds like Minnie Mouse. I guess you just can't judge a book by its cover.

Eventually, the crowd begins to disperse leaving us to pack up our stuff.

"I've grabbed the feedback cards," Heather says, "And I'm about to order an Uber to take me and Mir home."

"Get a cab and let me know what I owe you tomorrow."

"Don't forget this," she says, grabbing the gong from the bar top.

"Is that yours?" Harry says, suddenly appearing at my side, his gaze anxiously flicking between Beckett and myself. Actually, between Beckett and where I've slid the gong under my arm.

"It's mine," I answer defensively. "Well, I just borrowed it."

Beckett sets off laughing as Harry looks like . . . well, I'm not sure what he looks like. Like he's going to explode or maybe be sick?

"Jesus, Beckett." He blows out a harsh breath. "Only you would be so blasé about something this old."

"Oh my God. Is this an antique? I thought it was something you picked up on your holidays." Because it's so ugly.

"Harry deals in art. He's got a gallery in Belgravia. I think I told you that?" Beckett says, still chuckling. "He also has a bit of a passion for antiquities."

"Here, take it!" I shove it at Harry. "If it's damaged, please don't tell me." Because suddenly *I* feel sick.

"I'll go and . . . stow this somewhere," Harry begins.

"The car should be outside," Beckett suggests.

"Olivia, it was lovely to meet you. Your drunken employee, too. She was rather sweet."

"Thank you for babysitting." And I mean that sincerely. "I like him," I say, looking up into Beckett's inscrutable expression as Harry disappears through the door.

"Maybe we'll have him around for dinner one night soon."

"I'd like that." Really, I would. "I could cook. And you could pretend to wash dishes."

"What is the point of paying someone to do something only to have to do it yourself?" His gaze slides to a sleepy Miranda as Heather coaxes her out from the booth.

"If only we were all as clever as you."

"Yes, if only. The world would make much more sense."

"You keep telling yourself that," I reply, patting his chest before reaching for my purse. "Could you help them into their cab or whatever? I just need to close out the tab." I pull out my company credit card, kiss him quickly on the lips and turn to the bar again. Only, as the cash register has been closed out already, I make my way downstairs to the main bar. The eyewatering tab settled, I slip a sizeable tip into the tip jar. I pull my purse higher on my shoulder as I turn and walk straight into a wall of unfamiliar chest. *It's so strange how I know this isn't Beckett without even looking up into his face,* is the thought that crosses my mind right before I open my mouth. "Sorry, I wasn't watching where I was—'

"Olivia?"

I don't know who is more shocked, Luke or myself. He certainly looks shocked. Meanwhile, I think my jaw has become unhinged.

"What are you doing here?" The words, when I find them, sound more accusatory.

To Have and Hate

"I came with some mates for a drink." He indicates behind him to where two men sit with talented attendee Prudence and another two women from tonight's event. *So much for our success.* "How are you?"

"Good. I'm good." I seem to be nodding quite a bit, and quite rapidly, as I try to process his appearance.

"You haven't returned any of my calls." His words are surprisingly soft and hold a trace of hurt rather than accusation. "I thought we were friends."

"Yeah, well, I thought that, too. But then I discovered I was just a bit of entertainment for you and your stepdad." I never was one to beat around the bush, so to speak.

"I'm sorry?" He straightens, brushing a hand through his floppy fair hair. "I'm not sure I follow."

"Don't you?" I wish my words were a rapier because then I'd poke him with it. How dare he make me feel dirty, used and disposable while they laughed, while they played me. Well, who's laughing now?

"Ols, I'm totally confused." His answer is low and urgent and there's something unsettling in his tone, not that I have time to dwell as he hurries on. "Is this about me not coming to the party Mark threw, because, Jesus." He blows out a violent breath. "Do you think I want to celebrate you being with someone else? Someone other than me?"

"That was never going to happen."

"Well, you made that infinitely clear," he retorts, matching my anger now.

"You don't get to play the injured party." Incensed, I punctuate the words with my finger, violently poking the air between us. So much for Regency style social cuts. I'm sure the Duchess of Devonshire didn't stand around arguing like a fishwife.

"Really? Because from my viewpoint, things obviously look a little different. But at least I don't have to watch the bastard swanning around the office like the cat that ate the fucking canary anymore."

"What are you talking about?" Though no need to ask who the feathers belong to.

"He got rid of me as part of the deal. Didn't he tell you? Majority ownership of the company for him and a huge fuck off handshake for me. As of this week, I don't have to look at him ever again. But you know what hurts the most? We've been friends for a long time, you and me, but you just dropped me. You didn't lose any sleep before moving on to the next man who could dig you out of the shit."

"That's not what happened." My cheeks sting almost as though he's struck me.

"Anna and I aren't together—did you know that? We're going to co-parent and I'll support her and the baby, but you didn't even give me a chance to get my head around things before you fucked off and married him."

"Because you left me no choice!" I yell.

The whole bar falls quiet at my pronouncement.

I was never going to be his friend, not after learning I'd been nothing but a joke. He left me high and dry, in no position to do anything but marry Beckett . . . The man suddenly standing at the door behind Luke, his expression murderous.

40

OLIVIA

"I don't know what he's been filling your head with, but maybe you should pick up the phone next time I call." Luke's voice is pitched softer, like he knows Beckett is behind him, or maybe like he knows I'm about to leave.

I find myself nodding jerkily, my shoulder brushes his arm as I pass. I don't look back but sail through the door as Beckett steps aside to let me through.

"What is he doing here?"

The air outside is crisp with the promise of frost, Beckett's words just a little puff of white in the air. I wish I'd remembered to bring a jacket as I rub my bare upper arms. It won't be long before sidewalks will be covered in a carpet of leaves, crisp beneath our feet. And then what? We won't be crunching along these streets together when the snow falls. *Will we?* I swallow thickly over the riot of thoughts as I notice the ever-present Mercedes parked on this side of the street, a couple of car lengths away. I glance at it distractedly and back at him.

"It was a coincidence, I think." I'm surprised how even my voice sounds. Such a contrast to my noisy mind. *He no longer works at JBW and that's somehow Beckett's doing. As for the rest . . .*

"Didn't you say that Luke knew about his stepfather's plan? My pitch and—"

"Why are we talking about this now?" He pivots on the leather sole of his shoe, turning to face me. I do likewise more slowly, my mind still trying to sort through the puzzle pieces.

"Because we haven't talked about it before, I guess."

"It didn't matter to you. You weren't interested in anything but revenge."

"No, revenge was mainly your thing. *Your* hard on."

His firm *hmph* becomes visible in the air. "You have no idea what makes me hard." The edge to his words almost feels like a blow. Does he mean that I don't— "Not sexually. In other ways you don't understand. You *can't* understand."

"I understand someone stole the toys from your crib." In a motion that's more him than me, I turn swiftly and begin moving in the opposite direction of the car, away from his horrible words. Away from him.

"Olivia," he growls, then repeats in a yell as my feet thunder against the pavement so hard, I'm surprised the heels don't snap. "Stop." Feet scuffle against the sidewalk, his hand reaching out to grab my arm.

"Get off me," I demand, pulling away. "I need time to think." To process. Because something isn't right.

"You're not stomping your way through the streets of London alone, no matter how fearsome you think you are."

"Stop telling me what to do. Stop treating me like a child!" I realise we're actually tussling. He's not hurting me, but he's not letting go of my arms, either.

"Then stop behaving like one. What is this about? One minute you're fine, then *he* turns up and suddenly you're like this."

"Like what? Like angry?" I step closer, eyes narrowed. "Do I not fit the mould? Am I too disobedient?"

"I doubt you've been obedient a day in your life."

"I'll never bow to you."

"You'll do just as I tell you and when I tell you to." His words are bullets, his tone barbed.

"Fuck you." I turn but don't get very far as he pushes me into a nearby shop doorway. The brick wall beneath my back is shockingly cold and the stench in the small space acrid and choking. Beckett steps in after me, and though the darkness swallows me, light from a nearby lamppost turns his eyes to coal while casting his high cheekbones in stark relief. He has never looked more frightening.

"What did he say to you?" he grates out through gritted teeth.

My pulse begins to pound. I thought I'd seen him angry before but this? This is different. This is the apex predator without a cage, his anger as real as the breath that caresses my face. I shuffle back, my instinct pure self-preservation as he follows, his movements dark and threatening, the kind of threat that sends a thrill skittering across my skin. He isn't going to hurt me. I know that. But the shimmer of excitement that he could is undeniable.

"What he said is none of your concern." I find myself lifting my chin, my answer defiant but not without a tremor.

"Why the fuck were you talking to him?" His voice deepens, his anger coming off him in icy waves.

"Again, that's got nothing to do with—"

"I am your husband." He doesn't shout, but his words are no less piercing.

"In name only," I whisper.

Reaching out, he places one hand on the wall behind me, the brush of his sleeve against my shoulder a jolt of electricity. A jolt of awareness of how close he is. Leaning forward, he joins me in the shadows, his words more powerful with the absence of light.

"The husband whose name you cry out in the dark." His lips touch my cheek, his hand sliding up my thigh, dragging my dress with it, dragging a stuttering sigh from my lips. "You won't see him again," he whispers. His teeth graze my jaw as his fingers tantalise the soft skin of my inner thigh.

"You can't stop me."

"Don't tempt me, darling. There are no depths I won't sink to get what I want."

"To get your hands on what you want?" His agreement is more purr than word as his hand ghosts between my legs, his whole body stilling as I reach out and grasp his wrist. "Tell me the truth, Beckett. Tell me any truth."

Tell me you own the company ahead of time.

Tell me Luke had a hand in that fucked up business.

Tell me you love me.

Tell me something!

"I don't need to tell you anything."

"Then I'm walking." His hand moves from between my legs as he straightens, the streetlight revealing him in all his handsome glory. But I don't have time to appreciate this because I'm walking. Slipping around the side and out into the street. I head in the opposite direction of the car, my eyes scanning the roads for a passing cab. I can't stay here, not with him. Not like this.

"Olivia," he calls after me. I don't hear his footsteps. "Where are you going?" he demands.

"Home." I throw the word over my shoulder like an accusation. "*My home*." His place doesn't hold interest for me. Not tonight. Not with him.

"You can't leave." My heart begins to beat as his footsteps sound behind me again.

"Fucking watch me," I mutter under my breath, hiking my purse higher on my shoulder as though worried he'd steal it.

"Get in the car," he demands, spinning me suddenly to face him.

"Go fuck yourself."

"Then you leave me no choice." His free hand feeds into his inside jacket pocket, pulling out his phone.

"What? Are you going to call my mom?" Despite my mocking tone, inside I'm trembling.

The light from his screen washes his face as he swipes it with his thumb. "I'm calling my lawyer. Braunstein, Beckett here. I find myself this evening in position of requiring a filing for divorce on the grounds of abandonment."

"Are you kidding me?" I almost screech.

"Yes, Olivia left me this evening. Yes, she forfeits her company."

"You can't do that," I whisper. "That wasn't our deal."

"That was exactly our deal," he retorts angrily, unheeding the man on the other end of the line, a man in another country. "If you'd sought proper advice, you'd know about this."

"I did not sign up for this shit."

"Yet it's your signature on the paperwork."

I press my hand over his, ending the call. "You can't do this, Beckett. Abandonment isn't leaving for one night because I need time alone." Because I can't stand the sight of you.

"You don't get to decide. As you so nicely reminded me, this isn't a real marriage. We don't play by those terms. You are the junior partner, signed to certain requirements, and one of those requirements is to remain by my side for as long as I have need of you."

"For six fucking months," I growl, anger and frustration washing through me. I try to pull my arms from his fingers when they tighten like a vice. "That was the deal."

"Yes. And recess hasn't arrived yet, so you'll get in the fucking car." He releases me and I step immediately to the kerbside, watching as cars pass. Watching and waiting, willing him to make sense. Any kind of sense.

"I'll come home with you, because I have to." My eyes cut to his angrily. "But I'll get a cab. I don't want to be anywhere near you."

I sense rather than see or hear his deep sigh this time. "Please, Olivia. Just get in the car. I'll tell you whatever you like."

41

BECKETT

THE DARKNESS of the car wraps around us, the sweep of the tyres against the road the only sound made. Cars at night are like a private world, and we are each existing in our own separate one tonight.

How had it come to this? Yelling in the streets, hurling threats. Never before has someone made me feel like she does. Angry and exasperated, wired and alarmed. Like I want to put her in a box and protect her from all harm.

Including from me.

The headlights of the oncoming traffic sweeps over her face, washing her alternately in light and darkness over and over again. This journey is torturous. I fucking hate it and yet I never want it to end. Because of what it might represent. But we eventually arrive at the gates, and shortly following, the front of the house.

"That will be all for tonight, Dobson." Olivia's body turns towards me in surprise. As the driver's door closes with a quiet *click*, I hear her intake of breath but beat her to speaking. "That first night, in the car. In this car." I turn my head to where her hand rests against the leather, though I resist reaching out to touch her as the interior light dims. I'm thankful for the lights in the garden tonight, I find. "It took every ounce of my strength to leave you."

"But you did leave." Her tone delivers the unspoken. *You managed just fine, you prick.*

"I wanted you. I had to have you, but you came to me from him." I look at her then. Those mossy green depths betraying nothing.

"That's not how it happened," she answers softly.

"Yes, it is. You said so yourself. You'd waited so long for him to be available and you thought that night he was. Then I stumbled in."

"You hardly stumbled." A laugh, short and sharp. "I doubt you've stumbled once in your whole life."

"Yes, because my whole life is an exercise in perfection."

"No, because your whole life is an exercise in control. You want to control everything around you. Including me."

"Control is an obsession. An alternative to addiction, or perhaps a more acceptable one."

"You can't live your life like that."

"There are more harmful things to be addicted to." *Like you.* "But we were talking about Luke. What did he say to you earlier?"

"That's still none of your business."

"Whatever he said has confused you. I can see it in your face." *Taste it, almost.* "But perhaps it takes a manipulator to truly know one. You see, behind that boyish charm, Luke isn't the man you think he is. I doubt he was ever that man, even back at university. He plays people, women in particular, for no other reason than kicks. I suspect he's a narcissist. He was playing you and I had to be sure you weren't going to let him."

"So you manipulated me into marrying you." A statement, not a question. "That makes no sense, not even if you thought you were protecting me."

"I would be lying if I said my reasons were altruistic. Luke would've fucked you. Played with you a little before moving on, leaving E-Volve to go under. I saw we could help each other, and I was honest about my plans. I was my true authentic self, as they say over on Instagram."

"You were, are, the devil. The terms you offered me..."

"Were necessary. I didn't promise anything I couldn't deliver." I didn't promise her love because it wasn't part of the plan. If it had been, I still would've neglected to say so because she deserves better than my love.

"So you just decided I was better off being manipulated by you." I'd expected anger, not coldness. Horror, not resignation. "Does playing God get you off?"

"I haven't heard you complain about the compensation yet. Any of it."

"I'm sure that makes it all better in that screwy head of yours." She reaches for the door handle. "But you'll just have to forgive me because it makes no sense in mine."

"Stop."

"Don't worry. I'm not going anywhere, just inside the house. I'd like to drink a cup of hot tea then get into bed. Alone. I'm pretty sure the contract didn't explicitly mention us sharing a bed."

"I'm not finished yet." With a sigh, her hand slips away, her spine connecting with the leather again.

"You promised me six months."

"Yes, it's all in the contract." She sighs wearily.

"JBW became mine this week."

"What?" She sits straighter. In the dim light, her gaze whips to mine. "How?"

"I think Luke's stepfather is preparing to leave his wife. It's what I assume has compelled him to sell quickly." And at a good price.

"And you didn't tell me because you're keeping his secret, why?"

"How can you be so oblivious?" The truth will set you free? I don't think so, but it is flying fast. "I didn't tell you because I knew you'd leave me. And I'm not ready for that, Olivia. You can't leave yet."

I have never felt as vulnerable as I do right now. More vulnerable than being arrested and subsequently spending a night in the custody suite of a police station, more vulnerable even than entering rehab. And it is sickening. I feel shame and yet a strange sense of relief because she hasn't run screaming. And she doesn't look like she's about to as I watch conflicting impulses come into existence and fade across her beautiful face. Then she's leaning forward, cupping my cheeks in her hands, her lips a soft slide against mine.

"I get it. And it's okay to feel vulnerable. It's okay to be—"

I cut her words off, my mouth covering hers as I pull her across my lap with a sound somewhere between a moan and demand. Her legs slide over mine, the flare of her dress settling over us like the bloom of a flower, the smell of her perfume surrounding us.

"We're picking up where we left off."

Her smoky words echo under my lips, her head thrown back as I work my way down her neck, skimming my tongue across her collarbone. But I don't reply. I can't open up anymore because I already feel torn apart. Flayed.

Her hands scramble against my belt as I reach to expedite things, tilting her in my lap as she pulls my cock free from the confines of my clothing.

"You have such a beautiful cock."

My laughter is a thing of joy, a sound that rings free in the confines of the car. She beams back at me wickedly as I wrap my hand around the back of her neck, pulling her in for another kiss. Frantic and fast. Teeth and tongues. Sighs and compliments about the satin and steel she holds in her hand. My mind goes hazy around the edges as her mouth finds my ear and she whispers, "I need to feel you inside me."

Need.

To.

Feel.

I growl a feral growling sound as I find the zipper of her dress, pulling on it before wrestling the sleeves across her shoulders, almost restraining her until she pulls one arm free. My heart thumps and my dick pounds as she pushes it to her waist. The sight before me is like a fantasy, this languid eyed creature, all lush curves and fuck me mouth. She pushes up on her knees, sliding her arms around my neck, her fingers teasing the soft hairs at my nape as she presses her breasts against my face. *Like I need the hint.* She moans as I bite over the gossamer fabric, sucking her nipples into hard points as my fingers slide across her hot centre in a bare caress. Her sigh plays along my face as I push the scrap of lace to the side. As I grasp the base of my cock, she sinks down, taking me to the hilt.

Fucking sublime.

I can't touch enough. Suck enough. Fuck enough, as I buck up into her body, bowed and open to me. We are wild and unrestrained by everything but the confines of this space, this thing that has built between us is too painful to express in any other way. And the pleasure is too great to prolong as my thumb finds her clit, her detonation around my cock dragging me with her.

Her arms still around my neck, her heart seems to beat in time with my own. I want to stay here forever, let the world carry without us, let it pass us by. But at the hitch in her breath, I know we can't, so I cut off her words for a second time tonight.

"Darling, let me take you to bed."

42

OLIVIA

I WAKE TO AN EMPTY BED, the same as usual. When I roll over and check my phone, it's already gone nine. But it is Saturday. Saturday following a big night. I stretch out, testing the aches. The overworked muscles of my stomach and thighs and the way my wrists seem to still bear the press of his fingers.

Last night was . . . a revelation. I felt his need for me. Saw the raw truth of his vulnerability. We barely spoke yet we seemed to say all we needed to without words. It doesn't mean we're fixed, but maybe that we have a chance beyond our fucked-up beginnings.

It's such a paradox, I reflect as I stare at the ceiling. As individuals, we're so reluctant to reveal our weaknesses, yet when we do, the results yield such intimacy. Like last night, because the experience wasn't just sex. It was about closeness and understanding. Acceptance. Reassurance. Love.

Love we couldn't speak of. Or at least I couldn't.

I know that makes me a fraud because Beckett isn't the only one hiding. In my defence, last night was not the time to call out my love in the throes of passion. That I think we can have more than six months is something that needs to be said in a sane space. *Sane, not mad with need.* It should be discussed and understood as both a truth and a risk, not misconstrued as the result of some mind-blowing fucking.

I am ... reluctant to get out of bed. Another human weakness, and not a physical one. It's not that I particularly want to spend my Saturday in here, but because I'm avoiding the difficult things I have to say.

I love you.

I think you love me.

We need to talk about what we're going to do.

But eventually, and with a deep breath, I slide my legs out of the bed and opt for a quick shower, wincing a little as I take in the state of my appearance in the mirror. My hair looks like an angry autumn bush and my cheeks pink from his stubble. I'm going to need more than a scarf to hide this web of sucking marks.

Need. Desire. Signs of a night well spent.

I take myself off to the shower with a smile on my face.

Slightly restored and wearing the work out leggings I don't work out in, I take myself downstairs, coming up short at the sight of a monogrammed suitcase in the hall. A leather weekend bag and Beckett's laptop bag are placed next to it. My stomach flips but I try not to examine what this might mean.

"Beckett?" The rooms I pass bear no sign of him and his running shoes haven't been abandoned at the top of the basement staircase. I find him in the kitchen, the broad outline of him dark against the bank of windows. Weekend Beckett in well-worn jeans and a pale blue shirt is a sight to behold. "Hey, what's up?"

I don't make my way across the space to be near him. Don't slide my hands around his waist as I rest my head against his strong back. I don't say *good morning* or *how are you* or *did you make coffee yet* because a God-given sixth sense tells me something is very, very wrong with this picture. This moment. As he turns, his expression is confirmation. He's so frighteningly handsome, but he also looks like he hasn't slept in a week.

"I didn't want to wake you. Though I thought I might have to."

This is kind of a running joke between us, like the hours he doesn't sleep have been passed on to me for use. "If sleeping was an Olympic sport . . ." His eyes slide away, his ghost of a smile slipping, the ghost becoming closer to a wraith.

"I'm awake now. Are you going to tell me about the suitcase?"

"There's no easy way to say this, but I'm leaving."

"For how long?" Wrapping my arms across my chest, my fingers clasp my forearms, like I somehow sense my heart needs the extra layer of protection right now. "Is it work?"

He shakes his head. "I haven't decided how long I'll be away. But my lawyers will be in touch soon to confirm the details of the settlement."

"I don't understand," I answer dumbly, because I really think I do. Or part of me does. The logical part of me understands he's leaving for good, but it makes no rational sense. "I thought last night—you said you weren't ready for this to be over."

"In truth, I'm not sure I'll ever be ready. If I stay, the next few weeks will be unhealthy. For us both. You have to believe that."

"But it doesn't have to stop at six months. We could—"

"Stop." The intensity of the word cuts across the room. "This is the way it has to be."

"That's bullshit, Beckett. You can't just leave me without any fucking explanation."

"All that I owe you was written into the contract. Into the prenup. There's nothing else to say."

I feel like I'm going to be sick because he can't mean it. He can't be so cold. Can he? And now I know why my arms are banded across my chest. It's because it hurts to breathe.

"I know I said six months. But now I don't need you anymore."

More words are said. Something about the house. The lawyers. Being served. I don't take any of it in, not as he steps closer, and the morning light hits him just right. He looks perfect, but it's an illusion. A trick of the light.

What he is isn't perfect but perfectly fucked up.

"Olivia. Did you hear what I said?"

"You're a coward," I whisper, unable to look at him. He presses his lips to my head as though he agrees, and then he's gone.

I feel everything in the coming days. The wind is too cold, the sound of the traffic too loud, and the three flights of stairs to get to my front door are enough to make me stay up there. I feign a case of flu and croak down the phone on Monday morning to tell Mir I won't be in. Turns out crying until you literally have no more tears to secrete is a really good way to make you sound like you've been ill.

Is grief a kind of illness?

I hang on to the knowledge that heartbreak turns to anger, not that I've ever experienced a breakup like this. In fact, I wonder if anyone else in the world ever has, because on top of feeling like utter shit I'm also balancing the weight of the knowledge that I only have myself to blame. Yes, he's a total bastard, the way he'd handled things, but the state I'm in is my own fault. I shouldn't have fallen in love with him—I shouldn't be feeling anything because it was all supposed to be pretend.

I should be furious.

Why aren't I?

Where is my damn angry stage?

Breakups are the pits. Sadness is debilitating. And painful. And the ache in my heart weighs me down, like the muscle has been filled to the brim with concrete.

By Tuesday I've stopped crying, though I still look like I've been sick. *Puffy eyes. Red nose. Pallid skin.* When I get to work, the crew avoid me like I'm a plague carrying rat, which means they leave me in peace, and I get to do the stoic thing of throwing myself into my work like a tragic artist. But you can only pretend to be recovering from illness for so long. Or not, as the case may be, because as the weekend rolls around, the *Evening News* is out with the E-Volve speed dating article with images in all its CMYK glory. The pictures of the *Lust Island* guys along with a candid shot of Beckett hugging me like he's trying to absorb me.

I don't spend the weekend in bed, but I do spend it staring at the article and remembering. *Remembering everything.* The way his gaze devoured me in the mornings as I dressed and how in the darkness his soft words and kisses had slid over my skin.

I also remember how he said he didn't need me anymore and that I need to remember more than anything.

The blame is squarely on my shoulders. Just as I'd accepted the blame for the state I'd gotten my business in. I'd known from the beginning what to expect. Beckett hadn't sold me lies. I'd just lied to myself.

Angry. I need angry. Why isn't that stage here yet!

"We haven't seen Beckett around for a while." Mir places a latte on my desk. A latte from the bean-to-cup machine Beckett had arrived with one day, making Miranda his biggest fan. As much as I want not to drink it on principle, it would be ridiculously churlish.

"Thanks." My eyes flick up from my laptop for the briefest moment and find her expression expectant. Oh, she asked me a question, didn't she? *Beckett.* "He's been busy." Busy being anywhere but with me. He packed a bag. I bet the bastard went on vacation just to get away from me. I go back to hammering the keys in an attempt to stave off more tears. Maybe I really should have insurance on my laptop, like Jorge suggested. I'm not ready to talk about Beckett or our breakup. I'm not ready for the knowing looks, sympathetic murmurs and banal comments.

He's not worth it. It's his loss. He doesn't know what he's missing.

Maybe if I repeat these enough myself, I'll start to believe.

It's been ten days since he left, so I guess he's not the only one that's a coward.

"Ols, I hope you don't mind me saying this, but you look like a bag of bones."

"That's what happens when you've been ill, Mir. You can't

keep anything down, so you lose weight." I shouldn't be using this tone with her, and I feel especially awful as she slides a chocolate cookie next to my coffee. She didn't do anything wrong, so why am I taking it out on her?

It's his fault. Or it's my own.

Depending on which way the wind blows.

My phone rings as I'm leaving the office on Sunday. I slide it from my pocket and look at the screen because I'm screening my calls these days. When Reggie called yesterday, I ignored it, texting her immediately to say I had laryngitis, just to give me a few more days to pluck up the courage to speak to her. Explain. Maybe I'll even tell her the truth.

But this call? For the first time in a long time, I answer it.

"Luke."

"Hey, Ols. You answered!"

"I did." I lean back against the window of the coffee shop next door to the office, preferring not to walk and take this call, especially if the talk turns to Beckett. *I wonder how long it took him to tell the folks in his office about us.*

"How are you?" That's not a careful enquiry, more a casual one.

"Oh, you know. Busy."

"I heard that matches dot com are sniffing around."

This is true. In the absence of Beckett sitting in on our haphazard board meetings, he'd sent his proxy. Bob. An older man who sits on a few company boards, apparently. Anyway, he has a contact who has spoken to *his* contact, and now we're waiting for *that* contact to patch us through.

"I'm not sure you're one hundred percent right," I answer halfheartedly. "But let's just say that things are looking good." In some aspects, at least.

"Excellent! I always knew E-volve had legs." Legs he tried to

To Have and Hate

kick out from under me. Maybe. It's not a line of enquiry I've had much energy to consider. "Hey, I just called to say I'm at *Greens*. I wondered if you'd like to meet me for a drink."

I move the phone from my face and sigh. I'd rather spend time with Hannibal Lecter.

"Come on. Just a drink. We didn't get time to talk when I saw you the other day. And the stuff you said? Well, I haven't been able to get it out of my head."

"Listen, Luke, I'm really tired. I was just heading home." I don't have the energy to wade through any more shit. "Can we just do this another day?"

"Please, Ols. We need to talk about this. Clear the air. I won't lose you as a friend. I can't—I need you."

I sigh again, not hiding it this time. Maybe this is bigger than just Beckett said/Luke said. Maybe I ought to give him the chance to explain before I wipe him entirely from my life.

"Give me ten minutes," I answer wearily. "But I'm only staying for one drink."

Greens, as it turns out, is situated at the Shoreditch end of Hoxton, so it takes me longer than I'd imagined it would to get there. I find Luke sitting outside under an awning strung with lights. The floor is covered with fake grass and the furniture is wooden. But the rustic décor seems to have brought all the hipsters to the yard because the place is buzzing.

Luke stands as I approach the table, though wisely senses I'm in no mood for a hug.

"I'm so glad you came," he says pushing a large glass of white wine my way. A pint of lager stands in front of him.

"Like I said, I can't stay long." I sit and busy myself with my purse so as not to look at him. It looks like I can manage to muster anger at someone. "What is it you wanted to talk about?" I bring the glass to my mouth for a sip. It tastes metallic, but it's not the wine, it's me. Everything tastes wrong lately. Feels wrong, too.

"About the other day, before you rushed off, I wanted to apologise. I was wrong to say those things. I'd had a few beers, and that's a crap excuse, I know, but I was angry. I didn't mean to make it sound as though I wasn't happy for you."

"It doesn't matter," I murmur, my gaze sliding to a nearby table of girls, at least one of which seems to be interested in Luke. I narrow my eyes in their direction, sure I recognise one or two of them from somewhere.

"I was trying to be happy for you." As he says this, he strokes the condensation from his glass with his thumb, his eyes captivated by the motion. "But I suppose I was jealous. Angry, too. Angry at the world. Anna and I are never going to be anything to each other, and I fucked up my chance with you."

"What's done is done," I offer lamely, and I wasn't going to do this, but what the fuck. "Beckett told me Mark had no intention of investing in E-Volve."

"What?" Luke's head comes up, his gaze hitting mine hard. "How the hell would he know that?"

"Because Mark told him, apparently."

"Well, I know nothing about that," he blusters, raking a hand through his hair. "Honestly, Ols. My part was over as soon as I got you in through the door. I don't even work there anymore. And that's Beckett's doing." That sounds like deflecting to me. "He hasn't been in the office lately, I heard."

"You still keep in contact with them?" I swallow thickly. Does he know about us? Beckett has no incentive to keep things secret, but on the other hand, he isn't the sharing kind. And he's definitely not the fishing kind, like the man in front of me.

"Yeah, I do. I made good friends at JBW. I'd worked there since leaving uni, after all. But my new job is pretty cool, too," he adds a touch defensively.

"I'm happy for you." And I'll be even happier when this afternoon is over.

"I know it's not like senior partners are in the office nine to five anyway. Mark never was," he adds with an unimpressed snort. He reaches for his glass, taking a deep pull, leaving a foamy white trail under his nose. "But Beckett is apparently there even less than Mark was."

"But he's still there?" I hate how this comes out as a question and not an answer. Hate that I'm desperate for information.

"Yeah, I just wondered what's going on with him."

Me and you both, Luke. Me and you both. "You could always ask him," I reply instead.

"Ask the bloke who fired me?" He snorts.

"I thought you said you got a golden handshake?" Or a fuck off one, as he'd called it.

"I did, but he still got rid of me," he answers defensively. "I loved working at JBW—I didn't want to leave."

"So why do you think he made you?"

"Because of Mark. He had it in for me because of him."

Or maybe because Beckett was right. Maybe Luke is a manipulator, too. A narcissist? I can't see it. But did he have a hand in any of the other stuff? And do I really care right now? What I do care for is a trip to the bathroom. Too much coffee and my bladder is threatening a revolt.

"Do you want another drink?" I ask as I stand.

"Yeah, cheers. That'd be great."

"I'll be right back."

I'm in the bathroom stall when I hear the outer door swing open, the noise of the bar carrying in then shutting off again. Heels totter and girls giggle, but I'm not really paying attention. I'm digging in the bottom of my bag for a tissue because the universe is picking on me. *The dispenser is empty.*

"Where did you disappear to?" I still at the sound of her voice. I know this voice. This is the squeaky deep-throater from the speed dating night. What's her name again? "You didn't look to score, did you?" That's it—the incongruously named Prudence!

"It depends on what you mean by score," the second voice answers in a smug tone.

"Like, as in charlie."

Jesus, does everyone in London do cocaine?

"Nah. I've got someone hooking me up later."

"So, where've you been?" Prudence asks as I return to my tissue quest. I'll hide in here for as long as it takes because I'm in no hurry to speak to either of them. I'm also not exactly looking Instagram perfect right now, which is important since I seem to have become the face of the brand.

"I've been inside, having a drink with Marnie."

"No, *before* that," Prudence says. "We couldn't find you."

"You wouldn't believe it if I told you, babe."

"Try me."

"Hey, don't go stealing my lines!" The other woman giggles. "Anyways, I was like, in a totally skeevy supply cupboard, full of mops and cleaning stuff."

"What or *who* were you doing in there?"

"Who, definitely."

"It was that guy from the speed dating thing the other night, wasn't it?" At this I still. Wasn't Luke sitting with the girls right before our altercation? "You totally shagged him, didn't you?" Prudence squeals.

I do not need to hear this. Or maybe I do. Maybe I need to hear it all.

"Strike when the iron is hot and all that." She pauses for a beat, and I almost hear her sigh. "I've had better, though."

"Ooh, shame," Prudence replies, absolutely gloating.

"It really is. He's a looker, and we were vibing and we had chemistry and all that the other night, didn't we?"

"Yeah, for sure."

"Anyway, I saw him in here earlier."

"In the ladies?"

"No, you idiot. Out in the bar. We had a drink and a chat. And we snuck off to do the dirty deed. You know how horny wine makes me."

"I know how horny city boys make you," her friend answers snidely. "Lawyers and traders and stuff."

"Totally. I'm a slut for a man with a big . . . bankbook." The pair break out into dirty sniggering giggles. "Sadly, that was the only big thing about him. Apart from his ego."

"How's that, babe?"

"Well, he's blown me off for the next hour because he needs to deal with his ex. You remember that American who ran the speed dating thing we went to the other night?"

That. Rat. Bastard.

"Where you met him, you mean?"

"Yeah. Well, apparently, they had a thing going on before she got married."

That fucker. That douche bag!

"Oh, I saw that article! I follow her on Insta. Her New York wedding post was so cute!"

"Unfollow her," her friend bites back. "She's a total ho-bag. She's already cheating on her husband with Luke."

"I thought you were doing him?"

"Just casual, babe. He's hooking us up with coke later, yeah?"

"Oh!" Prudence gasps with delight. "I remember now! She's the one that got her claws into that tasty bit of stuff from JBW? The millionaire? We saw him on the speed dating night, remember?"

"Beckett something or other," the other woman agrees. "They say he's richer than a millionaire."

"What comes after a millionaire?"

"Are you being serious?" From Prudence there's no reply. She can't really be a teacher, can she? "He comes from old money. Now, there's a man I'd let take me *anywhere*, if you know what I mean. And I bet he doesn't have a dick like a pencil."

"Oh, no. Luke took you in the cupboard and you didn't even

have fun?" Prudence sounds thrilled, despite her faux-sad tone. This pair can't be friends. Frenemies, maybe.

"He was all talk and no substance."

"Babe, little men need love, too."

"I know," she says with a resigned sigh. "I'm meeting him after she's gone. It's good to keep your options open."

"You're still gonna see him after he blew you off for his ex?"

"He's finishing with her as we speak. Besides, the greedy bitch already has her man."

Only, I don't. And now I'm beginning to wonder if this is part of the reason, while also wondering if I'll get away with killing Luke.

"No!" Prudence cries suddenly, as though she's just heard her dog died. "I've just realised where I've seen him before."

"Who, Beckett?"

"No, Luke. He fucked Amelia a couple of months ago. He even called later crying because his ex is pregnant and her dad is absolutely threatening to get out the shotguns. They've got to get married because her uncle is the Archbishop of Canterbury or something."

"Really?"

"He's something religious, anyway. I told Amelia that it sounded like he was chasing a pity fuck. But you know what they say. If you lie down with dogs, you get up with fleas."

"Good job we screwed standing up," she says with a snicker.

"Where'd Amelia meet him anyway?"

"That dating app she's just signed up for."

My stomach hits the floor. This is like some great big cosmic clusterfuck.

"E-Volve?"

"Nah, it was that other one. The swipey one."

"Tinder?"

"That's it."

So much for sisterhood. So much for evolving. And so much for fucking romance!

To Have and Hate

But at least my purse yields a squashed and very sorry looking packet of tissues from the bottom as the pair of nitwits finish retouching their makeup. Once they've left, I wash my hands and stride out to the bar.

Oops. I mustn't forget Luke's pint of beer. What the hell, I'm feeling generous. I'll order him two.

He looks up from his phone as I approach the table, his eyes merrily twinkling at the pint glass I carry in each hand.

"Are you joining m—" He doesn't get any farther than that, unless you count a lot of yelled *Jesus* and *fucks* as he jumps from his seat. To be fair, I did order the really cold stuff. And I had the bartender put ice in.

"What the fuck, Ols!" he yells, on his feet now and standing like a scarecrow. *Head bowed, his arms held out and all of it dripping.*

"There." I place the glasses down on the table, before straightening and brushing away the beery splashes from my outfit. "You are the kind of man who gives *man*kind a terrible name, Luke." I announce this loudly, the crowd around us beginning to jeer. "Ladies, take a good look at this pretty face. Remember it, because behind the mask hides a liar and a cheat. And if you're still tempted, if you just can't resist a pretty face, you should know I have it on good authority . . ." I point to the girls sitting at the same table as Prudence, "that he also has a pencil dick."

Pulling my purse higher on my shoulder, I leave to the sound of cheers. English drinkers are easily entertained. They get super excited if someone behind the bar so much as breaks a glass . . .

43

OLIVIA

BACK OUT ON THE STREET, my footsteps are quick and light on the pavement. No stomping for me. No more dragging my heels or moping. And no more tears. I'm done with all that. And after tonight, no more beers because my shirt reeks of the stuff. I don't think I'll ever be able to drink it again.

I suddenly realise what I should've done. I was waiting for anger to come to me, when what I should've done is reached inside, past the sadness and grief and what ifs, into the very heart of me.

I'm looking at this all wrong.

I'm not the woman who was blackmailed into marriage.

I'm the woman who married a man to get what *she* wanted.

I've had the power all along, and I am the woman who will have her say.

All that I owe you was written into the contract.

Oh, Beckett, you are so very wrong. And you are about to discover just that.

I hail a black cab in the middle of the street, almost falling into the seat in my haste to get in. I give the cabbie Beckett's address, but the minute the door closes, fear starts to creep back in. What had felt so certain, so right outside on the street, begins to feel like the opposite. But there's no going back as the taxi merges with the evening traffic. There's no going back because, from now on, I need to move forward. If he doesn't want me, fine. I'll learn to live with that. I mean, it'll still hurt, because I love him. But I need him to hear that. I need him to know, to look at me as I tell him. And I need him to hear what a prick he's been.

If he's home.

He packed a case, my mind oh-so helpfully supplies.

Luke was most likely lying. Maybe he hasn't been into the office at all.

He's probably gone on vacation to escape this exact scenario; his ex turning up on the doorstep, full of drama.

After all, this isn't his first marriage rodeo.

Or maybe I won't even get as far as his front door.

Maybe he's already changed the codes for the gate. And I'll look like an idiot.

"You visiting someone, love?" the cabbie asks, pulling me from my riotous thoughts.

"Er, yeah. You could say that." Some would say visiting. Some would say delivering a smackdown.

"It's a nice area."

"It is." Furtively tipping my nose to my chest. Yep, I still smell like a brewery.

"Got to have plenty of money to live 'round here."

"Really? I wouldn't know. Oh, look, we're here."

The cabbie pulls a little past the keypad and I lean out of the window to key in the digits. My relief is great as the gates begin to open slowly.

His Mercedes is parked at the top of the driveway. I take that as a promising sign as I pay my fare and step onto the path.

I ring the bell.

And I wait, straining to hear signs of life from inside.

I ring it again, keeping my finger on the buzzer longer than is usually necessary.

But the door remains closed.

Doubt starts to creep in. I should've thought this through better. Planned to come another day. He might not be here, but I could come back on a weekday morning and catch him leaving for the office.

Except he'll now have security footage of me being here. He might change the gate code.

Unless he really has just gone away indefinitely.

But no. He has what he wanted all along. JBW. He wouldn't leave now.

So maybe a vacation? Or maybe I'm just losing my mind.

With a heavy sense of failure, I lean my back against the front door and figuratively shake my fist at the universe. Then fall backwards as the door swings open.

"Olivia?"

"This was not how this was supposed to work," I grumble from my position on the floor. I look up, wondering if I've ever felt more foolish than this.

Probably.

Definitely.

Beckett looks . . . sweaty. And unreasonably delicious in his shorts and a T-shirt, the fabric moulded to him like a second skin. I've obviously disturbed him from working out. But how dare he smile down at me with that sinful half smile of his.

Just like our first encounter, I find myself being lifted. But unlike our first encounter, my ass is throbbing so hard I'm pretty sure I'll never get to sit on it again.

"You've lost weight." Of course, the first thing that comes into my head flies out of my mouth.

"A little," he agrees.

"You should hire a cook. To feed you," I add, as though the qualification is necessary.

"Olivia." My name on his lips is . . . distracting. "I'm so pleased you're here," he adds softly, completely throwing me. I mean, throwing me more than seeing him standing here, not the sharp and thorny Beckett of our last meeting but the charming one.

To Have and Hate

The one whose eyes sparkle with something that could be fondness. You know, rather than the souls of the damned. This is not the version I'd expected. And this is not going the way I'd planned.

Guns blazing? They're still in the holster.

"Oh? Maybe you won't be so pleased when you hear what I've got to say to you." That's better. Angry words and an appropriately snarky tone.

"Maybe not, but do you think I could speak first? Would you mind?" I shrug magnanimously. Or maybe immaturely, but as he reaches for my hand, I snatch it back. He nods as though understanding before leading me deeper into the house.

"Please, sit down. I just need to get something."

We're in his office. He'd fucked me over that Bauhaus desk last month. *God, this feels so weird.* I take a seat on the edge of one of the two chairs opposite the desk. Beckett makes his way to the other side, opening a drawer and pulling out a folder.

Paperwork.

My heart sinks. This is where he serves me with divorce papers. I've saved him the trouble of serving me by presenting myself. While examining my idiocy, I somehow didn't notice he'd moved and is now in front of me, his ass resting on the edge of the antique desk, his long legs stretched out between my chair and the next.

"First, I need to tell you I'm sorry."

"I'm sorry, *what*?" I'm pretty sure my response would've been heard three boroughs wide.

"I can say it that way if you want, but it really makes no sense."

This makes no sense. And whatever I was expecting, this isn't it. I mean, not that I don't want to hear it. "You don't say sorry. *Ever*. Remember?"

"Apparently *ever* was an overstatement. And I do recall saying it to you once before."

"Before snatching it back!"

"Look, do you want to hear this apology or not?"

"Go for it," I say with a little huff, crossing my arms over my chest. The way his eyes track the lift of my breasts does nothing for me.

Also, I'm lying.

"I'm sorry," he begins. "I'm sorry for walking out. I panicked but, as it turns out, I needed the time to clear my head. To work a few things out."

"Apologies don't come with qualifiers," I retort. "Or else they're really not really apologies."

"Are you going to let me finish?" he asks a touch disdainfully, which just lights the fire under my boiler.

"That depends. Are you going to get to the point sometime soon?"

"I'm sorry I mistook passion for obsession." His jaw flexes and his brows draw together in that fierce way of his. I think his expression has less to do with the discomfort in issuing apologies, and more with the way I'm looking at him. So I strive for an outer nonchalance while inside, my temperature has spiked.

Why do our sniping interactions turn me on?

"And I'm sorry I didn't share how I felt with you."

"Anything else?"

With an annoyed little pout, he twists his upper body, reaching for the paperwork from his desk. "I'm sorry I didn't tell you that I loved you."

Ohmygod. He loves me? But he didn't even look at me when he said it. What's with that?

"You've no comment?" he asks, turning back. "Nothing to like to say?"

I shake my head. I'm still processing here!

"Then you should also know I'm sorry you didn't get to say it first. That I didn't get to hear you say it."

"Who said I was going to say it at all?" I answer with a little flounce.

To Have and Hate

"You were going to, and I let my fear shut you down."

"If you say so."

"I do. Do you know what else I say?"

I open my mouth, but no words come out, not as he drops to his knees in front of me. Not as he places the paperwork on my lap and lifts my left hand, producing my diamond wedding band before me. The wedding ring I'd left behind.

"I say, stay married to me, Olivia. Not for a contract or a company. Not for six months or six years, but forever." His gaze burns with sincerity. Which is just as well, considering his next words. "Say yes, darling. You know you want me, or why else would you keep falling at my feet?"

"You really are . . ."

"The perfect person for you."

"I was going to say prick."

"Of course you were," he replies with an amused twist to his lips. "I know I'm a prick, but I'm *your* prick. To have and to hold . . ." As he slides the ring back on my finger, he sends me an inciting look. "Whenever you like."

"Seriously? That's your grand declaration? Am I supposed to swoon right now because I get to hold your dick whenever I feel like it?"

"You know it's your favourite part of me, darling."

"I might hold it over a fire on a stick," I mutter, staring down at my ring.

"Just be with me, Olivia. Let me love you forever and I promise you I'll do whatever I can to make you happy . . . short of roasting my dick over an open flame."

I laugh and I cry, my heart fit to burst because there really is no other answer than this: "Alexander William Beckett III, you are going to regret this because I'm going to torment you for the rest of your life."

EPILOGUE
BECKETT

I LEFT her that awful day, as she said, a coward. But didn't go very far. A weekend in a hotel to wallow. A weekend where I almost decided I was better off being addicted to cocaine than I was her. A weekend where I tried to persuade myself she was better off without me. That she deserved someone stronger. Someone whole.

I came back to an empty house. Four cold walls. A pristine kitchen; no kettle or cups littering the benchtops. No used teabags dumped in the sink. A bedroom that would never again witness her joy. Her wedding ring on the dresser. A hair tie on the windowsill with a knot of her red-brown hair tangled around it. Her perfume lingered. But she wasn't here.

I suffered a withdrawal I wasn't prepared for. As a fuck up, I deserved nothing but heartbreak and misery.

And she deserved so much better than me.

But I've never really been very good at denying myself. I've always gotten more than I deserved.

And that included Olivia.

Of course she chose to stay married to me...

It might've taken a hundred apologies, beginning with those whispered between her legs as she'd writhed in the chair in my office that afternoon. One leg hooked over my shoulder, the other trembled in my hand as I'd made good on my promise to love and take care of her forever.

Which is what we're doing today, in front of our friends and our family this time.

Oh—no. I don't mean I'll be eating her pussy in front of the congregation. We're doing something much more shocking than that. Today we're committing ourselves to each other for life. Again.

Perhaps shocking isn't the right word. Exhilarating, I think. Being married to Olivia will be a white-knuckle ride of sniping and fighting and make up sex. Of tender moments, of hot and heavy looks. And of such an abundance of love , love that will carry us through the years.

The air is crisp with the scent of fall, the garden a riot of colours to compliment my bride's lavishly autumnal hair. She has a smattering of freckles across her nose left over from our late honeymoon in Mustique. And a distinct lack of bikini tan lines under her stunning ivory dress.

I'd thoroughly recommend a private villa . . .

We're renewing our vows right here in our garden. Our garden. Our house. Our company in JBW. E-Volve is still all her baby, and it's well on the way to making her rich in her own right. Not that she'll ever have need of money, because as well as returning her wedding ring that afternoon, I'd also returned to her what was owed. The prenup torn, a post-nuptial agreement signed in its place.

You see, as I'd said to Olivia in the beginning, everyone has their price. And I'm worth nothing without her. So today we commit ourselves to the other. For better or worse. I'll endow her with my world, to the letter of the law as per the paperwork. She's welcome to it. She has my heart. I've surrendered it to her care. It's no use to me without her these days.

"There you are, my devilishly handsome husband." Olivia comes up behind me, wrapping her arms around my waist as she nestles into my side. As she tips back her head, I note the mischief lurking in the corners of her beautiful smile. "Do you think you might've burst into flames if we'd decided to do this in a church today?"

"Very droll," I reply. "I told you, I don't believe in a higher power, with the exception of the divinity between your legs."

"A blasphemer." Yet she offers me absolution as she pushes up onto her toes, her hand cupping my cheek as her lips find mine.

This woman. She is everything.

"You are my church and my chapel, my darling. And I'll worship you for the rest of my life."

ACKNOWLEDGMENTS

Bloody hell! This one really took a village!

Thank you to all for bearing with me while I stepped away and took care of other non-bookish things. I truly hope *Boliva* have been worth the wait for you.

To the usual suspects, as usual, my most sincere thanks. You went above and beyond, and at the risk of sounding Insta-schmaltzy, I truly feel blessed.

Drum roll, please!

Aimee Bow-ya. I love that you hate repetition and that your eyes see the stuff mine don't. Thank you great big heaps for the bathroom convo. It kind of took on a life of its own but the idea was yours in the beginning.

Lisa Staples. The queen of last-minute eye bizziling. Great catches. Great suggestions. The final Beckett response is on you. Love from the difficult prick to you!

Natasha Harvey, the Queen of OCD, thanks for paying attention to those *Death Becomes Her* moments and for the eye-bizziling, and the general *is-you-still-breathing* messages.

Michelle Barber for her Boo-Peeping and her championing of this pair. Also for the Boliva portmanteau. I love it!

To Elizabeth Barr, last but not least, the amazing keeper of rear end. A bit presumptuous on this one, but that's on me :D

Thanks to Jenny for putting up with my last-minuteness!

Thanks to the Lambs for putting up with my general lack of timing and surprise releases. And thanks to the people who pick up my books. I can't thank you enough for your kind messages, reviews, recommendations, and love you share for the people that live in my head.

To my family who astound me every day. In a good way! To M for his business helpings, his family stuff, and the endless supply of cups of tea. But not for making me feel like I've been out on the tiles when I admit I didn't go to bed last night. Other than that, we make a good team.

Certain liberties were taken in the writing of this book.

Re the Office of the City Clerk. If you care to check, paperwork needs to be filed in advance to obtain a marriage license prior to the actual ceremony. You can't just turn up on the day. But I'd like to think a rich bastard like Beckett would overcome such a mundane thing as queuing. It's not what you know, but who you ~~blow~~ know!

Second, the UK is a sticky place for prenuptial agreements, hence the pair jetting off to New York. There's also no such thing as a 'no fault' divorce here currently. As for a divorce filed for elsewhere, as it didn't come to that for *Bolivia*, I've used a sprinkling of poetic license here, too.

ABOUT THE AUTHOR

Donna writes dirty stories, according to her family. She hopes you find them funny, too.

When not bashing away at a keyboard she can usually be found hiding from her family and responsibilities with a good book in her hand, and a dog that looks like a mop by her feet.

She likes her humour and wine dry, her mojitos sweet, and her language salty.

You can join in all things Donna by signing up for her mailing list, or by becoming part of Donna's Lambs, her Reader Group over on Facebook, made fabulous by its members who are the best group of romance readers on the interwebz.

She might be biased.

Keep in contact
Donna's Amazon Page
Donna's Lambs
Donna's VIP Newsletter
mail@donnaalam.com
www.DonnaAlam.com

Made in the USA
Columbia, SC
06 October 2025